SECOND
SIGHT

Ryan S. Pack

Ryan S. Pack

ISBN-13: 978-0-9860564-6-8

Second Edition

My original dedication in the first edition of this book was to my wife, LuAnn. The more thought I gave it, the more I realized that she deserved this dedication be to her, as well, because without her continued love and support, there <u>still</u> wouldn't have been that first edition, let alone this one. So again to you, gràdh geal mo chridhe, I say thank you in the million tiny ways that I can.

(Oh, and we <u>really</u> need to get a car with a higher roof…)

<u>Chapter One</u>

By Thursday morning, he was positive that something had gone horribly wrong. He was pretty sure on Wednesday evening, but by dawn Thursday, he was sure. The fire that had been burning on the horizon since Tuesday night was still glowing and if anything, had spread even further, from the north to the west. He stood on the rickety porch of his rough wooden cabin, watching the sun struggle through the oily smoke that hung like fog in the distance. The smell of it had reached his cabin by midday of Wednesday, a harsh stench of diesel, rubber, and some sort of chemicals. He shook his head and continued to peer into the haze.

His name was Jeff Della, and on this Thursday morning in July 2008, he was twenty-three years old. His stood a hair under six feet tall, and was built like an Olympic swimmer. This was not due to any Olympic swimming (Jeff loathed swimming), but because of his constant physical labor. He fabricated rustic log furniture and beds from trees cut down one at a time from the 130 acre stretch of woods that he owned. He lugged each log back to the workshop situated behind his cabin, cut into the proper lengths, and turned it into the finished product.

Jeff wasn't a complete technophobe, but he had an inherent dislike to just about anything that had been produced since the early 1920's. Because of this, he didn't own an ATV, or a chainsaw, things that would have eased his burden considerably, given the lengths he sometimes was forced to drag the fallen trees back to his workshop. He refused to denude the forest in any one particular area, and would often spend several days scouting out just the right tree for each individual project. Once found, the tree would be marked and then Jeff would cut it down with an axe. After removing the limbs, reserving those that he would also use, he would then measure off the tree into equal lengths and cut it into pieces that he could manage through the forest back home.

This sort of process was guaranteed to build muscle tightly across his frame, and it had. After four years of doing this daily, Jeff could lift a hundred pounds with one arm as easy as if he were carrying a gallon of milk. He was sure-footed and graceful, qualities that came in handy when a one hundred foot tall pine tree suddenly gave up the fight with gravity and went from vertical to horizontal in the space of seconds. His only companion on these outings was his dog Waylon, a Siberian husky that was just as fleet of foot as his roommate. They could be found wandering the woods behind Jeff's cabin in all seasons and in all weather. They were completely at ease with each other, and needed no other company.

This hazy Thursday morning, Waylon sat at Jeff's feet, staring at the smoke in the distance. Jeff figured if it smelled this bad to him,

Waylon must be in hell. He reached down to rub the dog between the ears, and received a muted *woof* in return. Jeff turned back to his vigil. He brushed his blonde hair back out of his eyes with the fingers of his right hand. It was longer than usual, falling down to his shoulders. He kept meaning to get it cut, but kept putting it off for one reason or another. He wasn't a vain man, and although the few women that saw him on a regular basis found his hair to be attractive, he merely saw it as a hindrance. Should an errant strand blow into his eyes at the wrong time, and he could easily find himself lying under a tree instead of next to it. His beard he didn't mind, as it wasn't something that got in his way while he worked.

The eyes that now scanned the horizon were striking. They were blue, a cobalt blue that matched almost exactly the eyes of the dog at his side. Given that he was lucky to have them at all, he considered himself fortunate that they were as attractive as they were. They were, perhaps, the only thing about himself that he found to be so. He could look into his eyes in a mirror for several minutes at a time and not count it time lost. For a man that was so unconcerned with his overall appearance, such a vanity would seem odd. However, to Jeff, it was not a vanity at all, merely an affirmation.

When he was seventeen, Jeff and his father, mother, and younger sister had gone for an evening out in their hometown of Stone Grove, West Virginia. Stone Grove was a small town with a population of just over seven thousand. Situated in the coal fields, most of the men in town worked the coal mines, either in the deep mines or on the surface running loaders and the like. The rest drove the huge eighteen-wheelers that transported the coal to the barges for down-river transport or the power plants. Jeff had grown accustomed to having the giant trucks fly by on the narrow two-lane roads near his home from a very young age. Jeff's father, Ames, was a foreman at the coal mine located ten miles from their home. His mother Candice was a stay-at-home mom who sometimes gave piano lessons to the children in town. His sister Stephanie was three years younger than Jeff, and was incredibly impatient for next year, when she would leave what she called "Baby School", and begin attending Pullman County High School. Jeff, a junior that year, was *not* looking forward to having his baby sister in the same school as he, not because he didn't like her, but because she was heart-stoppingly beautiful, and Jeff knew it. He was already counting the number of fistfights he would be in his senior year as he attempted to keep the hormone-overloaded boys from his sister.

They had eaten at an all-you-can-eat buffet and then taken in a movie. They were nearly home when they had come around a curve and been hit head-on by large truck carrying an industrial disinfectant cleaner. The impact had thrown Jeff and his father through the windshield. Jeff had been saved massive laceration injuries by the fact that his father had taken most of the windshield with him as he had exited the vehicle. Jeff's mother and sister were killed instantly, their bodies crushed to a pulp by the high-speed meeting of metal. They had not even known that they were dying, Jeff was told later by a well-meaning doctor; everything had happened far too fast. Jeff supposed he should have been comforted by that bit of news, but at the time he hadn't felt particularly comforted, and told the doctor so. He had been less than cordial when he did so. Jeff's father had died equally quickly, only he had done so many yards from his wife and daughter. His short flight had ended with violent rapidity against a rock retaining wall on the side of the road.

The sole surviving member of the Della family had lain on the side of the road, both legs, one arm, and several ribs shattered. He remembered the panicked feeling of being unable to get a deep breath as his right lung had slowly filled with blood. Unable to move, he had lain there and watched as the truck driver who, as a result of the mass of his vehicle, had suffered nothing more than a bloody nose when it hit the steering wheel, staggered amongst the wreckage, staring stupidly around himself and repeatedly asking for someone named Margie. The man had wandered down the road about a hundred yards before his legs gave out and he simply sat, his legs splayed out, in the middle of the road. Jeff would later learn that the trucker had been far over the legal limit when he was given a Breathalyzer. The trucker was still sitting in the state penitentiary, as far as Jeff knew.

As he had lain there, Jeff had noticed a pool of liquid spreading out from the wreckage of the truck. He was afraid it was fuel, and expected to be burnt to a cinder at any moment. As the spreading stain had gotten closer to him, Jeff could smell the astringent aroma of the cleaner. His initial relief that he was not going to burn to death was replaced by pure agony a moment later. Unable to lift his head, the liquid had washed up against his face, filling both eyes before he could snap them shut.

The pain was absolute, a living thing. The rest of his injuries faded into nothingness. He felt as if his eyes had turned inward, grown razor sharp teeth, and were in the process of eating his brains out. His screams echoed off the hills and across the fields. The sound of the crash had been heard by the Della neighbors, but the screams were what brought them on the run. Jeff's neighbor Shawn was the first to arrive. He surveyed the terrible scene for a second, and then turned his attention to Jeff. Seeing the white froth covering Jeff's face, Shawn had glanced over at the truck and seen what it had been carrying. Although he knew that to move Jeff was to possibly kill him, Shawn reacted instinctively and pulled him out of the puddle of cleaner. Once he had moved him out of the way, he had crashed down to the small creek that flowed beside the road. He made trip after trip with water cupped in his hands to pour into Jeff's eyes.

He was still doing this when the ambulance and police cruisers arrived. The two paramedics that jumped out of the ambulance did a quick triage of the wreck and then went to work on trying to keep Jeff alive. By this point, Jeff was coughing up a pink froth, his rib having fully punctured his right lung. The medics had their hands full getting an airway in and immobilizing Jeff's legs and arm, and left his eyes to their own devices for the time being. Once they had Jeff fully immobilized and on the cot, one of them shined his penlight into Jeff's eye. The medic recoiled and motioned his partner to take a look. The other medic looked for a moment, shrugged, and told his partner to get it in gear. They manhandled the cot into the back of the ambulance and got underway to the hospital. The medic that remained in the back of the unit to work on Jeff en route felt his gaze drawn back to Jeff's eyes over and over. There was no pupil or iris visible at all. They looked like something from a horror movie. Where once a set of blue eyes had been, now there were nothing but red-black orbs. Jeff was spared the sight of the other emergency crews and police placing his family in body bags. He was spared the sight of the trucker, finally realizing the gravity of what he had done, weeping as he was none-too gently placed in the rear of a cruiser. Jeff was spared the sight of anything at all. He was completely blind.

Jeff had spent several months in the hospital, as his bones knit back together and his lung healed. He contracted pneumonia twice, and was very close to death on a couple of occasions. Throughout the entire ordeal, the doctors were insistent just how lucky Jeff had been. By rights, he should have died with his family beside the road that night. The fact that he was alive at all was a miracle, and he must think of it in that way. To keep his hopes up and a positive attitude was imperative for a full recovery, they told him.

Well, not a *complete* recovery. While the doctors were fully confident that Jeff's bones and lung would be fine in the fullness of time, given his youth, he would never see again. About that they were definite. His eyes had been far too badly damaged to ever be of use to him anymore. The cleaner was highly corrosive, and had not simply burned his eyes; they had eaten away at the lenses. Jeff spent most of the first three weeks in the hospital with bloody water leaking steadily out of his eyes, staining his pillow and giving him the look of a martyred saint, weeping tears of blood.

Jeff wasn't in the least concerned if he ever saw again. He wasn't concerned if he lived or not, so being able to see was of little import to him. He had loved his family very much. They had been closer than the other families that Jeff knew. There wasn't a Playstation to be found in the house. The same with cable television. It was something that Jeff's father had been disdainful of, and his wife had agreed with him. They owned a television, and a decent collection of DVDs, but these were watched rarely, and then only together as a family. There was no internet connection at the Della home. Jeff's mother and father believed that the influx of modern technology was taking its toll of the closeness of the family unit. Having spent the night with friends and seen how they interacted with their own families, Jeff was inclined to agree. Most of his friend's families were nice enough people, pleasant and good-hearted, but to Jeff's eyes, it seemed as if they were not so much families as they were roommates. One on the internet, another on the cell phone with someone, yet another playing something graphically violent on one of the many game consoles spread throughout the house, it was as if they barely acknowledged each other. Even during mealtimes, each member of the family would grab a plate and dash back to their respective pursuits.

On one occasion, Jeff watched in open amazement as Herb had grabbed his plate from his mother Andrea and headed back upstairs to his room to eat. Jeff had stood stupefied until Andrea had given him his plate and a smile. Jeff followed Herb upstairs, where he found him eating and watching "Being Human" on the BBC America. Herb was eating in his room. In his *bedroom*. The only way Jeff could even contemplate such an event happening at his house was if one of the family was too ill to come to the dinner table, and in that case, their dinner was more likely than not to be some of Candice's homemade chicken and rice soup, which she claimed to be able to cure everything from the common cold to malaria.

At home, dinner time was a time for talking about each other's day, how everyone was doing, and just generally catching up on each other's lives. Because he had seldom been exposed to the sort of lifestyle his friends lived daily, Jeff didn't grumble about having to spend time with his family. Just as he had been shocked at the actions of his friend's families, they had been at his.

Once when Herb was staying overnight, they had ended up lying on the living room floor in sleeping bags, talking late into the night. They had discussed everything from who was the hottest girl at school to what the chances of the football team, were of making the playoffs this season when Herb suddenly looked at Jeff and asked, "Dude, why does your family spend so much time together?"

Jeff had been totally unprepared for the question. He thought about it for a minute and replied, "I don't know. It's just what we've always done. Why doesn't yours?" As soon as he said it, he feared he might have crossed the line and insulted Herb, but the boy just laughed.

"Man, if I had to spend more than five minutes with my folks and my little brother, I'd jump off the high wall at the strip mine. Seriously, that would just freak me the hell out. I mean, I love 'em, but we're not, you know, exactly on the same channel when it comes to most stuff."

Jeff thought about that. It seemed to him that his family was on the *exact* same channel, and always had been. That was just the way it was. No matter how tired his dad might be after work, he always made time to speak with his wife and children, and not in the cursory way many men would. He genuinely wanted to know what was happening in their lives. Jeff just shrugged it off. His family was one way, his friend's another. Upon further thought, Jeff decided that even if some of those X-Box games *were* pretty cool, he wouldn't want to trade Herb's life for his own.

Losing an entire family in a fatal car crash would have been hard on anyone, but Jeff felt it a bit more viscerally than most. He hadn't lost the people that made sure the internet bill was paid, or that the latest video game was bought as soon as it came out, he had lost the companions that had made up the very heart and soul of his life.

The loss of Stephanie was the most difficult for him to accept. She had just been so vibrant, so full of life. Her fondest wish was to make the Varsity cheerleading team before she became a junior and now that wish was gone forever. No more chicken and rice soup when he was feeling under the weather. No more gruff hugs from his father, the smell of the coal he spent his days around clinging to his skin like aftershave. No more of the hauntingly beautiful way his mother had played "Moonlight Sonata" when the mood hit her. It was all gone. They were all gone. Jeff felt he should be all gone, too, but here he was, lying in a hospital bed drugged to the gills and staring into the darkness that was now his only sight.

Due to the extent of his injuries, he had been unable to attend his family's funeral. His Aunt Glenda had come in afterward and told him how beautiful it had been, and how Ames, Candice, and Stephanie were at peace at the right hand of Jesus now. Jeff had listened to her description, and then turned over painfully until his faced the wall. He had picked up quickly on how to locate where someone was in the room from the sound of their voice, and he knew that if he turned on his right side, he would be facing away from the chair next to his bed. It hurt like hell to lie on his right side, because of his ribs, but he did it anyway, ignoring Glenda until she left.

He ignored everyone else much the same way for the next month. He simply had nothing to say. The doctors would come in every day and update him on his progress, but Jeff would show no sign that he heard or cared. He would eat only enough to keep the doctors from threatening to put in a feeding tube. He lost weight, and began to look like a scarecrow. All the while, he wept his bloody tears.

After almost three months in the hospital, the doctors decided that Jeff had healed enough to go home. The only problem is that there was no one home to go to. With his parents dead, there was no one to help the blind seventeen year old boy take care of himself. Aunt Glenda and her husband Ralph had offered to take him into their home, but Jeff wasn't thrilled with the prospect. They lived over an hour away. Jeff could have cared less about graduating high school or missing his old friends, he just didn't want to leave the only home he had ever known. His father had kept a good life-insurance policy, and with his miner's pension he had insured that Jeff had plenty of money to take care of himself, but Jeff was blind. All the money in the world wasn't going to change that, and it appeared that Jeff was destined to live with his aunt for at least another eight months, until he turned eighteen.

Even then, what was he supposed to do? He would have enough money to do him, but what were his prospects? As he thought about the grim future stretching out before him, he did something that he hadn't done since the night of the accident. He wept. Not the bloody, watery discharge that had been leaking from his damaged eyes, but true tears. He wept silently through the night, finally drifting off to sleep from pure exhaustion just as the sky was kissed pink by the morning light.

A few hours later, at eight o'clock, one of the nurses that had been treating him came into the room to take his vitals and see how he was doing. As she went about her business, Jeff came slowly awake. Groggily, he turned his head to where he knew she must be standing and asked for a drink of water. She poured him a plastic glassful from the pitcher on his side table, and held his head up as he drank it. As she did, she noticed that the gauze that covered his eyes was soaked with red-tinted tears. Tears welled up in her own eyes at the thought of this brave boy that had not cried once since he had been brought into the hospital crying himself to sleep in the night. Gently, she laid his head back onto the stained pillow.

"Your bandage is wet. I'm going to change it and get you a clean one, all right?" she said.

Jeff just nodded.

The nurse left the room and returned with a new set of eye covers and some more gauze. She gently set about unrolling the wet bandage from his face until only the cotton eye covers remained. She very carefully pulled each one loose from his eyes, warning him to keep them shut to avoid getting anything into them until she changed the covers out. Jeff felt a rebellious wave of anger slip over him and with effort, pried open his eyelids.

What happened then was something that the doctors would never been able to explain.

When the nurse turned back to Jeff, a cotton eye cover in each hand, she found the boy looking at her. She gasped. The whites of both eyes were still the color of old blood, but his deep blue irises looked back at her clearly. The contrast between the red-black and the blue was unnerving. She opened her mouth to tell him that he needed to close his eyes, or she would have to irrigate them to insure that no foreign matter had gotten in when he spoke to her in a small voice.

"I can see you."

The nurse thought she had misunderstood him.

"No, honey, I need you to close your eyes, okay? I'll get these bandages on, and then get you some breakfast. You get out of here today. Won't that be nice? I'll bet you're sick of this old room."

"I can see you."

The nurse stopped and let that settle in. She looked down at him, and it *did* seem like he was looking at her, not just in her general direction. But she had read his chart. The blindness was permanent, no chance of regaining his sight without the possibility of major surgery later on, and even then the chances that he would ever see again were incredibly thin. There had just been too much damage done to the delicate eye structure. She smiled and walked back to him with his bandages,

"I'm sure one day you'll see just fine, honey. And then you can come back here and tell me how pretty I am, okay?"

She was shocked to find him looking right up at her, not where she had been standing a moment before. In that same quiet voice, he said, "You *are* pretty. I like your ponytail. It makes you look like a little girl."

The nurse was out of his room shouting for a doctor in seconds.

They kept him for a week longer, running every test imaginable on him. The optometrist that had made the initial diagnosis was named Stephens, and he was in complete denial. There was simply no way that this boy's eyes could have healed themselves like that. After being shown test result upon test result, he finally tossed the paperwork onto the desk and gave the attending physician a withering look.

"Look, I neither know, nor care, what sort of foolishness you're pulling. But if you've told that boy that he will be able to see again, I will personally see you brought before the board. That is the cruelest thing I've ever heard of anyone doing, and it is totally unprofessional. Now, I have several cases to see to today, and I am not going to waste anymore of my time with you."

The attending physician, a young doctor named Ribbon, merely held his hand out towards Jeff's room.

"This is no joke, I assure you. That you would even imply that I would give false hope like that to a child that has been through so much infuriates me, to be perfectly honest. Now, I'll tell you what. You go into that room. If, when you come out, you're not satisfied that Jeff can see you perfectly well, I will turn in my resignation to the board today, However, if… no, *when* you're satisfied that he can see, you will tender me an apology, heartfelt and sincere, or I will personally make it my life's ambition to catch you in town when we're both off-duty and kick the living shit out of you. Deal?"

The optometrist looked nervous for the first time. He glanced at Jeff's room and back at Ribbon. The man wasn't joking. He most likely would make good on his promise to locate Stephen's off the hospital property and stomp him. The man was furious. And, it was a small town. Stephens stalked into Jeff's room.

When he emerged twenty minutes later, he had the look of a man that had just survived a bomb blast. He walked up to Ribbon and held out his hand.

"I apologize. You were completely correct. That boy can see, and better than I can, at that. It's impossible, and it's a miracle, but he can most definitely see. Do you accept my apology?"

Ribbon smiled. "I agree with you. It *is* impossible, and it *is* a miracle. And yes, I accept your apology. Now, how in the *hell* do we document this?"

The two doctors walked off down the hall, trying to figure out just how to report that a boy whose eyes had been half-eaten out of his head three months earlier could now see like a hawk.

Jeff just sat in his room and stared at the wallpaper designs like he was viewing a masterpiece by Michelangelo for hours.

After his release from the hospital, Jeff had petitioned the court for status as an emancipated minor. Because he was due to turn eighteen in just a few months, it was granted. He moved back into his house, but in the end, no matter how much he loved his home, he just couldn't stand to live there anymore. Every corner held a new sadness, an old hurt. Each room still carried the scents and vibrations of those people he had lived and loved so well in them. Finally, after two years, he put it up for sale.

Between the money from the sale of the house and his father's life insurance, Jeff had managed enough money to buy the 130 acres of woodland with the log cabin on it. He had spent some more money renovating the cabin and building the workshop. He had bought a 1983 Dodge Ram from a farmer that lived not far from him for next to nothing. He had always enjoyed working with wood, and was quite good at building the log furniture that people commissioned him to make. He lived frugally, and had a considerable amount of money in the bank. On that Thursday morning, he had a net worth of just under one hundred thousand dollars. Not a fortune, but more than enough to keep him and Waylon happy for a very long time.

Jeff snapped back to the present and took his eyes from the smoky horizon. He looked down at Waylon.

"Well, big guy, what do you think? Terrorists?"

Waylon just looked back, his tail slowly swishing across the rough boards of the porch.

Jeff nodded. "Yeah, I figured about as much. See what happens when you don't watch CNN? You have no grasp of current events, my canine friend. You should really take a more active interest in the world around you."

Waylon took this in stride, gave another little woof, and padded down the steps and across the yard to where Jeff's truck sat. It was painted olive drab green with a thick black spray on bed-liner. To most people, the truck would have been ugly, but to Jeff it was a classic. What it gave up in esthetics, it more than made up for in dependability. The old truck had always gotten Jeff where he needed to go, in any weather, and he loved it. Jeff looked from Waylon to the truck and back again.

"Seriously? You think that it's a good idea to just go whipping into town and check things out? With *that* going on?" He flapped a hand to the northwest and its columns of smoke rising into the air.

Waylon patiently sat by the driver's side door and waited. Jeff let out a sigh, and turned to step back into the cabin to get his keys from the rack by the door. As he crossed the yard, he fixed Waylon with a piercing glare.

"Fine, but if we get into trouble, I'm holding *you* personally responsible, so remember it. We're not back here by this afternoon and working on that bedroom set the Hendersons wanted, and you get no hamburger. Dry dog food. *Cheap* dry dog food, pal."

Jeff made it to the door of the truck, and then stopped. He looked back at the smoke for a few moments, and then turned and headed back for the cabin. Waylon gave an interrogative bark. Jeff spoke absently over his shoulder. "Yeah, yeah, we're going, just give me a sec, you impatient ass."

He entered the cabin and walked into his bedroom. Like everything else in his home, it was simple to the point of being almost Spartan. His bed was one of his own creations, an oak ensemble that would most likely last far longer than Jeff himself would. Waylon had nosed his way back into the house and now stood at the bedroom door with his head cocked in that way that dogs have that convey more with a look than most people could with an hour's worth of conversation. Jeff grinned at him. Then he leaned over and pulled a long case out from under the bed. He laid it on the mattress and opened it up. It held a Ruger Mini-14, a .223 mm rifle that accepted the 30-round magazine that fed the standard U.S. M-4 rifle. Jeff took this from the case placed a magazine into it, worked the chamber, and laid it next to the case, and then added six more fully loaded magazines. From another compartment, he pulled out a handgun. It was also a Ruger. A P90, it was a .45 caliber pistol that held eight shots in the magazine. He took five more from the case. He placed one in the pistol and worked the slide. He ejected the magazine and opened a box of shells. He took a single shell out and topped it off, then snapped it back into the gun. He now had a .45 caliber handgun with nine shots, with thirty-two extra shells in the remaining mags. With the Mini-14, he had thirty rounds in the weapon, with one hundred and eighty rounds at the ready.

Jeff stood there looking at this display of firepower and began to second guess himself. Sure, there was something pretty bad going on, but he was just driving the seventeen miles to town to ask a few questions, not entering a combat zone. Or was he? That was the problem. He had no idea what he might find in town. That decided him. Taking a duffel bag from his closet, he placed the extra mags into it. He took out his Fobus paddle holster for his P90 and clipped it onto his belt. He slid the handgun into it. The Mini-14 he slung over one shoulder by the strap. He would place it on the gun rack when he got to the truck. If he had no problems, he'd simply drive to the small general store that stood on the outskirts of town, ask his questions, and haul ass back home. No one would question him carrying his handgun. People carried their guns around all the time. The rifle would be in the truck. No problems there.

So, if everything was kosher, it would be a simple trip to the store and back. He needed some dog food and milk, anyway. No harm, no foul, and he would sleep better tonight than he had since Tuesday night. If there was a problem, well... he'd at least be able to deal with it. Better to have it and not need it than to need it and not have it. He left the bedroom and headed back outside. He paused to lock his door and then went to his truck. He opened the door for Waylon, who clambered in like an old pro and took up his customary position on the passenger side of the bench seat. Jeff placed the rifle on the rack attached to the back window of the truck and climbed in. He slid his seatbelt on and glanced over at Waylon.

"You just remember whose idea this was, buddy. I'm not kidding about that hamburger. Never doubt me."

Waylon stared blandly back. Jeff shook his head, started the truck, and backed out of the driveway. He turned right onto the road and headed toward town. He was feeling a little embarrassed by all the firepower he was packing, but shook it off. If there was a problem in town, it wouldn't be one that two hundred and fifty-one rounds of ammunition couldn't handle, he was sure.

He had never been more wrong in his life.

Chapter Two

Jeff drove slowly down the two-lane blacktop road that led into town. As he drove, he played back the last two days in his mind. He rubbed Waylon's ears absently as he drove, a small line furrowed between his brows as he thought.

Tuesday had been a carbon copy of every other day of his life of the last four years. He had risen with the sun, as was his habit, fed and watered Waylon, and eaten a simple breakfast of oatmeal and toast. His single vice was coffee, and he drank it by the pot, several times a day. After their morning ritual of food and some playtime, he and Waylon had headed out into the woods, in search of just the right tree for the bedroom set that Marsha and Jackson Henderson had commissioned him to fabricate.

They had been near the rear of the property line at around one o'clock, when there had been a sudden flash, as if lightening had shot across the sky. Waylon had given out a surprised yip, and Jeff had stared into the blameless clear July sky. Jeff looked at Waylon, who looked right back.

"Waylon, what the hell was that?"

If Waylon had an opinion, he kept it to himself. Jeff shrugged and headed for the tree he had marked for the job ahead. He was busily attacking it with his axe when he heard a loud, hollow boom echo across the woods from the north. Waylon cut loose with another yelp, and looked accusingly at Jeff, as if to say that this was all *highly* improper, and he didn't much appreciate it, thank you very much. Jeff looked back at him helplessly.

"Hey, dog, don't look at *me*. I've been right here with you the whole time. Jeff climbed to the top of the ridgeline and looked north. There was nothing to see, at least not then. For several minutes there were smaller booms that sounded, but after about fifteen minutes, the quiet returned to the forest. Jeff remained on the ridge for another quarter of an hour, but saw nothing else. He turned and loped back down the hill to the tree he had been working on. He looked over at Waylon.

"Don't ask me, bub. I don't know what that was. Coal mine's south of here. There's nothing up that way but more forest until you get to the river, and then more nothing until you get near Huntington. So your guess is as good as mine. However, none of this stimulating conversation is getting this tree down. So, if you'll excuse me, those of us with thumbs have work to do."

Waylon flipped his head at Jeff and took off through the woods to find something to occupy his time. Jeff grinned as he hoisted the axe to his shoulder. "Touchy, touchy", he said under his breath.

The rest of the afternoon was spent in first getting the tree down and then getting its limbs off. Jeff marked the length of the trunk for cutting the next day and headed for home. It was almost six o'clock, and he was getting hungry. As he headed back home, he turned his face to the sky and emitted a shrill whistle.

"Hey, Waylon, you coming with me, or what? We're having chili tonight, but I'm not above eating it all myself!"

Within seconds the underbrush shook as Waylon came bursting through. He ran up to Jeff's side and gave him his best doggy grin. Jeff returned it with one of his own.

"You're such a big baby, you know it? You know I wouldn't eat all the chili without giving you some. C'mon, you goober. Let's go get cleaned up and grab some grub."

They walked home through the early evening stillness. Jeff set the axe on its hook in the workshop and placed a leather cover over the blade. He would sharpen it again in the morning before they started back out. He was methodical, and took care of his tools. After cleaning up with a quick shower, Jeff and Waylon set about making a kettle of chili. With Waylon acting as foreman, Jeff added spices and hot sauce until it was just right. They left it to simmer and went out on the porch to enjoy the cool breeze that usually passed through the hollow about that time of evening.

They made it to the porch, and Jeff stopped dead. The sky in the north was glowing dully. Jeff had seen that sort of glow before, when there had been several forest fires burning during the dry season a few years back. Whatever had made that loud boom earlier had apparently also caught one hell of a lot of trees on fire. He estimated that the fires were many miles off, and of no urgent concern to his house or woods. They might even be on the far side of the river, which would be a lucky break for him if they were. He wondered why he hadn't heard the National Guard helicopters shuttling back and forth to the river with their huge water bags slung underneath. That was one of the best ways to kill a big fire in these parts. Use men to make a firebreak, and then inundate the fire with water from the river flown up in those big choppers. But he had heard nothing that day, not even an airplane, now that he thought about it.

The first tendrils of unease made their way into his mind. Shrugging his shoulders, he and Waylon went back in and made short work of the pot of chili. After the meal, Waylon broke wind, a long, trumpeting sound that seemed to go on forever. Jeff fixed him with a gimlet eye.

"That's it, big boy, you're bedding down in the living room tonight."

Waylon managed to look sheepish, at least until Jeff cut loose with some gas of his own. Jeff shot the dog a guilty look, who was staring at him blandly. Under his breath, Jeff said, "All right, all right, we're *both* sleeping in the living room tonight. You happy?"

After dinner, Jeff had turned on the radio to see if there was any news about the fire. He didn't own a TV. His concern mounted when he couldn't get anything from most of the station he knew were in range. The low hiss of white noise seemed to mock him as he dialed back and forth. He finally found a local FM station that was coming in loud and clear, playing country music. He relaxed a bit. The smoke from the fire was probably messing with his reception, he figured.

He listened to the radio for the better part of an hour before he began to get nervous again. The station was coming in fine, music and commercials, but there was no news to be heard. In fact, there hadn't been a deejay come on once since he had turned the radio on. He remembered that the station had made a pretty big deal about a year ago about how they were going to a pre-programmed format, and that the deejays would only be necessary for local news and weather. With no deejay, Jeff got neither. He listened for about another hour and finally gave it up as a lost cause. At around eleven o'clock, he and Waylon had bedded down in the living room to go to sleep.

Jeff didn't get much sleep that Tuesday night. He slept fitfully, waking often. Waylon seemed to feel the tension as well, although whether he was picking it up from Jeff or from something else, Jeff didn't know. Every so often, the dog would raise his head and let out a tiny whine. They remained like that, tossing throughout the night, neither of them ever falling into a deep sleep.

Wednesday morning had not improved. For the first time, Jeff could see the smoke that the darkness had hidden. His sense of unease deepened. He turned the radio back on, but could still only get the one station he had gotten the night before. Although he couldn't be sure, it seemed to him that the station was repeating itself, the songs and commercials in the same order as the night before. He shrugged it off. The thing was programmed to play the popular songs, over and over, and the businesses probably paid for their ads to run for at least a week at a time, maybe a month.

Because he could think of nothing else to do, Jeff went ahead and sharpened his axe and went to work on the tree he had felled the day before. A more social animal would have probably been in town asking questions by Tuesday night, but Jeff had gotten so used to living with just Waylon that he didn't consider traveling into town to get some information. He just went about his work. By that afternoon, he had hewn the trunk into manageable pieces and was lugging them laboriously back to the workshop, one at a time. He got most of them done before deciding to knock off for the day. It wasn't like him to leave a task unfinished, but this particular tree had been a great distance from the workshop, and he was edgy.

He called Waylon to him, and the dog gave him a questioning look.

"Yeah, it's a little early, but you're not the one lugging those big bastards through the woods, are ya? As a matter of fact, aren't you guys bred to haul sleds? I bet I could whip up a harness in no time and you could just trot these bad boys right up to the workshop for me."

Waylon gave him a decidedly unpleasant look that included a great many teeth. Jeff smiled affably.

"Or I could break down and buy a four-wheeler. Either way, okay? Let's see if we can refrain from tearing off my balls, what do you say, buddy?"

They had returned to the cabin and eaten a light meal, just a bacon sandwich for Jeff and some raw bacon for Waylon. Once he had finished, he stood from the kitchen table and glanced at his watch. It was nearly four-thirty. He approached the radio and reached out for the knob. His hand hesitated. He gritted his teeth in annoyance at himself and flipped the radio on. The sound of music immediately sprang into the cabin. Jeff released a breath he hadn't realized he had been holding and went back to the kitchen table and sat down. He petted Waylon as they listened to Big and Rich exhort the world to save some horses by riding some cowboys. Jeff grinned. The song went off, and after a few seconds of silence, there was an audible click and Big and Rich were back for an encore performance. Jeff's grin disappeared. He listened to the song through, listening to those horses and cowboys. The song went off. That click sounded, and Big and Rich returned.

The station played the song fourteen times by Jeff's count before he turned off the radio. He looked down at Waylon.

"I think we might be in some trouble here, big boy."

Waylon seemed to agree. They spent the night in the living room again, where Jeff could see out the north-facing windows and keep an eye on the progress of the fire. As far as he could tell, it had continued, unabated. The whole of the sky from the north across to the west was now aglow. They slept even worse that night.

Jeff glanced in his rearview mirror. He had not passed a single vehicle, coming or going, since they had left the cabin. This stretch of road wasn't Interstate 64 by any means, but there was usually *some* traffic on it. He hadn't really noticed it at first, but the closer he got to the general store, the more he realized that the road was pretty much deserted. He glanced over at Waylon, who was hanging his head out the window and smelling the air. He must not have enjoyed it, because he pulled his head back in and whined back in his throat. Jeff rubbed the dog's head again and spoke soothingly to him.

"I know, bub. It'll be all right. We'll figure out what's going down once we get to Sam's. He knows everything that happens in this county before it happens. All will be well."

Sam Merchant owned and operated the general store. He was a crusty, foul-mouthed eighty-something man that enjoyed nothing better than to opine about just how quickly the world was going to hell. Jeff wasn't just making idle conversation with Waylon about Sam's penchant for knowing everything that happened in Stone Grove. The old man knew who was sleeping with who, who was about to lose their house to the bank, and every other lurid detail about the folks in Stone Grove with frightening accuracy. It wouldn't have surprised Jeff to learn that Sam had somehow wire-tapped the entire phone system in town.

Jeff crested the final hill before the store and hit the break instinctively. Waylon, unprepared for the sudden stop, was flung into the floorboards with an angry bark. He clambered back up into the seat and gave Jeff a murderous look. It was lost on him, because Jeff's eyes were locked on the scene that lay before him at the bottom of the rise. The general store was right where it should be, and everything seemed to be in order there, but there were no less than four vehicles in the ditches around the store. One truck had run off the road and into a power line. Instead of staying in the vehicle, which would have shielded the driver from the electricity, the man had gotten out of his truck and walked straight into the snapping tangle of downed lines. Jeff was surprised he couldn't smell the man's burnt body from where he sat.

The drivers from the other vehicles had gotten out, as well, but no one had apparently thought to call 911 to get help for the man in the truck. It was hard to tell from where he sat, but Jeff thought that, judging from the state of the body, the man had been there for quite some time. Maybe even a day or so. There wasn't much left that looked human. Smoke had stopped coming from the man, and there was a bare patch of ground around him that had burned clean away.

Jeff blew out a breath and took his foot from the brake. He drove slowly down the hill and eased into the general store's parking lot. He turned off his engine, and sat for several minutes, gathering his thoughts. He looked around at the other wrecked cars. Most were minor, but besides the truck, at least one of them looked like it could have been a fatality. It was a small Mazda, and it had apparently hit the ditch on the far side of the road at some speed, jumped into the air, and landed on its top. Jeff looked closely at the vehicle for a moment, and then realized that his assessment of the wreck's fatal nature had been correct. Lying inside the car, sprawling on the roof was the driver. From the angle of the body, Jeff could tell that the man was not merely injured, but dead. A great splash of blood had hit the side window. Again, Jeff realized that this hadn't happened recently. The blood had dried to a dark maroon. Jeff felt his tension raise another notch.

He ran through the facts as best he could. There were two dead men within 200 feet of him, and no one had done anything about that. There were four vehicles that no one had sent a wrecker for. There was no crime scene tape, no indication that anyone had been here in an official capacity to deal with what was quite obviously a mess. He loosened his grip on the steering wheel, realizing that he was holding it in a white-knuckled death grip. He turned his attention to the front of the store. It seemed to be okay. The lights were on, and the "Open" sign hung in the window. Jeff opened the door of the truck and stiffly got out. Waylon ran across the seat and jumped out on the ground next to him. He continued to whine quietly, looking around at the dead men.

"I know how you feel. This is *très.* freaky. Keep your eyes peeled, okay? I'm not about to let my guard down, so don't you."

Waylon looked at him like he'd lost his mind. There was no chance of letting *his* guard down, the dog's eyes seemed to say. They stood there in the parking lot for a moment, surveying the scene. Apart from the crackle of the downed lines and the stench of burnt ozone and roasted human flesh in the air, things seemed to be fairly safe, at least so far. Jeff stepped away from the truck a few paces and then stopped. It might seem safe, but from what he had seen so far, things were a few light-years from all right. He went back to the truck and got the rifle from the gun rack and stuffed two extra magazines into his back pockets. Re-checking to see that the rifle was ready to fire if he needed it, he started back towards the general store's front entrance. He paused just outside the door, listening intently. There was no sound coming from inside, no bustle of movement or talk. He stood like that for several more minutes, and then slowly pushed open the glass door.

His life was saved by a puddle of what looked like a soft drink by the front door. As he stepped in, his foot slid forward on the sticky liquid and he went down to one knee. At that same instant there came a roar from his left behind the cash register. In some small room in his mind a voice calmly reported that someone had just fired a shotgun at him. Jeff had one hand on the door handle, the other on his rifle. This turned out to be a good thing, because had he been holding the rifle with both hands in a ready position, he most likely would have fired the entire clip towards the source of the gunshot, and cut Sam Merchant in half. As it was, he let out a breathless scream and flung himself onto the floor. Glass from the front door pattered down around him. The shotgun blast had annihilated the upper pane of glass in the door. Jeff began to wriggle forward on his belly, trying to put some distance between him and the shooter. Waylon barked madly.

Then Jeff heard the sound of the shotgun being racked with another shell, and he understood instantly that he had no chance of surviving a second shot. Lying prone on the ground, he presented a beautiful target. He heard Sam screaming.

"Now, you sumbitches! Now! Try me now! I'll blow your Gawd-DAMN heads off!!!"

Jeff screamed right back.

"Jesus, Sam, don't shoot me! I've been coming here for years, so DON'T YOU SHOOT ME!!!"

There was a pause, and Jeff breathed out a quick prayer of thanks. He risked raising his head from the floor and looking over at the counter where Sam was standing. The man was weaving and holding the shotgun so tight that his fingers were bloodless. When he spoke, his voice cracked in an old man's waver.

"Jeff Della? Is that you?"

Jeff stood the rest of the way up, holding the rifle one-handed with the barrel pointed at the floor in case Sam viewed that as enough of a threat to finish what he had started when Jeff had entered the store.

"Of course it's me, you old bastard. What the hell is wrong with you? You shooting at all your customers today, or did I win a special lottery or something?"

He began brushing the broken glass from his clothing, noting that he was now covered completely with sticky soft drink residue from his mid chest down. This might have been a blessing in disguise, because he wasn't completely sure he hadn't pissed himself when the shotgun had gone off. He was beginning to get angry as he brushed the glass away. The initial surge of adrenaline was giving way to the shakes, and they in turn were giving way to anger. He was scared, he was covered in glass, he was sticky, and he was *pissed*, figuratively and quite possibly literally. He was about to turn on the old man and vent some of this rage when he noticed with alarm that Sam was weeping openly, tears cutting tracks down the wrinkled landscape of his face. Jeff's anger vanished in an instant and he instinctively went towards the old man.

"Sam, come on, buddy, calm down. What's the matter? Are you hurt? Did someone try to rob you? What?"

As he neared the old man, Jeff noticed that Sam smelled pretty ripe. He also looked like he'd missed a few meals and hadn't slept in a few days. His tears continued to roll, and he stumbled to the counter. The shotgun went down on top of the counter next to the register, close by his hand.

"Son, how in the name of God did you get down here? Have you been walking the whole time? God, you must be starved, or thirsty. Get yourself some water from the cooler. You'll be able to tell it from the pop if you go left as far as you can, and then feel your way down to the third rack. That's all bottled water."

The whole time he was speaking to Jeff, he had been staring over Jeff's left shoulder. It was unnerving, and Jeff turned several times to look behind him, only to find no one there. Sam continued to speak, sitting down heavily in the easy chair he kept behind the counter.

"I just can't imagine it, all that way. You are one lucky fella. You could have fallen right off the Gawd-damn road there about two miles out from your place. That drop-off on the side of the road is damn near straight down. You'd a' broken your neck, sure's hell."

Waylon, who had been staking out the store, now padded back from the bread aisle and gave Jeff an interrogative bark. Sam's head swiveled towards the sound.

"Oh, you brought Waylon! Smart man, son. That dog'd never let you go off'n the road. How are you, you big furry sumbitch?"

Waylon, used to this term of endearment from Sam, went over to him to have his head scratched. Sam just sat there, staring off into space until Waylon licked his hand, and then Sam began stroking the dog's head. Jeff, still shaken from his brush with death, told Sam that he thought he'd have a cold beer instead of water, if he didn't mind. Sam laughed, the sound of crows in an autumn cornfield.

"Well, by Gawd, if you think you can tell the difference, suits me to the ground. You'll like as not wind up drinking a friggin' Yoo-Hoo, but suit y'self, son."

Jeff shook his head and walked back to the cooler. He opened it and selected one of the large, 24 ounce cans of Budweiser and walked back. He leaned up against the counter and popped the top and took a long pull. As he lowered the can, he noticed a look of surprise on Sam's face, his nostrils flaring.

"Damn, son, you got this place memorized better'n I do, an' I've owned her for longer'n you been alive. How'd you do that?"

Jeff was confused, and sounded it.

"Do what, Sam?"

"Pick the beer out, first shot."

"Well, I told you I was gonna get a beer, didn't I?"

Sam looked exasperated. "Well, yeah, I reckon you did say you's getting' a beer, but what I'm askin' is how you managed to pick it out so quick?"

Jeff felt his patience beginning to slip again. With an effort, he got it back under control. He took another long pull of beer and spoke calmly to the old man.

"Look, Sam, let's get some things worked out here. Okay, I've been through that door a couple of thousand times and you've never taken a pot-shot at me before. You damn near blow my head off, and the only thing you're concerned with is how I managed the mind-boggling feat of picking out a beer? Okay, listen carefully, because this might go too fast for you. First, I went to the cooler. Second, I picked out a beer. Third, I walked back up here and opened it. Now, does that about cover it? Can we get on to why you just tried to kill me, and why it looks like the friggin' Thunderdome outside? Christ Jesus, man, there's two dead men just beyond your parking lot, and one of them looks like an advertisement for why not to smoke in bed! Who gives a damn how I got the beer?"

It was Sam's turn to be pissed. He voice cracked with anger.

"Don't you get mouthy with me, young man. The world's gone right straight to hell in the last couple a' days, and I don't need your smart-ass comments. I wanna know how you picked out that beer s' damn fast, and I wanna know *now*!"

Jeff stood in open-mouthed wonder at the vehemence in the old man's voice.

"Well hell, Sam. I'm sorry I upset you. I picked the beer out by reading the damn label, that's all. Been able to do that since I was about three or four. I could have picked something else, I guess, but I thought a Bud would go down good. That's all. No harm, no foul, okay?"

Sam shot up out of his chair like he was on a spring. He almost overbalanced and went flat of his face, but he caught himself in time. Waylon gave out a warning bark and danced around the old man. With one hand on the counter and the other holding the strap of his overalls, Sam's face drained of blood and his eyes bulged. Jeff was immediately alarmed. Now, to top everything else off, the old codger was going to have a heart attack on him. Great.

"What do you mean, you *read* the label? How in the hell did you do *that*?"

Jeff was at a loss for words. He looked at Waylon for support, but the dog seemed as confused as Jeff was.

"I read the label, Sam", Jeff said slowly, talking as you would to a small child. "I read the label and picked out my beer. I've known how to read since I was a kid, like I said. You're starting to scare me, old timer. Have you had a stroke or something?"

Sam stumbled forward until he was right up against the counter, his face about six inches from Jeff's. His bloodshot eyes wandered all around, never settling at one point. This close, and the man's stink was even worse, but Jeff remained where he was as Sam reached out a hand and waved it around until he found Jeff's face. He laid his gnarled hand on Jeff's cheek and whispered to him.

"You *read* the label. You *read* it. You can *see*. Holy Gawd up in His heaven, you can *see!*"

Jeff raised his hand to cover Sam's. For the first time, the way the old man had been acting began to make sense.

"Yeah, Sam, I can see. Why can't you? How long have you been in here, not able to see? How long have you been blinded?"

Sam's answer chilled Jeff's heart.

"I've been blind since Tuesday, same as everybody else. You're the first person I seen in days that can see anything at all. Everybody's blind, son. Well, everybody 'cept you, apparently. Gawd help us all."

Jeff Della, the only man that could use his eyes, closed them.

Chapter Three

Jeff led Sam to the small room the old man kept at the back of the store. Jeff got Sam something to drink, and then set about making him something to eat. Sam had been eating what he could locate in the store by memory for the last two days, and once he had mistakenly opened what he thought was tuna only to find he was trying to eat a can of cat food. While Jeff prepared some hamburgers, Sam filled him in on what he knew.

"Sometime Tuesday afternoon there was this big ol' flash, like heat lightening. It lit up the store 'n everything. It left this big afterimage you know, like when somebody takes your picture when you ain't ready? Then things kept getting' darker 'n darker, and all the color went out. It was like I was a' watchin' an old black 'n white TV, and the picture tube went out. It happened so damn fast, Jeff. I mean. I was a' countin' the money over to the till, and that flash happened, and in just a few seconds I was blind as a bat. I waited for it to pass, but it never did." He began to cry. "No sir, it just never did. I can't see, an' I don't reckon I ever will again. Ain't this just an old bitch?"

Jeff rested his hand on Sam's shoulder and squeezed. Sam nodded at him and brushed the tears from his eyes with his fists, like a child. When he resumed his tale, his voice was slightly stronger.

"I heard them cars smash up out yonder, and I felt my way to the door and hollered. I hollered and hollered, seemed like forever afore anybody answered. Finally, I heard this woman hollering back. Turns out it was Mrs. Cracken from down the road. She said she couldn't see and that she'd wrecked her car and asked me to call 911 for her. Said she had her cell, but she couldn't see to dial the numbers right. I got right scared then, let me tell you, son. I mean, what's the chances, her n' me going blind at the same damn time? And what 'bout them others that had wrecked? Was they blinded, too? I could hear the power lines a' snappin' and crackin' over in yonder field, and I could smell that one feller a' burnin'. But what could I do? So I hollered back at her an' told her that I couldn't see neither. She sounded mad when she told me it t'warn't no joke. I told her that I was damn sure it warn't. She started a' cryin'. I asked her where she'd wrecked at, an' she told me that the last thing she'd seen was the ditch across road afore her sight went. So I hollered at her to come to the sound of my voice. I figured that she was right straight across from the store when she went into the ditch. So there I was a hollerin', and she was hollerin' right back as she made her way across the road to me." He laughed bitterly. "I bet we was a sight, the two of us screamin' like a couple a' lunatics. Anyhow, she made it over t' the store an' come in. We tried to figure out what to do next. We figured that callin' the 911 was the only thing we *could* do, so I made it over to t' phone. I punched in the numbers two or three times before I got it right. Musta been hittin' that damn pound sign there at t' bottom of the number pad, I dunno. Anyways, I heard the phone ring, and then there was a click. Then come on this recordin'. Said all the emergency circuits was busy. That scared the living hell outta me, boy. I mean, how many folks was tryin' to call to tie up the whole damned 911? The recordin' told me to hold, and somebody would be with me as soon as they could. I stayed on that damn phone for had to be a half hour or so." Sam shook his head in disgust. "That whole time, Mrs. Cracken was a' gettin' more 'n more worked up. Kept sayin' that she had t' get back to her young 'uns, 'cause she'd left the oldest to mind t' other two, an' the oldest was only thirteen. Said she had just run down here for some milk, 'cause she's a' makin' a cake, and she had everythin' she needed, 'cept for the milk, and she couldn't make it without t'milk, an'…"

Jeff cut him off. The man was starting to ramble. "Sam, let's leave the milk for a minute, okay? What happened with 911?"

Sam's gaze wondered around the room helplessly. When he spoke again, the note of strain was back in his voice.

"I tried to talk her outta goin' off on her own, Jeff. So help me Gawd, I did. Told her she wasn't in no state t' be wanderin' down t' road, and her blind like she was. Told her she'd be runned flat over by a semi afore she could get anywheres near t' her house. But she wouldn't listen. She just kept goin' on 'bout them young 'uns. Finally, she hugged my neck and told me to take care of myself, but she was a' goin' home. Told me Gawd would look out for her. She went out the door, an' I ain't seen her since." He let out a strangled sob. "Ain't seen her since, ain't seen nobody since, ain't seen *nothin'* since. Ah, Gawd, what are we a' gonna do, son?"

Jeff looked at the old man and felt his chest tighten with fear and pity. Clearing his throat, he spoke in a firm, reassuring tone.

"Well, Sam, first thing we're going to do is get some food in you. These burgers are about done. While I'm finishing these up, do you have a phone back here?"

Sam nodded. "Yeah, I got the cordless over t' the table yonder. Had it put in awhile back, 'cause I got tired of havin' to go through the damn store to answer the cussed thing ever' time it rang." He looked in Jeff's general direction, unshed tears making his eyes gleam. "Gawd bless you, son. Gawd bless you. I dunno what I'd a' done if'n you hadn't come along." He lowered his head and wept silently into his lap.

Jeff smiled at Sam, and then remembered that the old man couldn't see him doing it. So he repeated himself about getting some food into Sam. He turned to the table where the cordless phone sat on its base and picked it up. It was fully charged, he saw. At least the power was on. *But for how long?* He wondered. He shook that thought aside with a shudder and turned the phone on. He was thrilled to get a dial tone. He punched in 911 and waited. It started ringing. It rang and rang. Jeff let it ring for several minutes before he accepted the fact that no one was going to answer it. Whatever was going on, they were pretty much on their own with it. The prospect scared Jeff, but not as much as he would have figured it would. He guessed that spending so much time on his own had given him a self-reliance he didn't know he had possessed.

The two men sat across from each other at the small table and ate their burgers, while Waylon inhaled a few pounds of raw hamburger. They ate in silence, each deep in their own thoughts. The only sound in the room was the ticking of the wall clock and Waylon's grunts as he devoured his meat. Jeff was thinking that something like this wasn't a natural occurrence. This was deliberate. Someone, or something, had blinded the residents of a small West Virginia town for no good reason. The thought filled him with rage. He had always scoffed at the conspiracy theorists, making fun of their cock-eyed way of looking at the world. Every time a chemical spill occurred, or the Northern Lights were visible this far south, they were squalling that the government was up to something underhanded. Maybe there had been something to it, he thought. *Something* sure as hell had done this. Only humans seemed to be affected. Waylon was proof of that. This was a targeted operation against the people of his town, and if the government didn't have anything to do with it, why the hell weren't they here in droves, with their Blackhawk helicopters and mobile hospitals, setting up aid stations and taking care of their citizens?

Jeff felt a wave of black hate rush over him at his government. Where the hell were they? Why weren't they helping clean this mess up? There were seven thousand souls in Stone Grove, and if not one of them could see, it would be anarchy. He needed only look out the front window of the store to see proof of that. Somewhere Mrs. Cracken was either wandering helplessly down the middle of the road, or she was dead. Who was going to help her get to her kids? Hell, who was going to help the *kids*, even if she did make it home?

Jeff got up and angrily grabbed the phone book from the table next to the cordless. He looked up the numbers for the closest F.B.I. office in Huntington, and punched the numbers forcefully. He waited for a moment and was rewarded with a ring on the other line. By God, someone in the Federal Bureau of Investigation was about to get one hellishly bad cussing. If they wanted to arrest him for it, fine. They could come and get him. He'd give them the address. While they were there, he would also point out that they might consider helping the seven thousand helpless people in his hometown.

Several minutes later, Jeff was forced to concede the fact that no one was answering the phone at the F.B.I. office in Huntington. The sons of bitches, they had cut off communications with the outside world! Well, by God, he had all day, and he'd call every official office he could find. He'd call the damned White House. Somebody was going to answer him, dammit!

He turned back to the phone book, jotting down numbers of various government agencies to call. Once he had compiled his list, he would start making some calls. Someone was going to give him some answers. Someone was going to come and help his town.

It still hadn't occurred to Jeff Della that the rest of the country may be in the same boat as Stone Grove.

Chapter Four

It was fortunate for Jeff that he hadn't thought about the rest of the country being affected, because that might have been the catalyst that sent him into the realm of panic. Besides, it wasn't that the rest of America had been blinded that Tuesday afternoon.

It had been the whole planet.

At the same time, all across the globe, the light that Jeff had dismissed as a freak lightning bolt had flashed. People all over the world, whether awake or asleep, were struck blind in that instant. Jeff didn't realize how lucky he was that he lived in such a small backwater town in West Virginia. Had he been a resident of New York, London, Paris, Moscow, or any other major urban area, he would have seen things that might have edged him over the line of insanity.

London was gone, completely burned to the ground. The dead lay scattered all along the Champs-Élysées, Eiffel Tower standing mute sentinel over the chaos below. In India, a nuclear power plant suffered a massive explosion, and the death toll from the resultant radiation was staggering. Planes crashed to the earth, scattering debris of metal and human parts for miles. Major highways looked like a vision out of the mind of Dante Alighieri. All over the planet, the sudden loss of vision had created an Armageddon, all without the first shot of a war being fired.

On Tuesday, July 8th, 2008, at exactly 6:45 P.M., GMT, the population of Earth was just over 6.7 billion people. By Thursday afternoon as Jeff and Sam were sitting down to their hamburgers, that number had dropped to 4.2 billion. In the space of two days, more than two and a half billion people had died, most in terribly violent ways. More people had died in two days than had in all the wars known to man in recorded history. And those numbers were growing daily.

In the White House, Jeff's call would have gone unanswered. The First Family was not exempted from the fate of the rest of America. The President, frantic to find his wife and daughters in the now-unfamiliar maze of the White House, slipped and fell down the staircase, snapping his neck and dying instantly. The Secret Service guards sat helpless as their wards wept, wandered, and died about them. In the Oval Office two men on the Presidential Security detail, men that had served together through two Presidents and had known each other for fifteen years, cast about until they had clasped hands. Both were devout Catholics, and deemed suicide a mortal sin. After ascertaining that no one was going to answer their clumsily-dialed phone calls home, they got around this roadblock by gripping hands and placing the muzzles of their weapons in each other's ears. They said good bye, counted back from three, and splattered their brains all over the rug with the Presidential Seal on it.

In London, there was not a single landmark left recognizable. The intense of heat from the unchecked fires, fires that had begun at the wharves on the Thames and turned into a firestorm, had reduced everything to twisted metal and ash. In Trafalgar Square, the statue of Horatio Nelson was a molten puddle of bronze amid piles of smoking debris. What Hitler had failed to do throughout the entirety of World War Two that unexplained flash had done in less than two days. The members of the Royal Family that had been in residence at Buckingham Palace that Tuesday now looked like the fallen, charred bodies of Pompeii. An hour northwest of the remains of London at Althorp, Northamptonshire, four black swans looked on in amazement as people that had come to visit Lady Diana Spencer's grave at Oval Lake milled about and fell into the water. For about an hour, the peaceful lake resounded with the cries of the frightened. Then, as they staggered off and silence returned, and the swans resumed their vigil over their fallen Princess, swimming gracefully around the bodies of the drowned.

New York City looked like a set from a post-apocalyptic movie by Thursday. The city contained over eight million people, all within a tiny geographic area. In places like this, such as Tokyo, the death and disaster that plagued the rest of the world was magnified a thousand fold. As with London, fires had begun springing up all across the city, and like London, barring a torrential rainstorm, the city was doomed to destruction.

In Africa, by the second day, the local wildlife had begun to understand that the bipedal creatures that had harassed and hunted them for thousands of years were suddenly no longer a threat. There was a rash of fatalities as lions and other carnivores began to hunt the blind populace. In all fairness, they were far easier to catch than gazelle and zebra. The terrified screams of the tribesmen echoed across the flat, sun-bleached savanna. A lion roared in primal triumph.

In areas of the world that were currently at war, the sounds of weapons being fired constantly filled the air. Soldiers, unable to fall back onto their training and having no chain of command, reacted much as Sam had done, by firing at any sound they heard. The number of fratricide events skyrocketed. Heavy caliber machine guns and explosive devices are deadly enough when used with deliberation, but when sprayed blindly, they make a much more of a mess.

A vast number of humans perished by things that they had taken for granted only moments before they lost their sight. Oddly enough, huge numbers of people died as a direct result of their hair dryers. The fact that many people were foolish enough to blow dry their hair near a sink or tub full of water was a contributing factor to this. Men fell from their riding mowers, tractors, golf carts, and ATV's and were subsequently run over, or died as they were flung from them. Women that were making a late lunch for their families suddenly found themselves being scalded or mutilated by various kitchen hardware. Children fell off jungle gyms and broke bones, where they lay screaming in pain. No adults rushed to their aid to tend their wounds.

The earth was dying, a mass extinction on par with the dinosaurs, all due to the loss of one of the five human senses.

While Jeff Della was angrily calling the agencies of his now-defunct government, the planet around him was strangling to death in darkness.

Chapter Five

After nearly an hour of fruitless efforts to reach someone, *anyone* in authority on the phone, an increasingly frustrated Jeff Della sat down at the table with Sam and ran his hands through his long hair over and over. He sat that way for quite some time before finally looking up at Sam. Thankfully, Sam couldn't see the panic and fear in Jeff's eyes.

"Sam, what in the hell are we going to do?"

Sam turned his head toward Jeff. "You're askin' *me*? Son, unless you missed a pretty good hunk of our earlier conversation, I'm *blind*. I can't do a damn thing. If'n you hadn't come by, I reckon I'd have sat here and starved to death, once the damned cat food ran out. I can't do anythin', 'cept sit here and feel sorry for m'self, and I'm a' doin' just fine at that, thank you very much. I reckon the question is, what're *you* gonna do? You have a pretty big advantage over the rest of us 'uns. You can at least see where you're a' goin'. That might not have meant one whole hell of a lot a couple a' days ago, but by Gawd, I reckon that makes you the Lord High King Poo-Bah around these parts now."

Jeff recoiled in horror. "Don't say that, Sam. Don't you even *think* it. I don't want to be Lord High King Poo-Bah of any damn thing except my 130 acres at home, with Waylon as the Crown Prince. I live up there by myself for a reason, old man, and I don't think you could pick worse candidate for a savior in this mess."

Sam shook his head. "Don't recall pickin' you for anything, son. I don't reckon anybody else in Stone Grove picked you for nothing, neither. Nobody tole me 'bout no 'lection. But by Gawd, *something's* picked you. You can see. The rest of us cain't. Adds up to me, son. You may not have volunteered for this here mess, but looks to me like you done been drafted."

Jeff sat back, his hands halfway through their latest trip through his hair, the enormity of what had happened finally settling in on him. He let out a pent-up breath and realized that he was shaking his head in negation very slowly, back and forth.

"Sweet God, Sam. What am I supposed to do? Go out and round up all seven thousand folks from town, find them places to live, keep them fed and watered, and make sure they keep from burning themselves up? You telling me that I've been appointed the fucking caretaker for the entire town???"

"Again, son, I ain't telling you nothing. I'm just pointin' out the obvious. You got a choice, of course. You can turn tail an' head back up that road to your place. Hell, you can fill up on ever' damn thing you'll need to live up there for the rest of your life, come to that. Who's gonna stop you? You walk right into the bank an' take you out ever' hunnert dollar bill in there, and you can use it to wallpaper that cabin of your'n. Even if there *was* somebody still a' workin' there, what are they gonna do, call the local boys in blue to come hoss your ass down to the jail? In what? They gonna just ask you politely to lead them to the jail so's they can lock you up? That's one choice. The other'n is that you do what you can. You can't take care of ever' body in town, that's obvious, ain't it? 'Sides, I don't reckon that there's near so many folks left in town as there was afore this, anyhow. Hell, they's two dead out my front door to hear you tell it, and I'll bet my Social Security that Mrs. Cracken never made it to her home place. And that's just right here within sight of this building. You think it's any better anywhere's else in the county? Anyways, that ain't the point, son. The point is, you got a gift that none of the rest of us got. How you use it's up to you. Ain't nobody gonna make you do nothin' you don't want to, an' that's a fact. If you want to go back up to your place and hunker down, then you go on. Just do me a favor and help me lug the edibles in here so I can eat for a bit. Maybe this won't last. Maybe we'll all be able to see come tomorrow. Who can tell? But if you do that, Jeff Della, you gonna be able to live with yourself, knowin' that you left the folks here to shift for themselves in the damned dark? You don't know what it's like, son. It's horrible, being blind. You're more helpless than any baby ever born. Maybe this is Gawd's justice on us sinners, I dunno. But I do know that what you decide to do right now is gonna be with you from now until the day you die, son."

Jeff looked over at Sam and said quietly, "You're wrong, old timer."

He could see Sam gearing up and getting ready to climb back onto his soapbox and held a hand out to stop him, and then with a quiet curse, remembered that the man couldn't see him. This was going to take some getting used to. He moved his hand forward until it was on Sam's shoulder.

"Hold on a second. I don't mean you're wrong about me making this decision, or living with it. I mean you're wrong about not knowing what it's like. I've *been* blind, Sam. I know *exactly* how it feels."

Sam's face showed his confusion, and then it cleared up.

"That's right. That wreck when your folks and little sister got killed. When was that, 'bout five, six years back?"

"Six. When I was seventeen," Jeff answered quietly.

"Yup, that's it, that's right. There was a big deal down to the hospital 'bout it. Called it a miracle. It was in the paper'n everything. I remember now. You was blinded by that diesel from the truck, right?"

"No, the cleaner the truck was carrying. It got in my eyes and about ate them out."

Sam was nodding. "Well, then I owe you an apology, looks like. You *do* know what it's like. But that bein' said, don't that make your choice a bit clearer? I mean, where the hell would you have been if'n them folks hadn't helped you back then?"

Jeff closed his eyes and rubbed his temples. He had the beginnings of one *hell* of a headache coming on. He asked Sam if he could get some Tylenol from the store. Sam laughed and asked him just how he'd stop him if he took a notion to. Jeff laughed back and went into the store proper from the back room. Waylon padded along beside him. He wandered the aisles until he found the Tylenol and took several, washing them down with a fresh beer from the cooler. Then he stood and looked out the store front and tried to assemble his rampant thoughts into some sort of order.

Again, the enormity of what he was facing came close to causing him to panic. Where was he supposed to start? Door-to-door? "Good afternoon, sir or madam, I was just in the neighborhood and was wondering if you might by any chance be blind. Oh, you are? Okay, then. What? No, that's been pretty much the standard answer so far. Well, is there anything I can get for you? Make the kids some dinner, maybe draw you all a bath? It's just that we'll have to do this in about 45 seconds, because that's how long I've got allotted to each house if I stand a hope in hell of covering the whole town before Christmas." *Jesus.*

As he stood there and looked out the window, he was totally unaware that he had begun crying himself. He shook his head in surprise when his vision doubled, and then trebled. There was a second of raw terror as he thought that whatever had happened to everyone else had finally caught up with him. Then he realized that he was seeing through a prism of tears, and he slapped them away roughly. Waylon whined and licked his hand.

"I'm okay, big boy. Just being a baby." He looked down at the dog. "What are we gonna do, Waylon? I'm sort of out of my league here, bub."

Waylon did what dogs do best; simply sat there giving comfort to his friend. Jeff was glad of it, and felt his mind begin to calm. He took several deep breaths and tried to look at the situation with a clear head. Yes, this was a disaster far beyond anything he could have ever imagined. Hell, even if he *had* been able to get the National Guard down here or someone like that, they would have had a tough time helping the entire town through this. The Guard wasn't coming. Nobody seemed to be on their way to help. *Ergo*, he was on his own. Okay, fair enough. He was one man. So, as one man, what should his first action be? Run like hell for Mexico? No, that one was out, at least for now. No, first he needed to figure out just how bad things were and what was the most important things that needed done. There was a phrase for this, he had heard on a movie once. What was it? Oh, yeah, *triage and damage assessment*. That was certainly what was needed here. He needed to do some major triage and damage assessment.

As he turned back to the living space in the back of the store, he noticed a row of maps on a rack near the front door. He walked over and took a look at them. Most of them were of the whole state of West Virginia. That was a bit too big of a picture for him at the moment, and he cast them aside. Towards the bottom of the rack he found some of the smaller maps of Stone Grove and the surrounding area. He took a few of these and another beer and headed back to Sam.

The old man was sitting just as Jeff had left him. When he heard Jeff come in, he homed in on the sound and cocked an eyebrow at him.

"So, you get your Tylenol? Maybe have you a good think out there?"

Jeff smiled. "Yeah, you old bastard, I did. Right now, I'm just trying to figure out what the hell I'm going to do about this shit."

Sam laughed. "Well, fair enough, son. Can't expect a man to be able to just jump right into somethin' like this cold. What are you a' thinkin'?"

Jeff spread the maps out on the table and studied them. After a few minutes, he spoke.

"Well, the best thing I can think to do is to try to cover the town like a grid. Do each section, one at a time. Find out who's still alive and who's not, for starters. And then, I'll need to start ferrying the folk still all right to one location. I can't be running back and forth across Stone Grove, trying to take care of the whole damn populace. If I can get all of them in one place, at least then I can have a better handle on things like getting them fed, stuff like that."

He glanced up at the clock on the wall. It read a quarter after two in the afternoon. He was shocked. Was it possible that he had only been here for a few hours? It had been weeks, at least. Shaking his head, he looked back down at the map.

"Sam, you have a ruler and a pen or pencil?"

The old man flapped his hand contemptuously towards the front of the store.

"You're in a frigging *store*, son. What do you think? Think we might have something like that around here?"

Jeff smiled. "All right, smart-ass. You get a can of cat food for dinner, you keep jacking with me." With that, he went back into the store and found the supplies he needed.

He returned and went to work on one of the maps. Within a few minutes, he had a picture of the town overlaid with vertical and horizontal lines. Each small square represented about a quarter of a mile. Christ only knew how many people lived within each of those squares. He wished he had a population density map of the town, and was about to head back into the store to see if Sam had any when he realized that he was being an idiot. Even if he knew how many people lived in each house, it wouldn't do him any good. Many would have been at work when the flash occurred, at school, or been out on errands and such. Damn. It looked like he was back to door-to-door. That would take *forever*. How many people would die on one side of town while he was knocking on every door on the other like the mailman from hell? He could feel the panic trying to edge back in and forced it back. *Only one man*, he told himself. *Do what you can.*

He voiced his concerns to Sam, not because he thought the old man would be able to help in any real way, but just to have a sounding board. However, when Sam answered him, Jeff felt like the world's biggest ass.

"Why you doin' the door-to-door thing? I mean, yeah, if you wanna be thorough, then that's the only way to do it, I reckon. But why don't you just pull into each neighborhood and lay on the horn? Get out an' holler that you're there to help, but you need ever' body to come outside to where you can see 'em, or give you some sort of signal or somethin'. I'm bettin' that anybody still able'll just about break their ass letting you know that they're there."

Jeff stood there with his jaw hanging open. Then he laughed and clapped Sam on the arm.

"Sam, you're a damn genius, and that's a fact!"

Sam just smiled. "No, son, I ain't no genius, I just got somethin' that you youngsters have lost over the last generation or two. Must been somethin' in the water, 'cause the whole damn lot of you seem to have lost your common sense."

Jeff laughed like a loon. He was suddenly filled with a surge of energy. He began talking rapidly, rolling up his map and getting ready to head out. Sam stopped him short.

"Son, take a breath. Yeah, you got you a plan, and that's a start, sure as hell. But you go off all half-cocked now, and you'll be flat of your ass in an hour, guaranteed."

Jeff was impatient to be on his way, and it showed in his voice.

"Dammit, Sam, it's almost three now. I can have most of downtown done by dark if I get moving. These people need me, as you've pointed out *several* times now. Emphatically, at that. So, what, exactly, am I taking a breath for?"

"Well, for starters, just how many folks you reckon you can haul in that old truck of your'n? Even if you fill the back full, how many? Eight, ten maybe? Okay, there's that. Now, assumin' that ever' body is nice enough to just sit tight and wait on you to make about a million trips in your truck, where you plannin' on truckin' 'em to? You thinkin' 'bout bringin' 'em here, 'cause I ain't got much room for guests, as you can see. Or maybe you're plannin' on takin' 'em up to your place. You gonna let 'em pitch tents in your yard, or what?"

Jeff felt himself deflating, like a hot air balloon with a jagged hole in its side. Sam was right, he couldn't haul more than a dozen people at a time, max, and even then he had nowhere to haul them to. Jeff sighed. The initial energy he had felt swirled away like dust. Suddenly, he felt exhausted and overwhelmed all over again. Sam reached out to him, and Jeff took his hand.

"Son, it's all right. Your heart's in the right place, no doubtin' that. Now, you got to get your *head* in the right place."

Jeff took the breath that Sam had suggested. He thought for a minute and then said, "I could drive over to the school, and pick up one of the busses. Or one of the church busses, come to that. I could get a hell of a lot more people in each load that way. As to where to take them... hell, I don't know. The hospital, maybe? They've got plenty of beds, and some emergency generators. The power won't stay on forever, you know. Not with no one to keep it up and running. The hospital's got a cafeteria, we can stock up on canned food from the store..." He looked at Sam questioningly.

Sam couldn't see the look, but he could tell from the pregnant silence that Jeff wanted some input.

"Okay, the hospital sounds good. That's a start, anyway. But you're gonna need a lot more room than just the hospital. We're talkin' 'bout a bunch of folks here, Jeff. So, the hospital and where else? Needs to be someplace with plenty of room, and a place you can set up a kitchen and bath area. Also, it needs to be as close to the hospital as you can get it, or you'll be doin' just like you said, runnin' from one end of the city to the other. So, where does that leave us?"

Jeff looked back down at the map. He slapped his forehead.

"The damned high school, of course! Plenty of room to set up cots, it's got a cafeteria, and showers in the gym. Best of all, it's only about a block and a half from the hospital. I can shuttle back and forth between them with no problem."

Sam nodded. "Yeah, that would 'bout do, I reckon." He cast his eyes glumly at the ground at his feet. "I just hope that we'll actually need all that room."

Jeff wanted to tell the Sam that he was sure that they would, but he was afraid that the old man might be right. They sat in silence for a long moment, and then Jeff got up and headed for the front of the store. He looked back at Sam, concern showing in his eyes.

"Hey, old timer, are you going to be all right while I go do this? I'm liable to be gone for a long time, getting all this crap together. You okay here?"

Sam grunted. "Well, I wouldn't say no if'n you offered to bring me back a case of beer to keep me company while you're out gallivanting around the country. And maybe bring me my portable stereo in here, so's I can listen to me some music?"

"Hell, Sam, there aren't any radio stations up and running. I checked last night, and then again today on my way over here on the truck radio. You'll just be listening to static."

Sam managed a guilty look. "Well, it's a CD player, too, son. An' I've got me some CDs I listen to whenever I ain't got no customers, or at night when I'm closed. I figure I can play them, leastways until the power goes out on us. Just bring me that ol' stereo, and there's a cardboard box of CDs under the shelf beneath the register. Ain't no need in you goin' through 'em, I've got 'em pretty well organized, so's I can find what I want quick-like."

Jeff headed for the register and Sam called out to him, his voice echoing through the empty store. "Mind you bring my shotgun and that box of shells, too. I hope I don't need the sumbitch, but I'd feel better knowin' I had it."

Jeff yelled back that he'd bring everything and found the CD player. It was a surprisingly new model. Jeff had been expecting to find a relic from the early 90's that was almost as old as he was, but the stereo looked almost brand new, and was equipped with an EQ, Bass-booster, and multi-disc capability.

"Heavy, check out Grandpa's boom box, Waylon. I bet you Hank Williams and Ralph Stanley *rock* on this bad boy."

Waylon, who had been nosing around the Little Debbie display, looked up, woofed once, and then returned to his study.

"None of that crap, buddy boy. Chocolate is bad news for your species, my friend. So back off."

Waylon gave a final, longing glance at the display and headed back over to where Jeff stood, gathering up the stereo, CDs, shotgun, and shells. Once he had gotten everything together, he nodded his head toward the back room.

"Lead on, O Canine Companion of my Heart."

Waylon gave him another of his "Yeah, you're an idiot, but I guess you're *my* idiot looks and went back into the back room. Jeff followed and sat the bulky stereo and the remainder of his load on the table with and audible grunt.

"Christ, Sam, how many CDs have you got in here, anyway?"

Sam's head whipped around. "Here, now, you just hand that over! It ain't right to be pawin' through another man's property! Show some respect to your elders, by Gawd!"

Jeff totally misunderstanding Sam's request, silently handed the man his shotgun and the box of shells. Sam felt the items and looked confused. His face clenched in anger, and he spouted "Not the shotgun, you little smart-ass! You gimme my CDs!"

Jeff was taken aback, but laughed nervously.

"Okay, Sam, chill. Nobody is going to mess with your CDs. What's the matter with you, anyway? You think I'm going to steal your damned CDs? Hell, my truck doesn't even have a CD player in it. Even if it did, I wouldn't want to listen to a bunch of old dead dudes beating a banjo to death with a…"

Jeff trailed off as he finally got a good look into the box containing the CDs. Like a man in a trance, he began to flip through them one at a time. The silence in the room became a palpable thing. After what seemed an eternity, he turned to Sam, his eyes huge with disbelief.

"Godsmack, Sam? Let's see: we got Korn, Limp Bizkit, Pantera… here's some Metallica; Master of Puppets, my personal favorite, Megadeth, Alice in Chains… and oh, my sweet Jesus Christ wearing a polo shirt, you've got *Motörhead* in here! Lemmy Motörhead, by God and all his Apostles! Samuel Merchant, you're a fucking *metalhead*!!!"

Sam, who had been sweating and looking wildly around during this inventory of his listening material, now firmed up his jaw and replied in a gravelly voice, "What a man listens to in his free time ain't nobody's business but his own, by Gawd. Now, before you get any ideas 'bout givin' me shit 'bout my music, I'd like to remind you that I'm a' holdin' a damned street howitzer, and even blind as hell I can turn your head into meatloaf from here."

Jeff held up his hands in a useless gesture of surrender. He was grinning like an idiot, but Sam couldn't see that, either. When he spoke, there was genuine respect in his voice.

"Sam, I think this is quite possibly the coolest thing I have ever seen in my whole life. Man, the thought of you head-banging to 'The Ace of Spades' will give me something to look forward to forever, I shit you not. Hell, I just wish I knew about this secret of yours a long time ago. We would have had a hell of a lot more to talk about. You ever hear of Velvet Revolver?"

Sam snorted in disgust. "You think I'm an idjit, boy? Of course I've heard of 'em. After Guns 'N' Roses broke up, Slash, Duff McKagan, and Matt Sorum went in with Dave Kushner from Wasted Youth an' Scott Weiland from Stone Temple Pilots to form Velvet

Revolver. Weiland left back in April, though, so who knows what'll happen there. You want my opinion, they'd a' done better with somebody else on lead vocals. Weiland just wasn't the right fit for that band. But that's just me. Maybe they'll find 'em a better singer now that he's out of the picture."

Jeff was silent for so long that Sam began to look concerned.

"You still there, boy?"

"Yeah, I'm here, Sam. I just cannot *believe* I'm having this discussion. This is one of the most surreal things I've ever been party to. How old are you, Sam?"

Sam's chest puffed out with pride.

"I'll be eighty-seven come August the fourth, boy. Somethin' 'bout it?"

Jeff shook his head. "No, sir, not one thing. It's just to think that I've known the coolest old fart in America for years, and I never had a clue. It simply amazes."

Sam lifted the barrel of the shotgun threateningly.

"If you're a' goin', I suggest you get on with it, boy, afore you go an' piss me right off."

Jeff backed out of the room, the dopey grin still plastered to his face.

"I'm going, I'm going. You sure you'll be all right?"

"I got me some food, some beer, some tunes, and a 12 gauge that'll take the head clean off a man at twenty yards. I'm livin' the American Dream, boy. Go tend to y'business."

Jeff turned and began to gather some supplies. He got several bottles of water, paused, and then got a whole case. Folks might be thirsty. He grabbed some of the Little Debbie's that Waylon had been eyeing earlier and took it all out to his truck and put it in the bed. He came back in and grabbed some of the emergency first aid kits that were designed for the glove box of vehicles and took them out, too. It wasn't a trauma kit, but it beat the hell out of duct tape. He looked around, trying to see if there was anything he was forgetting. Finding nothing else he could use at the moment, he headed for the door.

He stopped at the busted glass of the door and yelled into the back to Sam.

"I'm out of here, old timer. You should be all right until I get back. I'll be back over this way by dark, one way or another. Try not to be too drunk to walk, what say? I don't want to pack your big ass to the truck."

Sam's voice carried from the back of the store.

"You still here, you little peckerwood? Go on, get outta my store!"

Jeff couldn't resist a parting shot.

"Try not to lose your balance when you start head banging, all right? You'll fall and hurt yourself."

Jeff vacated the store quickly, stopping only long enough to snag his rifle from where he had leaned it against the wall. He didn't leave quite fast enough to miss some of the most colorful curse words he had ever heard, however. He laughed as he and Waylon walked over to the truck and climbed in. He started the old Dodge up and reversed out of the parking lot and onto the road. He looked at the storefront one last time before putting the truck in gear and heading out.

"Motörhead. I *will* be *damned*."

Chapter Six

Jeff drove down the road towards town. He was not emboldened by what he saw. There were several more wrecked vehicles on both sides of the road. As with the accidents near the general store, some of these looked to be no worse than fender-benders, and others looked deadly. He was greeted with proof positive that at least one accident had resulted in fatalities about three miles from Sam's store. He was forced to drive slowly around a two-car collision that had left one man flung across the hood of his car, his head nearly ripped from his shoulders, and the driver of the other car still strapped into her vehicle with blood all down the front of her blouse. How long had she sat there slowly bleeding out, unable to see, waiting for help that would never come? Jeff shuddered as he went past. Car wrecks were, for obvious reasons, very low on his list of favorite things.

Jeff had nearly made it into town when a thought suddenly surfaced in his mind and popped like a bubble. There was a school for the blind in town. It wasn't a very large one, being in the sticks like they were, but he remembered reading about it in the newspaper. There had been hell raised over the taxes it was going to take to fund the thing, and the whole town was up in arms. According to the town council, there simply weren't enough blind children in the area to necessitate a school catering to their disability. It was sad, to be sure, but that money was needed elsewhere, so very sorry.

It turned out that there were more blind children around that anyone had at first thought. Jeff had read that more than twenty families from the tri-county area had arrived at the town council meeting with their blind children in tow to encourage the funding of such a school. Although many of the families resided in other counties, they said they were willing to pay a set amount from their own pockets to help get the little school up and going. The town councilmen had felt themselves backed into a corner with the whole deal. To deny the funding was one thing, but to do so faced with more than twenty blind children between the ages of five and sixteen staring blankly in their direction was another altogether. Had they nixed the school right then, they would have made Ebenezer Scrooge look like George Clooney.

Both sides were saved from a political debacle by a young attorney that happened to know about a federal subsidy that would enable the county to build the school at a much lower cost than originally thought. After a quick recess to check the figures, the town fathers were able to march back into the council chambers and magnanimously announce that ground breaking ceremonies for the new school would commence in less than six months.

The school, called Second Sight, was about a block and a half from where Jeff sat in his truck. As he thought about it, it seemed more and more likely to him that if anyone at all might be able to lend him a hand in this Herculean endeavor, it would be those that hadn't lost what they had never had in the first place. Having lived their whole lives in the darkness, the events of last Tuesday would not have affected them quite so badly. He could vaguely remember seeing the small white van from the school in town, taking the children out on field trips. He had once seen the lot of them at Sam's store, eating ice cream bars with obvious delight. They were being monitored by an older Hispanic man and a young redhead. Jeff had been in a hurry to get to the hardware store for some polyurethane, but the redhead had been enough to cause him to do a double-take and wish that he had not been in too much of a hurry to stop. Regretfully, he had continued out of the store.

He sat at the intersection just before the city limits now, rethinking his plan of attack. The initial plan of getting on a bus and laying on the horn was still a valid one, but if he had some help, things would undoubtedly go a bit smoother. If nothing else, the blind kids could help keep the rest of the folks calm. *Jesus*, he thought, *I depending on kids to keep the adults in line.* Blind *kids, at that. What a clusterfuck.*

He turned left down the street and headed for the school. He stopped short of it and turned off the truck. He took a long look around, but could see no movement. The class might have been on a field trip, for all he knew. With a sigh, he climbed out of the truck and waited for Waylon to jump to the ground. He looked at the rifle on the gun rack and almost closed the door when caution stopped him. Yes, he was going into a school for blind kids. The Mini-14 might be a bit of overkill, considering he still had his .45 on his hip, but then again, he had almost gotten his head blown off going into a store he'd been doing business with for years earlier in the day. Better safe than decapitated: that was his motto. As he has at Sam's store. he grabbed the rifle and stuck a couple of extra mags in his back pockets.

He and Waylon went up the short gravel walkway towards the school's main entrance. He stopped at the doors and looked inside the wire-covered glass windows on the door. It was dim inside, almost dark. That made him think that there was no one there at first, but then he looked down and noticed that the doors had been chained shut, from the inside. That struck him as very odd. He knocked on the door and called out.

"Hello? Is there anyone there? I've come to help, if I can. My name is Jeff Della. I live outside of town. Hello?"

He tried for several more minutes with no result. He looked down at Waylon and shrugged.

"Well hoss, it's back to Plan A, I guess."

They turned and started back toward the truck when Jeff heard a muted sound from inside the building. Turning back, he saw a dim figure separate from the shadows and make its way to the door. He stood at the entrance to the door and waited until the figure came closer. As it did, he could make out that the redhead from the field trip was coming to the door. She moved so sure-footedly that he at first thought she might be like him, unaffected by the flash. But then he remembered her that day at Sam's store. She had been slow and cautious then. She stopped just shy of the doors and cocked her head to one side, listening. It struck Jeff that he had seen Waylon do that very thing on countless occasions. After a few moments, she nodded and spoke through the safety glass, her voice muted.

"Do you have a dog out there?"

"Yes, ma'am, my Siberian husky, Waylon."

"Are you alone, besides the dog?"

"Yes, ma'am. Just the two of us. We were wondering... I mean *I* was wondering if maybe I might be able to help you folks. See, the thing is..."

She held up a hand to stop him. She resumed her cocked-head stance for a moment, and then asked him a question that he was totally unprepared for.

"Do you work in the deep mines? Underground?"

He stammered for a second and then got himself together.

"Well, ma'am, I've got to say that is an odd question, given what's happened, but no, I don't. I make furniture. Out at my place outside of town. As a matter of fact, I believe I see one of my chairs sitting in that room just off to your left. I don't know where you bought it, but it definitely looks like one of mine."

She stood very still. After a moment, she asked him his name.

"Della, ma'am. Jeff Della. Like I was saying, the thing is, I can still see. I know that's a bit weird, but I promise you it's true."

She nodded again.

"I know you can. I heard your truck pull up. I don't think you'd be out driving if you were blind, Mr. Della." She spoke with no surprise in her voice at all, which set Jeff back on his heels a bit.

"Ma'am, you do know what's happened, don't you? I mean, about the flash and all?"

The redhead nodded again. She still displayed no surprise that Jeff was unaffected by it, and that was becoming a bit unnerving. He wasn't sure what sort of response he had been expecting when people found out he could still see, but this definitely wasn't it. Christ, he hoped that the woman wasn't slow or anything. That would complicate things greatly. He spoke very slowly and carefully.

"Okay, ma'am. Well, the thing is, I can still see, so maybe I can help you folks. Do you understand? Maybe I can give you a hand with whatever you need. Do you understand? I can see to get supplies, help with cooking, things like that. Do you understand?"

"Mr. Della, why are you repeating yourself? And more to the point, why are you speaking to me like I am three years old? Is there something wrong with you?"

Jeff, who had just been wondering the same thing about her, turned beet red.

"No, ma'am, there's nothing wrong with me. I'm just sort of surprised that you're *not* surprised that I'm not blind like everybody else, is all. I'm sorry if I offended you."

That seemed to satisfy her. She stepped to the door and placed a key in the padlock that held the chains. Just before she turned it, she turned her face to his. They were separated by less than a half inch of wired glass, but Jeff found himself slightly breathless as he looked into her eyes. They might not have functioned properly, but they were the most beautiful shade of emerald green he had ever seen in his life. When she spoke to him, her voice was low and slightly frightened.

"I shouldn't be doing this, Mr. Della. We all agreed that we wouldn't open the doors for anyone. But you can see, and you're right, that would be a great help to us. By opening this door, I'm placing our lives in your hands. Please remember that. *Please*, be a good man." She then turned the key in the lock and he heard the chains rattle to the floor. She pulled the door open and stepped back, allowing he and Waylon to enter the building. They stepped through into the cool dimness of the front foyer. Sure enough, sitting in a small office to the side was one of his chairs. He remembered fabricating it about a year ago. He looked around the small, neat foyer and was startled by the sound of the chains rattling behind him. He turned to find the young woman reattaching the chains to the door and padlocking them again. Once she had completed this task, she turned to face him.

He was once again taken in by the beauty of her eyes. With her red hair and green eyes, she could have been the poster child for Irish tourism. She looked to be about his age, or maybe a little younger, with a slight build. She stood about five foot four, and was full in all the right places, as far as Jeff was concerned. He realized he was ogling her shamelessly, and she couldn't see him doing it. He felt bad about it and hastened to cover his shame.

"Ma'am, it's not that I'm ungrateful or anything, but it's a little late to be locking the door, isn't it? I mean, I'm already inside. And why did you ask me to be a good man? I mean, I'm not an angel or anything like that, but I try to be a decent person. And to be brutally honest, even if I was a total jerk, the fact that I can see sort of offsets any personality deficiencies on my part, don't you think?" He gave her a small laugh to try to ease any tension the remark might have caused, but her face remained an impassive mask. He felt her gaze upon him, and even though he knew she couldn't see him, he found himself fidgeting and looking at the floor, stealing little glances at her face. For the love of God, he felt like a little kid that had got caught in the cookie jar! He steeled himself and looked her directly in the eyes.

"First, Mr. Della, would you please stop calling me 'ma'am'? It makes me feel like I should be your mother or something, and I don't quite think I'm old enough for such a thing. My name is Cynthia

Jordan. Call me Cyndi, or if you can't manage that, Cynthia will do. Secondly, simply because you can see most certainly does *not* excuse any 'personality deficiencies', as you call them. I've just allowed a man into our school, an *armed* man, if I'm smelling correctly, and I don't want to take any more chances than I absolutely have to. So, just understand this: we have worked this out beforehand. If you try anything, the children and Father Don will be out of here and gone before you can turn around twice. You have me at your mercy, of course, but you will not harm the children here. Are we clear on that?"

Jeff was unsure about how to answer the question so bluntly put to him. To buy himself a little time to figure out what approach to take with this woman, he asked, "You said you let an armed man in here if you were smelling correctly. What does that mean, if you don't mind me asking?"

She sighed. "You're attempting to change the subject, Mr. Della, and doing so quite badly. However, to answer your question, I can smell oil and gunpowder, and I assume that they are not some sort of aftershave you use. Now, I've answered your question, will you be so kind as to answer mine?"

Jeff cleared his throat. "Yes, ma'a…Cynthia. I apologize, it's just that I don't quite understand why you are so… well, protective, I guess, of the children. I mean, aside from the obvious reasons that we are all protective of children. Who *isn't* protective of children?

Dammit... I'm sorry. I'm rambling." He stopped talking for a moment to gather his wits. Cynthia waited patiently. Finally, he began again.

"Okay, Cynthia, it's like this: I found out earlier today that I'm apparently the only person on the planet, so far as I know, that can see. I also almost got my brains blown out by a guy I've bought dog food from for years, had to withstand a musical revelation that almost unhinged me mentally, and finally, I find out that if the people of this town are going to survive, they'll need me to do it. Following me so far, or are you wishing you hadn't opened the door?"

Cynthia smiled. "Well, you're two points up on interesting, I'll give you that. A point down on conversational style, but we'll see how it goes. Please continue."

Jeff looked at her dubiously. Well, all right, then.

"Okay, so I'm now the Caped Crusader, except I have no idea how to do it. The best idea I have come with so far was to get a bus and canvas the town, laying on the horn and asking anyone that was uninjured to come out to me, so I could round them up and take them to the hospital, or the high school." He laid out the plan he and Sam had concocted, finishing up with, "So, when I got to the intersection, I figured that if anyone in town might be able to help me, it would be you all, because of your familiarity with the problem. So, how am I doing now?"

"Another two points on interesting, and maybe one up on conversation. I haven't regretted opening to door yet, but there's still time for you to screw it up, so go on."

Jeff laughed. "Well, there's no going on to it, really. That's my plan, from beginning to end. Get everybody in a couple of central locations; take care of them the best I can, and then hope like hell whatever this is passes. Let me tell you something Cynthia, being the only person who isn't blind kind of sucks. I know that's a terrible thing to say to someone that's blind, but it's the God's truth."

Cynthia gave him a sad smile. "While I can empathize with your feelings on the matter, the truth is somewhat worse than what you seem to think."

Jeff cocked an eyebrow. "Worse? What in the hell could be worse than being the only man on the planet that can see?"

She sighed. "*Not* being the only person on the planet that can see, I'm afraid."

<u>Chapter Seven</u>

It took several seconds for what Cynthia had said to sink in enough for Jeff to make an even halfway coherent reply.

"I beg pardon? I'm not sure I caught that."

Cynthia gestured to the small office. "Let's have a seat. It seems that there are things you need to know."

That's got to be the understatement of the millennia. Hands down, thought Jeff as he followed her into the office. She sat down behind a tiny desk and motioned him to sit in the chair he had made. It was uncanny how well she moved, with such surety. If someone had told him Cynthia was blind, he would have been forced to disagree. *Well*, he thought, *this is her home turf. She probably knows it better than I know my own bedroom.* As they got situated into their respective chairs, Jeff was once again struck by Cynthia's eyes, but he was beginning to take in her whole person, and he continued to like what he saw. Snapping back to the matter at hand, he asked her again what she had meant by her statement about him not being the only person that could see.

Cynthia leaned back in her chair and fixed her eyes on Jeff's face. He knew she couldn't know exactly where it was, but she was remarkably close.

"On Tuesday afternoon, we were in class. Well, there were thirteen of us. Lucky, huh? There is as bug going around, and several of the students were out sick. So on Tuesday afternoon, when whatever it was happened, there was Father Don, eleven children, and myself in class. We were working on our Braille lessons. Actually, if it hadn't been for Father Don, none of us would have had a clue anything had happened at first."

Jeff interrupted her. "Father Don? Is he the middle-aged guy I see driving your bus around with the kids?"

Cynthia nodded. "Father Donald Martinez. He's a priest from over in Charleston. He moved down here when they opened the school. He's worked with blind children most of his adult life. We were very lucky to get him. He keeps this place going. He is the heart and soul of Second Sight."

"Okay, if he's the heart and soul, what does that make you?" asked Jeff with a grin.

He got one in return. "I guess that makes me the brain and nervous system. I keep up with our books up to date, and make sure that we have everything we need in the way of supplies and such. I also teach." She stopped and gave him a sly look. "You are definitely moving up in points for conversation, but what I've got to tell you is important, so let's keep the meet and greet for later, okay?"

Jeff said that was fine by him. In fact, he was willing to listen to her read off her grocery list as long as he could just look at her. His father's voice spoke up in the back of his mind, something that had not happened for many years.

I think some*body went and fell off the bridge over a girl.*

Cynthia continued. "Okay, so Tuesday afternoon, Father Don went blind, just like everyone else. We were about out of our heads over it. I got to the phone and dialed 911, but the officer I spoke with was as busy trying to get me to help *him* as I was getting him to help *me*. You see? He kept interrupting me, telling me to call the paramedics because he had suddenly gone blind. That frightened me very much, let me tell you. After I manage to calm him down enough to listen, I told him what had happened to Father Don. I could hear the radios going off in the background, and it was all the same thing. Officer needs assistance calls, every one of them. The policeman I was speaking to said 'Mother of God, what's going on here?' and hung up. I knew right then that help wasn't going to be coming anytime soon." She stopped and glanced in Jeff's direction. "That was actually a very intelligent idea, coming here. You're right; we *are* better prepared for something like this. With the exception of Father Don, nothing at all really changed for us. Anyway, we just sort of hunkered down, I guess. We could all smell smoke, but it was far away, so we weren't too worried about it.

We helped Father Don the best we could and waited. And waited. And then, just to mix things up a bit, we waited some more. You get the idea. We would hear people yelling outside, but we knew that there wasn't much we could do for them. In here, almost everyone can run through every room of this building full-tilt and not bump a knee. Once we step out that door… well, several of the children are from the surrounding counties and know nothing about Stone Grove except Second Sight. It seemed to me to be tantamount to a death sentence to let them outside, and if either of us adults went out and couldn't get back…" She let the comment linger. "As it was, staying low was just about the best thing we could have done, all things considered."

Jeff finally broke in again.

"Okay, hold up. I get the staying in part; that makes perfect sense to me. You probably kept those kids and Father Don alive staying where you knew the terrain. But why the chains? It's not like you had to worry about bandits breaking in, after all. What would they do, feel their way around until they found something worth stealing? I don't get it."

Cynthia blew and exasperated breath out. "Perhaps if you would let me finish, you would understand the whys and wherefores of the chains on the door."

Jeff once again felt like a school boy caught in the act. "Sorry, Cynthia. Please, go on."

"Thank you. We put the chains on the doors on Wednesday afternoon. We had been hearing what we thought was a vehicle somewhere across town off and on all that day. We couldn't be sure, because it was too far away. On Wednesday, though, we could hear it for sure. A big truck, like a four-wheel drive. Needless to say, we were ecstatic. We thought that help had finally come. I left the children with Father Don and headed for the front door. I wanted to flag whoever it was down before they drove away. The truck sounded like it was just down the street, near the intersection. I opened the door part-way and was about to go out onto the front step when I heard two men talking. Something about the way they sounded caused me to hesitate. I don't know what, exactly, but something in the first man's voice was just…off, somehow. He sounded like he was gloating. It just struck me odd, so I stepped back inside the doorway and listened with the door open just a crack. I listened for a few minutes and…" She trailed off, looking blankly into space. Jeff let her sit for a moment and then gently prodded her to go on.

"Cynthia, if someone was driving on Wednesday afternoon, then you're right, someone else besides me can see. It's very important that I find that person. His help would be invaluable to me right now. This job is just too big for one man to take on. Did you recognize his voice? Was he someone you know? If I can, I've got to try to find him just as soon as I can."

Cynthia jerked in her seat and flung her hand out to him. Surprised, he took it, and was shocked at the strength of her grip. When she spoke, she sounded panicky and scared.

"No, that's the absolute *last* thing you need to do. You have to listen to what happened next." She took a deep breath and relaxed her grip on Jeff's hand, but didn't let go. He was fine with that.

"While I stood there listening, I realized that I *did* recognize one of the voices. Just not the one of the man driving the truck. I recognized the voice of the other man. Do you know Officer Barnes? The Assistant Chief?"

Jeff thought about it for a moment and then it clicked.

"Kind of fat guy, balding, probably around forty or so?"

"Well, I couldn't tell you if he was fat or not, and I've never run my fingers through his hair, but yes, the age sounds about right." Her tone had taken on a bit of an edge. Jeff immediately apologized, and was amazed to find how much this woman's good opinion of him meant.

"I'm sorry Cynthia. I didn't mean any offense, it's just that I'm still not used to… well, all this. I've been around people that can see my whole life, so the way I talk is sort of geared for that. Of course you can't describe him, unless someone had described him to you. But I'm sure it's the same officer. What happened next?"

Cynthia's face softened. "No, *I'm* sorry. I shouldn't worry about you being politically correct. You came here to help, something you didn't have to do, and I jump down your throat because you ask one innocuous question. It wasn't fair, and I apologize."

Jeff grinned. "Okay, we've established that *I'm* sorry, *you're* sorry, and most likely the rest of *humanity* is sorry, albeit for different reasons. So, we're all sorry, we're all forgiven, and we're all best of friends now, okay?"

She turned those amazing eyes towards him. When she smiled, it only enhanced their appeal. In a soft voice that Jeff found incredibly sexy, she asked, "*Are* we best of friends, Jeff? I think just I might like that."

Jeff found it difficult to answer, because his mouth had suddenly decided to do its impression of the Sahara desert. He was once again profoundly grateful that Cynthia couldn't see him, because he wasn't sure he would have been able to cross his legs to hide his evident arousal without hurting himself. When he found his voice again, he said, "You betcha. Best of friends. We're like the Mickey Mouse club, minus the rodent. But why don't you finish your tale, milady?"

Cynthia's face lost its glow.

"Officer Barnes was on the street just across from us, from the sound of it. He had heard the truck at the intersection, and was waving his arms and yelling at it. I heard the truck engine stop and the man getting out. I could hear him walking down the street in heavy boots. They were clocking against the pavement so *loud*. Officer Barnes was asking the man from the truck who he was, if he could see... well, I'm sure you can imagine. The man from the truck didn't say a word, just stood there. I could hear him breathing, though, and it sounded like he had a respiratory infection or something. Officer Barnes started getting angry, demanding that the man talk to him. Finally the man said 'Well, well, if it ain't old Law Dog Barnes. How are you doing, Law Dog?' Officer Barnes must have known him, because he became very still and put his hand on his gun. He stepped backward and must have tripped and fallen, because the man from the truck started to laugh his head off. He was taunting Officer Barnes. Kept saying things like 'What's the matter, Law Dog? You having some eye trouble today?' Things like that. It was just horrible, the way he taunted that poor man. Finally, Officer Barnes just told the man to leave. When he wouldn't go, Officer Barnes must have pulled his gun, because the man from the truck laughed again and asked him how he expected to hit anything. Asked him if the police department had equipped their people with sonar with all that newfangled Homeland Security money. He said much worse, but I'm not going to repeat it. I could hear him walking up the where the officer sat in the street, those big boots clocking on the pavement. He moved around a lot, walking around so that Officer Barnes couldn't get an idea where he was, I suppose. Finally, the officer just asked him what he wanted. Officer Barnes just sounded so... *lost*. He sounded hurt and confused and just lost. The man kept circling him and making fun of him until Officer Barnes got mad enough, or scared enough I suppose, that he started screaming at the man, telling him to get away from him, things like that. Then, that man… he…" Cynthia trailed off, and Jeff was alarmed to see tears welling up in those wonderful eyes.

"Cynthia, what happened?" he asked softly.

She was silent for a moment longer and then took a deep breath and plunged through the rest of it like someone setting out to do a dirty task and trying to get it done as rapidly as possible.

"That man just walked up behind Officer Barnes and said: 'Give me a fucking D.U.I., will you? Well, let's see how many of them you can give out without your goddamned *head*. And that's just what he did."

Jeff took Cynthia's hand in is again and held it tightly.

"The man shot the police officer?"

Cynthia nodded somberly. "He just walked up behind him and shot him dead in the street in front of the school, just like that." Her voice sounded young and afraid, and Jeff wanted to take her in his arms, but was unsure how she would react.

"Cynthia, where's the body? It wasn't there when I go here."

She pointed through the lobby and towards a small grassy area enclosed by the school.

"We let the children play out there at recess, because there is no danger of any of them wandering off and getting lost. You can only reach the playground from inside the school, there isn't any door that leads to the street. After we were sure that the man in the truck was gone, Father Don and I went out and carried Officer Barnes inside and out to the playground. We used an old tablecloth to cover him with, and dug him a shallow grave out by the flower garden. It took us most of the night, but we managed to have it done by this morning." She stared off, a sad look on her face. "I just hope we were able to dig it right. I've never had to dig a grave before, and I didn't know how to do it." With that, the floodgates opened, and Cynthia sat silently weeping.

To hell with it, though Jeff, and he folded her into his arms. They sat like that for a long time, until the awkward position of their chairs made it uncomfortable to remain in the embrace. Breaking apart, Jeff wiped away the tears that remained in Cynthia's eyes.

"Do you know what I think?" he asked her.

"What?"

"I think that I'm very glad I remembered this place, and that I came here. You are incredibly brave to have done that. I can't imagine the courage it would take to go out there, knowing that man was there and what he had done. But you went anyway, and I think that is just incredible."

She looked confused.

"We couldn't just leave him lying there on the street, could we? I mean, he was a human being, not a bag of trash."

Jeff looked into her eyes. "Cynthia, leaving him there was just exactly what most people would have done. Most folks are far too wrapped up in their own problems to think of something like that. Most folks would have just went right on and left him lying in the street."

Cynthia shook her head forcefully.

"No, they wouldn't. Most people are good at heart. There are very few like that man that shot Officer Barnes. Almost everyone would have taken care of him if the situations were reversed."

"Maybe before the flash, but now, people are too busy trying to survive to bother with the niceties. Trust me, kiddo, things are different now. What you did for Officer Barnes was a very brave and… well, noble thing to do. Most people wouldn't have bothered, but you did. So, like I said, I'm glad I came here. With things the way they are now, I'm going to need all the nobility I can get around me. "

Cynthia laughed cynically. "Well, I don't *feel* very noble."

Unbidden, the thought shot across Jeff's mind. *Well, you should, because you look like a queen.* Out loud, he said, "So, since we've established that we're pretty much on the same side and my conversational skills are improving, do you think I might meet the rest of the gang? Get to know the whole crew?"

She laughed again, this time happily, and reached for his hand. He took it, and she led him through the lobby towards the staircase. He glanced back over his shoulder at the chained door. With luck, those chains might slow down an attacker for a few minutes, but the fact of the matter was that this was a school for the blind, not a fortress. Anyone that wanted in here bad enough was coming in, chains be damned.

Jeff sighed. As if everything else that was going on in the world wasn't bad enough, it now appeared that the only other human being in town that shared his gift of sight was also a stone cold killer.

Great. Just great.

Chapter Eight

Cynthia led him up the staircase to the upper floor of the school. Waylon padded along beside them, as silent as candle smoke. As they walked, it struck him odd that they would put a staircase in a school for the blind in the first place, and said so.

Cynthia gave him a look laced with ironic anger.

"Yes, you would think that a single storey would have been more practical, wouldn't you? We though so too, but the town fathers said that there wasn't enough land allocated for everything to fit in a single storey, so we got two. *And* no elevator, either, which has been fun. It just wasn't in the budget, and we couldn't get enough private donations to have one installed. I swear, I spend about half my time making sure the little ones don't go bum-over-teakettle down this ridiculous thing."

Her accent was definitely *not* West Virginia.

"Where are you from, Cynthia?" he asked. "Originally, I mean."

She grinned. "What, y'all don't think Ah soun' lak Ahm from 'round these parts?"

He grinned back.

"No, I definitely do *not* 'think y'all are from 'round these parts'"

She laughed. "I'm originally from Boston, but my parents and I moved to San Francisco when I was about four or five. We lived in California until I was eighteen, and then I went away to college."

Curious, he asked, "Where did you go to college?"

"I went to the Royal National College for the Blind in Hereford, England. There were only about two hundred of us there, altogether. I studied English and mathematics, mostly."

Jeff was impressed. "So, a Boston girl becomes a California girl, then an English girl, and winds up in… West Virginia? What part of that story did I miss?"

She laughed again. "That's pretty much exactly what my father said. He was… well, *distressed*, to say the very least that I chose Stone Grove, West Virginia to settle down. I think he had planned on me moving back in with them in San Francisco once I got my degree, but I wanted to travel around a bit. When I heard through a friend that Second Sight was about to open, and needed a teacher with real-life experience working with blind children, how could I say no?"

"I don't want to be rude or nosey, but it sounds to me like your family might be what around here we call 'well-off'. I can't imagine that it's cheap to send your kid to England to college."

"No, it isn't, and yes, you're right. We are what you'd call 'well-off'. My father got in on the ground floor when the internet boom started, and he made quite a bit of money."

"Really? How much money?" As soon as it left his mouth, Jeff realized how impertinent the question sounded. "I'm sorry, Cynthia, that's none of my business, and it was rude to ask."

Cynthia dropped his hand and elbowed him none too gently in the ribs. He let out a startled *oof!* that dissolved into laughter. She then took his hand again and continued down the second floor hallway.

"Well, it *was* incredibly rude, but I'll let it slide this time, since we're working on your conversational skills. If I chastise you too much, you'll clam up, and we don't want that. So I'll answer your question, as ill-mannered as it was. The last time I checked, my father was worth about thirty-eight million dollars. Satisfied?"

Jeff stopped dead in his tracks. His sudden stop caused Cynthia to be jerked off-balance. She nearly fell backward, where Jeff neatly caught her. He stood her upright, and then stared at her incredulously for a moment before he spoke again.

"You mean to tell me that you've got thirty-eight million dollars and you live in Stone Grove, West Virginia? On *purpose?!?*"

She elbowed him again, although not quite as hard.

"No, my *father* has thirty-eight million dollars, not me. And yes, I live in Stone Grove, West Virginia on *purpose*, you big dummy. How else could I live here? Accidentally?"

"No, I... I mean, it's just that...." Jeff stammered helplessly as he tried to organize his thoughts into something resembling a coherent statement. "I guess I just never met a millionaire before", he finished weakly. He saw the look on her face and quickly amended that to "The *daughter* of a millionaire, I mean."

She smiled. "Well, now that you have, what do you think of them?"

"I think that if all millionaires' daughters are as beautiful as you, then I hope that rich men are procreating rapidly."

He had answered without thought, and as he played back what he had said in his mind he was struck numb with embarrassment. His face turned an alarming shade of plum and for the third time that day, he was glad she couldn't see him. He couldn't have said something that sounded more like a pick-up line if he had tried. He waited with held breath for her reaction.

She stopped walking and turned to face him. With that eerie way she had, she seemed to look right at him, just as if she could see him as well as he could see her. When she spoke, her voice was low and a bit husky.

"Well, the conversational points are just *skyrocketing*, aren't they? Now, come on, let's meet Father Don and the kids."

She turned and started back down the hallway. With his heart in his throat, Jeff followed. He glanced down at Waylon, who had been watching the exchange with great interest.

"What are *you* looking at, furry ass?" he growled at the dog.

Waylon gave him a grin, and picked up the pace until he was alongside Cynthia.

"Goddamn dog", he muttered to himself.

They entered what appeared to be a recreation room at the end of the hall. There were two couches and several chairs surrounding a coffee table. Along the back wall were eleven bedrolls, the sleeping bag rolled up and each sitting atop a pillow. Next to these were eleven backpacks. Jeff was once again pleasantly surprised at the neatness of the room. It was hard to believe that eleven children had been sequestered in this room for three days now. Then he realized the need for such neatness. Without maintaining order, these children would be falling all over each other's belongings. Everything in the room had a place, and each child knew where that place was. As it was, the children's rec room looked more like a Marine Corps barracks, while retaining that indefinable quality that children so effortlessly give the space they occupy.

The adults had taken the two couches, and there was a marked difference between them. Even given his brief experience with the blind, Jeff could immediately tell the couch on the left of the room belonged to Cynthia, while the one on the right was Father Don's. Father Donald Martinez was a 58 year-old Hispanic man with salt and pepper hair and a boxer's build. Cynthia's couch mimicked the overall neatness of the children's bedrolls, her sheet and blanket neatly folded with her pillow stacked atop it, while Don's was a messy jumble of bedclothes. Graceful as he may have been before the flash, he was more than likely going to trip up in them and fall the first time he tried to get up if he didn't move them.

Cynthia led Jeff to the center of the room with her sure-footed grace and asked for the children's attention. It was unnecessary, because they had turned their heads as one the moment that Cynthia, Jeff, and Waylon had entered the room. They all now stood or sat, waiting expectantly for Cynthia to tell them what was going on.

"Father Don, children, this is Mr. Jeff Della. He lives outside of town. He wasn't affected by the flash like most people. He can see just fine, and he is here to help us."

This speech was met with silence ranging from hopeful to suspicious to outright hostile. Jeff stepped forward and cleared his throat.

"I'm very glad to meet all of you, and I'm very impressed at how well you've taken care of one another in this difficult time." It sounded like a politician's speech to Jeff, but he could think of nothing else to say. "I would very much like to help you, and I may need some help *from* you before this is over. Do you kids think you might be able to help me?"

One of the kids, a teen-age boy said with a bitter tone, "Help you with *what*? You want to learn to read Braille? Haven't you got anything better to do?"

This boy had been the hostile-looking kid. Jeff turned to him and asked," What's your name, son?"

"My name's Jamie Cummings, and I ain't your son."

Jeff felt Cynthia's warning hand on his arm and gently shook it off. He walked over to the boy until he was only a foot or so away. The boy looked to be about fifteen or sixteen, a few inches shy of six feet. His black hair stood in dark contrast to his milky-colored eyes. Jeff lowered his head until he was face-to-face with the boy.

"No, Jamie Cummings, you most certainly aren't my son. If you were, I would bust your ass for talking that way to your elders, just like my dad did mine. So, what's your deal? Do you dislike me in particular for some reason, or are you just a punk to everyone?"

Jeff heard Cynthia's audible gasp, and Father Don's low grumble of protest as he tried to extricate himself from his blankets. Jeff knew that he was being harsh, but he did *not* have time to jack around with this kid playing "Who's the Big Dog?" right now. Time was short, and things needed to be done.

Jamie didn't flinch or back up a bit, even when Jeff was right in his face. Whatever grudges the kid was packing around; he wasn't short on courage, something for which Jeff was profoundly grateful. They were going to need all the courage they could muster before this thing was over.

The boy stared defiantly back at Jeff, or at least in Jeff's general direction.

"I ain't a punk. I don't know you, one way or the other, but I know this: the last guy that could see around here blew a cop's head off in the street. So you'll just have to *excuse* me if I don't kiss your ass just because your damned eyes work, right?"

Cynthia gasped. "Jamie! Mr. Della is here to help, and furthermore, you need to watch your language in front of the other children."

Jamie barked out a sarcastic laugh.

"Yeah, Ms. Jordan. The world's coming to an end, but let's make sure that the kiddies don't hear any bad words they might repeat."

By this time, Father Don had managed to make his way clear of his bedclothes and was standing uncertainly next to the couch with one hand on the arm.

"Jamie Cummings, I don't take to that kind of talk *amigo*. Now, you apologize to both Mr. Della and Ms. Jordan for being an insensitive little *cuto de pablo*, all right?"

Jamie had the good grace to look abashed at speaking like that to Cynthia, but his distrust of Jeff remained unabated. He simply stood there staring off into space for a bit until he finally mumbled, "Sorry, Miz Jordan."

Father Don was an old hand at the waiting game, and he stood there patiently. The silence grew heavy and uncomfortable, but the priest looked like he was prepared to stand there for the next year or so, if that's what it took. Finally, Jamie spit out a "Sorry" at Jeff and did a neat about-face and walked to his bedroll. It still amazed Jeff how easy these people made it seem to move about.

"Okay, then. Like Ms. Jordan said, my name Is Jeff Della. I answer to Jeff, though. Mr. Della was my dad's name, so try not to confuse me, okay?"

The joke was weak, but it brought a ghost of a smile to a few faces, especially the younger ones. Jeff looked at the children, eleven of them; each better equipped to deal with what was going on than any other adult in town, except Jeff.

And, of course, the cheerful, neighborhood cop-killer.

Jeff snapped his fingers and said cheerfully, "Okay, guys, I'd like to get to know you all, so how about you tell me your names?"

Cynthia stepped forward to do the honors. She called out their names in order, from left to right. How she knew where they were standing in relation to her was a mystery to Jeff. *I may never get used to this*, he thought.

"Jeff, this is Paul, Christy, Charlie, Gennie, Brandon, Mike, Randy, Rebecca, Glendon, and Angie. And, of course, you've met Jamie. This is all of the students that were present on Tuesday. Like I said, there was a bug going around, and several of our kids were out that day." Her face took a saddened cast. "I only hope that they're all okay."

Glendon spoke up. "They're fine, Ms. Jordan. They were at home, right? *Nobody* knows home like we do." An Asian-American boy, Glendon was a rarity for small-town West Virginia. His parents lived a couple of counties away and drove him to school each say before setting off to work. Glendon's sunny smile dimmed as he remembered that his parents were somewhere out there, blind and alone. A pall settled over the children as their thoughts turned toward home.

Jeff pulled them out of their funk by announcing that he required some volunteers. The children all looked towards him with interest.

"Okay, guys, here's the deal: there are a bunch of good folks out there that need our help. They can't see, so they can't take care of themselves. We need to do what we can to help them. Now, I've worked out a plan to get them all to a couple of central locations, where it'll be easier to care for them. Here's what I think we should do…"

Jeff spent several minutes explaining in detail his plan. The children and the adults alike listened carefully. His experience with children limited to his own sister and the younger siblings of his friends, it was a little unnerving to have so many children listening with such quiet reserve and intensity. He would have figured at least the younger ones would have been squirming halfway through his spiel, but they all remained perfectly motionless until he had finished. Living life depending so greatly upon hearing must have had a bearing on their concentration, he supposed.

"Well", he finished up, "what do you guys think? Does it sound doable?"

The group all seemed to pull closer together without moving a muscle. Father Don had made his way over to where Jeff was standing and felt around until he located the man's elbow. He nodded toward the hall, and the two of them walked out of the rec room. Once in the hallway, Father Don spoke so quietly that Jeff had to lean in close to hear what he was saying.

"A couple of things, Mr. Della. First off, let me tell you from the bottom of my heart that I am thanking God Almighty for you right now. If you hadn't shown up when you did…" He left the comment hanging. "Second off, they need a minute or two to hash this out. It's odd to watch, because sometimes they do it without saying very much, which can be unsettling to someone not used to it. It still unsettles me at times, and I've dealt with the blind for over thirty years. Anyway, they need to come to a consensus. It's not like with you and me. Well, if I could still see, I mean. With the sighted, people tend to look to a strong leader to make decisions. I mean, even in a democracy, we've still got the President, right? With the blind, you can't put your faith in what you see, because you can't. So, you develop another way of seeing the world and each other. That group of kids in there is from just about every ethnic and social background coming or going, but they are all the same, so you understand? It's almost like a collective society, in a way. A hive or something. I don't know exactly how to explain it. I'm not very good with words, which is funny when you think about it, me being a priest an all. Bottom line is, they'll figure about your plan, which by the way is better than anything *I've* come up with, and if there are any holes in it or ways to improve it, they'll figure them out. And I've never met a better organizer than Cynthia Jordan in my life, hands down. She's the best. So let's give them a bit to do their thing. In the meantime, why don't you tell me a little about yourself?"

Jeff found himself giving Father Don the condensed version of his life story while Waylon sniffed about from room to room. When he was finished, he turned to Martinez and looked at him closely. The priest was staring off into space, but the compassion was clearly evident on his features.

"Son, I'm so very sorry about your family. God has truly tested you."

Jeff, who wasn't so sure about God in general, declined comment. Instead, he asked Father Don what his story was. The priest looked surprised at first, and then pleased that someone wanted to know.

"It's a pretty simple story, really", he began. "I was born and raised in a little town on the Texas-Mexican border called Roma. My mom used to joke that we were all Italian-Americans. My dad was a carpenter and my mother was a homemaker. I have a brother named Greg and a sister named Linda. My mom's American, my dad moved to the U.S. back in '56. My grandparents on my dad's side weren't too crazy about their oldest son marrying an Anglo, but he was in love, and that was that. I felt the calling of the church from an early age. Choirboy, the whole works. I was ordained on my twenty-third birthday. My mom and dad were so proud of me. I stayed in Roma for a while, and then decided that I wanted to move around a bit and see some of God's miracles here on earth. I wound up working with blind kids in an orphanage in Oklahoma City for a while, and it seemed like I had a knack for it. So, instead of settling down to a parish and tending my flock, I just sort of drifted from place to place and worked with the blind. I figured that *they* could be my flock, and my parish just happened to cover the whole country. I was in Charleston a few years back when I heard about Second Sight. It seemed so odd and out of place, a school for the blind in this tiny town in coal country, so I decided to check it out. I was only going to be here for a few months, but before I knew it, a couple of years had gone by. I love this place. I love the kids, the town, all of it. I had pretty much decided that this was going to be my final destination, right here in Stone Grove. Helping with the kids, reading my Bible, just…" He trailed off and turned in Jeff's direction.

"I just realized it. I'll never read my Bible again. Ever. I've seen God's word for the very last time." Tears threatened to well up in the priest's eyes for a moment.

Jeff clapped him on the shoulder.

"So you're telling me that they don't have a Bible in Braille here, Father?"

Martinez looked confused. "Well, of course there are. There are two… no three that I know of. But I can't read Braille, son."

Jeff smiled. "Well, then I guess it's lucky for you that you live in a school for the blind, isn't it? I feel reasonably certain that one of those kids, or Cynthia can teach you to read Braille, don't you think?"

Martinez's eyes cleared and he laughed.

"I knew I was going to like you, son. Talk about not seeing the forest for the trees! Of course, I can't see either, anymore. I'm pissing and moaning about not knowing how to read Braille in a school for the blind! Mary, mother of God, protect me from my own ignorance."

They walked back down the hallway, still chuckling. Waylon had found something interesting in one of the rooms and was giving it hell up and down the hallway. It appeared to be the head of a mop, but Jeff couldn't be sure, so quickly was the dog whipping it back and forth.

Cynthia appeared in the rec room's doorway and softly called out for the men to join them. Jeff and Martinez walked back into the room, where it appeared that not one of the children had moved an inch. Jeff looked at the group apprehensively. He suddenly realized just how much he was counting on these people to help him. Cynthia looked his way and smiled.

"Well, as far as your plan goes, we can't find much wrong with it. It's a good plan, but there is one flaw. It's just too massive in its scope and size. You're planning to keep a town of seven thousand alive and healthy all by yourself?"

Jeff was taken aback. "Well, I had kind of hoped I could count on you guys for some help."

"No, of course we'll help, that's not what I mean. I mean that most of the work is still going to have to be done by you. Driving supplies in, getting medicines, water, everything. You'll have to be the one to locate and ship all that stuff in. I'd love to help you out, but the state of West Virginia declined to give me a driver's license. Do you really have any idea just how huge an undertaking that is going to be, just logistically speaking?"

Jeff stood with his brow furrowed. "Well, yeah, I know it's going to be a big deal, but what are my other options?"

Cynthia turned to the children. "Kids, Jeff and Father Don and I are going into the next room to discuss some things. Randy, you and

Angie are in charge of today's reading. Let's get at least two chapters done, okay?"

The children all found seats on the couches and chairs as the two older children picked up a large book and began to take turns reading, their hands flying across the pages. Cynthia motioned Jeff into the hall, and then took Father Don by the arm and led him out behind them. They went into the next room, one that looked like a storage room. Filing cabinets and various pieces of equipment from several different computers, printers, and even an old typewriter lay strewn about. Cynthia closed the door and turned to face Jeff.

"This is going to sound heartless, because it *is* heartless. The simple truth is that you cannot take care of seven thousand people, not even with our help. It just can't be done."

Jeff thought back to what he had seen at the general store and said, "I don't think it will be anything like seven thousand. There were countless fatalities the first day, and more since. As much as I hate to admit it, there may be a couple of thousand folks already dead." He looked at the floor as he admitted this last.

"Okay, let's say you're right. Say that two thousand have died since Tuesday. That still leaves you with five thousand people. I personally think it was much more than that, but I'm a realist bordering on a pessimist. But here is the cold hard truth of it, Jeff: if there were only two thousand people left, you *still* couldn't take care of them all. You just couldn't. There's no way you could keep that many fed, clothed, and clean. And without cleanliness, there will be disease. Let's say we save two thousand people. Each of those people will need two thousand calories a day in food. Do you realize how much that is? That's four *million* calories, per *day*! Can you imagine how difficult that would be to truck in daily if you had a whole workforce to help you? And that's every single day. Now, you can lower their caloric intake and lessen the amount of food you have to bring in every day, but by doing that, you'll be lowering their bodies' ability to fight off infection and illness. And that's just *food*, Jeff. What about water? Most people lose about ten cups of water a day, just going through their normal routine. You get a lot of that back through your food, but not all. A person will normally replace about four cups of water a day through their foods, so that leaves about six cups lacking. Now these people are going to be much more sedentary than they were before, but they are still going to sweat, to cry… they'll lose that water. So, let's be optimistic and say that you only need to provide four cups of drinking water per person, per day. That's eight thousand cups per day; there are sixteen cups to the gallon, so that's five hundred gallons of water, per day. And that's just drinking water, Jeff. Not to mention water to bathe in, or to clean with. No bathing, no cleaning… you're right back to disease. And in those conditions, a sickness would spread like wildfire, and there would be almost nothing you could do about it but watch them die. Are you following me here, Jeff?"

Jeff was in a state of shock. He had expected this to be a big job, but Cynthia's cold math had left him breathless. Five hundred gallons of water *a day*? How was he supposed to keep that much water in constant supply? Sure, the water mains worked right now, just like the electricity, but for how much longer? What happens when he turns the tap and nothing but air comes out? And that was just the *water*, for the love of God. Four million calories a day? And for God alone knew how many days? The cooking, the cleaning, the bathing, the help feeding... what the fuck was he going to *do*? He could just see himself lugging five hundred gallon jugs of water to the hospital and the high school every day he was strong, but it would take him all day, just to get the water to the townsfolk. He suddenly felt very small and alone.

"Jesus, Cynthia... what in the hell am I going to do?"

Her jaw tightened. When she spoke, her voice was cold, nearly devoid of emotion.

"You save those you can and you let the rest...die."

Father Don gasped. "Cynthia, you don't mean that! You *can't* mean that!"

She whipped toward him like a striking viper. "What else would you have him do, Don? He can save some, or he can save none. Those are the choices. If he tries to save them all, everyone will die, whether from dehydration, starvation, or disease, they will all die. So will Jeff, if you want to be honest about it. Even if he's in incredible shape, two or three weeks of that sort of labor, and he'll die of exhaustion. And we're saying that it's only two thousand still alive. What if I'm wrong and he's right? What if there are more like five thousand people out there? Then everything more than doubles. Can't you see that?"

Martinez looked hurt and shocked at the younger woman.

"I can't believe I'm hearing you sentence thousands of innocent people to death like this, Cynthia. They will all *die* without help!"

"Yes, just like most of them will die, even *with* help, including those doing the helping. When a communicable disease breaks out, do you think that the caretakers will be immune? No, Don, it'll be the *children* that will die, trying to help Jeff help those people. You would be sentencing *them* to death. Besides, it isn't *us* that has sentenced mankind to death, it's whatever caused this in the first place. Man or God, or whatever, *we* didn't do this. We're just stuck trying to clean up the mess. And, before we get any deeper into the theological ramifications of all this, may I remind you gentlemen that there is a murderer roaming around out there, as well? What are you going to do, just go up and ask him for a hand, tell him that it's all right he executed a police officer in front of our school. You going to tell him that we'll just keep that to ourselves if he'll pitch in lugging the fucking *WATER*???"

Cynthia spun on her heel and walked to the corner of the room, where Jeff could watch her shoulders shake as she silently sobbed. He wanted to go to her and comfort her, but he was still too mired in his own shock and dismay at the truth of her words.

Father Don simply stood, his jaw hanging open, his sightless eyes bulging in their sockets. The overall effect was to make him look slightly slow, like a mentally retarded child that had grown to manhood. The three of them stood in a triangle, each locked into their own thoughts. The horror of what was to come had begun to settle in on them.

Cynthia was right. In order to save some of the lives of the people of Stone Grove, they would have to let most of them die. But who were they supposed to save?

Ryan S. Pack

Chapter Nine

Jeff had told Cynthia and Father Don that he needed to take a walk and think things over. He nodded at their warnings to stay away from the windows and not draw attention to himself and walked back downstairs. The rifle was still slung across the back of the chair in the room he and Cynthia had first sat down to discuss the situation. He picked it up and slung it over his shoulder. With things being what they were, the handgun didn't seem to be enough protection anymore.

He motioned for Waylon to stay put, and walked to the front door. He looked up and down the street. He could see nothing. He ran back upstairs and asked Cynthia for the keys to the chains on the door.

"Why?" she asked. "What are you going outside for?"

"I've got some supplies in my truck. Water, food, things like that. I want to bring them in. Also, I need to get my extra ammunition for my rifle and handgun. All that stuff is in my truck."

Cynthia looked skeptical. "I'm not so sure it's a good idea to be running in and out of here, Jeff. It might bring attention to us. If that man comes back…"

Jeff looked at her grimly. "If that man comes back, I'll blow his damned heart out."

Cynthia managed to look shocked and appalled at this. "How could you just *shoot* a man like that?"

Jeff found himself furious. It happened instantly, like someone had thrown a bucket of boiling water over his mind. His voice dripped with sarcasm as he replied.

"You know, it seems to me that you were just informing me that I needed to let a few thousand innocent people die slow and horrible deaths a little bit ago. So now *I'm* the bad guy because I said I'll kill a man that murdered a blind cop in the middle of the street? You know what? You're priorities are a little fucked up, lady."

Cynthia drew in a sharp breath and, with a shaking hand, dug the keys out of her pocket. She hurled them toward Jeff, who reached out and caught them instinctively. She turned and, for the first time since he had met her, stumbled as she made her way back towards the rec room. She had gone about six steps when Jeff caught up to her and held her by the arms. She struggled weakly against him, tears rolling freely down her face.

"Cynthia, I'm sorry. I didn't mean for it to come out that way. It's just that I'm… well there's just been a lot for me to process today. You guys have had three days to get used to this stuff. I've had since this morning, okay? I know what you said is true. I understand now that I can't save everyone. I get it, all right? But you need to understand something. Somewhere out there right now is a man that has absolutely no problem killing defenseless people. You have all told me this, and I believe you. Now, what exactly do you suggest I do if I run across this guy? Take him to the police station? Ask him nicely to please stop killing folks? Cynthia, there *are* no police stations anymore. Hell, there are no *police*. There's only a bunch of blind people trying to survive. I'm going to try to help as many of them as I can, but I can't do that with some crazy son of a bitch wandering around behind me, shooting anyone he feels like. If I see him, I'm going to kill him. In fact, one way or another, before much longer I'm going to find him if I don't happen across him while I'm trying to get things done. If I can, I'll find him, and I'll ambush him. I'm not interested in being fair. I'm not going to try to catch him and lock him up. He'd just be one more mouth to feed, and I don't have the extra time or energy to deal with that. As far as I'm concerned, he gave up his right to life when he decided to use this clusterfuck as an excuse to do whatever the hell he wants to instead of helping. So, I'm not sorry about what I said, but I am sorry about *how* I said it. Okay?"

Cynthia nodded her head and wiped the tears from her face. She tried a smile. It was a sad affair, but it was better than nothing.

"I know", she said. "It's just that I like you. You come along like the White Knight in a fairy tale to help save everyone, and I kind of enjoyed that image. The White Knight usually kills the dragon, but not with a rifle."

Jeff laughed. "Would you rather I challenge him to a duel? We can go get those old Civil War sabers from the wall in the library and kill each other like real men."

Cynthia slapped at his arm. "No, you idiot, I don't. I just *hate* all this. I hate what it's made us all become. God, Jeff, I just said that we are going to have to let most of the people in this town *die*! How am I supposed to live with myself, knowing that I'm part of something like that?"

Jeff kissed her gently on the forehead. "You'll live with it the same way we all will, Cynthia. One day at a time."

He left her upstairs and went back to the front door. After checking the street again, he quietly opened the door and stepped outside. It was getting late in the day, and the light had taken on the heavy glow of the beginning of a summer twilight. He held the rifle in both hands, his palm sweaty against the pistol grip. Despite his claims to Cynthia, he wasn't really sure if he could simply gun down another human being. The fact that he was most likely going to have to do that very thing before much longer didn't make him feel any more at ease.

He crossed the street in a jog, and began ferrying the supplies he had gotten from Sam's store back to the lobby. After he had finished with them, he ran back one last time and grabbed his duffle bag of ammo. As he was closing the door, he thought he heard an engine in the distance. He stood motionless and waited. Very softly, in the distance, he could hear the low growl of a truck motor, and the squeal of tires as someone pulled out. In the oppressive silence that had covered the town like a blanket, there was no way of telling how far away the vehicle was. Jeff relocked the door and began carrying the supplies upstairs.

The kids were thrilled, with the exception of Jamie Cummings, with the bounty of Little Debbie cakes. Jeff was pretty sure at this point that the boy wouldn't be thrilled by anything less than news that Jeff had been eaten by wolves by the side of the road. That bothered him, because he needed that kid. He was big enough to be useful on the labor end of things, and seemed, for all his gruff demeanor, to be plenty intelligent. Jeff gave an inward sigh and set about placing the supplies along one wall, where everyone had access to them. He put them in order and told Cynthia how they were stacked so she could get what they needed by touch.

After he had gotten everything situated in the rec room, he called for Cynthia and Father Don to accompany him into the hallway again.

"Listen", he said, "I have to leave for a while. I need to go back across town to the old general store and pick up a friend of mine."

Martinez's head came up. "Old Sam Merchant? The guy that runs the store?"

"Yeah. I left him there this morning and I told him I'd be back for his as soon as I could get everything set up." He looked around forlornly. "I had expected to have half the town either in the hospital or over at the high school by now, but I'm glad I came here first. If I hadn't, I would still be running around like a chicken with its head cut off, trying to round up folks. Or I'd be dead, thanks to our local psycho." He sighed. "Either way, I've got to go pick up Sam. While I'm there, I can get some more food and water. Can you think of anything else we might need?"

Cynthia spoke up immediately.

"We need propane tanks for cooking. The big ones if you can find them, but we have an attachment hose on our grill that lets us use the small ones, too. I guess you'll need lanterns and candles. We won't have much use for them, but *you* might. Bleach, too. We can use it to sterilize the water if we need to. We've got a pretty well-stocked first aid cabinet, so I think we're good there. But if you want to grab some more medicine, we can probably use it. Tylenol, Benadryl, stuff for stomach cramps, the usual." Her voice dropped lower. "I know that it would be pointless for you to bring us guns, but I would feel better if we had *something*. Knives, machetes, something like that. If that man comes back while you're gone, I don't want to have to try to defend these children with my bare hands."

Jeff had a momentary image of Cynthia decked out like Red Sonja, dressed in a skimpy leather outfit with a broadsword slung across her back. He found the thought unbearably sexy and blushed furiously.

"I think I can find something that will work", he said. "Sam has just about everything that can be had in that store. I seem to remember a pretty large selection of knives in a display case back there in the rear of the store. I'll see to it that both of you have one, and something suitable for the older children."

Cynthia shook her head. "Not just the older children, *all* the children. In normal circumstances, I'd ask for a mental evaluation before I would suggest arming an eight year old kid, but circumstances are far from normal. The children need something to give them a fighting chance, if something were to happen to the adults."

"Okay, you're right. Even the little ones need some sort of protection. I'd like to find some Mace or something. Something that shoots pepper spray in a wide pattern, so they didn't really have to aim too much. I just don't know exactly where to locate something like that. They don't exactly advertise it at Walmart, and even old Sam doesn't keep anything like that handy. I don't think", he added with a grin. "I'll run over there before it gets totally dark. I don't want to be advertising myself with all my lights on. It's bad enough that bastard might hear my truck."

He looked at the two people standing before him, one blind since birth and the other blind since Tuesday. These two people were all that stood between death for the eleven children in the other room. He suffered a moment of indecision. He was torn between his word to

Sam that he would be back to get him, and leaving these people to their own devices while he was gone.

Cynthia seemed to sense his hesitancy.

"Go on, go get Sam and bring him back. I'll stay downstairs and listen for your truck, so you won't be exposed on the street for too long."

"What if you hear the truck, think it's me, and let that killer in instead?"

Cynthia gave him a haughty look. "You think I can't tell the difference between a Dodge and a Ford?"

"How in the hell did you know I was driving a Dodge?" he asked incredulously.

She blew out her breath, puffing her cheeks like a trumpet player.

"The same way I've been able to tell the difference between my mother's footsteps and my father's since I was a little girl, you dummy. I'm *blind*, remember? Us blindies can hear *really* well. Goofball." She flapped her hand at him and told him, "Go on, get going. I don't want to stand in the downstairs foyer all night, if that's okay with you."

Jeff smiled again and called out to Waylon. The dog came bouncing out of the rec room, where he had become a big hit with the kids. He cocked his head at Jeff quizzically.

"Yeah, fuzzball, we're going back over to get Sam. You up for that?"

Waylon glanced back into the rec room and at Jeff again.

"Oh, so that's how it is, huh? Traitor. Fine, stay here and let everybody fawn all over you while I'm out doing slave labor under extremely dangerous conditions. I'll remember this, though. Ask me for some more hamburger later and see what happens."

Cynthia came over to Jeff and reached out for his hand. He took it, and they walked downstairs together. Father Don had already begun to make his way back into the rec room to hang out with the kids.

"Will you be all right without Waylon?" she asked.

"Sure. The big baby is just after all the affection he can get. He's an attention hog, always has been." He gripped her hand reassuringly. "No, really, I'll be fine. It would be cramped up front with Sam and Waylon both, anyway, and I don't want to hear them arguing over who gets the window seat."

Cynthia laughed, and then grew sober.

"You'll be careful?" she asked. "Nothing heroic and such? The White Knight getting his ass back to the blind children is the next chapter in this fairy tale, you know. His *uninjured* ass, by the way."

"Yes, ma'am, ass returning to children in an uninjured condition, got it."

She slapped at him again. "I told you to stop calling me 'ma'am'".

"Well, I'll work on it, but if you don't quit beating on me, I'm going to have to report this. Domestic violence is a very serious matter. Love doesn't have to hurt, you know. I have my rights."

She grinned and flashed him those amazing eyes again.

"Love doesn't have to hurt, huh? Getting a bit ahead of yourself, aren't you? We haven't even been on a date yet, unless you count giving me a Little Debbie and a bottle of water a date, and if that's the case, let me assure you that it will our first and *last* date".

Jeff felt his chest tightening and his ears burning. Getting his nerve up, he said, "I think I can do better than a Little Debbie and a bottle of spring water. Maybe after we get all this taken care of you'd be willing to give it another try?"

Cynthia just stared at him blankly. He felt his stomach drop to his shoes. *Had to push it, didn't you*, he thought. *Why didn't you just play it cool? Stupid-ass!*

"Jeff", she said, "did you just ask me out?"

"Christ, Cynthia, I'm sorry. I know it was too forward. I don't even know if you're involved with anyone else, and it was arrogant of me to even…" He stopped as she reached up and found his face, and then placed a finger over his lips.

"You just asked me out on a date. I just wanted to make sure that was what it was. It seems to be the end of the world the last time I checked, and you asked me out on a *date*. You are such an odd man."

Jeff played back what had just happened in his head and realized that she was right. The whole world was ending all around them, and he had just off-handedly asked her if she'd like to go out. Go out to what? The movies, maybe some popcorn? They could no doubt find a good seat. Of course, he would have to tell her what was going on, since she was frigging *blind*. The whole thing suddenly struck him as the stupidest, funniest thing he had ever heard anyone say in his life, and it had been *he* that said it. He burst out into gales of laughter. Full-bodied laughter, springing up from the soles of his feet and slamming out of the roots of his hair. He whooped and bellowed laughter to the roof beams. Waylon stuck his head out of the rec room, looked at Jeff and seemed to shake his head helplessly. The dog then turned and went back into the room. This just made it worse. Jeff was laughing so hard now that his legs felt boneless, and he was afraid that he might just collapse where he stood if he didn't get control over himself.

While Jeff was carrying on, Cynthia remained motionless, a little grin playing at the corners of her mouth. After several minutes, he had settled down into occasional hiccupping giggles. She took his hand again.

"Better?" she asked.

Wiping tears of hilarity from his eyes, Jeff said, "Yes, I'm okay. I'm just an idiot. The end of mankind, and yet that international playboy Jeff Della maintains his dashing good looks and undeniable charm with the ladies."

This sent him back off into another bout of stifled giggles, and he managed to blow snot all over his fingers while clapping his hand over his mouth. He hastily wiped his hand on the seat of his jeans as they continued down the staircase. They made it to the foyer and Cynthia paused.

"Well, your sense of timing is quite possibly the worst in the world, but in answer to your question, yes, I think we might arrange something. Seeing as how we'll be spending a great deal of time together for the foreseeable future, anyway. Maybe we can have a candle-lit dinner of Chef Boyardee Beefaroni with a nice red wine, what about that?"

Jeff could feel the stupid grin on his face grow larger. "I think that may be the most romantic evening I can imagine. Of course, my evenings mainly consist of eating with my dog and listening to the radio, so my sense of romance may be a bit off. Maybe you could help me with that. Since you've already taken my conversational skills under your wing, anyway."

She smiled at him and squeezed his hand again, briefly but firmly. She began to flip through her keys until she came up with the one for the lock on the chains. She had placed it in the lock when she turned back to him, her face serious.

"I mean it, Jeff. You watch yourself. It's too late today to start rounding up the townsfolk. If you come across any that you can help without exposing yourself too much, then by all means, go ahead. But don't go looking for anyone except Sam. Tomorrow we'll get started trying to sort out how we're going to get this accomplished. Tonight, we need a good meal and a good night's sleep."

She gripped his arm tight enough that it almost hurt. "And do *not* go on some commando mission looking for the man in the truck. It's a small town, and your paths will cross soon enough. Just get Sam, some more supplies, and get your ass back here, just as quick as you can."

Without thinking, Jeff stepped in and kissed Cynthia. It wasn't a long, deep kiss, but neither was it something that could have been mistaken for the kiss reserved for a sister or favorite female cousin. When he stepped back, he saw with amusement that he wasn't the only one capable of blushing around here. She just looked toward him and said, "Thank you. That was nice. Now, get out of here."

He laughed. "Sure, kiss 'em and then show 'em the door. My momma warned me about women like you."

Cynthia gave him a come-hither look and said, "Sweetheart, your momma didn't even *know* about women like me. Now beat it."

Jeff went across the street in the failing light of the evening. When he got to the truck, he turned back and saw the vague shadow of Cynthia standing in the darkened foyer. He waved, knowing that she couldn't see it but not caring.

He got into the truck and rechecked the bolt of his rifle to ensure there was a round in the chamber; he then did the same thing with his handgun. He had taken a couple of magazines for each weapon from his duffel bag, leaving the remainder upstairs by the supplies he had brought with him. He had no intention of getting involved in a firefight with anyone tonight. If things got hairy, he would fire his weapon empty and then drive like the Devil himself was after him.

He turned on the truck, congratulating himself for maintaining the vehicle. The engine wasn't silent, but it was fairly quiet for an older model. He put it in gear and slowly pulled away from Second Sight. As he drove to Sam Merchant's store, he found himself preoccupied by Cynthia Jordan, and those incredible eyes.

Chapter Ten

He pulled into the general store's parking lot about twenty minutes later. He parked his truck on the far side of the lot, where the store itself obscured the truck from view from anyone passing by on the road. Jeff climbed out and was instantly uneasy. The tiny hairs on the back of his neck rose and all his muscles tensed. He didn't know what exactly was wrong, but he had no doubt that *something* was. Something had happened. Something bad.

From the darkened depths of the store there came nothing but silence. Jeff had half expected to pull into the parking lot and hear the thrashing sound of heavy metal blasting out of the storefront. Instead he heard only the evening insects tuning up for their nightly symphony.

He slowly made his way to the front of the store, looking left and right across the parking lot and the fields beyond. The cars remained where they had wrecked, and another hot July day had not improved the look of the two fatalities. At least the electric lines had stopped snapping the corpse of the first driver, although the stench of burnt human flesh still hung oppressively in the evening air. The man now resembled something from a carnival haunted house, a blackened mummy. Jeff noticed with a rising gorge that even the man's *teeth* were burned in the remains of his gums. He looked away quickly and turned his attention to the storefront.

The last time he had entered the front door, he had nearly had his head taken off by a shotgun. He had no desire to repeat the experience. He wanted to yell out to Sam, but was restrained by a sense of foreboding. If there was anyone inside that meant him harm, they already knew he was in the parking lot. He saw no reason to give them even more advance warning of his arrival.

He stood in the parking lot trying to decide what to do when he realized that he made a beautiful target to anyone wishing to shoot at him. Standing in the middle of an empty parking lot, the sun going down directly in front of him, he could see little through the glare, but to anyone looking at him from the store he would have made a perfectly silhouetted target.

He hunkered down with his rifle gripped in his hands, feeling like an actor in a war movie. A *bad* actor in a war movie, at that. He could shoot both his weapons with a good degree of accuracy, because it was a hobby of his to target shoot at a range he had set up behind his cabin. But his knowledge of tactics were limited to what he had seen on TV and movies, and news pieces showing soldiers in Iraq or Afghanistan going about the business of war. Beyond that, he was winging it.

He duck-walked to the wall of the store beside the door way and risked raising his head for a quick peek inside. He could see nothing more than what he had seen when he left. He sat with his back against the wall and tried to figure out what to do next. If he simply walked through the front door, he ran the risk of either frightening Sam and repeating the shotgun incident or maybe having someone else playing Sam's part in that particular scenario. That someone else was there, or had been, was something Jeff was certain of. He didn't know how he knew this, but he wasn't about to question it. The feeling was just too strong, more of a certainty. He suddenly found himself wishing he hadn't left Waylon at Second Sight. The dog's heightened senses would be very handy to Jeff right about now.

He racked his brain to come up with something resembling a plan. The sudden realization that Sam might be hurt or dead inside galvanized him into action. Taking a deep breath, he rolled through the store's half-opened front door, picking up more broken glass as he did so. He came out of the roll with his rifle up, trying to look everywhere at once. While it was dim outside, inside the store the darkness seemed complete. He fervently wished he had a flashlight and suddenly realized that he had all of them he could possibly use, not six feet away on a shelf. Sliding over to the rack on his knees, he found himself praying madly that the batteries would be at the very least close to the flashlights. The thought of fumbling through the darkened store to find batteries while an unknown threat stalked him filled him with dread.

He reached the shelf and sent a thank you to God, if he was listening. There were several flashlights on the shelf, and a great many of them required that the batteries be bought separately. However, he found several in packages that included the batteries with the lights. He tore into one of these and fumbled the batteries into the rear of the light, cursing silently as his clumsy hands failed to engage the threads of the end cap at first.

He was still looking wildly around every few seconds, his imagination in overdrive. He could see his tormentor creeping towards him, a crazed madman wearing night vision goggles like the villain in "The Silence of the Lambs". Jeff didn't look much like Jodie Foster, and he was certain that he wouldn't be able to fire with the same kind of super-human accuracy that she had displayed in the movie, hitting his target in the dark. A toddler crawling toward him right now stood an *excellent* chance of having an entire thirty-round magazine emptied at it.

He finally got the end cap on the flashlight and clicked it on. It wouldn't work. He cursed again, this time out loud and in a high, near-panicked voice. He realized that he had put the batteries in upside-down, and spent a tortuous minute rectifying this. When finally he managed to get the flashlight to work, he played it across the entire store, row by row. He was dimly aware that he was once again making a target of himself, but at the moment he couldn't give a damn. He *had* to see what was going on. He felt a huge wave of empathy for all the people that had lost their sight so suddenly. They had no flashlight to end their fear. Their darkness was permanent. The thought nearly made Jeff weep.

Once he had satisfied that the store proper was empty of threats, he began to creep towards the back room where he had last seen Sam, the flashlight in his left hand, and the rifle unsteadily in his right. *Should have left the rifle and used my pistol,* he thought. There were no lights on, but then again, there wouldn't have been any need of them for Sam. Suddenly, Jeff realized that *all* the lights in the store were out. The neon signs in the windows, the street lights, everything. It was nearly completely dark outside by now, and there were no comforting pools of light in the parking lot like islands surrounded by blackness, keeping the dark at bay.

He understood that the power had gone out here. The electricity had been on at Second Sight, but here there was no juice. Jeff had no idea if the downed power lines at the wreck had overloaded a transformer, or if this was just the beginning of the end of the electricity in Stone Grove. At the moment, he was still too tense and freaked-out to consider the possibility that *all* the power in town might be out before the sun rose in the morning.

He edged up to the door separating Sam's private quarters from the rest of the store. He placed his ear to the door and listened for all he was worth. After several seconds, he realized that he could hear something, but he couldn't figure out what it was. It was a wet, organic sound; that much he was sure of. His imagination gleefully supplied the mental image of a brain-eating zombie chowing down on poor old Sam's head. Jeff shook off the image and, with a deep breath, prepared himself. Prepared himself for *what*, he had no idea.

"Sam?" he stage whispered through the door. "Sam? You in there? It's Jeff. I'm back to get you. You okay?"

The only reply was that wet, slobbering noise. Jeff gripped his rifle so hard that the plastic pistol grip gave a loud crack. Jeff let out a tiny screech and jumped about a foot off the ground at the unexpected noise. He cut loose with a flood of profanity that would have done a pirate proud and then stood there, trying to get his heart to regain something that at least approximated normal.

Finally, he felt like he had himself under a bit more control. *That old bastard is sound asleep in there with his headphones on,* he thought angrily. *He's got Pantera's "Cowboys from Hell" on repeat, and that noise is his old ass snoring.* Having convinced himself that he had given himself a serious case of the willies for no good reason, he straightened and opened the door, tossing it open harder than he needed to in his anger. It hit the wall and bounced back, but not before Jeff had caught sight of Sam.

He was not listening to his boom box. He didn't have on headphones. And he was *not* snoring. Jeff threw the door back open and rushed into the room, crossing it in three huge, shambling steps. In the harsh bean of light from the flashlight, the blood running down the sides of Sam's mouth were hellishly vivid, almost black. His shirt was soaked to his skin with blood, and a puddle of it had formed on the floor around his seat. The wet, snoring noise Jeff had heard was the labored sound of Sam trying to pull air into his destroyed lungs.

But the man was alive, and he was aware. His sightless eyes flitted about the room, but he was obviously trying to form words. His blood-smeared lips opened and closed. His hand hung weakly in the air, trying to reach out for Jeff. Jeff slid to his knees in front of Sam and grabbed his hand, all the while making soothing noises to the man. There wasn't enough light for Jeff to see just how badly Sam was injured. In the calmest voice he could manage, he said, "Sam, I've got to get some more light in here. The power's gone, and I can't see very well with this flashlight. I've got to go get a few more and turn them on so I can see better, okay? You're doing good, old hoss; just give me a minute to get some light going."

Sam shook his head weakly and tried again to speak. Jeff leaned down so that his ear was nearly touching the old man's lips. In a husky, choked whisper, he heard Sam say, "Lantern."

Jeff looked around. "Where is it, Sam? In the store, or back here? I need to hurry, pal. If it's a new one in the store, I don't have time to put the mantles on and shit like that."

Sam shook his head again and waved his hand vaguely towards the closet across from where the chair sat. Jeff figured that Sam had this room memorized from living her so long that he probably could have found anything he needed in the dark. Jeff turned to the closet and opened it, expecting a chaotic jumble of old man's paraphernalia. He was surprised to find a very organized space, with shelves neatly stacked with various kinds of outdoor equipment and fishing gear. On the second shelf stood a lantern that ran on the small sixteen and a half ounce propane bottles that so many things had been modified to run on these days. *Got to get some of these to take back to Second* Sight, *Cynthia said she needed some,* he thought almost incoherently. He pulled it from the shelf and sat it on the table in front of Sam. Jeff hadn't used this type of lantern before, preferring the old liquid fueled pump models. He was afraid that it would take some sort of special procedure to start, but it had been made to be operated by children from the look of it. He turned the knob and heard the hiss of propane. Pushing a button sparked, and flame flared up. Within seconds, there was a constant, bright light filling up the small room.

When Jeff turned back to Sam, his first instinctive wish was that it was dark again. The man was covered in blood. It was splattered in ropy splashes on the floor, the table, and the wall beside him. A spilt-second glance told Jeff that Sam could not live. Even if they had been sitting in a shock-trauma unit, Sam had no chance of survival. Kneeling back down in front of the man, Jeff looked helplessly into his eyes. They stared back into the nothingness that was his world now. Each breath was more labored than the last, and blood continued to well out of his mouth with each exhalation. Jeff felt the prickle of tears in the backs of his eyes, and his throat closed. He forced it back open and spoke.

"Sam, what happened? How did you do this to yourself?"

Jeff looked all about the man and realized that the wound was on his chest. He was about to pull the shirt back to see what had happened when Sam's hand gripped his fiercely. Jeff looked back into Sam's face to see the man giving him a look of pure fury. His mouth was working again, and Jeff leaned in again to hear what he had to say.

"Did nothin' to myself… sumbitch shot me…sumbitch come in an'…" The rest of Sam's sentence ended in a gurgle of fresh blood that ran down the corner of his mouth and down his neck.

Jeff felt a surge of red fury spring through him. There was only one "sumbitch" currently in the business of shooting helpless blind men that he knew of. He looked back at Sam and said, "Was it a man in a truck? Did it sound like a truck outside?"

Sam nodded weakly. In his failing voice, he said, "Thought t'was you, comin' back… hollered to come on back… sumbitch come in… laughin'… shot…"

Jeff was now shaking with anger. Sam had heard a truck and thought that Jeff had returned to pick him up. Thinking nothing more, he had yelled at the man from the truck to come on back. The bastard had, and… well, what he had done was perfectly evident all over the room. God-*damn* it. Sam was still talking. Knowing time was not on his side, Jeff listened closely.

"Told me… glad he found me… told me…he'd get me for sellin' him that ol' chainsaw…said I sold it to him knowin' it was broke…sumbitch…I *told* him it was old 'n broke…sum-*bitch*…"

Jeff was having trouble following the man, and was beginning to think he was delirious when it dawned on him that Sam was talking about selling the man something some time back.

"Sam, do you know who did this to you?"

Sam nodded. "Sumbitch...Oscar...Dan...Dan... dammit....Oscar *Daniels*!" This last was followed by a spray of blood that misted the air between them. Jeff racked his brain for a minute and came up with a face. He looked back down at Sam.

"Are you talking about the guy that drives that souped-up Ford F-150 with the flashy paintjob, works the deep mine? The one that stays drunk all the damn time and is in the 911 report in the paper every other week?"

Sam nodded.

"And he came in here and fucking shot you because of a *chainsaw*???"

Sam nodded again, a painful grin on his face. When he drew his breath, it sounded like someone wringing out a sponge.

"Ain't... that... 'bout... a bitch...son?"

Sam's grip on Jeff's hand tightened for a moment, and then fell lax into his lap. As Jeff looked on, Sam breathed out his last tidal breath. It seemed to last for hours to Jeff.

And then it was over.

Jeff had no idea how long he sat like that, kneeling in front of Sam, the dead man's blood soaking into the knees of his blue jeans. Finally he looked groggily around, like a man coming out of a deep sleep. He stood and took a step back. From this angle, he was able to see perfectly what had occurred. The man from the Ford, one Oscar Daniels by name, had entered the store and been hailed by Sam. He had walked back to Sam's little room, taunted him about an ever-fucking *chainsaw*, and then shot the helpless old man through the lung at point blank range. Then he had turned and just walked off into the night, on to find whoever else in this town that had ever pissed him off and do the same to them. Given the number of times as Daniels had been in trouble, and the general distaste in which the town held him, Jeff imagined that the list was fairly long.

Is that what he had been doing this whole time? Just driving all over Stone Grove and killing everyone that had ever crossed him? The only other man in the whole town that could see, and he was systematically killing people on his shit list? What the hell kind of deal was that? How many had he killed? And how many more were left on that list? Once he finished taking care of all his old grudges, what next? Maybe some recreational rape? Or maybe he'd gotten a taste for the killing and would just start killing at random, assuming that he wasn't doing that anyway. The fact that the cop he had killed had arrested him and he thought that Sam had sold him a faulty chainsaw argued that he had an agenda, though.

Jeff could not remember ever being as angry as he was right now. Not even when the drunk tucker had killed his family had Jeff been this angry. This wasn't a logical anger. It wasn't even anger, really. It surpassed anger a thousand fold. This feeling just nodded at anger as it strode past. A short while earlier, Jeff had been concerned that he would have a hard time killing another human being, even in self-defense.

Now, he couldn't wait to find Oscar Daniels. Jeff was sure enough of his marksmanship to know that when the time came, he wouldn't miss. No, he would be able to put a round right through Daniels' knee, from a goodly distance off. After he was on the ground, Jeff was going to see just how many 5.56 mm rounds he could put into that drunk fuck before the man finally gave in and died.

Jeff was willing to bet that, with careful enough aim, he could put a great many rounds into the man before hitting anything vital.

Jeff turned to the bed in the back of the room and pulled off the blanket. His whole body was shaking, a fine tremor that was so fast that he felt like a cell phone that had been set to vibrate. As gentle as a mother putting her baby to bed, Jeff covered Sam's body with the blanket. He took one last look at the outline of an innocent old man that had done nothing to deserve having his chest caved in by a large handgun in the dark, and turned to go.

As he reached to door, he said over his shoulder, "Rest easy, old hoss. I'll see to it you're paid back. In *full*... A fucking *chainsaw*."

It was a pitiful epitaph, but Jeff figured that Sam would not only understand, but agree whole-heartedly.

Jeff went back into the store, the lantern in one hand and his rifle in the other. His earlier fear of being seen had disappeared like fog in the sun. A very large part of him wished that Daniels would see the light and think that Sam had managed to make it out into the store and come back to finish the job. That would suit Jeff right down to the ground.

Jeff began to load the truck with the things that Cynthia had requested. He went heavy on the canned food and bottled water, and got all the rest of the first aid equipment he could locate. He gathered all the candles in the store and all the lanterns and flashlights, as well. He found several pallets of the small propane canisters in the back storeroom, and he took all of these. He looked over his provisions and nodded. This would do for now. He needed to get back to the school.

But first, he had one more stop to make.

Chapter Eleven

It was quiet on the road on the way back into town. Jeff kept his eyes open and listened as best he could for the sound of the other truck. He was driving without headlights, the three-quarters full moon providing enough light to drive by, as long as he went slowly. Apparently, Daniels had business on the other side of town, or he was asleep somewhere. *Hell*, thought Jeff, *he may have someone in Charleston he needs to kill for short-changing him at a 7-11.*

Jeff's fury had not lessened, but it had changed in nature. The heat that seemed to radiate from every nerve in his body had stopped. It had been replaced by a cold vacuum, almost a complete lack of feeling. It remained there, however, and he knew that when he got his chance to unleash it, Oscar Daniels was going to scream so loudly that his eardrums were going to burst. And he was going to die *blind*. Jeff swore that to himself. That son of a bitch would die *blind*.

Jeff cruised into town, but instead of taking the turn that would take him back to the school; he drove straight on to Main Street. About halfway down the street was a store fronted by an olive drab awning. Jeff pulled in front of it and killed the engine. He got out of the truck and again stood listening. Nothing but the insects of the night. He turned and went to the door of the shop with the green awning. As he had hoped, it was unlocked. He opened the door slowly, kneeling down as he did so. He was learning. If the shopkeeper was present, and in the mood to open fire, he would hopefully spray his ammunition over Jeff's head, instead of through it.

After several minutes, Jeff was satisfied that no one was going to open up on him, and he walked inside. He had taken the time to exchange the small flashlight he had been using at Sam's store with a four-battery job with a light that lit up a room like the sun. He played the light around the shop, looking at the wares. He took another step and was hit by the soft slap of the smell of decay. He walked over to the counter and found out why the proprietor had not decided to shoot at him. The man lay sprawled behind the counter; a 9mm clutched loosely in one hand, and a very large smear of blood and brains on the wall behind him. He had opted out.

Jeff found it ironic that this man had taken his own life. The man's name had been Simon Robertson, and he had been a survivalist. He had a conspiracy theory about every event on the evening news, and had constantly talked about the long over-due revolution. Faced with a true catastrophe, he had simply taken a gun and blown his head off. Jeff shook his head. It wasn't any of his concern. This man was dead, but what he sold was about to come in very handy.

Robertson had run an Army surplus store, like the ones found in almost every city in America. The United States military had produced a vast amount of equipment, and much of it found its way into stores like this one. Jeff looked around, not really sure where to begin. He felt pretty well armed. He knew his weapons, and was familiar with them. There were racks of AR-15 carbines and AK-47 assault rifles, but Jeff didn't feel like he had the time to familiarize himself with an entirely new weapon system. He did feel that it was time for some upgrades to his existing weapons, though.

His Mini-14 accepted standard AR magazines. Jeff looked around until he found the backpacks and duffle bags. He chose a large backpack covered with straps called MOLLE by the Army, according to the tags on it, which meant "Modular Lightweight Load-carrying Equipment", straps that allowed a person to add more accessories to the pack as needed. He took the pack to the display case that housed the clips and broke the glass with the butt of his rifle. He took out ten more clips for his rifle, and then cast about until he found the clips for the handguns.

He was disappointed in what he found. There were only three magazines for his particular model of handgun. He again thought about changing weapons. There were Glocks, Sigs, Smith & Wessons, you name it, and the man had it. After a few moments, he decided against switching. He knew his Ruger P90, and three more clips would suffice.

Moving on to the ammunition, he went heavy on the hollow points and soft tipped shells. Jeff had done his fair share of hunting, and he knew that full metal jacketed rounds passed straight through flesh, doing less damage. Hollow points and soft-tips, though, would expand and cause massive damage when they entered flesh and bone. He also took several boxes of 12-gauge double-aught buck shotgun shells. He didn't have a 12-gauge yet, but he soon would.

He passed the hunting rifles with their impressive scopes. He had no desire to shoot Daniels from across the county. This was going to be a very up-close and personal job. He stopped at the shotguns, looking over his choices. He chose a Remington with a pistol grip, collapsible stock, and a fore grip. Attached to the stock was a place to insert five extra shells, and the sling was also covered with small loops to hold extra ammunition. Satisfied, he tried to strap the shogun to the pack, only to find it wouldn't work. He was about to set it aside to take out to the truck separately when he noticed a holster designed for shotguns, also covered with MOLLE straps. After some futzing around with it, he had it attached to the side of the pack, and the shotgun fit into it snugly.

He now turned his attention to the accessories for the assault rifles. His Mini-14 wasn't technically an assault rifle, it was more of a rifle one would expect to find a farmer using to keep varmints down, but it was chambered in 5.56, the same as the U.S. military's caliber, and used thirty-round clips. As far as Jeff was concerned, any of the accessories for the AR-15's should work just fine for his rifle. He scanned the vast array of equipment and briefly wished he had familiarized himself with this stuff long ago. Again, he was relying mainly on what he had seen on TV and movies.

He thought about what he needed in order to accomplish his objective. Okay, he would need a sight that could give him quick target acquisition. The optics he had seen U.S. soldiers using in Iraq and Afghanistan hadn't really looked like traditional scopes that Jeff was used to. He looked around at the selection and found something that looked like what he had seen on those weapons. It had a small screen instead of a tube. He fooled around with it for several minutes before giving up and breaking out the instructions. It took batteries, he found. Luckily, Robertson had a large stock of these. Placing the batteries in the optic, he turned the dial on the side and immediately a bright red dot appeared in the window. Jeff smiled. This could come in handy. He laid it to one side and continued to peruse the accessories. A flashlight that attached to the rifle seemed like a good idea, so he chose one of those as well, after reading the directions to see what sort of batteries they used. *I'm dealing with one hell of a lot of batteries tonight*, he thought. Again, he was in luck. Robertson had obviously been a big fan of keeping plenty of batteries for the toys he sold.

Jeff thought about getting a laser sight for his rifle, as well, but decided against it. It seemed to him that lasers worked both ways. You could see where you were going to shoot, but the target could see where the shot was coming from also, so… no laser, then. He took his rifle behind the counter to a workspace to attach all his new acquisitions. He was flummoxed by the fact that everything seemed geared to fit a certain kind of base, and he had no such base on his rifle. He walked over to the rack of assault rifles and saw immediately how the system worked. These were called Picatinny rails, according to the merchandizing information. They accepted most accessories, and made changing things out much easier. His rifle had nothing like this on it. Well, damn.

He was about to give in and pick out one of the AR-15's when he saw a display case full of receivers for various weapons. He walked over and shined his light into it. After a few moments of searching, he found just what he was looking for. It was a receiver for a Mini-14 that would replace the one on his rifle, but this one was covered in Picatinny rails. He grinned again.

In a matter of a few minutes, he had changed out the receiver and was adding the scope and the flashlight to his rifle. It was a quick and easy process, and he had his newly revamped rifle done in about ten minutes. It was only as he was about to sling it over his shoulder that he realized he had overlooked a big problem.

His nice new sight looked bad-ass on his rifle, and when he had shouldered it, the bright red dot had shown up great. He was able to keep both eyes open and still track targets. He liked it. However, as with any new scope or optic, it didn't come pre-sighted on target. He wouldn't know if the damn thing was accurate without taking it out into the street and shooting the hell out of something, adjusting the sight with every shot. If Daniels was anywhere near town, he was *bound* to hear that. Again, that didn't really bother Jeff, but that much gunfire would scare the hell out Cynthia and the kids. It might even give Father

Don a heart attack. He could imagine their horror when the night around them suddenly erupted into massive amounts of gunfire. And if this sight was like any other scope he had ever used, it would take at least one box of ammo to get it sighted it properly.

He was trying to think of how to deal with this dilemma when his gaze passed idly over a rack of cases. The sign above them said "SAVE AMMO!" in big letters at the top. Under this, in smaller letters, it said, "Why spend money on ammo getting that scope dead-on? These laser bore-sighters will pay for themselves the first few times you use them!!!" Jeff looked upward and sent out a silent "thank you". He took one of the cases from the rack and opened it. It was pretty self-explanatory. You chose your caliber, and then turned on the laser that was encased in a brass cover that was shaped like that bullet. You chambered the laser into the barrel just like you would a regular bullet, and then lined your sights up with the red dot.

Jeff took the 5.56 bore-sighter and tried to turn it on. Of course, it required batteries. He shook his head. Fortunately, the case contained the batteries, as well. Soon, Jeff had the bore-sighter in place. He stepped outside the shop and looked through the sight. There, against a brick wall about seventy yards away, was a bright red dot. He turned on the sight of his rifle and now there were two red dots, about an inch apart in the little window. Using the adjustment knobs, he soon had the two red dots perfectly overlaying one another. He turned off the sight and took the brass bore-sighter out of the gun and turned it off, as well. Now, at least in theory, the red dot on his sight would be dead-on at about seventy yards. Jeff nodded, satisfied. He turned and went back into the store.

He repacked the bore-sighter and placed the case in the backpack. It seemed to be a handy little tool, and worked with every caliber from .17 HMR up to .50 BMG, according to the accompanying paperwork. All of that meant nothing to Jeff, but being able to sight-in a gun silently seemed to be a good idea to him. He went back to the military equipment and soon had more MOLLE gear attached to his pack. He started to add a canteen, but found a very handy little specimen called a Camelbak, which appeared be a backpack converted into a 3 liter water container, complete with a tube that ended with a mouthpiece that you could turn on and off, and simply bite down on the receptacle at the end and drink as if from a long straw. To this, he added several magazine holders, and some very nice little first aid kits. The kits were much handier than the ones from the general store, and were better equipped. Jeff added some water purification tablets that he found and several boxes of what were advertised as MRE's, or "Meals, Ready to Eat", meals that might come in handy. He found several drop-leg platforms that attached to his belt and were snapped around his leg with elastic bands. These, too, were covered in MOLLE straps, and soon he had a holster that would fit his P90 and the magazine holders attached to them.

He looked around to see if there was anything else he might need. There were racks and racks of military clothing, but Jeff saw no need to look like a soldier. He wasn't one, and didn't feel any need to impersonate one. Besides, what good was camouflage in a world where only one other person could see him? His eye happened across a table bearing knives of all kinds, and remembering Cynthia's request, he walked over to see what could be had.

There were several machetes, so he took two. There were survival knives as long as his forearm, but they seemed a bit much for children. There were, however, several lock blades with assisted opening devices, and some drop-point daggers that he figured the kids could handle. He gathered all these up, along with a few sharpeners and put it all in the backpack. He shouldered it, and was surprised at how heavy it was. It was all the ammo, he figured. He was walking out of the store when he noticed something behind the glass of the main display case, the one right next to the cash register. He walked over for a closer look, and began to grin. He broke this case as well, and gathered up the case within. He checked the instructions to make sure he was good on the right kind of batteries, and then stuck it in his pack. He made his way to the door, the grin still on his face.

Maybe he wasn't as good a shot as Jodie Foster in that movie, but he was willing to bet that with a set of night vision goggles, he would have had a hell of a lot better chance taking her out if he had been the villain. That's what got the villain killed, playing around with her by staring at her through his night vision goggles while she stumbled around in the dark instead of just shooting her.

Night vision goggles like the ones Jeff Della now had in his backpack.

Chapter Twelve

He circled the school twice and came in from the opposite direction from which he left. He pulled up to the front door and got out of the truck, scanning the surrounding buildings quickly. He ran lightly up the walkway towards the door. He heard the chains being removed before he got within ten feet of the door. Cynthia was there instantly, her head cocked to one side, listening intently.

"Why are you alone? Where's Mr. Merchant? Is that *your* blood I smell?"

Jeff brushed by her and sat his heavy backpack down on the floor next to the door. He turned and headed back to the truck. Over his shoulder he said, "I'll explain later. Right now I need to get this stuff in here."

He made several trips, nearly running as he shuttled the supplies to the school. On his last trip he heard a scream, rising, rising, and then abruptly cut off. He stood motionless and waited. After several minutes without any more sound, he finished ferrying the supplies into the school. He then drove his truck about half a block down the street and parked it. *No sense advertising my presence at the school,* he thought. He ran back to the school. Once inside, he took the chains from Cynthia and replaced them himself. Looking around, he saw a soft drink machine against the wall. The power was still on here, and the machine lit up the foyer with a soft blue light. He crossed the room and unplugged the machine. It was heavy, but he was able to lug it into position in front of the door. Once he was satisfied that it was pushed as far against the door as it would go, he stepped back and began to gather the boxes he had brought from the general store.

Cynthia had been silent throughout all of this, but now she spoke up.

"Jeff? Do you want to tell me what's going on? I'm pretty sure you just shoved a Pepsi machine across the room in front of the door, unless you suddenly felt a need to redecorate. Where's Mr. Merchant?"

Again, Jeff told her he would explain later. He grabbed a box of propane tanks and headed up the stairs. Waylon met him at the top of the staircase, jumping ecstatically around his feet. Jeff absently spoke to the dog and continued down the hall. He took the box into the rec room and placed it against the wall next to the supplies he had brought in earlier.

He made several trips up and down the stairs, barely acknowledging the several attempts to get him to talk to anyone. He just kept muttering, "Later. I'll explain later." By the time all the supplies were neatly stacked against the wall, Jeff was beginning to feel the first warning twinges of pain from the leg he had broken in the car wreck when he was seventeen. When he did too much and taxed the leg for extended periods, it would sometimes begin to throb. If he continued to punish it, it would soon be difficult for him to walk. He rubbed it absently as he stood looking around the room at the expectant faces turned towards him. Looking down at his hand, he noticed that it was smeared with Sam Merchant's blood. He grimaced as another jolt of rage shot through him.

He took a breath and then said, "Give me just a second, guys. I've got to take some Tylenol for my leg. It hurts." He went to the first aid kits he had brought and was rummaging around when Cynthia touched his shoulder and handed him four pills. He hadn't heard her move.

"Here", she said, "these are 500 milligrams. I get headaches sometimes."

He thanked her and popped the pills into his mouth and took a drink of bottled water. If he had known he was going to be putting his leg through its paces today, he would have brought his Voltaren gel, a topical pain relieving gel that he rubbed on his leg when it gave him trouble. *If I had known what I was going to be doing today, I would have stayed at the fucking house in the first place*, he thought angrily. He shook the thought away. It wasn't the fault of these people that he was here. He had made his decision, and now he would stick by it.

He considered taking the adults out into the hallway to discuss what had happened since he had left and decided against it. Things were what they were, and as hard as it might be, these kids needed to deal with it. He turned towards them.

"Sam Merchant it dead. He was shot to death by the same man that killed Officer Barnes. The man's name is Oscar Daniels. He's a coal miner and apparently also a psychopath. Why he can still see is a mystery to me, but I'm not feeling too happy that the only other person in town that can see is such a prick."

The younger children inhaled, waiting for Father Don or Cynthia to chastise Jeff for using that bad word. When neither said anything to him, the kids looked confused and scared. If it was all right to use bad swear words in front of them, things must be *really* bad. Jeff continued, passing a hand over his weary face.

"All right. Here's the deal, as I see it. We can't save this town. Cynthia, you are completely right about that. I figure that we may be able to bring as many as we can here for now, and move over to the school or the hospital later. But the number of people that we can save has lowered drastically. We may be able to handle a hundred people, split about 70-30 between the kids and the adults. I just can't leave the kids to die. The adults we save will need to be people with specialized skills. Doctors, mechanics, things like that. They may not be able to see, but they can use me as their hands. So, starting tomorrow, I start canvassing town for the folks we're going to try to keep alive."

He paused. "Well, maybe not starting tomorrow. Saturday, I'll start gathering together our little flock. Yeah, Saturday should work."

Cynthia stood with her brows furrowed.

"I know I have no right to second guess you on this, especially since I'm the one that said we'd have to let most of the people make do on their own, but why wait an extra day? Every day we wait is that much longer for people to get hurt or killed trying to take care of themselves. Shouldn't we start first thing tomorrow? Or maybe even tonight?"

Jeff closed his eyes and leaned back against the wall.

"There are a few reasons for waiting, Cynthia. First, my leg isn't going to take much more abuse before it locks up on me completely, and if that happens, I'm down for at least a week. We can't afford that. Also, I am totally exhausted. Second, when I go out to gather folk up, we're going to need to be ready to help them once they get here. If I was to fill this place up with folks tonight, what would you do for them? No beds, no real medicines for the sick or injured, no food prepared... you follow me?"

Cynthia nodded. "Yes, I can see that makes sense. And I'm sorry. I should have realized that you would be tired, emotionally and physically. But... if you sleep like a log tonight and rest your leg, wouldn't you still be able to start tomorrow while we're setting up here?"

Jeff shook his head, his eyes still closed.

"No, I can't start tomorrow. You all *will* need to get everything ready that you can tomorrow, though, you're right about that. Second Sight will act like an aid station. We'll bring folks here, make sure that they have some food and water in them, some meds if they're hurt, and then transition them to the hospital later. It's only about two blocks from here, and the school van will let us take people over in larger groups than my truck would."

"Okay" said Cynthia, "That makes sense. We know Second Sight, so we can get around here just fine while you're out finding people. We can have this place turned into a way station in no time and be ready for just as many people as you can find. But I still don't understand why we can't start tomorrow. Well, I guess *we're* going to start tomorrow, but why can't you?"

"I can't help find people tomorrow. I'll be busy."

Cynthia finally let some of her exasperation show. "Doing what?" she asked testily.

Jeff finally opened his eyes. Although she didn't know it, she would have been glad that she was blind so she couldn't see the cold hatred that burned in them. In a dead voice, Jeff said, "Finding Oscar Daniels."

It was nearly midnight when Jeff finally managed to lay down. They had moved another couch into the rec room from Father Don's small office. Jeff lay on his back, rubbing his leg. Waylon had come over and given him a slobbering kiss and laid his furry head on Jeff's chest. Jeff stroked the dog for a while, and then Waylon padded back over to his new fan club. The kids fought over who Waylon would sleep next to until Jeff assured them that the dog would wander back and forth among them all night.

Cynthia came over and sat on her own couch. Jeff sat up and began to ruffle through his backpack. He began laying out boxes of ammunition, along with his other acquisitions. She listened to him humming quietly under his breath as he worked, loading each of the magazines and fitting them into their custom holders on the MOLLE gear. Jeff loaded the shotgun and added ammo to the rack on the side and the sling. He pumped the action, and then added one more shell to top the weapon off. Cynthia remained silent.

Jeff told the children to come over to his couch. They came willingly enough, although Jamie Cummings still shuffled resentfully. Jeff gave him a bland stare. He was going to have to do something about the boy, and quickly. Once the children stood surrounded the seated Jeff, he began to remove the knives he had gotten at the surplus store. He took out a dagger from its sheath and asked the children to come to him, one at a time. He took their hands and ran them down the handle of the knife, and then very carefully around each to touch the blade. Most of them pulled back instinctively when they felt the keen edge under their fingers. Jamie did not. Instead, he flicked his thumb over the edge, testing its sharpness. Again, Jeff was favorably impressed. He *really* needed this kid. Younger than some of the others, he had courage enough to spare for all of them.

Placing the dagger back in its sheath, he then took out the assisted-opening lock blades and familiarized each child with how it operated. Once he was satisfied that they could work the knives without hurting themselves, he handed them out. Each of the younger children got a lock-blade. He spoke earnestly to them.

"Now, I want all of those in your pockets. They attach with the little clips on the side to the inside of your pocket, so they won't fall out. I don't want to see them out any other time, unless you're lying down to go to bed. Then, you lay them beside you, *closed*, for the night. If I see one out any other time, it's gone, and you won't get it back. Don't be using them to clean your fingernails, whittling, anything else. Got it?"

The younger children all nodded.

"Okay then, go on over and play with my dog, but don't let me catch any of you giving him chocolate. He wants it, but it's bad for him." He lowered his voice. "Also, you feed him chocolate, and gets very gassy. And you most certainly do *not* want that, kiddos, let me tell you. Now, beat it."

The kids went back to their play with Waylon giggling at each other at the thought of a farting dog. They glowed with pride that they had been trusted with real knives, just like the adults used. Jeff now turned to the older children. There were seven of them, four boys and three girls, ranging in age from fourteen to sixteen. To each of these except Jamie he gave one of the daggers, showing them how to loop the sheaths through their belts and fasten the retaining strap. The same warning was given to them about having the weapons out at inappropriate times. They went off to sit with the younger kids, ostentatiously to watch over them, but in reality they just wanted to play with Waylon too.

Jamie stood dejectedly by the couch and then turned to go to his bedroll. Jeff could tell that the boy felt he was being punished for being a smart ass to Jeff earlier. Before he could take more than a few steps, Jeff called him back. The boy turned, his face a perfect mix of suspicion and hope. Limping a bit, Jeff got up from the couch and asked Jamie to follow him into the hall. Jamie followed slowly, obviously not sure what was about to happen.

Once they were in the hallway, Jeff turned to the boy and laid a hand on his shoulder. Jamie tensed up, but didn't shrug the hand off. Jeff took this as a good sign.

"Jamie, I'm really curious. Is there something about me specifically that bothers you? And if so, what is it? There are not many of us here son, and we need to have each other's backs. I'd like to know that you've got mine, because I assure you that I have yours."

Jamie stood stock-still and stared into space over Jeff's shoulder. When he spoke, his voice was low.

"I didn't think you would come back."

Jeff was surprised. "Of course I came back. I told you I was going to, didn't I? It took me longer than I had planned, but of course I came back."

Jamie gave Jeff a look that was cynical far beyond his years.

"And I guess everybody that has ever told you they were coming back always did, huh?"

Jeff began to understand. His voice soft, he asked, "Who left you, son? Was it your dad?"

Jamie tensed up, anger bubbling just under the surface of his face. "Have you been talking to Father Don? He isn't supposed to talk about what we talk about to anyone. It's a 'seal of conversation', or something, he said."

"It's the 'seal of the confessional', Jamie, and no, he hasn't said a word to me about you, I swear."

The boy's suspicious look encompassed his face totally.

"Then how'd you know about my dad?"

"I made a few educated guesses Jamie, that's all. You were openly hostile to me the second you met me. That tells me that you didn't trust me. That either means that you didn't trust me in particular, or just men in general. Since you didn't know me, I figured it was more of a 'men in general' kind of thing. Then a minute ago, you asked that question about people coming back when they say they would. It just added up. Nothing secret about it."

Jamie turned slightly away from Jeff and leaned against the hallway wall. He spoke in a flat, declarative tone.

"My dad took off on my mom and me when I was twelve. He told us he was going to a seminar somewhere. He was some sort of big deal at the coal company, and he had gone on them before. We didn't think anything about it, really. He was supposed to be gone for three days. He didn't call at all, and my mom got worried, so she called his supervisor. The guy was just as surprised as mom was. Said he was about to call her and ask where dad was, because he hadn't come in to work for a few days. That wasn't like him, his boss said. My mom about lost it. She called the bank and found out that he had cleaned out the account, took everything but fifteen hundred dollars. He had put the house in mom's name, though. I guess we owe him for that, at least. If he hadn't done that, I don't know what we would have done. We sold the house and moved from Huntington down here to Stone Grove. Mom works for the realtor in town. She's his secretary, I guess, but she's studying to get her realtor's license." The boy stopped and turned his face towards Jeff. "I just don't go for the whole 'trust' thing very well. At least that's what Father Don tells me. My mom says the same thing."

Jeff moved over until he was close enough to the boy to reach out and touch his arm. Jamie turned towards him, using the radar that had replaced his sight.

"Jamie, you don't know me very well. Hell, you just met me today. I don't expect you to throw yourself in front of a train for me, but I need to know that I can count on you if things go south on us. Can I count on you? All I can promise you is that I will do my best to not disappoint you."

Jamie thought it over for a moment, and then smiled. It changed his entire face. If the boy knew how dramatic the change was, he would smile a lot more, in Jeff's opinion.

"Okay, chief, you're on. I'll watch your back, and you watch mine. Deal?" He stuck his hand out.

Jeff grinned and took it. "You got a deal, Jamie."

The boy kept smiling when he said, "Of course, having me watch your back would be kinda like having Helen Keller compile a mix tape for you, you know."

Jeff laughed. The boy turned back towards the rec room but Jeff held onto his hand.

"Hold on a second there, big guy. If you're watching my back, I'd feel better about it if you had more to defend us than your smart-assery. You want this?"

He held out the last knife, a long-bladed Bowie with a heavy leather grip. He took the boy's hand and placed the knife into it, grip first. Jamie slid the knife out of its sheath and inhaled as he felt the long, sharp blade. He grinned at Jeff.

"This isn't a knife; it's a damned short sword!" He laughed and carefully slid the knife back into the sheath. "Thank you, Jeff. And I know, you catch me picking my teeth with it and it's gone. Gotcha."

The two made their way back into the rec room. Jamie headed slowly over to the children, threading his new knife through his belt. Jeff went back over to the couch and sat down. Father Don and Cynthia were sitting comfortably, making small talk. When Jeff sat down, Cynthia nodded towards the end of the room where the children had gathered around Waylon.

"You did very well with them", she said. "It was just the right mix of seriousness and keeping it light enough to not scare them. I think you'll be pleasantly surprised how closely they follow your instructions. Thank you for doing that. I hate to think of arming a bunch of blind children, but we have a responsibility to help them protect themselves if something happens to us."

"Speaking of you", Jeff said, "I didn't forget you two, either. Here." He opened the pack again and removed the two machetes from the surplus store. He gave one to Cynthia and the other to Father Don. As the two of them checked out the sharpness and length of their weapons, Jeff began "Now, if I catch those out anytime except when you're lying down to sleep, then I'll..." He got no further. Cynthia, with her unfailing sense of position, gave him a perfectly aimed kick to the ankle. They all laughed.

"What did I tell you about that domestic violence, young lady?" Jeff asked archly. She smiled back.

"Right, I'll work on it. Maybe I can get into some counseling. You know, try to curb my violent tendencies."

They children were beginning to show signs of sleepiness. Eyes glazed and yawns broke out like wildfire. Cynthia announced that it was time for bed, and all the children took turns brushing their teeth and heading to their bedrolls.

Waylon rambled back and forth between the kids as they got situated, giving out good night licks liberally. The children could sense when the dog was closing in on their faces and were able to avoid getting any open-mouthed kisses.

Father Don heaved himself from his couch and made his way slowly over to where the children lay on their mats. He knelt on the floor in front of them and folded his hands together. In his deep voice, he began;" Now I lay me down to sleep..."

As one, the children ran through the rest of the litany. Jeff was surprised to see that even the older children were saying it, and with no detectable sarcasm. At seventeen, he would have been horribly self-conscious of saying what he would have been considered a baby prayer, but the older kids showed no such reservations. They finished the prayer in perfect harmony, asking that God bless each of them, and to look after all those that had fallen victim to the blindness that had engulfed the world. There was a slight pause, and then the tiny voice of eight year old Christy Lowman spoke up. "And God bless Mr. Della for coming to help us and bringing Waylon, who smells a little like a rug but is very cuddly."

Jeff felt tears sting the corners of his eyes at this unexpected sweetness. He blinked them back and growled at Christy with mock anger. "I think I remember telling you that my name is Jeff, young lady. My dad's name was Mr. Della."

Christy giggled into her cupped hand. The children began to settle in and were all sleeping in an amazingly short period of time, by Jeff's reckoning. Of course, they had been through a great deal the last three days, and were probably at least as mentally exhausted as Jeff himself. Sleep was the best friend of those who can achieve it without nightmares, especially during times of great stress or emotional turmoil. It for good reason that pain-dulling morphine had been named after Morpheus, God of Sleep. Jeff only hoped that he could slip off as effortlessly as the children had. He doubted it, however.

He continued to lie on is back, rubbing his leg rhythmically, trying to coax it into easing off. He couldn't afford to be laid up right now. He could drive back over to his place and pick up some of his Voltaren gel, he supposed. He needed some more clothing, anyway.

While he had felt a deep respect and admiration for Sam Merchant, wearing blue jeans crusted with the old man's blood wasn't exactly his idea of the height of fashion. He had left home that morning expecting a small trip into town to see what was going on, so he hadn't dressed for the Apocalypse. Not that he knew what the appropriate dress code for the end of the world was, but he was willing to bet it wasn't something that had been covered in Cosmo. Maybe he should have grabbed some of the fatigues that he had seen at the surplus store. Well, maybe tomorrow. He wasn't up to another trip anywhere tonight. One more go-around with the clutch on his truck, and his leg would most likely pack its bags and leave, anyway. He sighed, trying to will the pain away.

Cynthia had remained on her couch throughout the prayer and now sat with her head cocked to one side, listening intently to Jeff. He had noticed she was in that posture for quite a while, but wasn't sure what she was listening to. He just assumed that she had been making sure that all the children had been participating during Father Don's evening prayers. He was once again surprised by her perception when she asked, "Is it really bad? Your leg, I mean."

Jeff let out a rueful laugh. "How the hell did you know I was thinking about my leg? Was mind-reading one of the courses offered in Britain?"

She smiled. "No, I can hear you rubbing your leg and making little noises. It sounds like it hurts."

"Yeah, it does. If I overdo it, I almost always wind up paying the price. The bone healed all right, but I can always tell when it's going to rain. I'm in pretty good shape, but when I broke it, the bone was pretty much shattered. I'll be okay." He reached over and patted her leg. "Thanks for thinking about me, though. Waylon usually just gives me a 'Get off your ass' look whenever I hurt myself", he said with a laugh.

Cynthia laughed back, and then seemed to come to a decision. She got up and walked gracefully out of the rec room and into the darkness of the hallway. Jeff could hear her walking down the hall. He started to get up, but then realized that she was much better off in the dark than he would ever be. He lay back down and waited for her to return.

She did, about five minutes later. In her hand was a small black bag. She walked unerringly back to her couch and sat down. She unzipped the bag and began to feel around inside it. "Damn", she muttered. Then she handed the bag to Jeff and said, "The tie-downs for the bottles have come loose, and I can't tell which is which. You'll have to find it."

Jeff took the bag from her and asked, "Find what? What am I looking for?"

She just grinned and said, "I think you'll know it when you find it."

Jeff pilfered through the jumble of bottles. They were medicines, and none of them were over-the-counter. Jeff found bottles for high blood pressure medicine, which had Father Don's name on them, as well as some medicine for high cholesterol. He had just about exhausted to bottles when he came across a bottle near the bottom of the bag that was about half-full of Percocet. They were prescribed to Cynthia, and were almost a year old. He looked at her quizzically.

"I'm just guessing here, but I assume you're giving me some pain meds, right? Because I think my blood pressure and cholesterol are pretty much under control."

She laughed again. "Well, if you say so. But yes, I thought maybe some of those might help you sleep."

Jeff opened the bottle and shook two of the pills out into his hand, hesitated, and then put one back. He wasn't sure just how deeply he might sleep under the influence of two of them, and he might need to be able to wake up quickly in the night. Remembering a trick that a nurse had shown him after the accident, he broke the pill in half and washed it down with a gulp of bottled water. The medicine would get into his bloodstream quicker this way. He thanked Cynthia and then asked her what had happened to her that she needed the pills in the first place. She turned a brilliant crimson as she spoke.

"About a year ago I was getting out of the shower when I fell and twisted my ankle pretty badly. I didn't break anything, but it swelled like an inner tube. The doctor prescribed them for me for the pain, along with some topical stuff. It quit hurting fairly quickly, so I didn't need all the pills. I suppose I should have flushed the rest, but I figured that someone might need one sometime."

Jeff was again confused by her expression. "Cynthia, this may not be any of my business, and if so, tell me to shut up, but you look very embarrassed right now. If you turn any redder, your face might start smoking. Why are you embarrassed about twisting your ankle?"

Cynthia actually *did* turn redder, but there was no sign of any smoke just yet.

"I twisted my ankle because I did something very stupid, if you must know", she said primly.

"What, taking a shower? What's stupid about that? I've fallen getting out of the shower dozens of times."

"You're not blind."

"Okay", he said, not following. "All the more reason why *I* should be the one embarrassed about it. Hell, you can't see what you're doing. You've got a perfectly good reason for falling. *I'm* just clumsy."

Cynthia took a deep breath. "I was in the shower when the phone rang. I was expecting a call from my mom, so I had the phone on the towel rack. It was my mom, and I told her that I would call her back when I got out of the shower. I *thought* I put the phone back on the towel rack, but I guess I must have missed, because it fell on the floor. I didn't hear it fall because of the water from the shower. When I got finished, I stepped out of the tub and right onto the phone and over I went. I should have been more careful."

"Jeez, Cynthia, don't be so damned critical of yourself. Everyone makes mistakes. Christ, if I had to go through life without being able to see and the worst thing I did was twist my ankle coming out of the shower, I'd be tickled pink with myself."

She sighed and lowered her voice almost to the point where he couldn't hear her.

"Well, you wouldn't be tickled pink if the damn EMT that showed up to take you to the E.R. found you naked and sopping wet on the bathroom floor."

The mental image had a two-pronged effect on Jeff. On one hand, he couldn't help from emitting a stifled laugh, which earned him a venomous look. On the other, the thought of Cynthia naked and sopping wet *anywhere*, bathroom floor, kitchen table, you name it, woke up his lower anatomy for the third (or was it fourth?) time since he had met her. Seeing her look, he was quick to apologize.

"Sorry, Cynthia. Really, I am. It's not funny, but it *is* funny, if you know what I mean. And trust me, you have no reason to be embarrassed about the EMT seeing you naked. Was it a he or a she?"

"The EMT was a man, a young one from the sound of it. Why?"

"Then you made his day, I guarantee you that run was the best one he had all year."

"Oh, ha-ha, I'll just bet it was. I bet he couldn't wait to get back to the station and tell all his buddies about the stupid naked blind lady in the bathroom floor. You can be a little mean sometimes, Jeff."

He could see that he had hurt her feelings and hurriedly tried to repair the damage. "You're not following me, Cynthia. You didn't make his day be being some dumb blind chick that fell. Unless he was *totally,* out-of-the-closet gay, you made his day because he got to see an incredibly attractive young woman naked and wet. Trust me. As a man, I speak for my species when I say that the thought of you naked and wet, regardless of the circumstances, would be a treat."

Cynthia turned even redder, but with a tiny smile. Father Don, who had been listening in, now growled at Jeff.

"Watch it, young man. I may be blind, but I've still got a mean left hook."

"Yes, sir, I read you loud and clear." To Cynthia, he said, "I meant no disrespect, okay? Just honest appreciation. Do you forgive me?"

She had kept her little smile. "Well, since you say it *that* way, I guess there's nothing to forgive, is there?"

Father Don now turned his growl toward Cynthia. "Don't *encourage* him, for goodness sake!"

They all shared a laugh. After a few moments, Cynthia turned back in Jeff's direction and asked, "Are you really going to track down this Daniels man tomorrow?" Her face was serious and solemn.

Jeff looked down at the gear he had gotten together and his newly-improved weaponry. Nodding, he said, "Yeah, I guess I am. I just don't see any other way around it. We can't do what needs to be done with a psycho like that running around loose killing whoever he feels like. There aren't any jails anymore, Cynthia. I can't make a citizen's arrest and turn him over to the proper authorities, because the proper authorities have ceased to exist. So, yes, I am going to track him down. When I do, I'm going to kill him. It's better than he deserves. I hate that he's made this necessary, and when I think of how much help another set of working eyes could be here, I get *furious*." He turned to Martinez. "Is what I'm doing a sin, Father? I mean, I know it must be, but what I'm asking is how *bad* a sin, I guess."

Father Don sat musing. He took his time thinking it over. Finally, he spoke.

"Jeff, the way I see it is this: what you're doing isn't that much different than what soldiers have to do every day. I've spoken with a great many soldiers, both going to and returning from the war. It's mostly the ones heading to war that worry that what they are going to have to do is a sin. The thought that they might have to take a human life, whatever the circumstances, weighed heavy on their hearts. With the ones that have returned from the war, very often they felt the anger you're feeling. They were angry that the people that they had to kill had forced them into the situation. I suppose it's been that way throughout time." He shook his head sadly. "I'm not going to get off on a theological rant. If you want that, read some Thomas Aquinas. I'm just going to say that if the situation wasn't what it is, I would tell you that you are about to commit a mortal sin. That said, the situation *is* what it is, and I think you're doing the only thing you can. You didn't ask for this. You didn't ask to be placed in this position, and you *certainly* didn't ask for Oscar Daniels to be the kind of man that he is. He has chosen to take advantage of this tragedy, and compound the problem. All I've seen you do is try to ease the suffering." He reached out to Jeff until Jeff took his hand. "I think you are a good man, Jeff Della. You have helped when you didn't have to. You could have turned around and went right back home, but you didn't. You're here, with us. If I came across hard on you earlier, I'm sorry. I am just now really coming to grips with this situation myself. You do what you have to do tomorrow. If it's God's will, you will succeed, and we can try to begin rebuilding. Insofar as whether what you're doing is a sin… I'm not sure. But I *do* know that this man Daniels has committed sins, at least two, and that both of them were mortal. Let God decide who's in the right of it. But since you've got a priest with you saying go for it, I think we can safely assume that you're covered."

Jeff looked at his rifle knowing that tomorrow, if everything came off right, it would end a man's life. He looked back up into the sightless yet compassionate eyes of the older man and said, "God willing. Okay, I guess that will have to do."

They all laid down on their couches, and soon the sound of Cynthia and Father Don's breathing deepened as they slid off to sleep. Despite the Percocet and his exhaustion, it took Jeff much longer to fall asleep. When he finally did, he tossed and turned throughout the remainder of the night, making small, frightened noises in the back of his throat.

In the small hours of the night, Waylon got up from his place among the children and padded over to his friend. He laid his muzzle on Jeff's chest and listened to the man's broken dreams.

Very gently, the dog licked the single tear that slipped free from Jeff's right eye. Waylon lay down on the floor next to Jeff and curled into a tight ball, his eyes open and alert.

He remained that way until the sun began to brighten the eastern sky.

<u>Chapter Thirteen</u>

The object of the discussion taking place at Second Sight had indeed been out of town that night. Had he known, Jeff could have sighted in every gun in the store and set off explosives on Main Street. Oscar Daniels was forty miles away, looking up an old acquaintance who owed him some money from a poker game played four years ago. The man had won, according to the other players that night, but Oscar was certain that the man had somehow cheated him. So, he was going to collect his winnings now, with interest.

The fact that money was useless meant nothing whatsoever to Daniels. He intended to take the four hundred dollars off the man, and then shoot him in the face. End of story. There wasn't any logic to what he was doing, but to Oscar Daniels, logic had always been something akin to China, heard about but never actually seen.

On that fateful Tuesday afternoon, Daniels had been a thirty-eight year old coal miner who had been three times divorced and more in trouble with the law than out of it. His crimes had always been just this side of serious enough to keep him from doing any real time. He had spent several weeks in jail on alcohol and drug related charges, but both his small-time status as a user and abuser and his willingness to rat out anyone he thought would get him off the hook had kept him from any real time.

Oscar had managed to retain his job at the mine only because of his older brother, who had gone to college and returned with a degree that ensured the big-wigs at the mine needed him. His older brother had argued Oscar's case with their superiors on numerous occasions. The latest had been the DUI that Officer Barnes had given him. It was still in court, but Daniels had been informed that if he was found guilty of the DUI (his third in the last two years) that he would no longer be employed by the Stone Grove Mining Corporation. Oscar had gone to his brother to intervene, just as he always had, but had left his brother's office both shocked and furious. His brother had told him that this was it. If they found him guilty of the DUI, there were simply no more strings left he could pull.

Oscar had been thinking about that very hard on that Tuesday afternoon. It was a week until his court date, and barring a miracle, they were going to find him guilty. He had blown almost three times the legal limit, and had resisted arrest, all of which was caught on the cop's dashboard camera. No, they had him dead-to-rights, which meant a mandatory 90 day stay in jail, the loss of his license for five years, and now, apparently, no job. He had no children from any of his three wives, thank God, but he had bills, and plenty of them. No, barring a miracle, by the end of next week, he was done for.

And then: a miracle.

Oscar had been down in one of the four shafts that led into the deep mine that afternoon. He had stopped in at one of the small storage buildings that sat at intervals along the shaft that contained various safety equipment, first aid supplies, emergency food, and bottled oxygen in the event of a cave-in. He had stopped in not to check to see that the supplies were up to date and ready to go, (which was his responsibility), but to smoke a joint and see just how much lead he had managed to steal from the maintenance shed topside. They used the lead as counter balances in the truck tires that transported the coal off the mountain, and Oscar had found it to be the perfect consistency for melting down into bullets for his .44 caliber 1851 Confederate Navy black powder pistol. Being a thrifty man, as well as a thief, he saw no sense in buying the lead, cheap as it was, when there was literally a ton of the stuff lying around in the maintenance shed.

He was looking over his take that day and puffing away on his joint when he heard the shift foreman coming down the shaft. Oscar had groaned out loud. He was caught, dammit, caught again and there was no getting out of it. There was no way the foreman would miss the smell of the pot. Oscar *might* have managed to persuade the man that the long, rectangular sheet of thick lead had been found lying on the floor of the shaft and that he was taking it back. A "You know how sloppy those mechanics are" kind of thing, but the pot was going to end him, right there. *Great*, he thought, *they can add* this *to my goddamn DUI charge. Son of a BITCH!*

He had just slumped his shoulders and sat on an upturned plastic bucket, waiting for the foreman, who sounded like he was about ten yards away, to get there and tear open the door. The foreman, a man named Granger, had had it in for Oscar since he had started working at the mine. Granger had made it no secret that he believed that Oscar was a hazard to the other miners, was lazy, stupid, and incompetent, and that the only reason he had the job in the first place was because of his big brother being so tight with the management. Well, this would be the final nail in his coffin, no mistake about it. Oscar had sat on his bucket with his joint in one hand and his lead in the other and was amazed to find himself about to cry. Well, goddamn it if that son of a bitch would see him *crying*, that was for sure! He reached up to wipe the tears away when he realized that both hands were full. He was about to put down the lead and take care of himself when the knob of the door began to turn. Furious, Oscar did the only thing he could think of: he covered his eyes with the hand holding the lead.

The knob was still turning when Oscar felt, more than saw, the pulse of light. His eyes had tingled for a second, and they began itching like he had gotten soap in them. He lowered his hand and dropped the lead to the floor and began to wipe his eyes. They were burning now, as well. There was an eye flush kit mounted on the wall of the shed, as mandated by OSHA, and Oscar used it to clean his eyes out. Once he had finished, they still stung a bit, but he could see all right, and most of the burning was gone.

Remembering Granger's impending entrance, Oscar turned defiantly towards the door. *Hell,* he thought, *if I'm going down, I may as well slug the shit out of that son of a bitch while I'm doing it.* However, Granger was a large man with very large arms, and Oscar wasn't quite as brave as he liked to think he was. Looking around, his eyes fastened on the lead on the floor. He picked it back up and held it in his hand. He figured that no matter *how* big and bad Granger thought he was, five or six pounds of lead to the bridge of the nose would probably stop his clock for a bit. Oscar would just have to time his blow exactly right.

He was still waiting four or five minutes later when he began to wonder why Granger hadn't come through the door. He could still hear him out there, along with several of the other miners, their voices raised in alarm. Not the smartest person to grace the planet, Oscar's first thought wasn't that something bad might be happening to the mine, something that might require him to get the hell out of it rapidly, but that it was entirely possible that he might just get away with smoking a little pot and swiping some lead, after all. He stuffed the lead into his pocket and snuffed out the joint under his work boot, shoving the roach under the plastic bucket he had been using as a seat. Fixing a look that he hoped was just the right amount of alarm and curiosity on his face; he opened the door to the shed and climbed down the three metal steps to the shaft floor.

The look of curiosity and alarm changed into one of abject stupidity as he looked around himself. The men in the mine with him were stumbling around with their arms out in front of them, falling over themselves and banging into walls. Granger was yelling at the top of his lungs for everyone to *stay still, dammit!* At first, Oscar thought that they were just trying to screw with his head, because they knew he had been getting high in the storage shed. But the more he watched, the more he realized that the men in the mine couldn't see at all. He thought back to the moment when his eyes had burned and thought that whatever had caused that was most likely the cause of *this*. Only this seemed to be much worse. Whatever had hit these men so hard, Oscar had only gotten a small dose of it inside the shed.

Being the kind of man that he was, Oscar did what he did best: he looked out for number one. He sprinted down the shaft towards the opening, hoping like hell that he hadn't gotten enough of whatever it was in his eyes to do any permanent damage. He gave no thought at all to the men that remained in the shaft until he neared the exit. Once topside, he could find another foreman and explain what had happened. Hell, if he played this just right, he might come out of this looking like a hero. Visions of newspaper articles danced in his head. "Brave Miner Rescues Blinded Co-Workers", that sounded pretty good. Maybe he might even make it on WSAZ, the local news at six! Let them try to convict a damned hero of a DUI! This might just work out pretty sweet for him after all.

However, what he saw topside made the events in the shaft look like kids on a playground. In front of his incredulous eyes, a loader and a rock truck both ran off the high wall and plummeted out of sight. The sound of them slamming into the ground hundreds of feet below was enormous and deafening. Men were running about the outside of the mine, screaming and panicked. A fire had begun to fully engulf a semi that had slammed into the side of the hill, and its driver was writhing on the ground, the oily diesel flames slowly covering his body. No one rushed to help him. The chaos on the hilltop was complete.

For a moment, Oscar wondered if the marijuana that he had been smoking had been laced with something. He had bought it from a man that had been selling him weed for years, and it seemed unlikely that the man would have sold him laced pot on purpose. If you wanted a little extra, you paid for it. However this had been its normal price. Maybe the man had gotten mixed up when he had gotten the large baggie out and measured Oscar's portion.

Oscar wondered around the hilltop, avoiding the screaming, flailing men as best he could. This was not something he was prepared to deal with. He had taken the mandatory safety classes to get his miner's card, and they had covered everything from mine collapses to CPR and first aid, but this… what the hell *was* this?

He had finally made his way to his vehicle, a Ford F-150 that had cost more than his single wide trailer, and was his pride and joy. It was jacked up and had huge tires on it. It destroyed his gas mileage, but he didn't care because it was also *bad ass*. He started the engine and sat there, hoping that the rumble of the engine would drown out the screaming outside. It didn't, so he turned on his CD player. With a stereo system that was likewise more expensive than most of his other possessions, Trace Adkins succeeded where the engine had not. Oscar sat there listening to Trace extol the virtues of a "Honky-Tonk Badonkadonk" for a bit, and then shook his head to clear it. He put his ride into gear and headed off the hill. He had no real plan at this point, but was just running on auto-pilot.

His trip to town convinced him that whatever had happened was not relegated to the mine. All over Stone Grove, cars were wrecked, there were a few fires, and people ran about like the ants he had burned with a magnifying glass as a child. He stopped for no one, content to simply watch the carnage from his Realtree camouflage-covered seats. He watched in amazement as a woman pushing a baby carriage in front of her ran off the sidewalk full-tilt and was slammed into by a Volvo that had been rolling down the street without a driver. The woman and the baby were flung across the hood of the vacant car and onto the road. The woman twitched a few times and then laid still, her blood pooling slowly around her. The baby came out of the carriage, bounced onto the pavement once, and came to rest against a street light. It didn't twitch at all.

Oscar Daniels watched all this as Trace Adkins gave way to Toby Keith. Toby informed Oscar the he loved his bar, which seemed like an astoundingly good idea to Oscar. He turned down the street and pulled into a small bar set in the middle of a cracked pavement parking lot. He killed the engine of his truck and walked across the blazingly hot asphalt towards the front door.

He had nearly arrived at his destination when a man he knew vaguely from hundreds of beer-soaked nights came tearing out the front door. The man (Kevin, was that his name?) ran blindly into the parking lot and stuck the front end of a parked GTO. Oscar could hear several of the man's bones crack. The man began screaming as he lay on the hot pavement, clutching his abdomen. For some reason, the man's screams had done what the cacophony of yelling had been unable to do to this point: it got under Oscar's skin and pissed him off. He wasn't concerned about the man's welfare; he just wanted him to shut the hell up. How was he supposed to enjoy his beer with this idiot *caterwauling* just outside the damn door?

Oscar walked over to the man, who had managed to roll onto his side and was scooting across the lot like a crawdad, screaming with each breath. Oscar strode up to the injured man and stood looking balefully down at him. When he finally spoke, the contempt was evident in his voice.

"Hey, why don't you shut the fuck up? Nobody wants to hear that shit. Keep it down. I'm going to go enjoy me a beer or three, and I don't want to hear none of this shit while I'm doin' it. Got it, dumb ass?"

The man turned his head toward Oscar, hope lighting up his blind eyes.

"Mister, I'm hurt, I'm hurt real bad. And I can't see. Mister, please, you got to call 911. Oh, dear-to-God, I'm hurt so *bad!*"

The man took a sobbing breath, which must have caused him great pain, because he cut loose with another scream.

He was drawing a breath to let out another when Oscar Daniels committed his first murder.

Before the man could release his pent-up scream, Oscar casually brought one of his heavy work boots down on the man's throat. The steam-engine whistle that had started to make its way out of his throat was cut off as cleanly as turning off a TV with a remote. The man made several gurgling noises in his chest, but nothing could rise past his shattered windpipe. His face a bruised purple, and he convulsed on the pavement for the better part of a minute. Oscar just watched him, his face never changing expression. Once the man had stopped moving completely, Oscar nodded with satisfaction and turned to head back towards the bar.

It could be argued the he was acting in a state of shock. His actions up to that point certainly pointed in that direction, but by the time he was halfway across the parking lot, a look of panic settled on his face and he jerked his head around on his neck so fast it popped with a little machine-gun sound. He was certain that any second the parking lot would fill police cars and he would be staring down the barrels of many, many guns. Guns held by men that had more than likely arrested him at one point in time or another, and hated his guts.

A lump rose in his throat, and for an ironic second, he could breathe no better than the man he had just killed.

With a shambling jerk, he turned towards his truck and began running. He had made it halfway there when he slowed from an all-out sprint... to a jog... to a walk... and then he stopped. He stood motionless, still about thirty feet from his truck with his head cocked to one side in an eerie imitation of Waylon, a dog he had never laid eyes on. Back and forth from across town came the sounds of rending metal, screaming people, and isolated popping noises as fires sprang up.

But no sirens.

There was nothing moving on the streets around him. The last vehicle he had seen moving had been the Volvo that had struck the woman and her baby, and that had been empty. He remained where he was, standing in that head cocked to one side stance, as the minutes slipped by. He stood there for half an hour (earning himself the beginning of a nice sunburn) before he was satisfied that no one was coming. 911 had not been called on him, and most likely wasn't going to be.

He turned once more and went back towards the bar. He opened the door and stepped into the cool dimness that caressed his sweaty face with a lover's touch. He inhaled deeply, taking in each of the myriad of smells he associated with this place, and loving each one. Stale cigarette smoke and the sharper tang of beer, the chalk from the pool cues, the faint underlying smell of peanuts and pretzels. He stepped up to the bar and was actually about to yell for service when he gave out a crazy-sounding laugh. Who the hell was going to serve him? Still laughing like a madman, he walked around the bar and pulled out several long-neck Buds from the cooler and set them on the bar. He then snagged a fifth of Jim Beam and made his way back around the bar to his stool.

The TV was on, some afternoon soap opera that he couldn't follow if he tried. He felt around the back of the bar until his fingers brushed the remote and then he began flicking through the channels, looking for something to watch. He felt a twinge of unease when he realized that if the TV still worked, that maybe what had happened was only local. Maybe he should go and hide the body. He thought for a few minutes, taking shots of whiskey straight from the bottle and chasing it with a long pull of beer. Finally, he decided to just let it go. If a platoon full of National Guard soldiers came tearing into the bar, he would tell them all about all the wrecks he had seen, and he had been sitting there, trying to get a hold of 911 ever since.

It occurred to him that if he *was* found in a bar drinking stolen beer and whiskey instead of being out in the streets helping, he might want to log a little time on the phone to prove he had been trying to call 911. This, of course, led to his next dilemma. What the hell did he do if he called 911 and someone answered? He could tell them about the woman and baby he had seen hit, that would give them something to chase. But didn't they have that call-tracing shit? If he called them, the number would show up here at the bar, and bang! He might be explaining the body in the parking lot after all.

He thought a little more (something that was growing increasingly difficult since he had, in the last hour, smoked a very large joint, slammed four beers, polished off at least a quarter of a bottle of whiskey, watched his hometown fall into chaos, and killed a man in the parking lot of a bar) and then his face lit up. He'd use his cell phone! Let them trace *that*, by God! Which, although Oscar didn't know it, they could, and easily. He dug the small pre-paid cell phone from his pocket and saw that the little window in the front had been scratched by the piece of lead he had placed in there earlier. He cursed bitterly. He couldn't afford another one of the damn things, and there were still a shit-pot full of minutes left on this one. With a resigned sigh, he flipped it open and dialed 911.

The phone was answered by an automated voice telling him that all circuits were busy. This pleased him to no end. Every so often he would stop channel surfing and drinking long enough to call again. He got the same response every time. He began to notice something about the TV, as well. The channels continued playing their programs, but the commercials began jumping oddly, showing half of one and then cutting short to begin another one. Soon, some of the channels stopped showing programs altogether.

Oscar didn't mind the loss of the TV channels. He was very much drunk by this point, and decided that he wanted to hear some music. He went over to the juke box and started digging around in his pockets for change. Suddenly stopping, he belted out his insane-sounding laugh again and went to the cash register. He opened it and emptied it of quarters and, after a second's hesitation, all the other money as well. The thought that money might very well be as useless as tits on a boar hog very soon never crossed his mind.

Suddenly several hundred dollars richer, and drunk as a monkey, Oscar went to the juke box and began plugging quarters into it until he had used them all. He spent several minutes laboriously making out the names of the songs with a drunk's myopic stare. Soon, the sound of country and southern rock music filled the bar. Oscar went over to the pool tables and attempted to play nine-ball. He made frequent trips to the bar to refill his beer and whiskey, and by 4:30 P.M. on that Tuesday afternoon, he was so drunk that he could barely stagger back and forth across from the bar to the pool tables.

Finally, a few minutes before 5 o'clock, he made his last abortive attempt to head back to the bar. The floor had taken a decided slant to the left, and he was afraid that if he didn't get a good grip on something, he would go sliding across the bar and out the front window. Thinking it might be a good idea to lay down for a minute and get his bearings, he clumsily climbed onto the pool table and laid his head on his arms. Within minutes, he passed out.

He lay on his side on the pool table the rest of that night. Around 1:00 A.M., he vomited all over himself and the green felt. The bologna and cheese sandwich and bag of Lay's potato chips he had eaten for lunch earlier that day came up in a gush, splashing all over his work clothes and the pool table. Had he been lying on his back he would have, in all probability, choked to death on his own vomit, saving the lives of several people. However, life is never that neat.

Oscar woke at well past noon the next day. It was not the most pleasant Wednesday he had ever faced. His eyes felt like they were full of sand and his head throbbed with each beat of his heart. He looked down at himself with disgust at the congealed vomit that had hardened to a mushy crust on is clothing. With great care, he climbed up and off the pool table. He stood unsteadily on his feet, swaying like a tree in a gale. After what seemed like an eternity, he managed to fight down the urge to vomit again. He looked blearily around the bar. The lights were still on, but the TV was broadcasting nothing but snow. Fragmented visions of the previous day shot through his mind like meteors, leaving painful afterimages of light and sound.

He made his way to the bar and looked dejectedly at the neatly stacked bottles. Hair of the dog was probably the only thing that would take away this wretched feeling, but he knew that there was no way he would be able to keep enough of the alcohol down to make *that* work. He stripped off his work shirt, its blaze orange visibility bands hurting his head just to look at. He stood there in his sleeveless t-shirt, pondering what he was going to do next.

He staggered over to one of the booths along the side wall and sat heavily down. He couldn't remember feeling this bad in his life. Even waking up in jail after his last DUI with a head that felt like it was full of shattered glass and angry maggots hadn't felt *this* bad.

He was sitting with his head in his hands when a sudden memory floated to the top of his mind and popped. His head jerked up, causing him to moan in pain, but he got up and made his way to the front door of the bar. He opened it and let out a low, hoarse cry as the blinding sunlight pounded through his head like a jackhammer. Forcing himself through the door, he peered across the parking lot.

Okay, so that had actually *happened.* The man he had killed lay where he had fallen. Oscar's mind was now moving much faster than he would have thought possible only moments before. There was a dead man lying in the middle of the parking lot of the bar, a dead man with the distinct waffle-tread of Oscar's work boot across his throat.

His hangover still present and accounted for, Oscar made himself go out into the hellish sun and walk over to the body. He stood looking down at it for several minutes. A day in the summer sun hadn't done anything to improve the man's looks. His face was swelling, and black bruises showed all along his back where his shirt had hiked up. He looked, in Oscar's humbled opinion, like shit. He also looked like a man that had had his throat stomped in.

A realization suddenly hit Oscar. The man was still lying here, and no one had come to collect him. It was then that he realized that no one was *going* to come collect him. Whatever had happened had changed all the rules, by simply removing them. Oscar could take off all his clothes and walk around on Main Street with his tallywhacker hanging out, and there wasn't anything anyone could do about it. *Christ,* he thought, *Screw running around naked. I just* killed *some son of a bitch, and nobody did* shit *about it.*

Oscar began to grin. Within a few seconds, the grin had widened into a face-lighting smile.

His head was breaking in half, he was about to puke, and he smelled like a hobo. He was also now able to do any goddamned thing he wanted, so it sort of evened out. He was about to head back into the bar and force some booze down his throat so he could enjoy his new-found freedom without feeling like total shit when his eyes happened upon the Rite Aid across the street. His smile now positively *radiated* good humor.

Stepping over the first of a great many people that would meet their ends at his hands, Oscar walked across the road and into the Rite Aid. He went straight back to the pharmacy and without hesitation crossed the counter. It took him almost a half hour to realize that he couldn't work the automated system that dispensed the pills. He finally got pissed and went over to a fire extinguisher on the wall. Taking it down, he swung it at the glass partition in the front of the medicine dispenser. Glass shattered, and he was soon pilfering through the various containers of medicines.

He finally found what he was looking for, and began filling the biggest bottles he could find with Percocet, Xanax, Soma, and Valium. He shook several of each out into his hand and went back across the counter to the soft drink cooler. He chose a large Gatorade, and washed down his take with slow, steady gulps of the re-hydrating drink. He went back to the pharmacy counter and piled all his bottles into a bag, and then headed out of the store.

He made his way back over to his truck and climbed in. He started it up and pulled out of the parking lot. He turned towards his home, a crappy single-wide trailer on the outskirts of town. By the time he was halfway there, the pills were beginning to kick in, and the hangover faded into first a faraway drone, and then disappeared altogether. He was nearly home when he saw a middle-aged man walking in the middle of the road, blood crusted to the side of his head. When the man heard Oscar's truck, he turned his head toward the sound. His expression was of a shipwrecked man finally seeing a boat sailing his way. Oscar gave out a loud, honking laugh and revved his engine. By the time the man understood what was about to happen, there was no time to do anything but throw his hands up in negation.

Oscar was doing better than sixty miles an hour when he struck the helpless man. There was a double thump that threw Oscar up off his seat. A fan of blood sprayed up on the windshield. Thank god he had installed those push bars on his truck! Oscar glanced into the rearview mirror and watched as the man's body rolled over and over until coming to a stop, face down in the middle of the street. Oscar pushed to button on his power windows and shouted out the side.

"*FUCK* the right-of-way laws, you dumb prick!"

Oscar Daniels was a man liberated.

He knew now that his DUI case was a thing of the past. Although he had murdered two people in the last twenty-four hours, his concern had kept returning to that DUI, and the possibility that he might lose his license. Without his ride, a man was nothing. That his concern for a DUI had overshadowed the fact that he was now guilty of multiple homicide would have been proof positive, had any been needed, of the years and years that Oscar's father had told anyone that would stand still and listen that his youngest son was "off in the head".

But even his father had never been aware of the depth of his son's mental problems.

No one had. Simply put, Oscar was just smart enough to realize that he was too stupid to commit any major crimes and get away with it. He would get caught, just as he had with the DUI. He was not one of the action stars he watched on TV, where even the villains were smooth and able to get away with everything from drug trafficking and murder to attempting to take over the world. While Oscar firmly believed that such men existed, he understood that he wasn't one of them. He'd get caught, just like he always had.

So he hadn't gone over that invisible line drawn in society's sand. He had pulled his time for various petty crimes, but he knew that to go over that barrier would be the end of him, and that he would rot for the rest of his life in prison over in Charleston. Prisons were meant for this very purpose, as a deterrent to crime, although they didn't always function that way. Most people simply knew right from wrong and followed what they believed to be the correct path.

Had the people of Stone Grove realized that the only thing that was keeping a homicidal madman in check was the fear of losing his precious truck, they most likely would not have been so blasé about Oscar Daniels, laughing at his latest run-in with the law, or poking fun at his strictly-held beliefs that what he saw on TV was as real as the sun rising in the east. To tell Oscar that wrestling wasn't real was to have a fight on your hands. No, had the townsfolk been aware of the tumor that had been growing in their community, held in check only by something as mundane as the fear of a lost license, they would have run Oscar out of town on a rail in a second.

But it was far too late for that now.

Oscar went on home, took a shower, and changed into his best "going-out Friday night" set of clothing. He pulled on his snakeskin boots with the two and a half inch heels, his black Stetson cowboy hat and, despite the heat, his leather vest over his purple silk button up shirt. A pair of jet black Wranglers finished his ensemble, and he quickly added his rings and necklace. Checking himself in the mirror, he admired his reflection.

"Very put-together, Mr. Daniels", he told himself. "You are one sexy son of a bitch." He tipped himself a wink and headed back into his living room. He was very high right now, and every movement he made seemed to be in slow motion, and he left contrails of light whenever he moved his arms and legs. It was a sight that he enjoyed immensely.

Even through the haze of drugs, Oscar had already begun planning his triumphant return to the town that had shit on him for most of his thirty-eight years. There were some bills come due, and he intended to collect on every damn one of them. Let them laugh at him now, the dumb bastards. He was the Lord of all Creation, by the simple expedient of being able to see. He was special, he was unique, and he was going to get what was by-God *his*.

Had he known about Jeff Della, Oscar would have wasted no time finding the man and killing him. He knew nothing about Della, and couldn't even pick him out of a crowd, but two men that could see in the kingdom of the blind was one too many. For Oscar to be special, he had to be the *only* person that could see. Having another simply wouldn't do. So it was fortunate for Jeff that he had remained at home as long as he had. If he had gone into town on Tuesday or Wednesday either one, chances would have been even money that Oscar would have heard his truck and sought him out. Luck had been with Jeff that Thursday, as well, because Oscar had taken to the road just after killing Sam Merchant to collect on his poker winnings.

Now, sitting in air-conditioned splendor in his run-down trailer, Oscar did something that he had never done in his adult life: He made a list. He wrote down the name of every person that had slighted him over the years. He considered doing it in alphabetical order, but that struck him as being just a shade too complex, so he settled for putting stars next to the names of the people that he felt had wronged him the worst. He would start with those and work his way backward. He was a man with a plan, and all the time in the world to execute it.

After finishing up his list, he went over to the bookshelf in the corner. (It did not, of course, contain any books. Oscar would read the Sunday comics from time to time, but that was about as deep as his literary interests ran.) On the second shelf was a wooden box. He took this and sat back down on his ratty, moth-eaten couch. He opened the lock with a small key from his key ring, and sung open the lid. Lying inside, nestled in plush green velvet, was his .44 Confederate Navy revolver.

While his home might reek of urine from the bathroom floor (Oscar thought of the toilet as a guide more than a necessity), and most of his belongings might be cast-off and second hand crap, there were two things that he owned that positively glowed with maintenance and love. One, of course, was his truck. The other was the black powder pistol that he now brought out of the box and caressed with a chamois cloth.

While black powder firearms were much harder to keep clean than smokeless modern weapons, not a hint of rust spoiled the deep bluing of the gun. The brass backstrap shined like gold. If one didn't know any better, it would have been easy to assume that the gun was a showpiece, something that had never seen a round fired through it.

That was, however, far from the truth. Oscar fired his pistol at least once a week, and if he could afford the powder and caps, more often than that. He was a very good shot with it. He molded his own bullets (mostly from the stolen lead from work), and could split a hair with the gun.

In his world of fantasy/reality, he was the Outlaw Josey Wales, Billy the Kid, Doc Holliday. Oddly enough, his grasp of reality was strong enough that just wanting to be like those men wasn't enough. You had to practice to achieve the kind of marksmanship they showed on "Tombstone", or "Young Guns".

So, Oscar had practiced.

Besides work and drinking, practicing with his pistol was about the *only* thing that he did. He had bought a cross-draw holster that angled the gun across his left hip, where he could draw and fire it with his right hand. With the constant practice, he was able to do this quite fast, indeed. He had been bitterly disappointed that the movies had either lied, or that those men from the Old West had simply been of a different breed, because while he could draw and cock the weapon so fast it was hard to track it with the naked eye, there was no chance of him hitting anything more than four feet away when he did.

As he had modified his draw, however, he had come to what he felt was a nice balance between speed and accuracy. His draw may not have been anything like Billy the Kid's, but by-God, he *hit* what he was aiming at, *every* time.

He strapped on the cross-draw holster rig, with its bullet pouch and powder flask, and stood back in front of the mirror. *Now*, he looked put-together. He touched the brim of his Stetson with one finger and went to load his pistol.

In an odd way, Oscar thought he *was* one of the heroes in his beloved movies. He was the lone man wronged, out to seek justice against those cowardly bastards that misused the law to get their way. It was a mark of just how quickly the man's dementia had come to the surface that he honestly felt like a man that would be respected for taking a stand against the powers that be. The man that had brutally murdered two innocent people, men that he had no quarrel with, was gone in his mind. In that man's place had stepped up the Lone Stranger. He laughed. "Lone Stranger", that was good. He only wished he had a badge to put on, just to complete his look. Maybe he could find one around town.

Find one he did, a day later when he executed Officer Barnes in front of Second Sight. He had wiped the blood and brain matter from the man's shiny badge and stuck it through his leather vest, just over his heart. He would have to take some Brasso to it later, though. Blood played the very hell with metal if you didn't get it all off.

Oscar had made his way through his entire list of locals, and was on his way out of town on Thursday evening to finish up the remaining names on his list. He had been disappointed to find that four of the names on his list, including the Mayor, had already been dead before he could redeem himself. Not allowing this setback to deter him in the least, he collected trinkets from each name on the list; a wristwatch here, a ring there. Even from those he found dead, he took his little souvenirs. From the Mayor's rotting corpse he had taken a tie-tack in the shape of an anchor. The Mayor had been in the Navy at some point, Oscar supposed.

Oscar had been en route out of town when he realized that his truck needed topped off with fuel. He was already out of town proper, and cursed because he would have to turn around and head back to the 7-11 on the outskirts of town. Then he brightened, remembering the gas pumps at the general store ran by that old son of a bitch, Sam Merchant. Oscar gunned his truck, heading for the store.

He was pulling into the parking lot when he remembered the chain saw he had bought from the old fucker a couple of years ago. The thing wouldn't work, no matter how hard Oscar tried to get it going. Hell, he didn't even *need* a damn chain saw. He had just seen it sitting on a display rack and bought it on an impulse. However, when he took the thing back to Merchant to demand his money back (It had only been twenty dollars, but it was the point of the thing), the old fart had reminded him of the "As Is" sticker that had been pasted to the price tag of the saw. Oscar couldn't remember any such sticker, and he told Merchant so. They had gone on, hammer-and-tongs, for almost a half hour before Sam had gotten tired of the argument. Sam enjoyed arguing more than anyone, but enough had been enough. With finality, he had told Oscar that the chain saw was sold, there were no refunds on "As Is" merchandise, and that so far as he, Sam, was concerned, Oscar could to shove the damn thing up his ass if he didn't want to take it and have it fixed.

Sam Merchant was an old man, but he was still brawny, and Oscar had been willing to bet that the bastard had *forgotten* more dirty tricks that Oscar had ever had a chance to learn. He probably had a baseball bat or something under that counter, maybe even a gun. At least this was what Oscar had told himself that day, storming out of the store. He was able to save face, and by that evening was even congratulating himself for not losing his cool and beating up a senior citizen. The truth of the matter, that Oscar was afraid that an old man would have kicked the shit out of him, was conveniently forgotten, as so much of what Oscar didn't want to deal with was wont to be.

Now pulling into the lot of the store, Oscar was tickled pink. He had forgotten all about that chain saw and his little dust-up with Sam Merchant. Now, if things worked out, he would be able to fill up his gas tank, grab an eighteen-pack of Budweiser, and kill the old bastard, all in one clean sweep. And that was just what he had done.

But he had taken the time to pull out his list and add Sam Merchant's name to it first, of course.

He had continued on out of town on his errands, a happy man. His music blasted so loud that he couldn't have heard Jeff's truck anyway, but they only missed each other by about five minutes. God was kind to Jeff, and didn't add the knowledge that had he been a few minutes earlier, he might have saved his friend's life.

Throughout the rest of that Thursday evening, while Jeff was arming himself and collecting provisions, Oscar was finishing up his list and heading back to Stone Grove. He wasn't staying at his trailer anymore. That place was for the *old* Oscar Daniels, not the Lone Stranger. *That* man stayed at the home of one of the wealthiest men in town, a mine owner that lived on a ten-acre spread in a house that looked like something Tom Cruise wouldn't have minded calling home.

Oscar was still cruising on pills and booze, and had been doing so pretty much non-stop for the last three days. The inevitable crash was coming, he could tell. This upset him. He had remembered several more names for his list, and he wanted to get to them as soon as he could. He was finding more and more of the people on his list were dead before he got to them, and that was *really* annoying. But the mix of alcohol and narcotics were beginning to wear him down, and if he didn't crash soon, he might drive his truck off the road and scuff the paint. That would simply not do.

He had resigned himself to the fact that he was going to have to bed down on the king-sized bed with its Egyptian cotton sheets in his new home and catch some sleep when an idea surfaced. Rite Aid was still right there, wasn't it? He grinned and headed back across town singing along with Travis Tritt. When he got back to the Rite Aid, he skipped back to the pharmacy, pilfered through the bottles again, and was soon headed back out to his truck with a giant bottle of Adipex, a weight loss drug that was the closest thing to speed that Oscar could lay his hands on right away. With a bit more careful canvassing of the town, he was sure he could find far more powerful drugs, although not at the Rite Aid.

He took three of the pills and headed back to his new abode. He was pulling into the driveway when his heart began trip-hammering in his chest and a greasy sweat broke out all over his body. *May have taken too much*, he thought. He didn't panic, though, simply shook out several more Valium to counter-balance the Adipex. He sat in the truck for twenty or thirty minutes, until his heart slipped back into a somewhat more normal rhythm, and then headed inside the house to find a bite to eat.

He cut loose with his ever-increasingly insane laugh as he realized that he had just taken several weight-loss pills and now he was *hungry*. Yep, it was surely a weird old world.

After making himself a roast beef sandwich and some chips, he headed upstairs to the master bedroom. He ate his dinner lying on the gigantic bed, watching a huge plasma screen TV. There was nothing on the cable, of course, but the previous owner had shared Oscar's love of action movies and Westerns. He was getting sleepy, but he hoped that there was enough Adipex in his system to wake him fairly early in the morning. Oscar fell asleep around one A.M. with the TV on, where

Clint Eastwood and Morgan Freeman were trying to decide who in the hell was shooting at them in a prairie field.

As he slept, Oscar Daniels' mouth curved into a slow, sweet smile. He had so much to do tomorrow.

It was good to be the king.

Chapter Fourteen

Sunlight filtered through Jeff Della's half-closed eye lids. He awoke to the sound of children playing and his dog jumping enthusiastically about the room. With an expectant groan, he sat up, waiting for the throb in his leg to take up where it had left off the night before. He was pleasantly surprised to find that, although it was stiff and very sore, it showed no signs of locking up completely as it had on other occasions.

He ran his fingers through his hair and gave out a huge yawn. Hearing this, Cynthia came over and handed him a paper plate and a plastic coffee cup.

"Good morning, lazy-bones. I was beginning to think you had overdosed on that medicine last night", she said.

He thanked her for the coffee and the plate of what turned out to be eggs and sausage. That explained the dream he had been having about breakfast with his family, he supposed. Setting the plate down on the table, he took a sip of coffee and asked her what time it was.

"It's almost eleven o'clock, big guy. You've slept the day away."

Jeff jerked with surprise. He must have been a lot more tired than he had thought. He couldn't remember the last time he had slept passed seven in the morning. He rubbed the sleep from his eyes and then attacked the plate of eggs and sausage. They were still warm, so breakfast couldn't have been that long ago. He figured everyone had slept in this morning. While he was stuffing his face with breakfast, Waylon came over and nuzzled his hand.

"Back off, fur ball. You can't tell me that nobody fed you this morning."

Cynthia laughed. "I don't see how that dog could be hungry again for at least a week. He's eaten off everyone's plate in addition to the plateful I made for him especially."

Jeff grinned. "You don't know my dog then, Cynthia. He is hollow from the back legs down. He has to be. I have no idea where else he fits it all, if not."

They exchanged pleasantries while Jeff ate, asking each other how they had slept. Cynthia asked Jeff how his leg felt.

"Well, it's not too bad right now", he answered. "I haven't been up and around on it yet, but it's tolerable for now."

Cynthia nodded towards the table in front of him. "I left the bag with those pain pills in it on the table in front of you. I told the kids that it was your medicine, and for them not to touch it, but I kept hearing someone messing around with it, so I came to check. It turns out you have a junkie dog, Jeff."

"I have no doubt", he laughed. "He gets into everything. He didn't actually get into any of the bottles, did he?"

Cynthia gave him an austere look. "Do I strike you as the sort of person that would engage in contributing to the delinquency of a canine, sir?"

"No, ma'am. He's just a sneaky dog, that's all. At least it wouldn't be contributing to the delinquency of a juvenile canine. He's seven, so we're good there, as long as PETA doesn't get wind of it."

Cynthia's face sobered. "Really though, Jeff, the pills are there if you need them. We need you up and around, not laid up with your leg in a cast."

He smiled. "Well, no cast yet, I don't think. I'll just take it as easy as I can on it for a bit. If it starts hurting too bad, I'll take a pill, I promise."

This seemed to satisfy her, and she went over to where the children were wrestling Waylon. Father Don made his way over to the couch and slowly sat down.

"'Mornin' Father", Jeff said. "How are we this fine day?"

The older man started to smile, but it turned into a grimace. "Well, I'm still blind. I keep hoping I'll wake up and this will all be a bad dream, but so far, no dice. I pray, and that helps. How about you?"

"About the same. I just keep hoping this thing will pass."

"'Take this cup from my lips'"?

"Yeah, something like that. Although it's looking more and more like I'm gonna have to drink that cup whether I want to or not." He sighed.

Father Don reached out in the now-familiar gesture, and Jeff took his hand. They gripped each other for a moment, each taking strength from the other. After a moment, they let their hands drop. Father Don brightened a little.

"Hey, do you think you might be able to round up a CB radio and a battery before you..." His face darkened. "Well, before you do what you need to today?"

Jeff matched his grim look. He could almost forget, sitting in this sunny room with a full belly and the sound of children's laughter, that he was intent on killing a man today. He shook it off.

"Yeah, I'm sure I could round up a CB and a battery. Why, though? I mean, if 911 is out, I doubt there are too many folks playing around on their CB's right now."

"Yeah, I'm sure you're right about that, at least locally. But I was thinking last night before I fell asleep. You can see and this Daniels man can see. That's two people just here in Stone Grove. It stands to reason that there are more out there, doesn't it? I mean, what are the chances that the only two people on the whole planet that can still see are sitting in the same little town in West Virginia?"

Jeff thought about it. "You're right. There *have* to be more folks like me out there, somewhere." He snapped his fingers. "I can do you better than a CB, though. How about a short wave radio set? Something with a bit more range? We can set up a CB base station here for starters, and then get ourselves a shortwave with a good sized tower. Hell, we can probably talk to people in Japan right now. There's not going to be a lot of traffic on the band." He grinned. "How's your Japanese, Don?"

"Probably about as good as your Spanish, young man", the priest replied.

"*No habla, senor.*" The men shared a laugh.

"So, you think you could hook us up with the CB first off? I could set it up while you're… well, you know. That way we can kind of get a foot up. I'd like to be a bit more proactive here. Just sitting around and reacting to what happens is no way to get through any crises, especially one of this magnitude."

Jeff reached over and patted Don's shoulder. "Consider it done, my friend. First thing. I know just where to get one, and I need to grab some more clothes, anyway. These are a bit ripe."

Don flapped a hand in the general direction of the bathroom. "Not much in the way of a shower, really. I mean, technically, you could call it one. It's a stall with a water hose in it. We used it for cleaning up, mostly. Cynthia has some shampoo and soap in there, though."

Jeff said that would be fine and slowly stood up, testing his leg. It gave out a short burst of complaint, but then settled down into a low throb. Yeah, he would be eating a pill or two today, that was for sure. He slid his feet into his boots, making a mental list of what he would need from the surplus store. He was certain that there would be a CB there, at the very least, and most likely a shortwave, as well. What sort of survival nut would be caught without those things?

He limped over to the children and spent a few minutes goofing around with them. Jamie Cummings was especially attentive to Jeff. It seemed that the boy had gone from hating his guts to a sort of hero-worship overnight. Jeff honestly wasn't sure which one made him more uncomfortable. Jeff told the kids that he was going to run a quick errand, but that he was leaving Waylon there as a guard dog. Waylon seemed to be agreeable to this, and thumped his tail against the floor.

Jeff headed back over to his couch and began to unload his new pack. He wasn't going to pack all this ammo and other supplies over to the surplus store. This wasn't the mission; this was just a quick errand. The real mission would begin later today.

Jeff emptied most of the contents of the pack and stacked them beside the couch. He kept plenty magazines for both his rifle and his handgun, though. Just because this was a quick twenty-minute trip a block away and back was no reason to get sloppy and wind up with his guts blown out.

He figured that he could fit a CB, battery, and maybe even a shortwave set into the pack, if they weren't too bulky. He hoped to find them still boxed up. They would take up less room, and he could assemble them here.

He shouldered the pack, holstered his pistol, and slung his rifle. He bounced experimentally on the balls of his feet to get an idea of how bad this little trip was going to hurt. The answering throb from his leg decided him. He shook out two of the Percocet and swallowed them with the last of his coffee, now cold. He was worried that too much would slow his reflexes, but not enough would leave him lying helpless in the street with a leg that was unable to support him. If that happened, he was a dead man.

He walked toward the door. Waylon got up to follow, but went back to the kids at Jeff's admonition to stay. Father Don looked around, trying to fix Jeff's location by sound and said "Pax vobiscum, Jeff."

Jeff had been a Baptist all his life, but he knew enough about Latin to understand and replied "And with you, Father", which brought a smile to the older man's face. Cynthia took Jeff's arm as they headed down the hall towards the staircase. On the way down the stairs, she said, "Same drill as before, right? You head out; I hang back and wait for you to get done. I hear you coming, and I'll have the chains off quick."

Jeff groaned and smacked his forehead.

"Yeah, that would have been great if I hadn't decided to remodel the foyer with the Pepsi machine last night. Dammit, moving that thing is going to kill me." He was truly glad for the Percocet now. This was *not* going to be beneficial to his leg in the least.

Cynthia drew in a sharp breath. "Oh, God, I forgot all about that!" She thought for a moment and then asked, "How bad is your leg, Jeff? I mean *really*, how bad?"

"It's been worse, I promise you that."

"Do you think you might be able to do a spot of climbing, if it meant that you didn't have to move that pop machine again?"

"Are you kidding? I'll climb this place like Spider Man if I don't have to jack around with that heavy bastard again."

She nodded. "Okay. Here's what we'll do. Almost all the windows here are small and covered with wire. They were made that way to keep any of the kids from going through them accidentally. But there is one window in the back of the cafeteria that is bigger than the others. You could fit through it, I'm almost positive. The thing is, it's set higher up than the others. Quite a bit higher, actually. I think they put it there to help keep the air flowing on hot days when we cooked lunch. From the inside, you won't have any problem climbing on a chair or a table and lowering yourself out. But from the outside, it's pretty high up, and you'll have to find a way to get back up to it. Sorry about this. I should have remembered the pop machine."

He laid his hand on her cheek. "That's all right, Cynthia. We've had quite a bit on our minds lately. Let's go take a look at this window of yours. Like I said, if I don't have to hoss that machine around again, I'll jump through that window like an Olympic gymnast."

The window wasn't as bad as he had feared. It was about seven feet up from the floor, which put about ten feet from the ground on the outside. He would definitely need something to get back in. However, he had no plans of leading any problems back here anyway, so he was content to clamber up on a chair and open the window. He dropped the pack to the ground, and then gave his rifle to Cynthia.

"Once I'm on the ground, you pass me my rifle, okay? I don't want to drop it if I can keep from it. I'm not sure how good those optics I put on there last night are sighted in, and I don't want to bang it up any more than I have to."

She took the rifle from him and held it. He was climbing back into the chair to lever himself out the window when she said his name.

He turned back around. With her radar precision, she stepped into up to him and brought her face close. Her eyes were closed and her mouth was slightly open, but it took Jeff several seconds to realize she wanted him to kiss her. When it clicked, he gladly acquiesced. They kissed, the rifle between them making it awkward. He was about to take the rifle from her so he could continue more thoroughly, but she stepped back primly and smiled at him.

"Don't get greedy there, stud. I was just wishing you luck, you know."

He grinned like a school boy. "Well, what do I get if I make it back in one piece? Because if you say nothing, I'll keep leaving so you have to wish me luck a *lot* more often."

She laughed. "Get your ass out the window, big guy. I've got a lot to do today, and I can't be standing around here toting your firearms."

Jeff gave her a mock salute, whether she could see it or not. "Yes, ma'am! Private Della will now execute your orders to the maximum of my ability!"

She giggled again, and then became serious. "Go on", she said softly. "Get this done, and then we'll worry about… the other thing. And then maybe we can start trying to really make a difference with some folks around here." *If there's any left*, she thought but didn't add.

Jeff couldn't resist. He reached in and gave her another brush on the lips, and then tuned and propelled himself through the window. He landed harder than he would have liked, but managed to take the brunt of the fall on his good leg. He turned up to the window. It looked one hell of a lot higher up from out here. Cynthia was reaching him his rifle. He took it and re-shouldered his pack.

"Okay, I'm out of here. When I get back, I'll have to find a step ladder or something to get back through the window. I shouldn't be gone more than a half hour or so, but just because you hear someone climbing through this window, don't assume it's me, all right? Stay out of sight in the kitchen. When I'm in, I'll let you know it's me. If you hear someone walking across that floor and I haven't announced myself, you cut their fucking head off, got it?"

The coarseness of his statement had the desired effect. She looked shocked for a moment, and then nodded. Her machete was slung across her back in a sheath, and she could get to it in seconds. Jeff felt better leaving, knowing that she would be on her guard. On her home turf, armed with a blade like that, sight wouldn't factor into it.

He hoped.

He headed across the lawn of the school and stopped by a tree, listening for a few minutes. The day had dawned clear and beautiful; as if the whole world hadn't fallen right the hell apart. The smell of the oily smoke from the horizon was even gone, a freshening breeze blowing it away. He hadn't seen any more huge plumes of smoke like he had those first few days, and hoped that the fires had burned out.

Snapping himself back to the present, he looked around. *Keep daydreaming, sweetheart. That's an excellent way to get yourself dead*, he thought.

Deciding that walking would be quieter, and therefore safer, Jeff left his truck parked at Second Sight. He walked briskly down the street, keeping close to the buildings. The Percocet were doing their job nicely. He felt barely a twinge as he broke into a slow jog. He stopped again at the intersection, his eyes trying to look everywhere at once. *If this is what being a soldier is like, I'm glad I never joined*, he thought. This was hellish, trying to cover every direction at once, and not knowing if a round was going to come screaming out of nowhere and slam into your heart at any second.

He took a few seconds to assert some control over himself. If he freaked out and froze in the open like this, Daniels could just saunter by and pop him at his leisure. Once he felt like he had it back together, he made for the surplus store at a dead run. Crossing Main Street was an exercise in pure terror. He just *knew* that was where Daniels was going to open up on him, while he was unprotected by the buildings. The twenty feet of pavement looked a mile wide to him.

He slammed into the door of the surplus store and dropped to the ground under the window. He lay there, trying to look around outside without raising his head when a small voice in his mind said *He's already in here with you. He knew this was where you were coming and he's already in here.* A terrified squeak jumped from his lips, and he spun around on the floor, trying to point his rifle everywhere at once.

There was nothing there. The only sound form the store came from the flies that were busily continuing their meal of Robertson. The man wasn't improving with the heat. Jeff had just been to shit-blind scared to notice before, but now the stench of decay was much more defined. Jeff climbed to his feet, cursing himself as a coward and a fool, and snagged a camouflage bandanna from a rack next to him. He clapped it over his lower face and tied it off around his neck.

Moving into the store, it was more difficult to see, his eyes having adjusted to the bright midday sun outside. After a few minutes, his eyes had acclimated, and he was able to make out the interior of the store. He looked around for a while and, sure enough, found a CB, a shortwave, and several emergency radios that worked one of three ways: good old fashioned batteries, a hand crank that supplied power, or small solar panels. These small radios had jacks for plugging in cell phones, but Jeff didn't think that would do much good. However, they also came equipped with lights, and might come in handy if they ran low on batteries.

He placed a new CB and shortwave radio set, still in their boxes, into his pack. He added five of the small emergency radios, as well. He lifted the pack, but the weight was not too bad at all. Now, he had to find some clothes. He looked around the store, hoping to find some blue jeans or even work pants but soon realized that, like it or not, he was going to look like a soldier if he got his clothing from here. He supposed he could go down the street to the men's store and pick out some new clothes, but after the fiasco of crossing Main Street, he didn't think he had the courage to do any window shopping around town today,

He grunted in disgust at himself as he pawed through the camouflage battle dress uniforms on the racks, looking for his size. He was going to hunt down a killer, huh? He couldn't even cross the damn street without nearly pissing himself. *Yeah, I bet you've got that bastard terrified, hero,* he thought. Then he realized that Daniels didn't even know that Jeff Della existed. *Great,* he thought, savagely pulling the BDU's from the racks. *You've got all the advantages. You know who he is, he knows nothing about you. You can draw him into an ambush, and he'll never even know you're there until you shoot him dead as hell, and you're* still *terrified, you chickenshit!*

He continued to chastise himself as he found several pairs of pants, shirts, and socks to add to his pack. After some more searching, he was able to locate some G.I. underwear and some olive drab t-shirts. He shoved all this into his pack and checked the weight. Still no problem so far. He looked around to see if there was anything else he might need. Once he left, he had no desire to ever return to this store again. His eyes traveled over the racks and displays until they settled on several bulky-looking vests. He walked over to them to check them out.

He could tell that they were army issue vests, with heavy ceramic plates inside them. The camouflage pattern was different than what was used by the United Stated, however. There were browns, grays, and different shades of green, but there were also shades of what was almost blaze orange. That struck Jeff as an odd color to try to conceal oneself with. He looked around the rack until he found the price tag, which contained a small item description. As it turned out, the vests were from Germany, and the pattern was called Flecktarn. Well, all right then. Apparently the German country side was full of blaze orange. Jeff really wanted to take one of the vests for the protection it provided. These things were supposed to stop assault rifle rounds. That orange bothered him, though. It might provide protection, but what good was it if it advertised his position to the person doing the shooting?

After a bit more debate, Jeff was about to give it up as a lost cause when he noticed several cans of flat camouflage paint, the kind people used to spray their boats and old work trucks. Grabbing a couple of cans of flat OD green, he tossed them into his pack and grabbed a vest that looked big enough to fit him. It was heavier than he expected, weighing almost as much as the backpack with the radio equipment in it. With a sigh, he pulled it on. It was heavy, and it was bulky, and it restricted his movement. But what it *also* did was stop the bullet that might slam through his chest and turn his heart into hamburger. He fumbled with the Velcro closures until it was tight enough to keep from sliding around on him, and then shouldered his pack.

He stood at the door of the surplus store for a few minutes, letting his eyes re-acclimate to the bright street. Once he felt ready, he took several deep breaths and raised his rifle to his shoulder, ready to fire. He sprinted out of the door and back across Main Street like a soldier in No Man's Land. Once again, he felt a terrified amazement at how long those twenty feet had seemed to have been. When he was against the buildings again, his breathing returned to something close to normal. He began moving back up the street toward Second Sight.

The extra weight of the pack and the vest were taking their toll on his leg. Even through the Percocets, the throbbing was back, with the new added feature of a lancing bolt of pain slamming up and down his leg with every third or fourth step. He sighed. His reflexes be damned, he was going to have to eat a few more of those pills once he got back to the school, or he would be laid up for days.

As he made his way cautiously down the street, keeping his eyes constantly roving from the street to the window and back again, he began to question his courage even more seriously. He had never really thought of himself as a brave man, but he had never considered himself to be a coward, either. Doctors and nurses beyond counting had told him how brave he had been after the accident, but Jeff had never considered that bravery, just simple blind luck. He laughed to himself. *All my luck is blind now*, the thought. He had lived where his family had died, nothing more.

In school, he had been in few fights, and most of those had been in primary school, which really only meant he had rolled around on the ground with another boy slightly rougher than he normally would have during recess. He was a fairly popular boy, and hadn't gotten into any fights in high school before the accident. After it, fighting wasn't much of an option. His choice of a secluded lifestyle after the accident had removed any possibility of hostility being brought to his front door. At twenty-three years old, he suddenly realized that not only did he not want to fight, he didn't know how.

And this wasn't a *fight*, dammit. This was something that went far beyond fisticuffs in the school playground or a scuffle in the parking lot of the local bar. He was planning to kill a man, if he could. More than that, he was planning to kill a man in cold blood from ambush. When he had been staring down at the ruined remains of Sam Merchant, the rage he had felt had been more than enough to make killing Oscar Daniels seem like nothing so morally difficult as stomping a black widow spider. It was impersonal even while it was the most personal thing that Jeff had ever felt. He shook his head. Even his own thoughts didn't make any sense about this, follow any set of logic.

He thought back to the cold, calculated manner he had told Cynthia and Father Don that he was going to find and kill Daniels. Yeah, he had sounded like a tough guy from an action flick when he had said that, and he was even willing to bet that they believed him, but they hadn't seen him skittering across Main Street like a little kid being chased by a bully, either. *Thank God they can't see, or they would know what a fucking fake I am*, he thought, and then realized just how heartless that little prayer had been. His self-disgust mounted.

A few minutes later, he was standing beneath the cafeteria window with his load of swag. He looked around for something to stand on to climb back in and realized that he should have done this *before* he had taken off, just so it would have been ready when he got back. He couldn't seem to plan far enough ahead to get anything right. Here he was, planning this incredibly tactical ambush of a murderer, and he couldn't remember to have a step ladder ready to get back into his base of operations. Yes, indeed, Jeff Della... super soldier.

He finally located a picnic table at the side of the lawn. Thankfully, it was one of the plastic models; otherwise Jeff wasn't sure he could have lugged it under the window. He fought it into position and climbed atop it. He almost lost his balance and fell as his leg gave him yet another high-voltage shot of anger, but after flailing his arms, he was able to retain his balance. Up went the self-disgust meter another notch. He shoved the window open and pushed his pack inside. It fell to the tile floor with a muffled thump. He reached in and lowered his rifle on top of it as gently as he could by the strap, and then began to make his way into the window. It seemed to take forever, and his leg was screaming at him by the time he slithered to the floor next to his equipment. He lay there for a moment, catching his breath, and then got up to close the window. As he was reaching up, he caught a glimpse of movement from his peripheral vision. He turned, accidentally putting all his weight on his bad leg.

Which, in turn, saved his life.

As he pivoted on his bad leg, it finally seemed to say to hell with it and give up. It crumpled under his weight, dropping him like a sack of grain to the floor. Had it not, the whickering blade of the machete that flashed over his head would have gone through it, instead. In his preoccupation with chastising himself for being a cowardly piece of crap, he had forgotten completely about his instructions to Cynthia. He hadn't announced himself in any way, except by making the exact noises someone breaking into a building would have made.

He lay on the floor, looking up as Cynthia recovered from her first swing and began to home in for her second. Jeff was so mesmerized by this sight that he quite nearly forgot to scream at her to stop. She looked like a Valkyrie, her flaming red tresses spinning out from her head and her green eyes intent on hacking this intruder into tiny bits. *Sweet Jesus*, he thought, *a blind woman has more guts than I do.* He was able to snap out of his trance when he saw that she had managed to correct the angle of her attack and was about to cut him in half.

"Cynthia, wait! It's Jeff! It's me, for God's sake!"

She let out a startled little scream of effort, and managed to heave the machete off target. It swished through the air to his right, close enough that he could hear the sinister little whisper as it went past. He had time to think that this was the second time in two days that he had nearly had his head taken off his shoulders when Cynthia fell bodily on top of him. She alternated between giving him blind kisses all over his face and slapping the shit out of him. He found himself laughing helplessly, which only lessened the number of kisses and increased the number of slaps.

"You stupid (*slap!*), ignorant (*slap!*), pig-headed (*slap!*), dumb ass! I could have (*slap-slap!*) killed you!"

Jeff managed to catch a hold of both her hands and keep her from ringing his bell any more. He took a breath to apologize, but Cynthia, now unable to slap, reverted back to the kissing. They stayed in that position for a bit, until both of them started laughing. Cynthia sat back, allowing Jeff to sit upright. She was crying, he saw, tears making her incredible eyes shine. Holding her hands in both of his, he said, "I am *so* sorry Cynthia. I mean it. I got caught up in what I was doing, and I forgot to call out. Entirely my fault. Forgive me?"

She gave him a look that told him that he most certainly on probation for a while, and then climbed off him and began carefully feeling around on the floor for her machete. She found it and finger-walked down the blade until she could grasp the handle. She slid the three feet of black steel back into the sheath and stood waiting for him to get up.

He made his way up the wall, using his good leg. He looked at her with something close to awe in his eyes.

"Where in the *hell* did you learn to swing a machete like that? Did your parents send you to a Mediaeval Arts for the Blind class when you were in England, or something?"

She gave him a scathing look. "Oh, ha-ha, funny man. You're lucky I'm not kicking your head around this damn cafeteria like a soccer ball right now, and you're going to *joke* about it?'

He apologized again; infusing what he hoped was just the right balance of begging and humility. She seemed to be mollified for the moment and asked him if he had gotten everything he had needed. Before he could answer, she asked, "And what in the hell are you wearing? It feels like you've got a concrete shirt on, or something."

He chose to answer last question first. "I'll have you know that I am sporting the latest in personal protective wear, giving the wearer greater survivability. At least that's what it said on the tag. It's also covered in a camouflage pattern called 'Flecktarn', which is obviously German for 'We think that blaze orange is a naturally occurring color'".

She gave him a blank look that bordered on agitation, so he quickly explained.

"It's a bullet-proof vest that soldiers wear. I found it at the surplus store and thought it might come in handy. It really does have blaze orange all over it, though, which I can't figure out to save my life." He stopped for a moment, thinking. "Uh… you know what blaze orange is, don't you? I mean I know you've never, uh…*seen* it, but…"

Her look dropped another few degrees.

"Blaze orange is the color that hunters wear when they are out in the woods so other hunters don't shoot them to death. My father hunted ducks, and I'm not an idiot, thank you very much."

He found himself apologizing again. He should be getting pretty good at it, considering all the practice he was getting. He quickly shifted the subject to his other finds, hoping to take her mind off his ignorance.

"And this is the CB, and here's the shortwave. I couldn't find a battery in the store, but we can probably rig something up from a car battery. I picked up some clothes so I could shower, but they are all military things, so I'm afraid that I'll look like a soldier once I out all this on", he finished, sounding slightly ashamed.

She looked confused. "What difference will it make if you look like a soldier or not? If anything, it will make the people you find feel even more secure."

Jeff grinned: finally a little pay-back. "And just *how*, exactly, will that make anyone feel more secure, Cynthia? It's not like they can *see* me, now is it?"

She gave him a baleful look and said, "Fine, point taken, Mr. Smarty-Pants. But really, what's the big deal about wearing military clothing?"

He stood leaning against the wall for a minute, trying to frame his answer. Finally, he said, "I just feel like an imposter, Cynthia. I'm no soldier. I found that out just trying to cross the street a little while ago." He went on to explain the terror that he had felt, and how his self-confidence had taken a nose dive in the last hour or so. He face burned as he admitted this, but at least no one could see it.

She reached out and found his face. She cupped her hand on his cheek and leaned in to kiss him once, very gently, on the lips. When she spoke, her voice was calm and compassionate.

"Jeff, you aren't a soldier, you're right about that. But that's okay. What you are is a good man trying to do the right thing. No one expects you to be a super hero, you know. You are feeling afraid and disgusted about the fact you are going to have to kill another human being. You think that's not a normal feeling? I would be worried if you didn't show some hesitation. I'm actually glad to hear you say this, because last night you sounded like you were looking *forward* to killing that man."

"Last night, I *was*." Jeff looked into her eyes. "*You* didn't hesitate just now. You would have taken my head off at the neck if my leg hadn't buckled. Maybe you're more of a super hero than I am."

She smiled sadly. "No, Jeff, I'm not. What I am is a blind woman that has several equally blind children that are her responsibility. Yes, I would have killed you if I could have. I just thank God you fell, and that you weren't hurt. But if you had been that Daniels man? Yes, I would have tried and tried to kill you. Not because I'm a super hero, but because I've got people depending on me."

For a moment, Jeff was stricken silent. In just a few sentences, Cynthia had summed up his problem perfectly. His courage wasn't the issue. His problem was that for so many years now, he had been responsible for no one but himself and Waylon, and Waylon was more than capable of fending for himself. Since he had been seventeen, Jeff had not felt the burden of responsibility that came with family or friends. His life had been solitary by choice, and now he found himself the only person capable of helping these people that had become so important to him. The terror he had been feeling wasn't directly related to the fact that he might be killed by Oscar Daniels. Having been close to death in his life, he accepted it as part and parcel of what had to be. What terrified him the most wasn't that Daniels might catch him unaware and kill him, but what would happen to Cynthia, Father Don, and the children if that happened. Without his eyes, they would be condemned to a brutally short life that would most likely end with their starvation, or worse.

He felt the weight of self-disgust lift from his shoulders, only to be replaced by the equally heavy weight of responsibility. Of the two, he found that the second sat far easier on him. It might even grow comfortable, given time.

"You're quite a woman, do you know that?" he asked her, covering her hand on his face with his own.

She grinned at him. "You don't know the half of it, big guy. Play your cards right and maybe you'll find out just how much woman I *am*."

He laughed. "Right, and have Father Don geld me with his machete? Methinks he wouldn't be quite so laid-back about such goings-on, do you?"

"He's my friend, not my father, Jeff. But this is a conversation for another time. Now, how much does all that stuff weigh?"

The question caught him off guard. "I don't know, probably twenty, maybe thirty pounds. Why?"

She let out an exasperated sigh. "Because your leg is messed up, and I need to know if I can carry all this stuff at one go, or if I'll have to make two trips, you big dummy."

He started to protest, but she stopped him with another kiss. "Fix the window back. And we probably need to put something in front of it that will make noise, so we can hear if someone tries to come through." She turned and felt around for his pack, and then hoisted it to her shoulder with almost no effort. The girl was strong, he had to admit that. The thought of what those powerful arms might have done to his head if she had connected with that machete sent a shiver up his spine.

He scouted around the cafeteria, limping like a sailor on a pitching deck until he located several large cans of tomato paste. He slid the window closed and then set the cans along the ledge. Anyone forcing the window up would catch the cans with the window edge, dropping them to the tile floor. It wasn't a professional alarm system, but the resultant noise would bring him running.

Using his rifle as a support, he made his way back up the stairs with Cynthia. It took him longer than he had hoped. His leg was going south, and going south quickly. They made their way back into the rec room and Jeff was almost bowled over by Waylon, who was glad as ever to see him. He rubbed the dog's ears for a minute and then sat down on the couch with an audible groan. Cynthia was there, the little black case in hand. He thanked her heartily and shook out three of the pills from the bottle. He broke them all in half and washed them down with a cup of coffee. Then, he lay back against the cushions of the couch and waited for them to kick in.

After a while, they did, and the pain in his leg faded away to a distant drone. While he sat there convalescing, Father Don began to unpack the CB and shortwave from their boxes. His hands moved with dexterous certainty with the various wires and buttons. He reminded Jeff of a soldier that could field-strip his weapon and reassemble it blindfolded.

"You look like you know what you're doing, Don", he said.

The older man smiled. "This was a hobby of mine when I was a kid. CB's, shortwave, HAM radios, all that stuff. We'll need a power source for these once the electricity dies, but these can be plugged right into the wall. We'll also need a big antenna for the shortwave, but the CB has one with it. I can have the CB up and running in about twenty minutes."

Jeff was glad that the man had found something to occupy him. It was harder on him than the others, because he was still getting used to being blind, something they had dealt with since birth. Having been blind himself, Jeff could empathize with the man totally. It was a helpless, depressing feeling.

While Father Don worked on the CB, Cynthia came to sit next to Jeff. She held his hand and they just sat there for a while, listening to the children play with Waylon, something neither they nor the dog seemed to grow tired of. Finally, she said, "What are we going to do now? I mean, are you going to be able to do what needs to be done, or do you need to rest your leg until tomorrow?"

Jeff thought about it. In a perfect world, he would spend the next few days taking it easy and rubbing Voltaren gel on his leg, laying around and listening to the radio. This wasn't a perfect world, however. He could feel the press of time. Every moment he spent sitting here on his ass, a baby could be starving or dying of dehydration just blocks away. The longer he waited, the higher the death toll was going to be.

But the simple fact of business was that he couldn't go about his job of finding survivors until he dealt with Oscar Daniels. An image, short but horrible, shot through his mind of him driving a van full of survivors when Daniels pulled alongside and blew his brains all over the windshield. That would be the end of *that* little rescue mission.

Finally, he sighed and gripped Cynthia's hand tighter.

"I need to do it today. We can't wait much longer, or there won't be anyone left to save. You know that." He looked at the clock. It was a quarter after three in the afternoon. Where had the day gone? "I'll let the pain meds kick all the way in, and then I'll see what I can get done. Hopefully, all this will be over, one way or the other, by tonight."

"Don't say it like that. Not one way or the other. You'll get him, you'll come back here, and tomorrow morning, we'll start to help people. Okay?" Her voice was strained, begging to be comforted.

"Okay. I'll get it done, and tomorrow we start the *real* work."

They sat on the couch holding hands as the sun softened into a glow that only Jeff could appreciate.

Chapter Fifteen

Oscar Daniels awoke that day at almost the exact same time as Jeff Della had. He felt much worse, however. The culmination of several days of constant drug and alcohol use left him feeling like he had been run over by a train. Fortunately, he had the cure. Within moments of waking up, he was gobbling various pills like a child eating candy. He lay back on the bed and waited for them to begin their work. Had they known it, the ironic similarity to the start of their day would have probably been totally lost upon the two men.

Oscar felt much better about a half an hour later, and was up getting dressed. He had changed out his purple silk shirt and black Wrangler jeans for a black silk shirt and black leather pants he had gotten from the men's store in town. Now decked out totally from head to toe in black, he told his reflection in a deep bass voice, "Hello. I'm Johnny Cash", and then went off into gales of laughter.

He went downstairs and got himself a beer from the fridge and then went into the large living room. He opened the doors to a massive cabinet that held an even larger plasma screen TV and popped in a DVD. He sat down on the couch, drinking his beer and watched Keifer Sutherland tell Emilio Estevez that he was *not* a god. Oscar replied in perfect time with Estevez, "Why don't you pull that trigger and find out?" Now, *that* was balls, by God. Oscar felt a twinge of disappointment that this kind of thing hadn't happened when he had gunned down Barnes. If he had thought about it at the time that was exactly what he would have said to the fucker.

Oscar worked his way through the rest of the movie and another twelve beers, and then decided it was time to get on with his business of the day. He reached into his pocket and pulled out his list. It was covered in crossed-out names, and had blood on it. (Another one of the reasons for the change of shirts. Blood ruined silk, he had found.) There wasn't much room left on the paper for any new names, but Oscar suddenly decided that he didn't *need* the list anymore. It occurred to him that this *whole* goddamn town had wronged him at one point or another, so to hell with the list. He'd just start knocking on doors.

Oscar had found that he absolutely *loved* killing folks. He had been disappointed to find the mine owner's family weren't at home when he had arrived there to claim the place, it would have been fun to kill them, too.

It was no wonder it was illegal. And he was a *natural* at it. The government always made the things that made you feel good illegal. *Not no more*, he thought. The days of the government fucking with his fun were *over*, baby.

And speaking of fucking… it had been quite some time since he had gotten laid. Oscar sat on the plush leather couch, rubbing his growing erection through his leather pants totally unselfconsciously. Yeah, he could find him a woman or two (Maybe even three, who knew?) today and have himself a grand old time. He could tie them up and toss them in the back of his truck and bring them back to his palace here and do… well, whatever he wanted to with them. Who was going to stop him?

Nobody, that's who.

With his day now planned out, Oscar headed out to his truck, snagging his pistol rig off the back of a dining room chair. He strapped it on as he walked across the room, stopping only to grab his bag of pharmaceuticals and another six-pack of beer. He stepped into the afternoon sun and squinted against the brightness. He fished out a pair of wraparound shades he had taken from one of his victims and put them on.

He walked to his truck and climbed in. He keyed the engine and sat enjoying the vibration of the big engine. He flipped through his CD holder and decided that today was a good day for Lynyrd Skynyrd. He spun his tires out of the driveway and headed into town, the sound of "Gimme Three Steps" blasting out of his massive speakers. He would head over to the east side of town first, he figured. That was where many of the upper-crust folks lived, and he wouldn't mind finding himself some rich bitch pussy to take back home.

Yes sir, it sure was good to be the king.

Chapter Sixteen

While Oscar Daniels was methodically planning to kidnap and rape blind women, Jeff Della was in Father Don's office, spray painting his vest. He had the window open and the door closed. The smell of the paint had been harsh enough on him, but to the blind folks in the next room, it had been overpowering. He carefully covered the vest with several coats, and was much happier with the look of the thing once he was done. He blaze orange was a thing of the past. The vest reeked of paint, but he figured it would mellow out eventually.

Having finished that task, he went into the small bathroom and stepped into the tiny cubicle that had been used to clean off equipment at the school. To his chagrin, there was not hot water, and the spray from the hose was cold enough to leave his teeth chattering. He washed himself off and even washed out his hair. Once he was done, he went to the sink and brushed his teeth with the toothbrush that Cynthia had gotten him. He stared at his reflection for a moment, debating on whether he should shave or not. He finally decided to hell with it. He was going on a manhunt, not a GQ cover-shoot.

He stepped into the GI underwear and a green t-shirt, and then pulled on his camouflage fatigues. Again unaware of the irony of his actions matching those of his prey, he looked at himself in the mirror, sang a few bars from the cartoon "G.I. Joe", and laughed.

He stepped out of the bathroom and walked over to where Father Don was working the CB. He had not been able to raise anyone yet, although he could have sworn that he had heard something just once, distant and crackling through the static.

"Any luck?" Jeff asked.

"Nothing since that one time, and I'm not even sure if I really heard anything or not", the priest replied. "Once we get the shortwave up, we'll see. And then we'll need a HAM radio, too.

Jeff clapped him on the back and told him to keep at it. He then walked over to the couch and began to think about what he needed to pack for his hunt. The ammo, sure. The night-vision goggles were something that he needed to fool around with until he got the hang of them, but he figured he could do that in one of the windowless closets in the hall. He attached his drop-leg platforms to his belt and snapped them around his legs. There were magazine holders for six clips of 5.56 mm ammunition on his left one, and the holster for his P90 and five more clip holders for it on his right. When he filled each of the holders and added his handgun, he walked around a bit to see how the added weight would affect his balance. He was pleasantly surprised. The platforms were snug against his leg, and didn't flop around like he had originally feared they might. Because they sat so tightly against his leg, they didn't seem to add as much weight. He wouldn't want to have to march fifty miles wearing the damn things, but he wasn't planning on that, anyway.

He checked his rifle again, turning on the red-dot sight and checking its brightness. It had an adjustment knob on the side that allowed him to make the dot brighter or dimmer, depending on the situation. According to the laser bore-sighter, the optic was dead-on, but Jeff wouldn't truly trust it until he had fired the weapon to see for himself. The shotgun was fully loaded and went into its scabbard on the pack. Jeff removed the extra fatigues from the back and replaced them with several boxes of ammunition for all three of his weapons, three MREs, one of the emergency radios, and several flashlights. He had no intention of being caught in the dark.

That reminded him about the night-vision goggles, and he took the box out to check them out. They came with a strap that fit over the head and held them in place, and a special attachment that would allow them to be clipped onto a helmet. Jeff had seen several Kevlar helmets in the surplus store, and now wondered if he should have grabbed one. *Screw that,* he thought, *enough is enough. I'm going after an asshole that shoots helpless blind people, not the damned Taliban.* He messed around with the straps on the goggles until they were secure around his head. The goggles were designed to flip up out of the way when they weren't needed. He attached them to the clip on the front of the strap, and flipped them down. He did this several more times to ensure that he had attached everything correctly, and then sat down to read the accompanying literature.

After he had read through the instructions twice, he placed the batteries in the goggles and flipped the switch. There was a soft hum as they powered up. Jeff put them back on and flipped the goggles into place. There was nothing but a solid green wall of light. He took them off again and checked to see if they might have had lens covers on, but they didn't. He peered back through them again and got nothing but that green. He turned them off and went back to the instructions. He couldn't root out the problem until suddenly it occurred to him that he was sitting in a bright, sun-lit room, trying to see through *night*-vision goggles. Laughing at himself, he headed into the hallway.

He stepped into the hall closet and closed the door. The blackness was complete, save for a tiny rim of light around the door facing. Putting the goggles back on, he flipped them down and turned them back on. They hummed briefly, and suddenly, the closet sprang into crisp, green clarity. He could read the tiniest words on the labels of the cleaning supplies. These things were *awesome*. He spent several more minutes looking around through them when he realized that he was just running down the batteries. He flipped them off and was instantly in the dark again. He opened the closet door and went back into the rec room.

Carefully placing the goggles back into their case, he slid them into one of the side pockets on the pack, where he could get to them in a hurry if he needed them. He filled his Camelbak with bottled water and pulled it on. He was impressed with the efficiency of the military equipment. Everything was modular, so it could be placed in any configuration the user wanted. It also made the best use of space. Nothing was bulkier than it absolutely needed to be. He understood that this system had come from trial and error, and that war was probably one of the harshest teachers.

Shouldering the pack and buckling everything together, he again walked across the room a few times. The weight was well-distributed. He still wouldn't want to do a forced march with all this crap on, but for his purposes, he thought it would work fine.

He took off the pack, but left his drop-leg platforms on. The holster was perfectly level with his right hand, and he could have his handgun out in a hurry if need be. He walked back over to the couch and sat down. He shook another couple of Percocets out and took them. He didn't want to be high, but he was deathly afraid that he was going to need his leg to work even more. He called out to Cynthia, who came over to him from the children.

"Hey, kiddo. Do you remember where I put those maps I had brought with me last night?"

She thought about it a second and then said, "I'm pretty sure you had them with you when you came back last night. Are they in your pack?"

He grunted in amusement. That was just like a woman, to remember a small a detail as that. Pilfering through the pockets of the pack, he found the maps, shoved down to one side. He thanked her and then laid one of the town maps out on the table to study it. He no longer felt like an imposter, but studying the maps reinforced the image that he was a soldier doing recon before a mission. Well, that *was* what he was doing, wasn't it?

He studied the layout of the town, trying to find the best place to set up his ambush. There were several dead-end streets, and Jeff would love nothing better than to lure Daniels down one of them and then block off the entrance with his truck. Unable to drive away, the man would have to go it on foot, which would give Jeff a much better chance of hitting him. He didn't want anything too close to Second Sight, though. There would be bullets flying, and he didn't want to chance the possibility that a stray shot could make its way through one of the windows here and strike someone.

He peered at the map for some time until he found a place that satisfied him, a dead-end street on the far side of town that would work perfectly if Jeff could lure Daniels into it. Having decided the where, he needed to work out the when and how. He continued to pore over the map, not really seeing it anymore. In his mind's eye, he saw the confrontation and the many possible results. In most of them, he wound up with a large hole in him. The bloody mess that had once been Sam Merchant's chest came back to him, hauntingly vivid.

He shook the thoughts away. Like Cynthia had said, he was responsible for something beyond himself. He looked up at those he was responsible for, and warmth spread across his chest. His mouth firmed into a razor line. He was going to find that murdering son of a bitch, and he was going to put paid to him. That was that, end of story. He had more important things to deal with than Mr. Oscar Daniels.

He checked the clock on the wall. It was nearly six o'clock. He should really get a watch, he thought. He stood and walked around the room making sure his leg wasn't in danger of stiffening up on him. He was walking towards the children, intent on getting in a little quality time with Waylon before the dog forgot who he was when he heard it. Clearly, through the open window, came the sound of the bass thump of a stereo, turned up very loud.

Everyone in the room stilled, like a group of people playing Statues. Heads came up in that familiar side-cocked position. Waylon gave out a low warning growl. Jeff hushed him. He looked around the room and was surprised to see that, although no one could look him directly in the eye, every face was turned towards him, expectant expressions on them.

Jeff again felt the weight bearing down on him. And again, it felt like a load that he could stand to bear. As the sound of the stereo faded, he was amazed at how calm and confident his voice sounded to his own ears.

"Okay, guys, that's him. Everybody just chill. He doesn't know we're here, and even if he did, he couldn't get in here." He smiled grimly. "Well, he might get in here, but getting back *out* would be a complete *bitch*."

The older children laughed nervously, and Cynthia smiled. Father Don just looked upset. Jeff set out to make everyone pull together as best he could. He was new to this leadership stuff, and he was honestly making most of it up as he went along.

"All right. Jamie, Glendon, Charles and Randy, front and center."

The boys made their way over to Jeff. He looked at them each in turn, trying to judge how well they were bearing up. Each seemed to be doing remarkably well. Jamie actually looked enthusiastic.

"Guys, hunker down here with me for a minute." They did, and he continued. "Here's the deal: I'm going to go out and find that douche bag, and I'm going to get rid of his ass." He lowered his voice while using the crude vocabulary, but remembering his own youth, he knew that cursing held an almost magical ability to bring young men together.

"While I'm gone, you four are my back-up. You guys are going to be the first line of defense if something should happen. You stay between anything that comes through that door and the other kids. Listen to Cynthia and Father Don, and back them up, too. Waylon stays here on guard. He's got better ears than even you fellows, and you've all got some *great* ears. Remember; keep your blades sheathed until you need them. I come back and somebody has cut somebody else's hand off, and I'm gonna be seriously pissed. We all on the same page here, guys?"

He got nods all around. He gave each of them a sector of the room that they were responsible for. There was only one door into the room, and anyone coming in would have a hard time against a forest of knives and machetes guarding the entrance, he told them. *Unless the son of a bitch can just stand out in the hallway and spray the room with a damned gun,* he thought but didn't add. He did, however, remind them that if they heard gunfire to drop to the floor and stay there until it let up.

He knew that he was giving them false hope, but he couldn't think of what else to do. If Daniels made it past him and somehow back-tracked him to this place, the only thing that dropping to the floor would do would be to make it easy for Daniels to shoot them, one at a time. But how could he tell these kids something like that?

The older boys took their position with grim determination. That taken care of, Jeff called the older girls over.

"Gennie, Rebecca, Angie, you guys are my second line, okay? I'm going to need you even worse than I need the guys. You've got the tougher job. I need you all to not only back up my first line, but I need you to also keep track of the younger kids and keep them safe and out of the way if something happens. Can I count on you guys, too?" Again, he got those solemn nods. God, these kids were something incredible. He couldn't imagine how he would have reacted to something like this at their age, even if he had been able to see. He touched each of them on the head and told them to take their places.

Cynthia came over and reached out for him. He took her into his arms without a single iota of self-consciousness. Had the room been full of people with 20/20 vision, he wouldn't have hesitated. They kissed, slowly and fully, taking full measure of their abilities. When they parted, the older kids gave a hooting applause. Jeff looked around and asked, "Were we *that* loud, guys?"

Jamie gave out a low wolf whistle and Mike Donner, only eleven, made pretend vomiting noises. Jeff grinned. "Yeah, I'll remember that Mikey, when you're a few years older and trying to do the same thing to one of these beautiful girls here, so bear it in mind."

Mike's face took on a look of disgusted incredulity. Kiss a *girl?* Not in *this* life, his face proclaimed. *Please, God,* Jeff prayed, *let this kid grow up and be able to find out how wrong he is about girls. Let them all grow up.* He fervently hoped that God was listening, but he was pretty sure that it was up to him to take the first necessary steps to insure that it happened.

Still holding Cynthia's hand, Jeff walked over to Father Don. The man had remained by the CB, twiddling the knobs and straining to hear something. He had studiously avoided taking part in the conversation with the children. Jeff kneeled down in front of him and asked him gruffly, "Okay Don, what's the problem?"

The older man was slightly taken aback by the direct question. His sightless eyes scanned the room. He kept his voice pitched so low that Jeff could barely hear him, from only a few inches away. It was better that way, Jeff had found. These kids had hearing that rivaled some comic book heroes. The priest's voice was tinged with anger, sadness, and regret.

"That was a nice speech, Jeff. No doubt bolstered their spirits to no end. Now, what do you think is *really* going to happen to them if that man finds us? Huh? You think he's just going to walk in here and be polite enough for us to cut him down with knives? I kind of doubt that, you know, and I think you do too. If he makes it past you and finds us here, he will *kill every child in this room.* He'll no doubt kill me, too, but at this point I can't seem to muster up enough give a damn to care. But there's Cynthia to consider, too. The kids, at least they'll die quick. With her, I imagine he'll probably take some time raping her before he gets around to killing her, too."

As he spoke, his voice took on a bitter edge that seemed so out of place coming from the man Jeff had come to know that he was silent a moment. Finally, he reached out and took Father Don by the arm. His grip was hard, but the older man didn't shy away.

"Don, were you really listening to my 'little speech' as you put it, or were you just waiting for your chance to get pissed off at me all private-like? I didn't blind you, old man, and neither did anyone else in this room." Jeff's voice was just as low as Don's had been, and just as angry.

"Jeff…" Cynthia started, her voice full of concern. Jeff cut her off. "Not right now, Cynthia. The good Father and I are talking. What about it, Don?"

The Hispanic man's complexion made it difficult for him to blush, but Jeff could still see his face darken. When he spoke, he was furious.

"If I could see, I would take you out in the yard and beat you like the punk you're acting like, you bastard. As a matter of fact, if you don't take your hand off me, I'll do it anyway, whether I can see or not."

Jeff didn't release the man's arm, if anything, he tightened his grip. He leaned in and spoke right into the priest's ear.

"Answer me, Don. Did you listen? I mean, really *listen* to what I told those kids?"

Father Don jerked his arm out of Jeff's grasp and said, "Yes. I heard you just fine. What the hell difference does *that* make?" The man had tears of fury standing in his eyes.

"Okay, Don, I'll tell you what difference it makes. If you were listening, you'll notice that I gave each of those kids positions well away from that door. Did you notice that?"

Father Don looked momentarily confused. He said, "Yes, I noticed that. I figured that you didn't want them to be in the doorway if that man just started shooting. Which would be all well and good if, like I said, he would come in politely and let us kill him, which he won't."

Jeff stood and turned back to the couch. He picked up his pack and brought it back over to where Father Don sat. Cynthia stood to the side, her hand nervously plucking at her necklace. Jeff knelt back down in front of the priest and said, "No, Don, I didn't tell them to stand clear of the doorway because of that. That would make sense, I suppose, but I'm not as stupid as you seem to think I am. I'm well aware of what will happen if Daniels makes it into this room. I may be young, but I'm not an idiot, Don. I kept them away from the doorway because that's *your* responsibility. Daniels isn't coming into this room, regardless of what happens to me, because *you're* not going to let him."

The priest gave out a strangled laugh. "Really? And how am I supposed to do that? Trust me, the old Holy Water and 'Get thee gone, Satan' only works in the movies."

"Yeah, I figured that. That's why we're not using Holy Water. I think that double-aught buckshot will be a better substitute, don't you?"

Father Don now looked completely confused, but some of his anger had leaked away, for which Jeff was glad. He needed the man angry and resolute, but only if it could be aimed at the right person. Jeff reached into the scabbard attached to his pack and brought out the Remington 12 gauge shotgun. He checked to make sure the safety was on, and then placed it into the man's hands.

Father Don gripped the weapon instinctively, so that it wouldn't fall. He ran his hands up and down it and then let out an exasperated sigh. Now his voice held more contempt that anger.

"You forgetting something, *amigo*? I'm still *blind*. This isn't any better than the machete. If he won't stand still for that, he's damned sure not going to stand still for this, now is he?"

"No, I doubt he would, if he knew you had it. In fact, I'll bet he would dance like Fred Astaire if he knew he had one of these trained on his ass. But he's not going to do any dancing, because he's not going to know you're pointing it at him."

"Well, that's good, since *I* won't know when I'm pointing it at him, either."

Jeff grinned. Now, the man was getting a little bit of his old banter back. Jeff welcomed it. Father Don felt useless and helpless, and Jeff was about to change that.

"All right, here's how this is going to go. When I leave this room, I'm closing that door. So, if there's anything anyone needs, now is the time to get it. Once it's closed, I'm going to set up some string on some of those empty water bottles. The other end of the string will be attached to the top of the door with tape. The door opens out, so when it's opened, the string will pull the bottles. They'll fall, and noise will be made. You follow me? Now, if it's me on the other side of that door, and believe me, you'll know if it is, all is well. If it isn't me, then whenever our friend opens the door, you're going to know. As he's opening the door, he'll be just on the other side of it, straight shot. That door isn't steel, it's just wood. It's not even solid wood, it's hollow-core. Not that it would matter if it *were* solid wood, not with the blast these shells have. If he opens it, you're going to blow him right out of his shoes." He overrode Father Don, who was about to start to point out his blindness again. "No, you *are* going to blow him out of his shoes. You're going to do it because from where you're sitting, you have a direct line-of-sight on that door. I'm going to set up something, some boxes or something that holds that gun dead-level with that door. Before I leave, I'll aim it and set it up. If Daniels shows up, you wait until you hear those bottles fall, and you just pull the trigger. The recoil is a bit of a bitch, so you'll need to have a good grip on it. Once you've fired that first time, you empty the fucker in that general direction. Sit just like you are now while you're firing it, or you might get off sight with it. Your first shot will no doubt gut that bastard like a trout, but you just go ahead and empty it anyway. There are five more shells in a holder on the side. Do you feel them?"

Father Don felt and nodded his head.

"Okay, each of them is facing down, so when you pull them out, you can just load them in the chamber without trying to figure out what direction they're in. You with me so far, Don?"

Again, the man nodded, a small light of hope shining on his face.

"So, the bottles fall, and Don pops the doorway. Then Don empties the gun. Then Don reloads and sits very, very still and *listens*. Everyone listens. You'll all be about half deaf from firing that thing inside a closed room, but you'll be able to hear well enough. If you don't take him out first time, you'll hurt him at the very least, and I mean hurt him *bad*. If he's still groaning out there, you make your way closer toward the door and fire some more, at a downward angle. You'll spray buckshot all over that hallway. Empty the gun again. There are more shells on the sling, you feel *them*?"

Father Don ran his hand down the sling and felt the shells in their holders. Again he nodded. Then he said, "If I'm still not sure, I hold still and I listen, right? Any more sound and I repeat the process."

Jeff smiled. "Yup, you got it in one." He reached out and took the man's arm again and this time the man didn't shy away. "You're blind Don, you're not helpless. You just make sure you're pointing that thing in even close to the right direction, and you'll do fine. Hell, those things were *made* for blind folks to shoot them."

Father Don looked at his feet, his face blazing with shame.

"I am so sorry, Jeff. I had no right to talk to you that way. And I didn't have any right to sit around feeling sorry for myself, either." He raised his head, his face now full of purpose. "Not that any of this matters anyway, you know. This is all just theoretical. You're going to find him, and you're going to clean his clock. God will be with you out there, and God will be with us in here. That's the truly wonderful thing about God, you know. He's the absolute master of multi-tasking."

Jeff laughed along with him. They got the shotgun set up on an end table and bracketed by a heavy book on each side. Jeff saw that the one on the left was *War and Peace* and sniggered. *I've finally found a use for that long-winded bastard*, he thought. Several attempts to read it over the years had left a lasting distaste for it with him. Once the shotgun was set up just right, Jeff knelt and peered down the sights. They were Tritium sights, and fairly screamed with neon orange and green. More importantly, they were aimed dead-on for the middle of the door. Jeff hadn't been joking. The spray pattern from the shotgun would fling high-velocity double-aught buck in a pattern that would splatter anyone standing on the other side of the door out of their shoes and halfway across the hall.

Jeff made his final preparations, checking everything a second, third, and fourth time. An idea struck him, and he called the youngest child, eight year old Christy Lowman, over to him. She came over with Waylon at her heels. Jeff was glad to see it. He had been counting on it, in fact.

"Christy, honey, can I ask you to do me a super-big favor?"

"Sure", she said, her voice golden honey.

"If Father Don has to shoot that big gun, the noise will be scary. It will scare Waylon bad. Do you think you could hold on to him *really* tight if that happens? Just hold on to him until all the shooting stops, and then he'll be fine. Can you do that for me?"

She assured him that she wouldn't turn loose of Waylon for anything. Jeff thanked her and gave her a kiss on top of her bright blonde curls. He wasn't worried in the slightest about Waylon being afraid of the shotgun going off. Waylon had been shooting with him hundreds of times, and was no more afraid of a gun than he was a butterfly. However, if he sensed a threat to the children at the door of the room, he would attack it, and by doing so, run straight into the line of fire. Jeff didn't want to think about coming back to find his dog ripped apart by a shotgun.

Finally, everything was in place. The bottles were attached to their string and the string was taped to the top of the door. Jeff shouldered his rifle and his backpack. It was hard to buckle shut over the Kevlar vest, but he managed. Cynthia followed him to the door. She would pull the bottles back into place once he opened the door, so they would be ready for when it was reopened. They stood in the doorway for a long, silent minute before Jeff finally said, "Are you sure that the kids can stay in their places as long as it takes? I mean, I may be gone a while. What if the need to go to the bathroom, or they..."

Cynthia shushed him. "They'll be fine. Everyone knows what to do. We'll all be right here when you get back, okay?"

Jeff looked dubiously past her at the children, all remaining so very still. Earlier, he would have thought that these last minute jitters were another sign that he was losing his courage, but he now recognized that he was simply worried about the children, not himself.

"All right", he said. "You guys have this under control. I'm going out the cafeteria window again, so there won't be any cans on the sill. But I'll close the window back, and if you all are quiet, you should be able to hear it being opened. That'll give you a few minutes to get set. Remember, he won't know what room you're in, so he'll have to check them one at a time. So make sure that Don holds his fire until those bottles *move*." He shook his head and said mainly to himself, "Hell there's no reason the bastard should have any idea where you all are, regardless. Unless you guys decide to start singing the hits of the '80's, he won't have a clue where I came from." He looked at her again, drinking her in as much as he could.

"If I'm not back by morning, then things have… well, they haven't worked out. If I don't get back, then you all…" He let the sentence hang unfinished. What *could* they do if he didn't make it back?

Cynthia reached out and kissed him once more, her lips soft and inviting. He *hated* this. He wanted to be here, with her and the kids, not out hunting a madman. But it was because of her and the kids that he needed to do it. He sighed.

She smiled when she heard it. "Go on, Jeff. Take care of this and get back here as soon as you can. You'll be back before morning." She turned to go back into the room and then paused. "Make sure you remember to let us know it *is* you, okay? I love Father Don, but I think I might be pretty upset with him if he killed you by accident."

Jeff laughed. "Yes, ma'am. I think that once a day is enough for me. I'll make enough noise that folks in Charleston will know I'm here. Cynthia…" He paused. *Hell with it*, he thought, *I may be dead by morning.* "I think I may be in love with you. I know that sounds stupid. You just met me yesterday. Shit, I shouldn't have said that. Just forget I said it, okay? I was just blubbering and I…"

Again she stopped him with a kiss. "We'll have to discuss this a bit more closely when you get back, won't we?" She answered herself. "Yes, I think that this needs to be investigated quite a bit further. So, why don't you hurry up and get back so we can do just that, what do you say?"

It wasn't as good as response as "I'm in love with you, too", but it beat the hell out of "Are you kidding?" With one final touch of her cheek, Jeff turned and started down the hallway.

God help him, he was on his way.

Chapter Seventeen

Oscar was having the time of his life. In his *old* life, he would have just gotten off work and been pulling into his driveway to take a shower and head back out to the bar. There, he would have done nothing more than drink too much and wind up with a hangover the next morning as he fought his way into wakefulness for *that* day's work. Here in his new life at a quarter past six in the evening, he had already killed five people. He hadn't found any good looking women yet, but he was confident he would. After all, he had all the time in the world.

He was sipping a bottle of Jim Beam that lay nestled against his crotch, following each nip with a pull of Bud. He seemed to have found just the right combination of alcohol, painkillers, and speed to make him feel invincible. The Adipex was doing a fine job of keeping him alert, while letting him feel all the wonderful effects of the other drugs at the same time. Although he didn't know it, his blood pressure was 210/100, and his heart rate was over 140 beats per minute. He was thirty-eight years old, and hadn't taken care of his body for almost any of that. A few more days of this, and he would most likely cease to be anyone's problem. His heart would explode in his chest and send him (along with his precious truck) into a ditch, where he would remain until Judgment Trump.

Of course, a few more days would also equate to many more deaths. Oscar had really found himself in killing. He had never been an imaginative man, depending on movies and TV to do his imagining for him. Even his daydreams were mostly just exact reenactments of those shows, only with him in the starring role.

But in killing he had found an outlet for himself. In a horribly macabre way, he was an artist, and death was his medium. Take the five people he had killed today, for example. They all reacted in much the same way at first, so pathetically happy that someone was there to help them. When he had first begun his killing, he had been very straightforward about it. Walk up, say something he felt was cool, and bang! One between the eyes, or maybe, if he was feeling like it, a gutshot to leave the victim screaming in agony as they died slowly.

Now, however, he had warmed to his role. He would knock on door after door, until finally he would hear the pitiful cried for help from the other side. He would then go inside (mostly he didn't even have to force the door- for whatever reason, folks didn't think to lock them) and locate the victim. Today, the five had consisted of four men and one woman. The men had ranged in age from a kid about seventeen or eighteen to an older man in his late fifties. The woman had perked Oscar's interest when he had heard a female voice drift to him through the door, but she had been hugely obese, and not attractive at all.

He had found one of the men first. After responding to his knock, Oscar had entered the house to find the man careening into every object in the room like a pinball machine on methamphetamines. The man had been weeping like a child. "Oh, thank God! Thank God, oh, thank God!" the man had said over and over again. In the earlier stages of his art, Oscar would have ended this calf-like bellowing immediately with a .44 bullet between the eyes. Not now, however. Instead of killing the man outright, Oscar had taken the man by the arm and led him to his couch. He hadn't even recoiled when the man had flung his arms around him and wept on his shoulder, even though the man reeked of body odor and terror. Oscar felt that the silk shirt might have to be replaced, though.

Oscar had spoken to the man quietly and calmly, identifying himself as a Federal agent of Homeland Security. There had been a terrorist act, he told the man. An unknown group had released an airborne chemical that had led to the *temporary* blindness of a large section of the Eastern Seaboard. Oscar apologized to the man that it had taken so long for Homeland Security to reach Stone Grove, but the appalling nature of this heinous act was even worse in the more heavily populated areas of the U.S. If he thought Stone Grove was bad, he told the man, he should see *Manhattan*. The weeping man told Oscar he understood completely, what a horror it must be, and did he say *temporary* blindness? Yes, indeedy, sir, temporary blindness. He should regain his sight within the next twenty-four to forty-eight hours. The man had begun sobbing so hard with relief that a string of snot had reached all the way from his nose to about an inch above the floor, where it hung like a pendulum. Oscar had watched it, fascinated, for several minutes before he had gotten the man's attention and, very gently, told him that he was only joking. You're going to blind the rest of your life, sir, he had told the man. The man's sightless eyes had opened wide in surprised outrage, and then Oscar had thumbed the hammer of his .44 back and put a round right through the left one. The hammersmash of blood, bone, and brains had splattered the wall behind the poor man, covering a Cubist style painting. That had only improved the thing, in Oscar's opinion.

With the teenage boy, he had claimed to be from the State Police, and had told the boy that the reason he was blind was the same reason that every other teenage boy in America was now blind: they had been whipping their weasel. Simple as that. "Didn't your mother ever tell you that if you jacked off too much, you'd go blind?" Oscar had asked the bewildered boy. Not long after that, he had grown tired of watching the boy swing blindly around the room trying to punch him in the face. The boy's face had been contorted with rage, and he had lost his ability to speak coherently, instead making primal grunts and screams as he tried to attack his tormentor. Oscar had given the boy on in the guts as punishment for trying to hit him, and had left him shrieking for his mother on the living room floor.

The woman had given him hope when he had heard her voice. When he had seen that she was just a fat, ugly old whore, he had gotten angry. However, even through his anger, he had not killed her outright.

Once he had gained access to her home, he had told her that he was the Voice of God, and that he had been sent to explain to humanity that the blindness had been visited upon them in reprisal for their sinful ways. Her sin, he told her, was gluttony, and she was doomed to an eternity in hell. The woman had grown completely hysterical, screaming for him to shut up, to go away, get out of her house, that she was going on A GODDAMNED DIET, he had no right...

Oscar had given her time to vent, and then told her softly that the Lord wasn't Jenny Craig, and his patience for her had run out. "You shouldn't have let yourself get in this shape in the first place. Didn't you know your body is a temple?" he had asked her. "It's GLANDULAR!" she had screamed back. "Of course it is", he had answered, and then blown a large, smoking hole directly between her massive, pendulous breasts.

While all of this proved (if any further proof was needed) that Oscar Daniels was a psychotic murderer, it also revealed something else. In his old life, Oscar had been a hum-drum, middle-of-the-road personality, not very bright, and with a limited imagination. In this new one, however, he was witty, quick on his feet, and able to maintain the stories he told his victims right up to the point that he killed them. Before, he wouldn't have been able to think up such stories, let alone keep up the façade of them as long as he wished.

Oscar had come out of his cocoon.

What emerged was not a butterfly, but some sort of horrid plague-carrying nightmare, but emerged he had. He was something else, something new. He was something more *there* than he had ever even dreamed of being before. It had taken the end of the world, but Oscar Daniels had been reborn into that which he was meant to be.

None of this came as any great consolation to his victims, who had spent their last few days on the earth in a blind terror, only to be slaughtered like sheep for no good reason at all.

Dead, after all, was still dead.

Now, at just past seven-thirty, Oscar was driving through the affluent neighborhoods on the east side of town, considering his options. There was still some daylight left, plenty of time for him to canvass the houses for the hot blonde that he just *knew* was hiding behind one of those doors. Then he could find a brunette and a redhead, and have a complete set.

He didn't know if it was the drugs, but the thought of a torture-laden ménage-a-tois didn't have quite the appeal to him that it had this morning. *Fuck it*, he thought. *I'll grab some bitches tomorrow. I'm just gonna go home and sack out. No more fucking Adipex tonight. That shit it making my chest hurt.*

He was turning into a driveway to swing his ride around and go back home when, during a pause between one Skynyrd track and the next, he heard a gunshot. He stopped, tromping on the brake. With one finger he stabbed the pause button on his CD player and powered down the window. He sat listening, but the sound didn't repeat itself. He shook his head, dismissing it. There had been quite a bit of gunfire during the first day or so after the flash, as people had fired at anything they heard in a panic. That had mostly died off, though, as folks had either managed to make it indoors to some food and water, or had been killed. He had heard only a few isolated shots on Wednesday, and none on Thursday, but he had been out of town quite a bit that day. There had been no shots at all that he had heard all day long today. Well, if it had been a shot, it was probably some bastard taking the easy way out. That bothered Oscar, because he sensed that his prey were growing thin on the ground, and every one that took themselves out was one less for him to harvest. He began to power up the window when, very clearly, came the sound of a rifle firing from across town. Oscar froze in place, listening intently.

This wasn't indiscriminate panic-fire. These were very deliberate shots, coming with clock-like precision. These were the shots of someone *aiming* and firing. And to aim, you had to be able to *see*.

Oscar was suddenly more furious than he had ever been in his life. His heart, already in the red-line, gave out a startled gallop. He pushed his hand to his chest absently. Had he been struck with a full-blown heart attack at that instant, he wouldn't have noticed until he was dead, so great was his rage.

Somewhere in town there was someone that could *see*! Some son of a bitch could *see*, in *his* town, Goddammit! The ramifications of this were completely lost on Oscar for the moment. He was too angry at not being special anymore, not being one of a kind. It wasn't *fair*, dammit! This was *his* time! This was *his* time, *his* town, *his* dream!

Taking his hand down from his chest, Oscar threw the truck in reverse and peeled out of the driveway, his window down, listening for the sounds of those hated gunshots. Every so often, he would hear them again, and would let the truck idle in neutral, trying to pinpoint their source. After a while, he felt he had a good idea where they were coming from, and he floored the accelerator, the truck's engine screaming as he shot across town.

The thought that he was driving into a trap, up against someone armed with a high-capacity rifle against his six-shot black powder pistol never crossed his mind.

Chapter Eighteen

Jeff stopped firing his rifle for a moment and listened. Yes, there it was, still across town but heading this way. The truck in the distance revved its engine, paused, and then revved again. It was obvious to Jeff that Daniels had heard him firing, and was now trying to locate him.

Jeff was lying prone on the third-storey roof of one of the town's banks. It was conveniently close to the dead end road Jeff had chosen for his ambush spot. He had climbed up here to try to hear better, listening for Daniels' truck. He had heard that, as well as the sound of what he thought was muffled gunfire, on several occasions in the last hour or so. After establishing that his prey was indeed out and about, Jeff set about getting ready to draw him in and put an end to him.

He had parked his own truck just adjacent to the entrance to the dead end road. It was a single lane that led to the back parking lot of the bank, and there was no other way out. It was also reassuringly far enough away from Second Sight that he wasn't worried about the school taking a wayward bullet. Once he had Daniels down that single lane road, he would pull his truck across the entrance, effectively sealing it. Then the shooting gallery would be open.

That thought had led to him remembering that he still hadn't actually field-tested the red-dot sight on his rifle. It was all well and good that the bore-sighter told him that he was ready to rock, but seeing a round hit exactly where he wanted it would give him much more peace of mind.

He had shrugged. What difference did it make if Daniels heard him now? In fact, wasn't that the point? Settling down into a prone position, he flipped on the red-dot and took careful aim at a building about fifty yards away. It was made of brick, and Jeff chose a lighter-colored one about halfway up the wall as his target. Taking a deep breath and letting it out, he slowly squeezed the trigger.

He found that he was justified in making sure that the red-dot worked in reality, not just theory when the round struck a point about a foot to the left and several inches low of the sight. When he thought that he might have gone into this without checking this thing first, he felt a shudder. Images of him spraying the parking lot all around Daniels as the man calmly lined up his deadly return shot ran through his mind.

Cursing under his breath, Jeff adjusted the knobs on the optic and tried again. This time, the round smacked home several inches closer to the brick, but still a little low. After some more adjustment, Jeff was able to hit the brick with each shot, dead-on. After a few rounds, it had stopped looking like a brick and began looking more like chalk smeared on the wall. Satisfied, Jeff had dropped the clip from the rifle and replaced it with a fresh one. From his pack, he opened a box of ammo and filled the one he had used to sight in the rifle and placed it in its holder on his drop-leg platform.

Since then, he had been shooting just enough to lead Daniels towards him. He was careful to time the shots with the pauses that came when the man stopped to listen. The truck grew closer and closer, until it sounded like it was almost on top of him. Jeff knew better, though. The truck had a big engine, and in the unearthly quiet that had fallen over the town since the flash, he knew that the truck was still a good distance away.

He looked at the western horizon, hoping he had planned this out just right. The sun was below the horizon now, but twilight was still bright enough to read by. He hoped it would get a bit darker before Daniels made it here. Otherwise, Jeff might have to lead him down the road personally, and that would, in his humble opinion, suck.

As it was, he turned his head and looked at the emergency radio he had set up in the parking lot. One of its many features had been a bright red strobe light that could be used as a signal in times of distress. If this didn't count as a time of distress, Jeff didn't know what did.

The light blinked merrily in the growing gloom. It was already very visible, and in a little longer, it would show up like a lighthouse. Jeff sat up clumsily in the heavy vest and grabbed his pack. He stood on the roof for a few moments more, listening to the sound of the truck rapidly approaching him. *Not much longer*, he thought.

He walked back to the door that led down the stairs to the ground floor. He flicked on his flashlight as he went down the steps. The power was still on in this part of town, but the bank hadn't had the lights on in the stairwell when the flash occurred. Jeff thought about flicking them on and decided against it. Dark was going to be his friend tonight. He checked the fit of the night-vision goggles again, for perhaps the hundredth time. He probably wouldn't even need them, he figured. There were street lights back in the parking lot of the bank. If he could have been assured that Daniels would turn down the alley, Jeff would have stayed up on the roof and picked him off from up there.

However, he couldn't be sure that Daniels would turn, and even if he did, he might smell a trap. Jeff needed to insure that the entrance to the alleyway was closed. If Daniels could just jump in his truck and drive away, Jeff would lose every advantage. That was something he didn't feel like he could afford.

As he made his way to the bottom of the stairs, Jeff was amazed at how calm he was. Now that it was actually happening, he seemed to have settled down. Maybe it was the Percocet, maybe it was the acceptance of his responsibility, Jeff didn't know. He didn't really care, to tell the truth, so long as he stayed as calm as he felt now.

He flicked off the flashlight and stood inside the darkened bank. He had timed it perfectly. As he stood there, he watched a huge Ford go tearing by. Jeff was afraid that Daniels was going far too fast to see the strobe, but was relieved a second later when the man slammed on his brakes and slid to a stop. The truck tore backwards in reverse and then he locked up his brakes again. Daniels whipped the truck into the alleyway and raced towards the flashing red light.

Jeff shook his head. He wasn't a tactical genius, but he was pretty sure he would have at least scoped out the situation before charging in like that. Well, if the man wanted to nail his own coffin shut, Jeff was glad to let him. Jeff slid out the door and ran lightly around to the driver's side of his door. Jumping in, he put the truck in neutral and began to push it towards the entrance. He didn't want to start it up and give himself away.

He received a pretty sharp twinge from his leg in reply, letting him know that it didn't appreciate this one bit. The truck was rolling well enough on its own now, and Jeff steered it into position. He tapped the brake and presto! Instant roadblock. He slipped back to his position by the bank. He intended to let Daniels climb out of the truck and go to the strobe, and then gun him down where he stood. The thought still sent a cold spike through his stomach, but not as bad as before.

Daniels came to a sliding stop and jumped out of his truck, running towards the strobe. Jeff took a deep breath and turned from the corner of the building and took aim at the man who had killed his friend and terrorized and already desolated town.

And stopped cold.

Daniels was kicking the emergency radio like a child throwing a tantrum. He began screaming. "Where are you, motherfucker? Huh? Where the fuck are you? Come on out here and take what's coming to you, you son of a bitch!" And then, with the absolute pinnacle of absurdity, he cried, "I'M THE ONLY ONE SUPPOSED TO BE ABLE TO SEE, YOU BASTARD!"

Jeff stood jaw agape at this spectacle. *This* was the man that had been the cause so much horror and grief? *This* fucking guy? He looked like an extra from *Blazing Saddles*, for the love of God! From his Black Stetson down to his silly pointed cowboy boots, he looked like a parody of an old Western villain. Sweet, merciful *Jesus*!

Daniels still hadn't noticed him, being so embroiled in his tirade against the unfairness of having someone else in town that could see. Jeff took another breath and stepped into the alleyway. The red-dot stood steadily on the center of the man's back. Jeff started to squeeze the trigger, but found that, no matter what the man had done, he was simply unable to shoot Daniels in the back. He raised his voice and yelled at the madman standing by his truck.

"Hey, you ugly Brokeback Mountain-looking *fuck!* This is for Sam Merchant!"

What happened next was nothing like what Jeff had planned. He had hoped that his shout would bring Daniels around to face him, and when it did, he planned on placing a 5.56 mm round straight through the fucker's black heart.

But that didn't happen.

Instead, Daniels turned on cue. Instead of standing in blank surprise, giving Jeff his opportunity to shoot him dead, however, the man made a dipping movement. The next thing Jeff knew, there was a huge blast of smoke and fire springing from the man's fist. Jeff had time to think *What the HELL is that*, and then he was flung backwards into the side of his truck by the force of several .44 caliber slugs slamming into his chest. It felt like a large man was slamming him with a ball bat in the ribs repeatedly.

Jeff fired instinctively, pulling the trigger of his Mini-14 several times. All his carefully laid plans had gone straight to hell in seconds, and he was pretty sure that he was about to die. The pain in his chest was getting worse. He refused to look down at it, irrationally hoping that if he didn't see the damage, it wouldn't exist.

Jeff's return fire had not hit Daniels, hadn't even come close, but it had given the man something to think about. As one of the rounds came close enough to him that he could hear the snap as is went by, he decided it was time to leave. He'd come back and kill this son of a bitch later, when the odds weren't so stacked against him. He turned and began scrambling back towards his truck.

Jeff tried to take a breath and couldn't. It felt like all the air in his body had been pushed violently out of him, leaving a painful vacuum. Black dots began dancing at the corners of his vision and he began to feel light headed. *I'm passing out*, he thought dimly, and then the horror of what would happen to him if he did made him draw a deep, involuntary breath. It hurt like hell, but his vision cleared, and he didn't feel so groggy. He looked up to see the glaring headlights of Daniels' truck bearing down on him at a high rate of speed.

Again, he fired instinctively. Luck was with him this time, however. As he depressed the trigger and felt the rifle thump against his shoulder, he remembered to keep the red-dot where he wanted it. Spider webs of broken glass raced across the windshield of the Ford, and dull noises that sounded like *bonk! bonk-bonk! bonk!* announced the fact that rounds were slamming into the metal of the hood, as well. Jeff continued firing until the truck was right on top of him and, at the last possible second, threw himself out of the way. He struck the ground rolling, his ribs screaming in protest.

Daniels slammed into Jeff's Dodge without slowing. Jeff's truck was old and built to last, but it was outweighed by the Ford by half. It slewed around sideways, the back quarter panel mangled. Daniels' forward momentum wasn't enough to clear the alleyway completely, and he had to floor it to get by the Dodge. The screech of metal sounded like a pair of Banshees singing a duet. Jeff watched the sparks fly as the two trucks did their drunken dance on the street, and then remembered the rifle. He brought it to his shoulder and began firing, ignoring the pain in his chest, the pain in his leg, the scream of rending metal, the end of the world.

He fired repeatedly into the truck. He was no more than thirty feet away, if that. The rounds smacked into Daniels' truck over and over, but the man refused to play fair and fall over the steering wheel and die. Daniels looked over at Jeff, his face a mask of pure hatred and madness. Incredibly, he flipped Jeff the middle finger before going back to work on getting his truck disentangled.

Now it was Jeff's turn for some complete, black fury. He rose to a kneeling position and dropped the clip out of the rifle. He had no idea how many rounds he had fired, but he wanted to be able to fire plenty more. He slapped a new magazine in the rifle and took very careful aim. His rifle barked again and again. He was finally rewarded by the uplifting and beautiful sight of Oscar Daniels slammed sideways in the seat, and a thin spray of blood fly up onto the window. *GOT YOU, MOTHERFUCKER!!!* Jeff's mind exalted. *Got-you-got-you-got-you GOT YOU!!!!!*

Daniels' sprang back up in the seat like a malignant Jack-in-the-box. His face had lost its sneer and was now contorted in pain. Jeff clambered to his feet and began walking towards the truck, firing as he went. Another scream from inside the truck announced yet another hit. It was over, the fat lady was singing, somebody close the curtains.

But then Daniels utterly amazed Jeff by dropping his truck back into gear and careening off down the street, weaving from side to side like a drunkard. Jeff, panicked that he might get away, began firing as fast as he would at the departing truck. He could see sparks fly and tail lights burst as rounds found there mark. The truck was still speeding away, however.

Jeff fired the rifle until there was an impotent little *click!* He stared at it stupidly for about half a second, and then dropped it to the ground and pulled out his handgun from its holster. The deeper, bass explosions of the .45 now echoed across the street. Jeff knew that he wasn't going to have any luck with the P90. As the truck rapidly retreated, the range grew quickly to the point where firing a pistol was a useless gesture.

Daniels slammed into a mail box and tore around the corner. Jeff, realizing that the man was getting away, holstered his handgun and snatched his rifle from the ground. He dropped the empty magazine and replaced it with a full one, working the charging handle as he ran to his truck. He climbed in and started it up, dropped it into gear, and floored it.

And then sat there as the truck refused to move.

He looked incredulously around. Jumping from the vehicle, he ran around to the back. The damage done was beyond what could be repaired on a street in the middle of town. Hell, the damage might be more than could be repaired if the damn thing was in a garage. The back tire was mangled, and it looked like the frame of the truck was bent.

Jeff listened to the sound of Oscar Daniels' truck as it faded into the night and then raised both his fists into the air and shook them in fury.

"God-*DAMMIT*!!!!"

Chapter Nineteen

Oscar Daniels had never been so hurt in his life. Emotionally, mentally, and physically, he had never felt anything like the pain that he currently had to endure. He was having a hard time keeping the truck on the road, weaving from side to side and almost going into the ditch on several occasions.

He was weeping openly, tears streaking his face like a child that had lost its best toy. He could feel warm blood soaking his shirt and his jeans, but he refused to look down to see how badly he was hurt. The pain was a living thing, a dragon that roared and spewed fire under his flesh as its talons tore into his bones. He wailed, and almost ran off the road again.

He was terrified that the horrible man that had hurt him so badly was still back there, closing in. His eyes kept going to rearview mirror, as they had done so many nights when he drove home from the bar drunk, deathly afraid that he would see blue lights. Now, he almost wished he *would* see blue lights. A policeman would keep that bastard from getting him; that was for sure.

And who *was* that son of a bitch, anyway? He had been dressed like a soldier. A terrifying thought went through Oscar's mind. Had he not used the ploy that he was from the government to torture someone just earlier today? Well, yes, but that was different. He had been kidding. But what if that soldier really *was* from the government? Oh, God, they must know about the killings and the drinking, and the drugs! Why else would that soldier have tried to arrest him?

But wait… *had* the soldier tried to arrest him? It didn't seem like it. He had yelled something, but Oscar didn't remember what it was, exactly. And he had sounded like a local boy, not some soldier from Washington. Besides, *one* soldier? Where were the rest of them? Where were the helicopters, the tanks, the Humvees? Goddammit, what was going on?

The more he thought about it, the more it seemed like that soldier hadn't been trying to arrest him at all. That box with the flashing light, that dead-end street… hell, seemed to him like he'd been… well… *bushwhacked!* Yes, by God, that's exactly what had happened! He had been bushwhacked by some mean soldier, for no good goddamn reason at all. He wept even harder at the unfairness of it all.

It was lucky for him that his newly acquired house wasn't much further down the road, because he was having a *really* hard time driving. He actually drove past the turn-off to the house at first, which involved the painful process of turning around. He finally got the truck pulled into the driveway and climbed out, screeching in pain. He looked at his truck and for the first time since he had been hurt, felt something other than sadness, betrayal, and pain.

He felt rage.

It flowed over him like some sort of magical curative, like the waters of that pond or whatever it was over in Europe that was supposed to cure you of the shit that was wrong with you. He still hurt, sure, but right now, he could care less.

Look at his truck.

His beautiful truck, so well maintained. It was ruined. The paintjob was destroyed, three of the windows were shot out, there were bullet holes all down the driver's side and across the hood (God only knew what damage had been done under *there*, the truck had been making odd noises and smoking all the way home), and the entire front end was bashed into an accordion of metal. Oscar was beyond fury. His eyes thumped in his head in time with his heart, which was pretty damn quick. He growled incomprehensibly in fury, and slammed his fist into his left leg.

Where he promptly struck the hole where Jeff Della had shot him the second time. Oscar Daniels slid bonelessly to the ground in a dead faint.

Several minutes later, Oscar came back to. He no longer felt as worried about his truck as he had before. Finally looking down at himself as he sat, splay-legged in the driveway, he couldn't make out how bad his injuries were. The black of his outfit hid the majority of the blood. He slowly made his way to his feet and staggered towards the house. He was almost halfway there when he realized that the bag of painkillers was still in the truck. He was going to need those tonight, for sure.

Whining like an old dog, Oscar limped back to the truck and snatched the bag from the seat. The dome light showed the pools of blood that had congealed on his seat and the floorboards. He felt a brief flare of fury shoot up, but had much more pressing concerns at the moment. He turned to the house and began his trek back.

It took him nearly twenty minutes to make it from his ruined truck to the large garden tub in the master bathroom of the house. On the way through he had grabbed several beers from the fridge, and had taken a handful of Percocets. He turned the water on and limped to the mirror to judge the damage as the tub filled.

He slowly unbuttoned his leather pants and slid them down. There was a small, neat hole on the outside of his left leg, about the width of a drinking straw. Red-black blood had caked all around it, held against the wound by the tight leather. The hole on the other side of his leg was a different matter. It looked like someone had taken a jagged ice cream scoop and hacked off a large hunk of his inner thigh. The bullet must have broken up into smaller pieces after exiting his left leg, because he had several tiny punctures in his right leg, as well. Both of them throbbed and burned like hell, even with the Percocets.

Oscar pulled off his leather vest as carefully as he could. This is where the worst of the pain was, and what scared him the most. From under his left armpit all the way across his chest was a fiery line that screeched at him, also in tandem with his heartbeat. Oscar was very much afraid that the first shot had taken him through the lung, maybe even clipping his heart. He wasn't coughing up blood yet, but if the bullet had gotten his lung or even *nicked* his heart, he was a dead man. Where was he going to go to get patched up? All the goddamn doctors were blind.

After dropping the leather vest to the floor (with another one of those straw-sized holes in it), he began the laborious process of unbuttoning the black silk shirt. His fingers didn't seem to want to cooperate, and even the smallest movements made him go weak in the knees in pain. After several agony-laden minutes, he had managed to get the shredded silk off. He took a shallow breath and closed his eyes.

When he opened them again, he was looking at a bloody mess. The round had entered his body under his left armpit, traveled around his rib (no doubt breaking it as it did), and existed his chest where his left nipple had once been. Now, there was only another one of those horrid, ice cream scoops of flesh gone. The silk hadn't been as effective as the leather pants in controlling the bleeding, and his whole lower chest and abdomen was awash in half-clotted blood.

He limped over to the garden tub, now full, and slowly lowered himself in. He gave out tiny shrieks as the water entered the wounds.

He knew about infection, though, having seen his older brother once pay no attention to a wound from stepping on a rusty nail. The resultant blue/black/green thing that had taken the place of his brother's foot, with its pus and blood and stench was more than incentive enough for Oscar to make sure that his wounds were clean.

After he had cleaned them out thoroughly, he washed the rest of the blood from his body and got out of the tub. He went to the medicine cabinet and found some triple antibiotic ointment and slathered it on all his wounds, and then wrapped each of them in gauze and medical tape that he found in the cabinet. Tomorrow, he would have to start a round of antibiotics to head off any infection that might already be making its way into his blood stream.

Oscar, now so weak from blood loss, fear, and Percocets, that he could barely walk, made his way into the master bedroom and pulled a long white terrycloth robe on, tying it loosely around him. He was on the verge of losing consciousness and could barely crawl up the bed. He was so cold that his teeth were chattering, but the only covering on the bed was the sheet and a very lightweight summer bedspread. Unable to climb out of bed to look for anything more substantial, Oscar lay in the giant bed, miserable. His last cogent thought before he slid unconscious was that, come tomorrow, someone was going to by-God *pay* for the damage to his truck.

Oscar had no real idea just how incredibly lucky he had been that night. Between the pain of his wounds and the destruction of beloved truck, no one could have possibly convinced him of it, but lucky he was. Both the rounds that had struck him had done so in places where centimeters meant the difference between life and death. The leg wound had missed the femur, which would have left him crippled for life, even if sepsis hadn't set in and killed him, by less than a quarter of an inch. The chest wound should have killed him dead on the spot, were it not for the shallow angle that the shot had entered. Firing from low to the ground up towards the heavily jacked-up truck with its massive tires had kept Jeff from killing Oscar that night. Had Jeff been firing level, or even close to level, the round would have passed through Oscar's chest, piercing his heart and both lungs, an instantly fatal shot. As it was, the angle of the shot allowed one of Oscar's ribs to catch much of the momentum of the round and curve it around his thorax, rather than through it.

When you couple that with the sheer volume of fire that Jeff had lain down, the odds of Oscar's survival were hard to calculate. Although neither man had bothered counting, Jeff had fired forty-nine shots at Oscar with the rifle alone, and another nine with the handgun. The majority of these shots had been form nearly point-blank range. While this might not have spoken well for Jeff's marksmanship (especially since Oscar fired only three times, and all three of these shots hit Jeff in the chest), it was a fact that both times that Jeff *had* shot Oscar, both should have been fatal. All of which goes to prove only one thing: Sometimes, you eat the bear and sometimes, the bear eats you. And still other times, you shoot at the bear enough times to take down a company of Marines, and the damn thing still crawls away to cause problems.

Chapter Twenty

Jeff had a long walk back to Second Sight. It hurt him almost as much to leave his truck sitting like a casualty of war as his chest did. However, he was simply sentimental about the truck in contrast to Oscar being simply mental about his. It had been a dependable old friend, and he hated leaving it sitting abandoned. What he would hate even more, however, would be for Daniels to suddenly decide to swing back around the block and give him another bit of run-and-gun.

Whatever else the man might be, he was a spookily good shot with that hand cannon. It had taken Jeff quite some time after the gunfight, by running it through his head over and over, to decipher that the man had been carrying an old black powder six-shooter, which followed suit with the whole cowboy vibe he had been trying for. The huge blast of fire and smoke had caught Jeff completely off-guard, not to mention the little side note of being shot in the chest three times.

Jeff rubbed his ribs with one hand, the other holding his rifle at a 45 degree angle, ready to come to his shoulder the second he needed it. As he rubbed, he congratulated himself on the decision to wear the vest. If he hadn't have worn the thing, he would be very, very dead right not. His mind went back to those three rapid thumps on his chest… he couldn't suppress the shiver than ran up his spine.

He still couldn't get over the man's ability to shoot. Things like that only happened in movies, didn't they? Had Daniels even aimed? It was obvious that he had, but damned if Jeff had been able to see him doing it.

All of which came back to the fact that Jeff was most certainly *not* a soldier. He had everything in his corner tonight; the element of surprise, tactical advantage, he had the man vastly out-gunned… sweet Christ, he had used an assault rifle and a .45 automatic and *still* only scored two hits. Even after expending more ammo than any three people should have needed. That crazy son of a bitch had fired three times and hit him three times, all with a gun that was state-of-the-art right about the time Robert E. Lee was having some scheduling conflicts.

Still, Daniels was hit, at least twice, and Jeff thought that he was hit pretty good. It was hard to tell for sure since the man was inside that gigantic truck, but the blood on the window and the screams were a pretty good indication that he wasn't in the best shape ever. On the other hand, Jeff had taken three rounds to the chest and was walking home, and not even limping too badly while doing so. When you got right down to it, which of them had been the better fighter? Daniels was lying somewhere right now with blood running out of him in at least two places, with no doctor to go to, and Jeff was skipping back to his base of operations with nothing more than some bruises, and a hard-earned lesson in the reality of gun battles.

The first and foremost lesson he had picked up tonight was simple: If the other guy is in the open, blow his damned head off. Don't get all chivalrous and wait for him to face you. If his back is turned, so much the better. Turn his lights out before he even knows you're in the same county. There was no danger of Jeff giving Oscar a warning again. The next time he saw Daniels, it would hopefully be from a scope while the man was taking a piss. His *last* piss, at that.

The second thing tonight had taught Jeff was that all those snide remarks he had made about himself as he had geared up were not as snide as he thought. Although he had nagged himself for "playing soldier", the simple fact remained that had he not been so equipped, he would be dead right now. Daniels had treated this whole thing like it was a movie, whereas Jeff had treated it like the real thing. Now, although both of them were worse for wear, Jeff was going to eat a good meal and sleep the sleep of the just tonight. He'd like to see Daniels try to pull *that* one off.

The third, and possibly most important, thing he had learned tonight hadn't really been a lesson *per se*. He had fired, and been fired on, in anger. He knew how he would react to that now. It wasn't something he could have taught himself, no matter how many military or police manuals he might have read. It was one of those things that can only be learned by doing, and he had done it.

The thing that absolutely amazed him was the disparate polarity of the whole encounter. It had happened in a second, maybe two, said one side of his mind. You're crazier than hell, responded the other, it lasted an hour, at the very least! Things had moved in hyper-speed slow motion. *Yeah*, he thought, *try explaining* that *statement to somebody*.

Jeff was so wrapped up in his thoughts that he didn't notice the man leaning against the light pole, even as he noticed him. It was something so natural, a man in that pose on a well-lit street that his mind refused to allocate the proper amount of caution to what his eyes reported. That, however, only lasted a second or so. (Or possibly an hour).

Jeff jerked his hand out of his vest and brought the rifle to bear on the man in one movement. The red-dot was still on, turned down to its lowest setting, but still giving off plenty of light to mark the man through the glass perfectly well. Jeff was about a half-pound of trigger pull or so from caving the guy's chest in when the man spoke in a pleasant, conversational voice.

"Hello. I don't know who you are, or if you mean me any harm, but I'd like to say up front that if you're plannin' on killin' me, I'd thank ya kindly."

Jeff jerked, and almost convulsively pulled the trigger. He managed to loosen his pull at the very last possible second. He stepped a little closer and watched as the man's head came up, swiveling around at the sound of Jeff's boots. Okay, he was blind, which took him down the threat level chart a step or three. Jeff stayed where he was, but tried to be as pleasant as this man had been to him.

"Well, I hadn't really planned on killing you, sorry. If you don't mind me asking, though... um...why, exactly, would you be thanking me if I was?"

The head continued to track the sounds Jeff was giving off. The man looked to be not much older than Jeff, possibly in his late twenties or early thirties. He had a head full of curly hair, either dark brown or black. Under the halogen lamp, it was impossible to tell. Even leaned up against the light pole with one knee cocked and his foot placed on the curb, it was easy to tell that the man was very, very tall. Jeff was no shrimp himself, but this guy had to tower over him by at least six or seven inches. His voice remained pleasant, but Jeff could detect a note of strain running through it.

"Well, fact is, I'm a Catholic. Ain't many of us 'round these parts, but there ya go. If I kill myself... well, that's Hell forever for me, now ain't it? An' if I go to Hell forever, I'll never see my Annie again. I just don't think I can deal with that." He turned his face towards Jeff, and he could see the pain stamped on the man's face. "I know they's somebody left 'round here that can see, 'cause I've heard him a' killin' folk an' rippin' up and down town in that big-ass truck. An' judgin' from the fact that it sounded like the O.K. Corral just a bit ago, I figure you're him. Dunno why you're not in your truck, but I reckon that don't matter." The man's face grew hard and determined. "I know you been killin' some folks hard, just shootin' 'em an' leavin' 'em to die slow. I also know you been killin' some folks outright. I can't make you do it one way or t'other, but I'd be obliged if you'd just do it quick and be done with it. But if you're of a mind to do it t'other way… well, I'll still be with Annie soon enough, I reckon."

The man stepped off the curb and slowly turned towards Jeff. He held his arms out to his sides and raised his face to the sky. He stood like that, perfectly motionless, while he calmly waited for the bullet that would either take off his head, or tear out his guts.

Jeff was bemused by this. He didn't want to string this man along, thinking he was about to die, but he simply couldn't help himself.

"You mind if I ask you a question?"

The man's face came back down, and now there was a touch of impatient anger in it. "Well, not one whole hell of a lot I can do to stop you, now is there?"

"No, but you can just not answer it, I suppose. I was just being polite and asking if it was all right to ask you."

The man's face now added confusion to the emotional stewpot. "You're a right odd kind of murderer, ain't ya? You'll gutshoot a man, an' leave him to die, but you wanna be polite? Beats any damn thing I ever heard of. Well, go ahead, ask your question. I'd like to get this here done."

Jeff couldn't help but grin. He liked this man. In his most polite voice, he asked, "If you're a Catholic, then you know that suicide is wrong. That's why you want me to kill you. But if you *want* me to kill you, isn't that the same thing as committing suicide?"

Anger now held the top honors on the man's face. "What kind of damned killer are ya, anyhow? I ain't out here for a fuckin' theological discussion!"

"I'm just genuinely curious. I don't get how asking me to kill you is any different than killing yourself."

"I didn't *ask* you to kill me. I said that if you were gonna, I'd thank ya kindly, and I will, if you'll ever get to it. If you walk off right now an' leave me standin' here, then I'll go on goin' on 'til I drop over or somethin' else happens to me, I guess. So, what's it gonna be? You gonna kill me, or what?"

Jeff couldn't let this man think he was Daniels any longer.

"Sorry, pal, but I'm not the guy that's been killing folks around here."

The man stood with a dumbfounded look on his face. "You mean to tell me I been tryin' to get another *blind* man to kill me? Son of a *BITCH*!"

"I thought you said you weren't *trying* to get me to kill you."

"Whatever! Damn it all to hell, if this ain't 'bout the stupidest one fuckin' thing I've ever seen..." He broke off, looking mildly surprised for a moment. "Say, partner, you best find yourself somewhere else to be when that fella does get back here. 'Less you got business with him, too. He'd probably kill the both of us same as he'd kill the one."

"I doubt he'll be back around here, at least for a while anyway. He'll be pulling those bullets I just put in his ass out for a few days, at the very least."

The man grew as still as stone.

"You tellin' me you can see?"

"Yeah, I can see. I mean, I used to be blind, but I got better, so now I can see just fine."

The man's expression melted into one of pure anguish. "You mean it goes *away*? You get your sight back?" Two huge tears rolled down his face. "Oh, Annie, honey, I'm so sorry..."

Jeff reached out to console the man who, not expecting to be touched, jerked back and almost fell. Jeff hurried to help him up, slinging the rifle. He talked rapidly as he helped the taller man up and over to the curb to sit down.

"No, that's not what I meant. I'm sorry; I should have thought how that was going to sound. No, I mean when I was a kid I was blinded in an accident, and I got better. They called it a miracle. It must have been, because I didn't go blind when everyone else did."

The man sat very still, tears falling silently down his face and onto the pavement between his shoes. Finally, Jeff asked, "What's your name, man?"

The man sighed. "Malcolm Connolly."

"You Irish?"

"Do I sound like I'm Irish to ya?" the man actually managed a weak grin. "My great-great-great-whoever-in-the-hell-knows granddaddy was Irish. Moved here around 'bout 1862, from what my Mama says. Back then, they's takin' folks right off'n the boats an' puttin' 'em in uniform to fight in the Civil War. They was two ports that he coulda put in to. If'n he'd went to New York, he'd a' been in the Grand Army of the Republic. But as it was, he wound up in Charleston, South Carolina, so he did his four years with the Army of Northern Virginia, right up to Appomattox, an' then he took off his butternut an' moved here to work the mines. Now you know my whole life history, an' who the hell are *you*?"

"Name's Jeff Della. I live out of town, over near the county line."

Malcolm was nodding. "Yeah, I know who you are. You make furniture and whatnot, make it outta raw lumber, what do you call it… 'Primitive', right?"

That surprised Jeff. "Yeah, I do. You buy something off me? I think I'd recall somebody as tall as you, big guy."

"Naw, it wasn't me, it was Annie what bought it. A big-ass chair, a recliner, like. Made it outta oak, I think."

Jeff made a conciliatory noise. "Was Annie your wife?" he asked gently.

Malcolm let two larger tear drops fall. When he spoke again, his voice was husky with emotion. "No, not yet, she wasn't. We was gettin' married come October. October the 26th. She wanted to do it sooner, get hitched in the spring, but I said no, we'd wait, an' now…"

Jeff grasped the man's shoulder and held it while he wept. Once the worst of it had passed, he asked as gently as he could, "What happened to her, Malcolm?"

He took a deep breath and wiped his nose with the back of his hand. In a tired voice he said, "She took to havin' seizures 'bout two years ago. They wasn't so bad at first, just *petite mal,* an' she took her medicine regular. She'd kept her condition regulated pretty well. After we all lost our sight, I made sure she kept takin' her meds on schedule. I could tell by my wristwatch what time it was. It chimes the hour, ya know. I was home from the hospital for lunch when it happened. We was all right at first. We was together, and we was home, so we was all right. But she had a spell. She had a spell, an' I was in the kitchen a' gettin' some water when she did. She fell, an' I couldn't tell where she was for a bit. It took me some time to find her, an' when I did…she'd…" he trailed off, more tears falling. Jeff waited patiently. He knew what losing someone was like.

When he was able to go on, Malcolm said, "I found her on the bedroom floor. She'd took a spell an' fell, like I said. But this time… this time, she fell an' hit her head on the side of the nightstand. She bled out. Bled out right there in my arms, Goddammit. I couldn't do nothin'. Compression bandages, even tried to start an I.V. Hell, *tried* nothin', I *started* the sumbitch! Had it goin' full bore, but she just… head wounds, you see…she bled out, an' wasn't a damn thing I could do about it. I couldn't see to put in any sutures, an' I didn't have my kit with me, so I didn't have no surgical glue, or…."

Again, Malcolm trailed off. Jeff had assumed that the man had worked at the hospital as a janitor or something like that. *Sounds like a redneck, so you automatically think he* is *one*, he thought. Then he asked, "What did you do at the hospital, Malcolm?"

He sighed. "P.A. worked in the E.R., same rotation as Doctor Randall. We got on real well. Could work a mass casualty like a house 'a fire, me 'n that man." He smiled wanly.

Jeff gripped his shoulder tightly. "Well, Malcolm, I am just as pleased as hell to make your acquaintance. You have no idea. How about we get out of the street, get a good meal into you?"

Malcolm looked incredulous. "Did you miss the first part of our little conversation, Jeff? I ain't rightly worried 'bout eatin' these days."

"I understand that, Malcolm. But here's the situation. I am sorry as hell about Annie, and tomorrow, first thing, I'll help you to do what's right by her, all okay? We'll take care of her together, and that's a promise. But tonight, I need you to come with me. I've got eleven kids and two adults that are just as blind as you are, and that number is going to start growing soon. I need you to help me Malcolm. Something happens to any of those kids, or hell, *anybody*, and I'm lost. I don't even know CPR, for Christ's sake. You are a gift from God, and that's the simple truth of it. One of the adults I mentioned is a Catholic priest, and he'll agree with me one hundred percent, I guarantee you that."

Malcolm moved back from Jeff's grasp and his face clouded with anger. "Again, you seemed to have missed somethin' from what I been sayin'. My fiancée died in my motherfuckin' arms and *I couldn't do nothin' to help her!!!*" He nearly screamed this last.

Jeff reached in and took his shoulders, both of them this time, and held tight. "I know, and I am so sorry. I mean that. I know how you feel. I lost my mom and dad and my baby sister all in one night. They died not a dozen feet from me. It was a car wreck. So I get it, I swear I do. But it's *different* now, Malcolm. You can't see, that's true, but you've got something else now. You've got *me*. I can be your eyes. Do you see? You can save so many lives. I'm starting to gather everyone I can together, and most of them are going to be in bad shape, and many of them, maybe even *most* of them will die if you're not there to help me. *Please*, Malcolm. You've got to come with me. You've got to help me, man. I'm in over my head here. I don't know shit about medicine. If it's not Tylenol, I don't get it. Without you, a lot of good people are going to die. I know you're hurting, but you are a gift from God, and I'm not even a religious man. What do you say?"

Malcolm looked helplessly at his feet. Finally he looked up in Jeff's direction. "What the hell *can* I say? I tell you to fuck off, an' let me alone, an' folks will die, just like Annie. I say okay, point me in the right direction, an' we'll get these folks took care of, and I gotta put aside all my hurtin' and help. An' helpin' is my ever-fucking *job*!" He let out an involuntary sob and hung his head lower.

Jeff did the only thing he could think to do. He put his arms around Malcolm and just held on until the man's storm had once again passed. Finally, Malcolm shrugged Jeff's arms off, but not angrily. "I told you, I was engaged. So keep your homo shit to yourself, got it?" he laughed through his tears.

Jeff laughed along with him, his own eyes a little moist. "Fair enough. I'll try to keep my erotic urges toward you in check, but no promises. So, you coming with me? I promise to keep my hands off your ass, at least until we get back to the school."

Malcolm got up, with some assistance from Jeff. He was skinny; as tall people often were, but he was almost to the point of emaciation. It had only been four days, but Jeff wondered how long it had been since Malcolm had eaten. They turned back down the street,

Jeff holding Malcolm's arm with one hand. He un-slung his rifle with the other.

"What school? The high school? That's not a bad idea. The hospital would be better, though." Malcolm said.

Jeff continued scanning the area. Just because he *thought* he'd put Daniels out of commission for a while, maybe for the count, didn't necessarily make it so. Talking to Malcolm while continued looking around, he said, "No, not the high school, although that was one of the ideas. The other one *was* the hospital, actually. No, the school I'm talking about is called Second Sight. It's the school for…"

"Blind kids." Malcolm finished. "Yeah, I remember them raisin' hell 'bout puttin' that place in. I was glad to see 'em do it. You got how many kids? Eleven? They all right? Physically, I mean?"

"Yeah, all fit as fiddles. Same goes for the adults. One of them is the priest I mentioned. His name's Father Don Martinez. The other's one of the teachers. Her name's Cynthia Jordan. Everybody except Father Don has been blind since birth, so they've done a lot better than most folks."

Malcolm nodded. "Yeah, makes sense. Hell, they don't miss what they ain't never had. How'd you end up there?"

As they walked, Jeff related everything that had happened to him since Tuesday, when he and Waylon had been out felling trees. As they neared the school, he finished up.

"So, that's why it sounded like Custer's Last Stand back there. That son of a bitch can shoot, I can tell you that. My chest still feels like somebody sat an elephant on it. But like I said, I got him at least twice, so he's not going to be as apt to be causing trouble as he has been. At least not for a while, anyway." He stopped, musing. "I'll have to finish it sometime soon, though. Even if I hurt him bad, he may pull through. I want that son of a bitch dead and buried. We can't be going around doing good works with that psycho running loose. But I'll find him. He's too damn stupid to keep a low profile." He was sure of that now. The man wasn't bright enough to be sneaky.

He was, however, dangerous. Especially with that damned pistol. Christ Jesus, what if he was that good with a rifle, too? If he could handle a rifle the way he handled that hand cannon, he'd be able to hit Jeff from Kentucky. Shit, one more thing to worry about. Well, he'd worry about it tomorrow. Fiddle-Dee-Dee, and all that. Jeff wasn't kidding with Malcolm, he had zero medical expertise, but that spray of blood on Daniels' truck window was enough to convince him that the man wasn't going to be a problem for the next few days, at least.

They made it to the back yard of the school and between them managed to get into the cafeteria window without breaking any bones. Standing in the cafeteria, Jeff yelled up the stairs, "It's me, and I've brought a friend!!! Anyone guarding the doorway with a very large shotgun would be much appreciated if they refrained from shooting either of us!"

The two men went up the staircase, where Jeff paused to yell again. "Everybody cool with me bringing a friend over to stay the night? Really, I'm not kidding about that shotgun!"

Father Don's voice came back through the door. "Okay, we're good. I've got the shotgun on safe and in the corner, so you should be all right." In a lower but still audible voice he said, "But what your dog does to you is not my responsibility."

Jeff grinned. A wave of relief rolled over him. He was *back*. He had gone into the lion's den and returned. A bit maimed on the edges, true, but alive. He hadn't completely succeeded in his mission, but he had left his mark on the man that had given them so much grief, and took him out of the game for a while. And he was by-God *back*.

He flung open the door and stepped backward, anticipating Waylon's leap. He was spot-on, because the dog hurled himself out of the room and tried to bowl his buddy over. Even prepared, Jeff was nearly knocked off his feet. The damn dog was almost as big as he was, after all.

He accepted some slobbery kisses and then told the dog, "All right, enough. The new guy is a homophobe, and he doesn't dig this kind of male bonding. Go on, get off me, you giant fuzz-ball!" The dog barked joyously and jumped in several complete circles. Jeff forced his way past Waylon and into the room, where he was nearly bowled over again, this time by Cynthia.

"You're back! You're back, you're back, you're back!" Each
"You're back!" was punctuated by a kiss. While not quite as slobbery as
Waylon's had been, they were far more enjoyable. He gave back as
good as he got, with the Greek chorus of wolf whistles from the
peanut gallery again.

After everyone was assured that Jeff was indeed back, and in
one piece, he introduced his new friend. "Ladies and gents, I'd like to
introduce Mr. Malcolm Connolly. P.A." Eight year old Christy asked,
"What's Mr. Malcolm got to pay?" and everyone laughed. "No, honey",
Jeff said, "P.A. It means 'Physician's Assistant'. He's just like a doctor,
only better, because he doesn't think he's God's gift to the world."

This was greeted with another sally of laughter. The tone of it
was relieved. Jeff knew that he had been tense going out, but he
couldn't imagine what had been going on in the minds of the people he
had left behind, with no way of knowing how things were going to turn
out.

Jeff introduced Malcolm to Cynthia and Father Don. The
priest, upon learning that Malcolm was a Catholic, raised his face to the
heavens and proclaimed, "Halleluiah! Finally, another civilized human
being amongst the barbarians!" Jeff growled at him and threatened to
throw his CB out the window, to which Father Don grinned like a
school boy and said, "Oh, I wouldn't do that if I were you. I've been
getting little twinges all day, and about an hour ago I got an actual

voice. It was garbled, but I could hear at least two words quite clearly. Everyone else agreed that they heard them, too."

By this time, Jeff was practically dancing with glee. "Well? What did they say, old man? Am I gonna have to beat it out of you?"

Father Don laughed. "Well one of the words was 'Nuclear' and the other one was 'Surry'."

Jeff stopped dancing. "How is that a good thing? I don't much care for the idea of anything nuclear near me, if that's okay with everyone."

"Don't you get it, Jeff?" asked Father Don. "If anyone would have been shielded from whatever this was really well, it would have been people in nuclear reactors. Also, nuclear subs, silos, anything like that. If the people on duty were shielded enough, maybe they didn't get whatever it was that got all of us!"

Jeff was still skeptical, but felt a cautious sense of optimism. "Okay, so we've got 'nuclear'. What the hell is 'Surry'? Sounds like the slurry ponds the mines use."

Cynthia chimed in. "Welcome to the wonderful world of useless trivia, Jeff. I just so happen to know that there is a reactor in Surry, Virginia. It's a place about seventeen miles to the north of Newport News. It's about three hundred and fifty or so miles away, as the crow flies." She beamed at him. "Don't bother asking me how I know. I told you, useless trivia. You don't ever want to play *Jeopardy* with me, good sir,"

Jeff was grinning again. He probably looked like an idiot, but no one here would mind that with the possible exception of Waylon, and he was used to it.

"Okay, folks, it looks like we might not be alone here, after all."

The cheer that went up was probably completely out of proportion to the possibility that any real help would come soon, but what the hell, *any* news these days was good news. Jeff joined in the cheer, his eyes clamped firmly on Cynthia.

He seemed to remember a certain discussion that she thought bore further investigation.

Chapter Twenty-One

By midnight, the rec room was filled with the sound of snoring. The stress of the day, coupled with the knowledge that the man that had been haunting them was hurt, possibly dead, had taken its toll on everyone present. The kids had fallen off to sleep like they had been gassed. Father Don had fiddled with the CB for a bit longer, trying to raise whoever had hailed him earlier before shrugging his shoulders and telling everyone that it was *way* past his bedtime.

Malcolm had indeed been without food for several days. Although still lost in the fog of grief over Annie, the smell of the spaghetti and meatballs that Cynthia had thrust under his nose had been sufficient to cause his stomach to overrule any other emotion at present. He fell to with a will, and ate three platefuls before begging off. "I eat one more bite, an' I'm gonna bust", he told Cynthia when she tried to fill his plate again. He was now lying on a pallet on his back, snoring loudly enough to drown out most of the rest of the sleepers.

Jeff was tired. He couldn't remember the last time he had felt so worn out. His ribs were throbbing in time with his leg. When he had removed the vest, fatigue jacket, and raised his t-shirt, he was greeted with three purple bruises about the size of his fist across his ribs and chest. He sent another silent thank you to God that he had decided to wear the vest. Without it, those dark, painful smudges would have been gaping holes, and most of his heart and lungs would have exited his back in a splatter. He dug around in the vest where the bullets had entered with his pocket knife and found the smashed and flattened lead balls, mushroomed and jagged from the impact. He stared at them for a long time, pondering the destructive power of something so tiny.

He sat back on the couch now, blowing out a long breath of relief. He had taken another Percocet, but only one. He figured that would be enough to let him sleep tonight. Tomorrow, he was going back home to gather some of his own clothing and personal effects. He figured he would be at Second Sight for quite some time, and there were a few pictures and other things he wanted to pick up from his place. He suddenly remembered that he would have to take the school's van, because his truck was a smashed ruin across town. He regretted that. He loved that old truck, he truly did.

Cynthia sat beside him on the couch, running her fingers through his hair at his temple. She did so slowly and methodically, and he found himself becoming more and more relaxed. It dawned on him that his mother had done this very thing when he was younger and couldn't sleep because of a nightmare or illness. The soothing, monotonous sweep of her fingers through his hair had always sent him straight off to sleep.

Jeff found tears standing in his eyes. He usually found a moment sometime during his day to send his thoughts and love to the family that he had lost, but he had been too occupied to do so for the last couple of days. It wasn't shame for having not thought of his family for a few days that now brought his tears, however. He couldn't remember a time since his family was still alive that he had spent so much time around other human beings. He had grown accustomed to his solitary lifestyle, just he and Waylon tearing around the forest.

But the last few days had exposed him to the sort of interaction among people that he had gone without for the last six years. Seeing Cynthia and Father Don with the children, hearing their joyful voices raised in laughter, reminded him forcefully of a time when he had been a *part* of a circle like that, not standing outside of it looking in. He hadn't known he had missed those feelings, any more than the children missed being able to see. At least he hadn't known he missed them until he had been immersed back into them. Now, only a few days since his life as a confirmed bachelor and loner, he couldn't imagine not being here with the children and friends he had made.

He couldn't even *begin* to imagine his life without Cynthia in it. Here she had been the whole time, just miles away from him, and yet it had taken the end of the world as they knew it for him to find her. If he could, he would have reversed what had happened in an instant, but the thought of losing her caused the selfish part of his mind to be glad that it had happened. That shamed him briefly, but he couldn't help it. She meant something more to him than what he had imagined. She wasn't just a fine-looking woman that he might take out a few times and then distance himself from her if it looked like it was becoming serious, as he had done of a few occasions before the flash. Jeff wasn't vain about his looks, but he knew that he was attractive to most women, and he was a man, after all. He had wanted to live alone, with all the freedom that entailed, not be a monk. Celibacy wasn't something that came natural to him.

With Cynthia, the thought of celibacy was one of the furthest things from his mind. But that wasn't it, however. There was a whole universe of other feelings that sprang up when he looked at her. With other women, he had seen a body and some company for a brief time. With Cynthia, it felt like Cadmus was sowing dragon's teeth of emotion in his heart and mind. Each time he looked at her, a new feeling came welling up.

He looked at her now, cutting his eyes so he didn't have to move his head. He didn't want her to stop running her fingers through his hair. She sat with a contented look on her face, one hand on his hair, the other playing with her necklace. Curious, he asked her, "What kind of necklace is that you're wearing?"

She jerked out of her reverie and turned to him with a smile. It wasn't her normal sunny one, though. This smile was tinged with sadness.

"It's a claddagh ring on a chain. It's a Celtic thing. My father bought it for my mother when he asked her to marry him. She gave it to me just before I left home after my last visit. I told her I couldn't take it, that it was hers, but she insisted. It was almost like she *knew...*"

Jeff could tell that Cynthia was on the verge of tears, herself. He knew that the chances that Cynthia would ever be with her parents again were astronomically small, but he wasn't about to say such a thing. To get her mind off of it, he said, "Okay, Ms. Trivia. What's a claddagh ring?"

She gave him a happier smile and an elbow in the ribs. Hearing his hiss of pain, she exclaimed, "Oh, Jeff, I'm so sorry! I forgot! Are you all right?"

He rubbed the tender area she had elbowed, breathing slowly. "Yeah, I'll live, you are *really* going to have to stop beating me, you know. It sets a bad example for the children."

She laughed and gave him a kiss on the cheek. "Really, I *am* sorry. I completely forgot about..." She waved a hand in the general direction of Jeff's injuries.

"Well, I'll let it slide this once, but one more time, and I'll have you before the judge, young lady. And that will make me look like the biggest pansy on the planet." Affecting a formal tone, he said, "Yes, Your Honor, I am aware that the young lady that assaulted me is blind. No, Your Honor, I couldn't seem to be able to overpower her and escape. She is a hell-cat, Sir."

Cynthia laughed again. "How do you know the judge would be a man? Not sexist are we?"

"No way, not this kid", he answered quickly. "And even if I were, I sure as hell wouldn't admit it with you still in elbowing distance."

She drew back her elbow threateningly, and to head her off, Jeff said, "Here, a present for you," and put the three smashed bullets into her hand. Her fingers instinctively wrapped around them. "What *are* these?" she asked, her confusion plain.

"Those, my good lady, are three bullets, fired from one almighty big horse pistol that slammed yours truly in the chest earlier this evening."

Cynthia hissed like a cat and flung the bullets across the room, where they made almost inaudible little tinkling noises as they hit the floor. Cynthia whipped around on him, her fury extremely evident. "You think that is *funny?*" she said, her voice barely above a whisper. "You get shot three times and you think that it's *funny???*"

Jeff felt like he had the time he had been wandering through the woods behind his house looking for the right tree when suddenly there was a rattle from his feet. He had looked down to see a large Eastern Diamondback Rattlesnake coiled up not six inches from his left boot. A dreamy sort of slow-motion terror had enveloped him as he looked at the death at his feet. Only Waylon's sudden arrival, which caused the snake to change targets, allowed Jeff to break the spell and slice downward into the snake with his axe so hard he had buried the head of it five inches into the ground. Pure luck had allowed the blow to land squarely on the snake's head, effectively splitting it in two.

Jeff felt that same cold terror now as he sat face to face with a viper he suddenly felt was much more dangerous. Very softly, he said, "Cynthia, I was wearing a bulletproof vest designed to stop rifle rounds. Bullets from a black powder revolver never stood a chance of penetrating it."

She pulled back and spat, "And if he had shot you in the *face*, smart-ass?"

Jeff had no answer for *that* one. Trying for a tactical withdrawal from this line of conversation, he said, "So, you were about to explain all about the claddagh ring to me, as I recall."

Cynthia shot one final evil glare his way, blew out a deep breath, and visibly calmed down. When she began speaking again, she took on the tone of a professor lecturing a classroom.

"The claddagh ring comes from an Irish fishing village of the same name. It first began being produced during the reign of Queen Mary II in the 17th century, but there are parts of the design that go all the way back to the late Roman era." She held the ring up for him to see. It had two hands on either side of a heart with a crown atop it.

"There are several meanings for the ring", she went on. "The hands represent friendship, the heart represents love, and the crown represents loyalty. It can be given in all sorts of situations, not just between people in love though."

He found himself interested. "Really? Like what? I mean, it doesn't look like the kind of gift I would buy a buddy of mine."

"Well, it all depends on how you wear it. If you wear the ring on your right ring finger with the heart pointing towards your fingertip, that means that you are unattached. Romantically, anyway", she amended. "That would be the way you would wear it if it were from a friend. If you wear it on your right ring finger with the heart pointing towards yourself, then it means that you are involved with someone. If you wear it on your left ring finger, either way, it means you're engaged or married." She ran her fingers over the ring. "My mom wore this every day since my dad bought it for her, twenty-two years ago. I couldn't believe it when she gave it to me. Dad had gotten her another ring for their twentieth anniversary, but Mom still wore this one most of the time." She stopped and turned her head towards Jeff. "Do you think she really *did* know something was going to happen? I don't mean that she had a vision or anything like that, but maybe just a feeling or something like that?"

Jeff shook his head. "I don't know, Cynthia. My mom's been gone for six years, but I can still remember how she just seemed to *know* things about my sister and me. I wouldn't say a word, but if something had happened at school, or was bothering one of us, she would be there asking what was up." He laughed. "Hell, half the time, *she* knew there was something wrong with one of us before *we* did. I think it's just a Mom thing."

They fell silent. Jeff took Cynthia's hand and held it gently between both of his own. They say that way for several minutes before he spoke again.

"Cynthia, what I said earlier tonight… well, I won't take it back, because I meant it. But I understand that right now isn't exactly the best time to be looking for romantic entanglements. I mean, I can tell you're kind of fond of me, unless you're just taken with kissing strange men at random." He laughed nervously. "What I'm trying to say, badly, is that I don't want you to feel pressured or anything like that. Or feel like you're beholden to me in some way, because you're not. I'm not going anywhere, so you can take your time and think about… well, everything."

He had been studying his lap throughout this, too embarrassed to look her straight on. She felt for his face and turned it to her. She kissed him once, very slowly and completely, and then sat back. "I *am* thinking about it, Jeff. Thinking about it quite a bit" She smiled suddenly, and lifted the chain off her neck. Undoing the clasp, she slid the ring off of it. Her fingers probed around the ring until it was facing the right direction, and she slid it onto her right ring finger, the heart pointing towards her. "There. I already knew I had a friend in you, and now, this says that I've got something a little more. We'll see how it goes, and maybe someday you can put it on my other hand. How's that?"

Jeff grinned. "I think that is just fine, that's what I think. Now, what do *you* think about another kiss?"

She laughed and very gently pushed him away. "I think I'm exhausted, and so are you, not mention wounded, to boot. I *further* think that it's time for bed. So, you'll have to make do with *this*…" She planted a small, chaste kiss on the corner of his mouth. "And then you'll have to get some sleep, you horn-dog."

Jeff made a token sound of disappointed protest, but stretched out as she got up and went to her own couch. Over her shoulder, she said, "Get some sleep, Jeff. We've got a lot to do tomorrow."

As he stared up at the ceiling, Jeff realized she was right. Everything he had done up to this point was just the preliminary for what was to come. Tomorrow, he was going to begin the Herculean task of trying to round up and care for the survivors of this thing. With an inward groan, he covered his eyes with his hand. When he answered her, his voice was heavy with resignation.

"I know, Cynthia. I know."

Jeff was awakened far too early for his liking by a large wet canine tongue in his ear. With a garbled shriek, he came halfway off his couch and landed in a sprawl. He turned his head and found himself eye-to-eye with a grinning Siberian husky. With a grunt of disgust, Jeff shoved the dog away. Waylon gave out a bark that sounded suspiciously like a laugh and danced away, back to the children. Jeff sat up and ran his hands through his unruly mop of hair. He was saved from a fate worse than death by a hand bearing a cup of coffee under his nose. He took it and looked around blearily.

Malcolm was sitting on the couch, grinning from ear to ear. Jeff eyed him suspiciously. "What are you grinning about, buddy?"

Malcolm's grin grew even wider. "You know something? You got a *remarkably* well-trained dog there. I was unaware that dogs was even aware what the human ear *was*, let alone its location."

Jeff was indignant. "*What???*"

The children broke out laughing. Malcolm joined in and then said, "The kids thought it'd be sweet if Waylon woke you up with a kiss. I just sorta mentioned that you might like one on the ear. Judgin' from the sound of your reaction, he took me at my word." The laughter in the room went up several notches. Jeff looked around, betrayal stamped on his sleep-puffed face.

"All right, I see how you guys are. See if I save the day anymore. I'm gonna sell the lot of you on Ebay, see if I don't."

The kids squealed with more laughter. Jeff grinned. It felt good to be a part of a group like this, it really did. Cynthia walked over with a plateful of pancakes, smothered in maple syrup. He thanked her and said, "I keep eating like this, and I'm going to have to buy new clothes."

She sat down beside him and kissed him lightly on the cheek. "I'm sure you can stand a few extra calories here and there. Besides, you'll need your strength today. Speaking of which, how are you feeling today?"

Malcolm put in, "Yeah, how are the ribs? Any trouble drawin' a deep breath? You still feelin' the pressure on your chest, like you was last night?"

Jeff held up his hands, a useless gesture. "Hold up, everybody. One thing at a time. Hell, I haven't even had my coffee yet." He took a drink from his cup, savoring the strong, reviving brew. He turned towards Malcolm. "Okay, big boy, you first: My ribs feel like a mule kicked me, but I can breathe okay. I'm sore, but I'm pretty sure I'll live. My leg still hurts a little, but I've got some Voltaren gel at the house that I'll pick up later. It helps."

Malcolm was nodding. "Yeah, that Voltaren is pretty good stuff. You can rub some on your ribs, too. That'll help with the soreness. Just make sure that you breathe deep as much as you can. If you get any sudden, sharp pains, or feel like you're having trouble breathin', you let me know right off, all right?"

"Gotcha, Doc. I'll keep you posted."

Malcolm stared off into space. "I need to get over to the hospital at some point today, too. I'm gonna need some supplies, and pack me up a few emergency kits. Gonna need some saline, some Lactated Ringer's, probably need some antibiotics, too…" He trailed off, making a mental list.

"You figure out whatever you need", Jeff told him. "We'll stop by the hospital when I head out to the house. We'll need to figure out for sure where we're going to set up our aid stations, or triage centers, or whatever in the hell you want to call them. I mean, what kind of shape are folks going to be in when we *do* find them, Malcolm?"

The man thought for a moment. "They're gonna be malnourished, dehydrated, sick with all kinds of different ailments. You name it. The flu, stomach viruses, the works. There's gonna be folks that are sick from eatin' stuff that's gone over, if I don't miss my guess. You said there was parts of town that had already lost power, didn't ya? Well, they'll be folks that's got sick from drinking sour milk, things like that."

"Wouldn't they know better than to drink something like that?" Cynthia asked, surprised. "I mean, they can smell it, right?"

"You get thirsty enough, you'll drink anything", Malcolm answered. "Plus, if the power's off, I'll bet that the water's gone down in some places, too. If that's so, then there's folks in close proximity to their own feces. That'll cause sickness pretty damn quick, all by itself. When we get set up, we're gonna need us clean beds, water, and lots of it, and soup. Tons of soup. People will need somethin' that's easy on their digestion. I wasn't in my right mind, eatin' as much as what I did last night. I'm damned lucky I ain't sick as a dog this mornin'. I think that the hospital will be our best bet. We can use the E.R. for its normal purpose, emergency treatment, but it can also be our triage station. We can bring folks through there, clean 'em up and make sure that they're not too sick or dehydrated. Once we get 'em straightened out, we can put 'em in the rooms on the second floor. That'll keep everybody together centrally located. We can go through the kitchen and see what we've got. The supplies should be fine, it's all canned stuff. We've got emergency generators, too. Power'll go out eventually, an' we need to be ready for it." He laughed. "Lights won't be much of a concern for anybody but you, Jeff, so the fuel for the generator should last one whole helluva lot longer. Anyway, I'll think on her and we'll get done what we need to."

Jeff reached over and put his hand on Malcolm's arm. His voice was gentle.

"We're also going to take care of Annie today, like I promised, Malcolm."

The man's eyes filled with unshed tears. "I'm obliged to you, Jeff."

"That's all right, man. It's the least I can do for you. Also, if you don't care, there's a friend of mine that needs taken care of, too."

His face clouded at the thought of Sam Merchant, who had died over the price of a chainsaw.

"We'll do it, Jeff. Eat some breakfast and let me have a bit to figure on what all we need to do, an' we'll head out." He got up and wandered slowly over to where Father Don sat at the CB, twiddling the knobs. That reminded Jeff, and he asked the priest, "Anything new on the CB?"

Father Don shook his head. "No. I tell you what we need is a shortwave, or a base station. Something with a lot more power than this. If I could have more power and a bigger transmitter and antenna, I bet I could really find out what's what out there."

"Okay, Don. It's on the list. First things first though. We've got to get a few things taken care of, and then it's time to help the folks around here. I'm going to be pretty busy, but I won't forget about you."

The man nodded and went back to his knobs. Jeff turned to Cynthia.

"How are you doing this morning, pretty lady?"

She smiled. "I am as right as the rain, Jeff." Her voice took on a concerned edge. "Are you *really* up to this today? I know that time is important, but you're hurt, and if you can't function, then you won't be able to do anyone any good."

"I'm fine, I promise. I am sore, but I don't even think I'll need any pain pills today. Some Tylenol ought to do me fine. And besides, we've gone over this, kiddo. Those folks aren't getting any better while we wait. How many kids are dying right now while I'm eating these pancakes?"

Her mouth made a small moue of distaste. "You certainly have a point. You *also* have really crappy ideas of what constitutes good mealtime conversational points."

Jeff looked at his half-eaten pancakes. He wasn't hungry anymore. "Yeah", he breathed, "you're right about that."

<u>Chapter Twenty-Two</u>

Less than three hours after he had awakened, Jeff Della was already exhausted again.

He had taken Malcolm and Jamie Cummings with him in the school van, leaving Second Sight in the capable hands of Cynthia and Father Don, along with the older children. They set up a similar protocol as they had the night before, with the shotgun aimed at the door and ready to go. When they returned, they would go through the process of clearly identifying themselves before they came into the upstairs hallway. Father Don had asked, half-jokingly, if they needed a password. Jeff had responded with, "How does 'Don't shoot me?' work for you?" Don had shown him where the keys to the van were located and then the four of them had manhandled the pop machine out the doorway downstairs.

"I'm sick of climbing through that damned window", Jeff said. "Anybody but us comes up those stairs, they'll regret it. I'm not sneaking out of here anymore; I'm leaving like a paying guest."

They pulled out onto the street and headed for Malcolm's house. Jeff drove them slowly through town with the windows down. He had left Waylon with the children, but he had taken his rifle, handgun and pack. He didn't expect any trouble from Daniels any time soon, but he wanted to be prepared. To Jamie, he said, "You've got the best ears, kiddo. I want you to keep them open. You hear anything at all, you let me know, all right?" The boy had responded immediately and sat perched on the edge of his seat with his head half out the window, listening intently.

The van was much quieter than his old truck had been, but it still seemed loud in the silence that blanketed town. They drove to Malcolm's house and stopped in the front. Jeff turned to Malcolm and asked him if he was ready.

"No, but I ain't never gonna be, neither. This has to be done. My Annie deserves better, an' I'm gonna give it to her."

Jeff clapped his shoulder again and they exited the van. Jamie walked alongside the men, Jeff holding on to one of his hands, and Malcolm holding on to the other. In this way, they went up the walkway and into the house. The soft stench of decay hit them with a slap as soon as they entered the door. Jeff realized that soon, the whole town was going to smell like this. It was a sobering thought.

Jamie, who had been living with heightened senses his whole life to make up for his lack of vision, was the most effected. He tried manfully to hold it in, but after a few moments he turned and vomited on the doorstep. He was apologizing even as he straightened up, terrified he had offended Malcolm and ashamed to have shown weakness in front of the other men.

Malcolm had reached out and found the boy's head, and had rubbed his hair. "It's okay, son", he said. "What we're buryin' here is just her body. Everythin' that made her who she was has gone on to Heaven, 'cept for what I keep in my heart. This is just what happens to bodies when they die, especially in the heat. You just stay here on the step an' let us take care of her, all right?"

Jamie's face showed a perfect balance of relief and shame. He agreed to sit out on the steps and listen for any danger. Jeff told him to give out a yell if he heard anything, and they would come running. The boy readily agreed. He sat down on the steps and resumed his listening position, something that reminded Jeff of the dog on those old RCA commercials.

Jeff and Malcolm went into the living room and up the stairs. The smell grew worse as they approached the bedroom, but Malcolm seemed to give it no heed. Jeff matched him step for step. He wasn't looking forward to this, but the man was going to help them save lives, and if this was the cost, Jeff was glad to pay it.

They entered the bedroom, and Jeff was overcome with pity. Malcolm had done his best for the woman that he loved. He had laid her on the bed and covered her with a soft quilt. A picture of the two of them together, lay atop the place where her hands met under the quilt.

Jeff could see how hard Malcolm had fought to keep Annie alive. There was blood splashed everywhere, it seemed. An I.V. bag and tubing lay on the floor, along with several compression bandages, all soaked with dried blood. Malcolm had fought like a tiger for her, and had fought blind. Jeff felt another surge of respect and admiration for the man.

Between the two of them, they picked her up and carried her gently down the stairs. Jeff had asked Malcolm if he wanted to locate a coffin for her and take her to the cemetery, but the man had declined. "We'll bury her out back'n the house", he said. "That's where she liked it the best, out by the hammock. I think that's the best place. She'd want to be there."

Jeff had agreed, and they took the woman's body out to where the hammock swayed gently between two trees. Jeff could see why Annie had liked it here. It was quiet and peaceful. It wasn't so bad a spot to be buried, as far as Jeff was concerned.

Malcolm had given Jeff directions as to where he could locate a shovel and a spade in the small shed in the back yard. Taking turns, with Jeff directing, they soon had a grave that was about five feet long and two feet wide. It was only about three feet deep, but Malcolm proclaimed it good enough. Jeff admired him even more. Malcolm's job was to take care of the living, not the dead, and he knew they were running out of time.

They lowered the quilt-covered body of Annie into the grave as gently as they could and began the painful process of filling it back up. Malcolm had to stop a few times as he gave in to his grief and sobbed.

Jeff, feeling helpless, only put his hand on the man's shoulder and stood there.

Finally, it was done. Malcolm recited the Lord's Prayer, and sang a verse of "Tears in Heaven" by Eric Clapton in a surprisingly beautiful voice. When he could do no more, Malcolm had turned away from the grave and staggered away. Jeff caught up to him in time to keep him from slamming into the side of the house, not that he thought the man cared at that instant. They stood in the back yard for about fifteen minutes, as Malcolm wept.

Getting back into the van, Malcolm said quietly, "Jeff, I got to thank you. Wasn't for you, Annie never woulda been seen to rightly. Thank you so much."

Jeff hugged Malcolm awkwardly with one arm. "You're welcome. I have to thank you for holding on and staying with us to help. I know how easy it is to want to give in."

Malcolm just nodded. They drove out of town towards their next stop, Sam Merchant's general store. Everyone was about to climb out of the van when Jeff said, "It's okay, you guys stay here. I can handle this on my own."

Malcolm looked concerned. "Jeff, you do much more luggin' and liftin' on your own, and you'll spring a rib. You best let me help."

"No, it's okay. I'm not going to be lifting anything heavier than a radio. It'll be fine, trust me."

Malcolm and Jamie looked confused, but said no more. Jeff got out of the van and walked to the doorway of the store. The glass from the window lay twinkling like diamonds from where Sam had shot it out. *Was that really just two days ago?* Jeff thought. *Is that possible?*

Taking a deep breath, he went into the store. The smell wasn't as bad here as it had been at Malcolm's, but it was there, nonetheless. The power was out, so the smell of rotting produce and meat from the cooler didn't help matters any. Jeff went to the little back room that had served Sam as a home for so many years.

Sam lay as he had been when Jeff had last seen him. In the dim light, he didn't look so bad at all. He looked more asleep than dead. Jeff knelt at the door way and spoke one last time to the old man.

"Sam, I'm sorry things turned out like this. I really am. I didn't kill that son of a bitch that did this to you, but I popped his floater for him, and I'm not done with his ass yet, either. If you can hear me, I want you to know that he's hurting and he'll hurt even more before I finish dealing with him. I just thought you would want to know."

He straightened and looked around. He saw the boom box and picked it up. He opened the CD player and saw that Sam had been listening to Linkin Park when he had died. He picked up the box of CDs and flipped through them until he found the one he wanted. Taking the boom box and the CD, he went out and sat them in the parking lot. He opened the CD and placed it in the stereo, and then he checked the batteries by flipping on the radio. The burst of static was explosively loud in the quiet day. Malcolm and Jamie both jumped, unprepared for the sound.

"It's okay, "Jeff called. "Just a few minutes more."

He walked back into the store and looked around until he found what he was looking for, a rack of fuel jugs. Taking two, he strode back out into the summer sun. He walked over to Sam had parked his Jeep Cherokee. He looked around the back of the Jeep and, sure enough, there was a section of hose about three feet long. Jeff grinned. That old bastard had been prepared for just about anything.

Jeff set about siphoning gas from the Jeep's tanks. Once he had filled up both jugs, he had four gallons of gasoline. These he took back into the store and began splashing everywhere. He emptied both jugs, pouring a small trail out onto the parking lot behind him. He stepped into the store one last time, picking out a Zippo lighter from the display case. The Zippo had the insignia for the band AC/DC on it. *Not quite,* Jeff thought, *but close enough.*

He left the store and picked up the boom box. He sat it in the back seat next to Jamie. The boy looked over, worried. "Jeff, is everything all right? I smell gasoline. *Lots* of it." Jeff assured him that it was okay, and then stepped around the van. He walked up to the trail of gas and struck the wheel of the Zippo. It lit the first time. Jeff wasn't a smoker, but he was sure that he would carry this lighter for the rest of his life.

He touched the lighter to the gas and stepped back as the almost invisible blue line of fire shot across the parking lot. He stepped back to the van and started it up. He pulled back out onto the road and drove to the rise where he had first seen the chaos on Thursday. He pulled over and parked the van again. He climbed out and opened the back door to pick up the boom box. He looked back at other two and said, "Things are about to get pretty noisy, so don't be surprised, okay?" He got two identical confused nods.

Nodding himself, he went to the back of the van and sat the boom box on the road. The general store was now fully engulfed, with muffled explosions coming out of it as propane tanks and God knew what else went off. Jeff reached down and flicked through the tracks of the CD until he came to the one he wanted.

Just as he hit play, the first of the underground fuel tanks went up. A gigantic roar tore into the bright summer sky and Jeff felt a wave of heat hit him like a slap in the face. Malcolm stuck his head out the window and yelled, "What the hell, Jeff???" Jeff told him it was all right, not to worry. Malcolm's head went back into the window, shaking in amazement.

The second tank went up. If anything, the roar was even louder than the first. Throughout it all from the boom box in a fierce counterpoint to the conflagration below, Lemmy Motörhead ripped his way through "The Ace of Spades".

Jeff stood smiling in the roadway with his hands on his hips, watching the general store turn into a fireball.

"Sam, you may have been a Baptist, but you just got the biggest fucking Viking funeral in the history of West Virginia. Thor himself would be proud."

They went to Jeff's house so he could collect his things, and as they pulled in the place that he had called home for the last six years he was amazed that it all looked as foreign to him as the dark side of the moon. What had been so familiar just a few days before now struck him as a place he might have visited once, long ago. He climbed out of the van and told Malcolm and Jamie to sit tight. He would only be a few minutes, he assured them. He went to the door and slid the key in the lock.

Inside, it even felt like a place that had stood empty for years, not days. He made his way into his bedroom and threw his other duffle bag from the closet onto the bed. He spent a few minutes going through his clothing, throwing it pell-mell into the bag. Underwear, jeans, pants, socks… what else? He stood in the center of the bedroom looking around. He grabbed his old leather jacket out of the closet and paused for a moment. He would be returning here before it cold enough to call for this, wouldn't he? Shrugging, he tossed into the bag. If he made it back out here, great. If not, he'd have what he needed.

Pushing the clothing down into the bag, he began pulling pictures off the wall. These he placed with great care into the bag on top of the clothes, wrapping each in a dishtowel. He went into the living room and stood, studying the walls. There was little here he actually needed. A few of his favorite books from the shelf, a knife his father had made from an old saw blade and deer antler, a small bracelet made of brightly colored beads of plastic, their luster dimmed with age and dust. This last had belonged to his sister. She had been wearing it the night of the accident, and a kindly police officer had brought it to Jeff about a week later, along with his parent's wedding bands. These, too, Jeff scooped out of small oak box on an end table.

He placed all these small treasures into the bag on top of the pictures and then headed back into the living room. Draped across a rocking chair that Jeff had made was an afghan that his mother had knitted. It was the first and last one she had ever made. She had started knitting as a hobby just before her death, and this was the first one she had started. It was unfinished, only about three-quarters of its length complete. Jeff had tied off the loose ends of yarn and brought it with him from his childhood home when he moved up here. A neighbor, an older woman named Nellie Singleton, had offered to finish it for him, but he had politely refused. The afghan wasn't finished because his mother *was*. That might have been a maudlin way of viewing it, but to allow someone else to complete the last thing his mother had been working on had seemed like a desecration. He gently took the afghan from the chair and carried it to the bag. Folding it, he placed it on top of everything else. The afghan kept everything from rolling around, and padded it, protected it. Just like his mother had done, he mused.

He went into the bathroom and grabbed his toothbrush, razor, shaving cream, and his tube of Voltaren gel. Malcolm had promised to get him all he wanted of it from the hospital, but this one was his, and he felt strangely possessive of it. He paused long enough to smear some of the oily gel on his leg and under his shirt across his ribs. In a little while, the pain there would be muted. He placed all his toiletries in the side pocket of his bag and closed it. With an instinctive grunt, he hoisted the bag to his shoulder. It was so light that he nearly threw it over his shoulder and across the room. He laughed. He had gotten accustomed to carrying much heavier bags in the last few days, he supposed.

He paused in the doorway, looking around once more. Had he missed anything? He hefted the bag again, feeling its lightness. Was this his whole life, one canvas duffle bag that weighed less than thirty pounds? He realized that this was, in fact, all that was important to him, and felt a little sad. Being able to pack your entire life into a single bag that wasn't even heavy enough to warrant thinking about was not much of a statement about the life that he had been leading. Again, he shrugged. This house was his past. His future sat outside in the van, waiting for him to get a move on.

He left the house, turning to lock the door. He stopped, fiddling absent-mindedly with his keys, and then turned and went to the van. Who the hell was going to break in to this place, sitting out in the middle of nowhere? Whoever it was, he silently wished them well and got into the van. He sat the duffle on the floor between the seats and turned towards his companions. "You guys ready?" he asked.

Malcolm turned to him. "If'n you're not gonna engage in anymore pyrotechnics, well, then I reckon we're ready."

Jeff laughed. "Nope, you play with fire and you'll piss the bed."

Jamie piped up from behind him, "If that's the case, you better put some plastic on the couch tonight, or you'll have to clean the cushions in the morning."

They all had a laugh at that, and Jeff keyed the van's ignition. Jeff had explained to them both about Sam Merchant, and why Jeff had decided that burning the old man's store was a fitting monument to him. Jamie was taken completely aback by the thought of a senior citizen rocking out to heavy metal music, just as Jeff had been. Jeff had grinned at the incredulous look stamped on Jamie's face as he had listed the contents of Sam's treasure trove of CDs. It felt nice to be able to relate something of Sam's personal life to these new friends, and Jeff figured Sam wouldn't mind being so remembered.

Turning out of the driveway, he glanced at his home once more in the rearview. *Home.* For Jeff, the word was just that, a word. At least it had been for a long time. He was leaving the place he had created for himself in the world, leaving land that he knew as intimately as he knew his own hands, but that feeling of being at a strange place lingered. The rec room where he had spent less than a week seemed a hundred times more fitting of the label "home" than the place he was now leaving. Jeff cut his eyes away from the log cabin and back to the road.

"Okay, boys, we're on our way."

They drove back towards town and met a bit of difficulty when they neared the site where the general store had once been. The fire had been intense, and there was debris lying all over the place. The road was full of it, most of it still smoking. Jeff pulled a face. Father Don would neuter him if he brought the van back on four flats, blind or not. Maybe giving Sam a Norse send-off may not have been the *best* thought-out plan Jeff had ever hatched. As he watched, a line of fire spread merrily across the field in front of the remains of the store. *What the hell*, Jeff thought embarrassedly, *it was a spur of the moment thing*. Now it looked like he might have to spend his day digging firebreaks to keep town from burning down.

As if in answer, a rumble of thunder sounded in the west. Grinning, Jeff gave out a silent "thank you" to Sam Merchant. It was a coincidence, but Jeff couldn't help but imagine Sam's irritated voice complaining about having to clean up a mess Jeff had made, what the hell was the boy thinking, was he an idiot, or what, starting a fire like that? Jeff laughed out loud.

Malcolm turned. "What's so funny?"

Jeff shook his head. "Nothing. I was just thinking about a friend of mine, that's all."

"Cool. You reckon this here fire'll burn itself out? I can smell it pretty strong."

Jamie agreed heartily. He had his hand clasped over his nose and was breathing through his mouth.

Jeff giggled again, and said, "I think we're in good shape. There's one hell of a thunderstorm building up. I think it's going to rain soon. That'll take care of the fire." As if in agreement, thunder rumbled in the distance. Jeff had a brief image of Thor flinging his hammer and Sam Merchant telling him that his aim was way off, here, gimme that thing, I'll show you how it's done. That undid him completely, and he began laughing like a loon. He was still laughing uncontrollably when they drove past the fire ring around the store. Malcolm turned to him and asked, "Jeff, can I tell you somethin'?"

"Sure."

"Don't take this the wrong way, or nothin', but you are one strange sumbitch, you know it?"

Jeff, who had just about regained control, now bellowed laughter so hard that a large gob of snot flew out of his nose and hit the windshield with a wet *splat*. He continued to break into helpless gales the rest of the way into town. Both Malcolm and Jamie just smiled, shaking their heads.

They entered town and drove to the hospital. With Malcolm giving directions, they entered the back bay of the E.R. The power was still on in this part of town, but the lights had started to flicker. Jeff didn't give it much more time before it gave up the ghost for good. Fortunately for them, the lights showed no unpleasant surprises. Everyone seemed to have wandered off. Jeff was glad. He was expecting to come across many more corpses before this was over, but he felt like he'd had enough to do him for a bit, if that was all right with everybody.

Under Malcolm's direction, Jeff filled several of the EMS bags in the E.R. with the supplies the P.A. thought that they might need as they began their search for survivors. They also made sure that the E.R. itself was in good shape and ready to accept any survivors they came across. Malcolm was more at home here, and could walk around almost as if he could see. He would point out this machine or that one and ask Jeff to turn them on and tell him what the readings were. It was all Greek to Jeff, but Malcolm seemed content with his answers. Within an hour, they were as ready as they could be.

Leaving the E.R., Jeff realized that the plan he had been working on with Sam Merchant three days ago was finally going to be put into action. The fact that the plan had been delayed by those three days sent a fresh wave of anger directed towards Oscar Daniels through Jeff's body. How many people had died in those three days that might have been saved if Jeff hadn't been wasting his time on that psychotic asshole? *You had better have bled to death, you bastard,* Jeff sent to him in a red dart of rage. *You had just better have. Because if I get another crack at you, I'm going to make it a point to shoot as low as I can. See how much trouble you can cause without any balls.*

The three of them climbed back into the van, and Jeff pulled his map out. Starting from the hospital, and working in ever-widening circles, they were going to save just as many folks as they could. He imagined the E.R. full to capacity and was simultaneously thrilled and terrified. Every new person that they found would become one more person that Jeff was personally responsible for. *Christ, I hope Don was right about that voice on the CB*, Jeff thought. *This is too big for me, and I know it.*

Shrugging, he remembered his grandfather's favorite saying about God never putting more on you than he thought you could handle. It was good to know *someone* had such confidence in him.

They turned out onto the street and headed for the first set of homes.

Here we go, Jeff thought.

Chapter Twenty-Three

Had Jeff known it, he would have been savagely proud of himself. Oscar Daniels was a man in a world of hurt. Even though he had cleaned his wounds several times, and raided the medicine cabinet to get some antibiotics that hadn't gone over, the holes in his leg and chest were bright, flaming red points of agony. They were hot to the touch, and Oscar lived in a constant state of terror that he would see lines of infection marching away from them. So far, there had been nothing like that happen, but it wasn't beyond the realm of possibility. Oscar wouldn't put it past that goddamn soldier to have been using some sort go poison bullets on him, the bastard.

Oscar's scream ripped through the house as he disinfected the wounds for the second time that day. No matter how many times he did it, or how many pain pills he had taken, the pain that shot through his body when the iodine hit his raw flesh was unbearable. Weeping openly, he applied triple antibiotic ointment to the bullet wounds and redressed them with gauze and tape.

He limped into the living room, huge tears rolling down his face. He stopped by the kitchen table to pry open the bottle of painkillers and eat three of them, pause, and then eat two more. He crunched them between his teeth and washed the whole chalky mess down with a long pull of beer. He made his way to the couch and sat down as frailly as an old man. He turned the TV on and tried to get interested in an old Western, but the pain from his wounds kept pulling his attention away. He finally gave up and stared out the huge picture window in the living room, looking at the gently rolling lawn and creek near the road.

He was more than just hurt, he was mad. Mad hell, he was fucking *furious*. Look at what had happened. All he had done was go to town looking for some female companionship, and now just fucking *look*. His truck was still sitting in the driveway, a complete ruin. He could see it out of the corner of the picture window, but avoided looking at it if he could help it. Seeing it in that shape sent a wave of pure grief washing over him, and more often than not, he would cry. It wasn't *right*, it wasn't *fair*! He hadn't been bothering anyone! Why couldn't folks just leave him alone? Why did someone always have to be fucking with him, making his life such a bitch?

He was sitting there wallowing in misery and self-pity when he heard a distant explosion, followed by a second one. His first thought was childishly hateful; *I hope some one got ALL BURNED UP!!!* His second thought, however, was more logical (at least logical for Oscar). Maybe that was the soldier! Maybe he had finished shooting up innocent folks just looking to have a little fun, and now he was blowing up half of the town!

A wave of civic pride rolled over Oscar. By God, there was someone blowing his town up! He couldn't just sit here and let that mercenary son of a bitch destroy his hometown! He half rose from the couch when his wounds screamed in protest. Sitting quickly back down, Oscar rapidly remembered that he *hated* his hometown, hated it with a *passion*. He grimaced at the fresh flash of pain that ran up and down his body, clenching his jaw and screwing his eyes shut.

After the worst of it had passed, no doubt aided by the narcotics running through his system, he opened his eyes again. He looked towards town, a frown line appearing between his brows. Yeah, he may not be the biggest fan of Stone Grove, West Virginia on the planet, but there was still the *point* behind it. He may hate the place, but still, to sit idly by and let some bastard destroy it seemed wrong to him somehow. He would have called someone about it if anyone was still answering their phones these days.

But they weren't. He knew, because he had stubbornly tried to call the police all night to report that bastard for shooting him, dialing 911 over and over. The fact that he couldn't even get a dial tone mattered not a whit to Oscar. He had been wronged, and by hell, *someone* was going to hear about it!

He sat now, thinking as hard as he could about what he should do next. It was obvious to him that he was on his own here. No one was coming to help. If this town was going to be saved, then by God, it would have to be Oscar Daniels that saved it. He doubted the town would thank him, but you never knew. The image of a statue of him in his Stetson on the courthouse lawn ran through his mind, leaving him grinning stupidly in its wake.

But what could he do? He was hurt, hurt *bad*, and he couldn't even get an ambulance out here to take him to the doctor. He supposed that he could load up on enough painkillers to make it to town himself, even though he would have to drive that fucking Toyota Highlander in the garage to get there. He made a disgusted face. Brought low, and that was a fact, to be reduced to driving a rice-burner around. But, in an emergency, you used what you had, he supposed.

Okay, so he could take enough happy pills to keep from hurting too bad, but then what? Just drive into town and find that soldier and go after him with his .44 again? Hell *no*. Oscar had hit that bastard three times; square in the chest, and the fucker had just gotten back up and kept pouring it on. *What if that soldier was like the ones in that movie?* he thought suddenly. The saliva in his mouth suddenly dried up. You could shoot those guys over and over, and they would just get right back up and keep coming. All you had to do was douse them in ice after it was all said and done, and they healed right up.

After a few minutes, Oscar shook his head. No, that was just make-believe, not like his Westerns. Those soldiers weren't real, they were just *actors*. No, that soldier had probably been wearing that body armor you saw the Army guys wearing all the time on the news. That would explain why his shots had failed to drop the fucker. His .44 was one hell of a weapon, but it wasn't designed to puncture bullet proof vests. It was used back during a time when men were *men*, by God. No armor for them, just high noon and a dusty street. Well, there was that one time good old Clint had worn a big piece of steel under his serape to screw with the bad guy's head, but that was different.

Okay, then were did that leave him? He was hurt, not using his own wheels, and shooting a gun that wouldn't do the job unless he got a head shot. Oscar didn't think that would be much of an issue, if he could get close enough to the son of a bitch. If he could close to within about twenty or thirty yards, he would turn that guy's head into a window. The only problem with that plan was actually *getting* within twenty or thirty yards. In his prime, without a goddamn hole in his leg the size of a roast beef and half his damn nipple blown off, Oscar could sneak right up on the guy. Not now, not hurt like he was. He shook his head. So what was he supposed to do?

He sat there for almost an hour, trying out various strategies and finding holes in each one. The problem was getting close enough to finish the bastard off. In a fair and just world, he would already be dead, dammit! Oscar had gotten the drop on him, and had hit him three square times. Life just wasn't fair, and that was a fact.

He turned his attention back to the movie, which was reaching the climax. The hero was taking aim at a stack of dynamite under a train trestle. He was down to his last bullet. As Oscar watched, the actor squinted down the length of his pipe-like sight and squeezed the trigger. The picture cut to the crosshairs lying over the dynamite, which went off with an almighty bang and sent the train full of enemy soldiers into the canyon.

Oscar let out a triumphant yell, which hurt his chest like hell. He didn't mind. Of course! He'd use a fucking rifle! He could work his way close enough to the soldier, wait for him to show his cowardly face, and then shoot him dead as Dillinger! He could take that bastard's head clean off with a high-powered hunting rifle. The previous owner had been an avid hunter, trophies hanging all around the house to prove it. Oscar had seen rifles in the gun case in the office the man had kept.

Getting up from the couch, Oscar headed toward the office, once again stopping by the kitchen table to chew a few painkillers. He popped a few Somas as well, just for flavor. He slowly made his way to the office and walked over to the gun case. It was a nice mahogany job, with frosted glass displaying an elk standing by a mountain stream. It was locked, which just went to show you how stupid some folks were. Oscar looked around and saw a big chunk of coal on the desk the man had obviously been using as a paperweight. Why in the hell someone would keep a chunk of that crap around like a gold nugget was beyond Oscar. He picked it up and threw it at the gun case. The glass shattered, and Oscar went over to it, careful not to step on any of the broken glass with his bare feet.

There were eight guns in the case. Three of them were shotguns, four were rifles, and there was a muzzle loader. He picked out the rifle with the biggest scope and took it from the case. He knew plenty about pistols, *his* pistol at least, but was not as familiar with rifles. He looked at the barrel and read that it was a .300 Weatherby. He pawed through the boxes of shells in the drawer at the bottom of the case until he found the right shells. Taking the rifle and the shells over to the desk, he sat down and swept the flotsam and jetsam on it to the floor. He opened the box of shells and took one out. He whistled softly. It was big enough to kill a fucking elephant, from the looks of it.

He messed around with the rifle until he figured out where the clip release was. Dropping it into his hand, he began to place shells into it. He was disappointed to find that it only held three. Well, he figured if you were shooting something this big, you didn't need to spray rounds all over the damn place like that soldier had done. He slapped the clip back into place and worked the bolt. Making sure the gun was on safe, he removed the clip and added another shell. There. Four rounds, each one looking like an anti aircraft shell. He picked up the rifle and slung it over his right shoulder, wincing at the pain the movement caused his chest wound.

He went back into the living room and sat back down on the couch. The movie had ended, the DVD symbol bouncing back and forth across the screen. Oscar didn't get up and put in another DVD. He just sat as the medicine he had taken worked its way throughout his system, giving everything a dream-like cast. He wouldn't try to go after the soldier today, it was too soon, and he was too hurt. One more night of rest, one more night to recover his strength, and then he would go finish this. He stretched out on the couch, the rifle lying on the floor next to him.

He was asleep within moments. In his dreams, he watched the soldier's head disappear in a red mist of blood and bone over and over.

He smiled in his sleep. It was a smile of contentment, as sweet as a child's.

Chapter Twenty-Four

Jeff Della leaned against the wall in the E.R., running his hands through his hair. He was past the point of distraction, and rapidly edging towards the fabled land of Panic.

It was just past ten o'clock in the evening. The fruits of his labor this first day were all over the place, some of them sitting in a catatonic stupor, some weeping helplessly, and others moving about, bumping into things. There were over fifty people in the emergency room at the moment, and Malcolm was looking as harried as Jeff felt. With a sigh, he rose from the wall and went over to give Malcolm a hand with their newest haul, an elderly woman that still wasn't convinced that she wasn't dreaming the whole thing.

There had been a disheartening number of houses that held no one at all, or worse, held their former occupants. The smell of the dead had stopped bothering Jeff after less than an hour, and even Jamie had become accustomed to it a little later. It was a simple procedure that they had worked out. They knocked on the door and announced themselves as being there to help. They stood on either side of the door to do this, visions of the shotgun arrangement back in the rec room vivid in their minds. If no one answered, they tried the door, kicking it open if locked. The smell of death was usually all the answer they needed, but Jeff felt compelled to at least *check* these houses anyway. The pitiful sights that he was rewarded with because of this attack of thoroughness were enough to guarantee that he wouldn't sleep soundly for weeks, he was sure. The children were the worst. There weren't as many of them as he feared, but he was looking towards the school with terrified eyes. The flash had happened in the middle of the day on a weekday, so most kids would have been in class. Had they been taken care of? If so, by who? He wasn't sure he wanted the answer to that question.

In several of the houses, they were met by not the sickly sweet smell of decomposition, but extremely agitated dogs and cats. Their owners had never made it home, and the last four days of enforced confinement had driven many of them at least near, if not over, the edge. When their knocking resulted in maniacal barking or yowling, they quickly edged back and Jeff would open the door, his pistol in hand. He didn't want to shoot any of the animals, but he wanted himself or his companions eaten alive even less. In most cases, the animals had gone streaking out of the houses and into the street, where they barked and growled until Jeff and his companions had moved to the next house.

After so many empty (or worse, full) houses without any survivors, Jeff was beginning to lose hope. It was the fifteenth or sixteenth house they checked before they finally found anyone alive. The first had been a woman in her forties, and she had been in pretty bad shape. With Jeff's help, Malcolm had managed to get her hydrated and stable enough to take to the van. She had been speechless throughout all of this, refusing to respond to any questions put to her. It was only when she was in the van and moving down the road that she had asked quietly, "Is this real?" They had assured her that it was. She began weeping then, and hadn't stopped for at least four hours.

And now he stood in the E.R., the cacophonous noise from the verbal survivors clanging in his ears like he was trapped in a pet shop full of insane parrots. He and Malcolm had agreed that they had their hands full with the people on hand, and that no more trips out would be able to be taken that night. As it was, it would be the middle of the night before these people could be squared away enough to be left alone for the night. Tiredly, he wished again he had at least one more person that could see to help him. Just *one*, that's all he needed. He sighed. He had also had a burning desire to sleep with Britney Spears when he had been fourteen, and *that* hadn't happened, either.

They had stopped by the school once in the early evening to give everyone an update on how things were progressing. Cynthia had again offered to help, but Jeff had told her that she was needed more where she was to take care of the children. Now, he almost wished he had taken her offer of help up. If things continued at the current rate, not just Cynthia but *everyone* at Second Sight would be over here, lending a hand. He looked longingly at the phone on the wall, wishing he could call her, just to hear her voice if for no other reason. The thought stopped him, and he shook his head. *Walkie-talkies, you ignorant dumbass,* he thought in disgust. *Just pick up some goddamned walkie-talkies. Jesus.*

He returned to the business at hand, and was soon immersed in the flow of movement that occurred as he and Malcolm made sure that each of their new charges were fit and uninjured. Each of the survivors had a tale to tell, and were pathetically eager for someone to listen to them. The stories were all different, and yet so similar, that Jeff had stopped really listening after the first few, just agreeing when it seemed necessary. He helped Malcolm make diagnoses and treat what he could. Most of the survivors were suffering from dehydration and slight malnutrition, although several had some fairly serious gashes where they had blindly blundered into sharp corners, or cut themselves trying to open canned food and the like. There was only one serious case in the E.R. at the moment, a fifty-something man that hadn't been able to take his insulin properly, and was edging towards something Malcolm called ketoacidosis. Jeff had no idea what that was, but he did know that diabetics needed to take their insulin, or they might die. Malcolm had started an I.V. on the man by touch alone, and had gotten Jeff to hang the proper bags of fluids and give him the proper medicines to inject into the I.V.s.

As they had gotten the survivors into order, treating them and getting fluids and food into them, Jeff had begun to feel like the little Dutch boy holding his finger in the dike. There were just over fifty people in here tonight. What the hell would happen tomorrow? Hell, the day after that? He tried to picture the hospital full to capacity and shied away in silent horror. He couldn't get his breath now, and this was just the *beginning*. Cynthia's frank appraisal of what it would take to save so many people was coming back to haunt him in spades.

They continued to treat and comfort the people that they had saved that day, and it was almost one-thirty in the morning before everyone was in a bed with instructions not to leave their rooms until someone came to get them the next morning. Jamie had given up the ghost around midnight, falling asleep in one of the couches in the E.R. waiting room. Malcolm and Jeff headed outside, standing by the bay door to the E.R. They blew out identical breaths of relief and weariness, and then laughed. Jeff stretched, arcing his back and then drawing a slight hiss of pain as the movement rippled across his sore ribs. He turned to Malcolm.

"Buddy, you think you can hold down the fort for a half an hour or so while I go over and check in on Cynthia and the kids?"

Malcolm smiled tiredly. "I can do you one better'n that, my friend. I can hold down her down until tomorrow mornin'. You go grab some sleep an' be back here around nine or so in the mornin'."

Jeff looked at Malcolm like he had lost his mind. "Are you nuts? Yeah, sure, I'll just fuck off and leave you here with fifty-plus blind folks. You can take care of them, no problem. Oh, *wait*, I forgot, you're blind too. What the hell?"

"Ain't nothin' left for you to do here, Jeff. Nothin' that requires eyes for, no ways. Mr. Peterson will live, or he won't, nothin' more you or me either one can do 'bout that." Malcolm was referring to the diabetic that was slipping in and out of consciousness. "So, what are you gonna do here tonight we ain't already done? Go on, grab some food and some sleep. I'm gonna do the same thing here." He felt Jeff's hesitation and said in a flat voice, "We can only do so much, Jeff. That's not somethin' I like admittin' any more than you do, but there she is. We got to deal with it."

Jeff still felt uneasy about the whole affair. "What if something happens? You just going to call me up and have me scoot over here to help out?"

Malcolm smiled. "Matter of fact, I am."

Jeff just stood there, confused. "What?"

"Take a look over there in that EMS room, back shelf beyond the equipment. Be careful, there's spine boards and such layin' everywheres."

Jeff went into the small room and flicked on the light. It buzzed feebly for a second, then brightened. On the shelf was a rack of hand-held walkie-talkie radios sitting in their battery recharging cradles. He laughed out loud. "Son of a bitch."

He came back out of the room holding two of the radios. He put one of them in Malcolm's hand and turned it on. He turned the other on and asked, "What's the range of these?"

Malcolm shrugged. "S'posed to be two miles with a clear line of sight. The school's only about three-quarters a mile from here, so we ought to be good. What channel is mine set on?"

Jeff looked and said "Three." He set his to match and keyed it up. The static came immediately from Malcolm's radio. "Okay, we'll give it a try. Once I get over to the school, I'm going to holler at you, so don't go to sleep until I do. I don't get an answer and I'm coming right back, deal?"

Malcolm nodded. "Yup. Go on. Don't worry about Jamie. I'm gonna go crash out on the couch right next to his, so he'll be fine. Just be back by nine or so, so we can get this lot fed before we head out to grab some more." He grinned crookedly. "Fun, ain't it?"

Jeff scowled. "Oh, yeah, best time I've ever had." He stopped and looked at Malcolm. "Listen, hoss, don't forget that son of a bitch Daniels is still out there somewhere. I may have hit him bad enough to kill him, but I won't be satisfied about that until I see his fucking body. You read me? You hear something, a vehicle or something, you holler at me right away, okay?"

"Yes, Mother. Come on, Jeff. We can't worry about everythin', or we'll go crazier than hell. If he's out there, then he's out there. Nothin' we can do 'bout it, not tonight. Let tonight take care of itself, all right? A little faith in the Lord might give you a help, you know."

"Yeah, I know", Jeff groused. "I'm trying. Okay, I'm gone. I'll holler at you as soon as I get to the school, so don't fall asleep until I do. I have to drive over here just because you fell out on guard duty and I'll feed you Alpo."

Malcolm laughed and turned back to the E.R. "G'night, Jeff. God bless ya."

"Good night, hoss. Sleep well."

Jeff got back into the van and started it up. He hadn't lost his sight, but his sense of smell seemed to be improving, because he could smell the faint odor of the survivors they had spent the day transporting. It was acrid and bitter. The smell of unwashed people, he guessed. *No*, he thought, *that's the smell of despair*. He could have done without that knowledge, but there it was.

A few minutes later, he was at Second Sight. He made his way up the stairs, yelling for Father Don to set aside the shotgun. It was late, but what the hell, better he wake up the kids than get his face caved in by a 12 gauge. He heard the muffled voice of Father Don calling that all was clear. Jeff keyed up the radio and said, "Malcolm, you read me?" He was rewarded instantly by a surprisingly clear version of Malcolm's voice replying "Yeah, dammit, now can I get some sleep?" Jeff laughed. "See you in the morning." Malcolm made a barely decipherable reply and the radio went silent.

Jeff entered the rec room and got his obligatory kiss from Waylon. Father Don looked his way and said, "Is that a radio I heard you using?"

"Yeah, Malcolm had several in the EMS room at the hospital. I should have thought about it before. We could have stayed in touch with you guys all day if I had, dammit."

"Language, mister", came Cynthia's voice from his side. "You're in the presence of a lady, remember." She went on, her voice turning serious. "You can't think of everything Jeff. None of us thought of it, either." She kissed him lightly on the lips and then turned towards Father Don. "Do you want to tell him, or do you want me to?"

Jeff looked from one to the other. "Tell me what?"

Father Don beamed at him, patting the CB like a favored child. "Guess what I've been doing while you were out saving the world, Mr. Della?"

Jeff held his breath.

Father Don went on without waiting for an answer. "I was worried that there wasn't enough antenna for this rig, so I fiddled around with the wiring and attached it to the old antenna that runs up the building next to ours. Works like a charm." He smiled proudly.

Jeff looked at him incredulously. "Are you insane? You could have gotten yourself killed, electrocuted, or some damn thing!"

"Ah, simmer down. All I did was run some wires", Father Don waved dismissively. "Now, do you want to hear my news, or not?"

Jeff sighed. "Okay, lay it on me."

"I was right about not being able to get enough signal. Once I was tapped into that antenna, I could pick up a lot better. And there *are* folks in Surry, Virginia. We were right about that. They cut in and out, but I also heard them mention the U.S.S. Ronald Regan. That's a supercarrier the Navy's got. Big thing, nuclear powered job. I couldn't make out what they were saying about it, but either way, there are folks out there, Jeff! We aren't alone! I've been yelling at them all day, but I can't tell if they were reading me or not. This thing's not very powerful. We've got to get a better set up going, so we can make sure that they know we're here. Other folks, Jeff. *Help*." He sat back, a pleased look on his face.

Jeff smiled. He would believe it when said help came charging over the horizon. But it was good to know that there were other people out there. In a confident voice, he said, "Way to go, Don. You are the man. And you're pretty cool, for an over-the-hill priest, I've got to say."

Father Don made as if he was going to toss the CB at Jeff, but grinned.

Jeff turned to Cynthia. "And how have you been today, pretty lady?"

She smiled at him, her emerald eyes shining. "I'm fine. You sound dead on your feet, though. Come sit down and let me get you something to eat. Beef stew all right?"

"Hell, *yeah* it is. I'd eat Waylon right now, I'm so hungry." At the sound of his name, Waylon raised his head and looked quizzically at Jeff. "Nothing, fuzz ball. Go back to sleep." Waylon thumped the floor with his tail a few times and lowered his head back onto his paws. Cynthia came back with a warm bowl of beef stew. From a can, granted, but it tasted just fine to Jeff. He looked up. "How'd you keep it warm? Surely you guys had dinner hours ago."

She nodded over her shoulder. "Sterno. I just lit it back when I heard you pulling in so it would be warm." She spoke matter-of-factly, but the thoughtfulness of the gesture touched Jeff.

"Thank you, Cynthia. You're awfully good to me."

She laughed softly. "Of course I am. A can of beef stew heated up over Sterno. I deserve a medal. One of these days, I'll *cook* for you, Jeff Della. Then you can praise me. Now, how did it go today?"

Between bites of his stew, he told her about his day. He finished the story at the same time as his second bowl of stew and sat back, rubbing his sore ribs but feeling contented.

"Wow, over fifty people? That's great, Jeff!"

"Yeah", he said, a note of concern creeping into his voice, "it is."

"What's wrong?"

He sat silent for a moment. Finally, he said, "It's like you said, Cyn. It's just fifty folks, and I'm almost dead. What am I going to do when that number doubles? Triples? God help me, what am I going to do with four or five hundred people in that hospital?" The fear in his voice was palpable.

Cynthia reached for his hand. "We'll do the best we can, Jeff. That's all we can do." She stopped with a smile. "Cyn? Is that just something cute you've decided to start calling me, or is it a hopeful bit of naïveté on your part?"

He was confused. "What? I don't follow you. Remember, you're dealing with a *very* tired white boy here."

She widened her eyes in mock shock. "You're *white*? Oh, my! I've never been so close to a *white* man before. My parents will be shocked and appalled."

Jeff snorted laughter into his cupped hands, trying to keep from waking the children. When he could speak again, he said, "Quit making me laugh, dammit! It hurts!" He chuckled again. "Now, really, what's the matter with 'Cyn'? Don't you like it?"

She grinned wickedly. "No I like it just fine. I was just wondering if it was something you were looking forward to on my part."

He was totally lost. "What?"

She blew out a disgusted breath. "You really must be tired. I hope that's it, because if you're really this slow, our conversations are going to suck. 'Cyn', 'Sin'. Get it? As in 'Original Sin'?"

It clicked. He laughed again. "Yup, you caught me. A little sin with you wouldn't come amiss." They both laughed as Father Don growled from across the room.

"Sorry, Father", Jeff said piously. "Would it be too sinful to request a small kiss from the lady fair?"

That earned him another growl from the supine priest, but it also earned him the kiss he asked for, so he considered it a fair trade.

After a while, they broke apart. Jeff lay his head in her lap, and she stroked her fingers through his hair at his temples again. He was nearly asleep when he roused himself groggily and asked her if they had an alarm clock.

She thought about it and said, "Well, my watch chimes the hours and half-hours, why?"

Jeff told her about needing to be at the hospital by nine or so. She assured him that she would set would be up. As he was drifting off, she also told him that she was going with him in the morning. He thought about arguing, but he was just too tired.

He was crossing that magical doorway between wakefulness and sleep when he thought he heard her say something else. It wasn't clear, and he was too far-gone to rouse himself again, but it seemed to him that she had spoken quietly, right into his ear. He drifted completely off to sleep with her words following him into the darkness.

"I'm falling in love with you, too, Jeff."

He smiled all night long.

Chapter Twenty-Five

Oscar Daniels was up long before the dawn. He had slept most of the previous day on the couch, waking at a little past three in the morning, stiff and sore. His first considered action was to eat some more pain medication and to take care of his wounds. The redness had subsided a bit, and the discharge from the wounds was clear, not yellow. He sighed in relief. No pus. This was a good thing.

He had gotten some coffee going in the kitchen, foregoing his morning beer. He had important business today, so he would lay off the sauce until he was finished with the soldier. He began to plan his day. He wanted to be in town, someplace well hidden before dawn so he could pinpoint where that son of a bitch was and put paid to *that* account.

He went into the master bedroom and limped into the walk-in closet. In the very back, he found what he was looking for. Several racks held camouflage clothing. *Two can play at this soldier game*, he thought. (The fact that he was going to be in the middle of town, where woodland camouflage would do him no good whatsoever never crossed his mind.) He took down a set of fatigues not unlike those Jeff had been wearing the night they met.

He slowly dressed, mindful of his injuries. He was moving a bit better today. He finished dressing and pilfered around until he came upon some boots, camouflage snake boots that reached almost up to his knees. The clothes were a bit tight on him, but not enough to be bothersome. The boots fit fine. He wriggled his toes experimentally. Yep, these would do just fine.

He went back into the kitchen and poured himself a cup of coffee. As he was drinking it, the lights flickered for a second, and then went out completely for a few more seconds. They came back on, but still flickered warningly ever so often. What was *this* horseshit? The damn power had better not go out. If it did, how would he watch his movies? Or keep his beer cold, for that matter? He glared at the lights, daring them to go off again. They continued to shine, but they still flickered.

"You had just better *not*", he informed them threateningly.

Taking his coffee into the living room, he checked the clock. It was almost four-thirty in the morning. He needed to get a move on if he was going to get into position somewhere in town before that chicken-shit soldier was up and prowling around.

He searched the house for the keys to the Toyota for almost a half an hour before he spied them lying in plain sight on the kitchen counter. He was getting angry, and that wouldn't do, not today. He needed to be at his best today. He shuffled over to the kitchen table and pawed through the bag of pill bottles until he came up with the

Valium. He shook out several and washed them down with some coffee. He thought for a moment, and then began filling the many pockets of the fatigues with bottles. He might start hurting later. Better to be safe than sorry.

He added the box of shells for the rifle to another pocket. He thought about leaving his pistol, thinking that it just didn't *look* right on all this military gear. In the end, he took it anyway, not being able to leave it. It was his security blanket, and besides he might need it at some point.

He headed out to the garage and climbed into the Toyota. It started right up, but he still pulled a grimace of disgust. It was a good thing everyone was blind. He wouldn't be caught dead driving this sort of thing normally. He pulled out of the garage and headed to town, his lights on low beam. He pulled as close to town as he dared, stopping on the outskirts of a shopping center on the edge of town. He would have to walk in from here. As he limped into town staying off the main streets, he tried to figure out the best place to set up to find the bastard.

He thought as he walked, thinking that the water tower on one of the hills in town would give him the best view. His injured leg screamed at that, however, so he decided to go somewhere closer. After a bit, his face lit up. He'd go to the high school! He could go up to the windows in the auditorium. They were high enough, and would give him a pretty good view of most of the town.

His destination figured out, Oscar trudged through town until he was within sight of the high school. He cheered up a bit at that. All this walking was playing hell with his leg. He stopped at the entrance to the school and took some more pills, and then headed up the stairs on the bleachers. As he settled in on the top step, sighing with relief to be off his leg, the first tendrils of dawn began to lighten the sky. He settled in, the rifle sticking out of the open window. He looked through the scope, aiming at a window in the hospital. The window zoomed into focus, looking like it was just feet away. Oscar grinned. Yes, sir, this would do just fine. Just let that son of a bitch come into view *now*.

His preparations complete, Oscar began to daydream. He envisioned himself taking that smart-ass soldier down. Then, he could get back to having his fun. And hell, when the police or whoever finally did show up, why Oscar could pin all those killings on that rogue soldier, couldn't he? After all, the man was going around shooting citizens and blowing shit up, so why couldn't he be guilty of the other stuff, as well?

Looking dreamily off into space, Oscar stroked the stock of the big rifle in his hands.

Yes, sir, this here was going to be a red-letter day.

Chapter Twenty-Six

Jeff again woke to the sound of children, and it made him smile. He sat up and rubbed the sleep from his eyes. Cynthia heard him moving and came over with the customary plate of breakfast. It was Pop-Tarts this morning. She said apologetically, "I didn't figure I would have time to actually make anything, and this seemed quick." He assured her it was fine and ate his with a cup of coffee. He looked around. It was daylight, but he couldn't tell what time it was. It had rained in the night, and it was still overcast this morning.

"What time is it?" he asked.

"It should be almost nine", Cynthia replied. Just then, her watch made a funny chime. She held up her wrist and smiled. "There you go. Nine o'clock on the dot."

He looked at the watch, curious. "How can you tell what hour it is? I mean, you can hear the chime, but how do you know what the actual hour is?"

"Each hour has its own chime, so you can keep track."

"Oh. That's pretty neat."

She smiled. "How else do you think us blind folk know the time, buddy?"

He laughed. "Are you sure about going with me today?" She had announced her intention to accompany him on today's outing while he had been eating his beef stew the night before. He'd thought about giving a token protest, but realized he really could make do with an extra set of hands.

Cynthia nodded. "Yes. We'll leave the radio you brought here and keep in touch with everyone that way. It'll be fine." She turned back to feeding the children.

Jeff played with Waylon for a few minutes and then stood. "Cynthia, if you're sure you're going with me, we need to get going. I don't like the thought of Malcolm over there by himself."

She nodded and told the children to behave and mind Father Don. Jeff gave the priest the radio and told him he would check in on him throughout the day. Father Don nodded, and went back to twiddling the knobs of his CB. *Gonna have to find a battery for when the power finally goes*, thought Jeff. If the man didn't have his CB, he would probably go nuts.

Jeff and Cynthia said their good byes and headed for the van. The day was already muggy. Jeff's face took a pained expression. Another day of checking for corpses did little to put him in a good mood. He was quiet for the ride over to the hospital. Cynthia seemed to understand, just laying her hand on his knee during the drive.

They arrived at the hospital and Jeff honked the horn. Jeff and Cynthia got out of the van and started towards the E.R. door. Jeff stopped and turned back. He reached behind the seat and pulled out his rifle. There wasn't any point in getting careless. They started across the parking lot. Malcolm came out of the bay door and came out to meet them. He was still in his element, and he moved much better than he had at Second Sight. Jeff almost raised a hand to wave before he checked himself with a grin.

"Hey, big guy, morning. How'd it go last night?" he called across the parking lot.

"Everythin' was fine. Most of 'em are still sleepin'. How 'bout you?"

"Like a baby. I brought Cynthia with me this morning. That okay with you?"

Malcolm laughed. "Hell, *yes*, it's okay! Another pair of hands around here wouldn't be turned down, let me tell you."

They met in the parking lot about thirty feet from the E.R. bay door. Jeff slung the rifle over his shoulder and clapped Malcolm on the shoulder. "You ready for another day of this?"

The man shook his head. "Not really. Matter of fact, I'd just as soon take an ass-whuppin' than do this again, but it's got to be done."

Jeff sighed. "Yeah, I know what you mean. Well, I figure that if we start where we left off last night, we can probably…"

He never finished the sentence. A bright red splash of blood flew from his head, splattering Malcolm in the face. Jeff's head rocked forward, and he fell in a boneless heap. He heard Malcolm's surprised yell, and Cynthia's scream.

Her wails followed him into the blackness, and he knew no more.

Chapter Twenty-Seven

Oscar had been nodding off when the sound of the car horn jerked him awake. He flailed about, not remembering where he was. Had the rifle not had its safety engaged, he would have blown a hole in the roof big enough to toss baseballs through. He looked wildly about. Remembering where he was, he jerked back to the window, hissing in pain.

He brought the rifle to his shoulder and sighted down the scope. The horn had come from a van sitting in the hospital parking lot. Oscar let out a silent whoop of delight and got ready. He flicked the safety off and waited for his shot.

He stopped a second later, however, confusion etching across his face. The man climbing out of the van wasn't the soldier, just some guy in blue jeans and an old work shirt. Getting out of the van next to him was a fine-looking redhead. By the way she walked with one hand in front of her, Oscar could tell she was blind, so no problems there. He put her in his mental rolodex for later inspection, and went back to the guy who had been driving the van. As Oscar watched, another man came out of the E.R. door. He wasn't as slow-going as the redhead, but Oscar could tell that this cat couldn't see, either. Again, no problem.

The two from the van started across the pavement, talking to the guy from the hospital. A few steps in, though, the van driver turned around and went back to the van, opened the door and pulled out a rifle. He then turned back to the hospital guy and the three of them stood there talking.

Oscar's pulse quickened. He didn't recognize that man, but he could recognize that fucking *rifle*! He ought to be able to; the son of a bitching thing had put enough lead into him! How this van guy had gotten it from the soldier was beyond Oscar, and he really didn't give a damn. Maybe he had killed the soldier, thereby depriving Oscar of his chance for revenge, or he was in it with the son of a bitch. Either way, he was a dead man. Oscar would ask his questions of the other two. After he got the answers he wanted, bang goes the hospital dude, and the redhead would be coming home with him. He grinned like a kid as he settled the rifle into position.

He watched as the van guy reached out and clapped the hospital dude on the shoulder. *Aw, how sweet*, he thought maliciously. The crosshairs of the scope settled on the van guy's head. Slowly squeezing the trigger, Oscar was simultaneously amazed with the recoil of the rifle and rewarded with the sight of the van guy's head spraying blood all over the hospital dude.

Now Oscar gave out an audible whoop of delight. He shouldered the rifle and scurried down the steps as fast as his bad leg would take him. He was out in the overcast sunlight in minutes, and limping like a madman towards the hospital.

A red-letter day, *indeed.*

<u>Chapter Twenty-Eight</u>

Cynthia sat moaning with Jeff's head in her lap. His blood was soaking through her pants. Malcolm was trying to take Jeff from her, to do something, but she couldn't let him go. She rocked back and forth, her tears scalding as they cut down her face. Malcolm was screaming at her, but she paid him no mind.

It wasn't *fair*. Not like this, not this man. He had tried so *hard*. Now, everything he was or would ever be was slowly soaking her pants. In a few seconds, he would just be one more corpse among billions. She tried to run her fingers through his hair like he liked, but the blood was too thick. She wailed, on and on.

She might have gone on that way forever had it not been for the horrible voice that came from behind her.

"Well, now... by God, I drilled *his* ass, didn't I?" Followed by a burst of insane laughter.

Cynthia knew in a heartbeat. This was the man that had cause so much pain in a world already full of torment. This was the man that had just killed Jeff Della. Oscar Fucking Daniels. *Him*. She gently laid

Jeff's head on the pavement and turned towards the sound of that gleeful, hateful voice.

"Oooo-wheee! *Drilled* his ass! Dropped him like a sack of potatoes, by God!"

Cynthia sprang like a cat towards the man. Homed in on his voice, she very nearly succeeded in clawing his face open with her nails before his danced out of the way. His laughter drove her mad. She flailed about, trying to connect.

"Damn, little lady, you are a spit-fire, ain't you? Yes, ma'am, I think you and me are gonna get along just *fine*."

"I wouldn't count on it. She's spoken for, you psychotic fuck."

Oscar and Cynthia both turned at the sound of this voice. Cynthia had time to whisper breathlessly, "Jeff?" before Oscar Daniels screamed his negation into the hot morning air.

Jeff Della, the left side of his face awash in blood, was very carefully aiming his P90 at Oscar. Jeff lay where Oscar had dropped him, but he had his pistol in hand, nonetheless. Oscar dropped the .300 Weatherby and clawed for his own pistol, but fast as he was, there was not a chance in hell that he was going to clear leather.

Jeff methodically fired his handgun into Daniels. The distance was less than ten feet, and Oscar wasn't the only one that was proficient with a handgun. Jeff fired the gun dry, watching with a clinical detachment as the .45 caliber slugs tore through Daniels' chest.

Somehow, the man managed to retain his footing and stood, swaying like a tree in a high wind. He looked down at the blood-roses blooming on the camouflage shirt and back up at Jeff. His mouth worked silently.

Finally, with his last tidal breath he said accusingly, "Dead…" and toppled forward onto the pavement.

"Yes", Jeff agreed, "you *are* dead, you son of a bitch."

Cynthia crawled over to where Jeff lay, and Malcolm came up the other side. When Cynthia tried to run her fingers over Jeff's face, Malcolm absently batted them aside so he could feel for the damage. Cynthia took Jeff's hand instead. It was cold, jarringly cold against the muggy air.

"Is he going to be all right?" Cynthia cried at Malcolm.

"I dunno. I can't tell where the goddamn bullet went in… Jeff, can you talk to me some more, buddy? Where's the worst pain?"

"Everywhere", Jeff said dreamily.

"Jesus Christ", Malcolm muttered. "Come on, come *on*…" His fingers probed all around Jeff's skull, trying to read the map of the man's head in his mind. There was just too much fucking *blood*…

Cynthia was weeping still, but she kept talking to Jeff. "If you don't get better, I won't feed your dog", she said, unable to think of anything else to threaten him with. "I don't care if PETA comes and takes me away *forever*, I won't ever feed him again!'

"Yeah, you will", Jeff replied in that same dreamy voice.

Malcolm frantically felt for a pulse at Jeff's carotid artery. It was there, but weak, getting so weak. The blood had slowed, as well; the flow timed with Jeff's failing heartbeat. "Goddamn it! Goddamn it! I can't fucking *see!*" His voice speeding up like a litany, he began saying. "Please God; let me see, just for a second, please God. Just for a second, God. Please. Just for a second, please God."

Cynthia felt Jeff's hand go lax in her own and she squeezed it as tight as she could, trying to force her warmth into him.

Jeff drew a fluttering breath and let it out. He inhaled once more and said in that same dreamy tone, "Say, isn't that a helicopter?"

Chapter Twenty-Nine

Jeff woke up with a staggering headache and cotton mouth. He tried to focus, but his eyes thumped in his head and watered. After several minutes, he was able to see clearly enough to make out that he was in a hospital room. *How in the hell did Malcolm drag me all the way up here without dropping me?* he wondered. He tried to call out, but his tongue was glued to the roof of his mouth. Looking around, he saw that there was a plastic pitcher of water on the bed stand. He grabbed it eagerly, but the movement caused his head to try to rip itself of his shoulders and run away screaming.

After a moment, he very carefully reached for the pitcher. There was a glass beside it, but he didn't give it a second glance. Bringing the pitcher to his mouth, he took a huge gulp and almost choked to death on an ice cube.

An *ice cube?* What in the *fuck?*

He hacked and coughed, each movement causing bright flares of pain to shoot out of his head through every orifice of his body. Jesus, he had to lay still.

He had just gotten himself under control when a man he didn't know walked through the door. The man was wearing a white doctor's coat, but he wasn't Malcolm. *Probably somebody Malcolm dragooned into service*, he thought groggily. It was only when the man looked him dead in the eye and smiled, and then picked up a chart and began reading it that things went from confusing to downright weird.

Because he could think of nothing else, he repeated, "What the *fuck*?"

The man grinned at him. "Well, hello to you too. And you're welcome for saving your life, by the way. Although that P.A. was doing a pretty fair job of it, all things considered."

Jeff was floored. He tried to say something, but several things kept coming out at once, and he just wound up making a wounded interrogatory noise at the man.

The man grinned again. "Okay, I can see you're not really all that up to speed, so I'll fill in the gaps for you, how's that?"

Jeff nodded dumbly.

"You, sir, are on board the U.S.S. Ronald Regan. It is a Nimitz-class supercarrier from what they tell me, but I'm Army, so what the hell do I know? I'm Captain John Hewes, United States Army. Formally of the 160th Airborne Special Operations Aviation Regiment, now part of what they are calling Task Force Ray Charles. I think it's a little uncivil to call it that, but that's just my opinion."

Jeff made another incredulous noise.

"Right. Sorry, I was off on a tangent. You don't give a damn what it's called, or who I am, or anything else. So, let's get to you. You are in stable condition, but it was touch-and-go with you for a bit. You are one extremely lucky man, in more ways than I can count. You can see, for starters, which puts you in a *tiny* minority compared to the rest of the planet. In addition to that, you were shot in the head by a *very* large caliber gun and you survived. Some of that was thanks to me." The man smiled fussily. "The bullet creased your scalp instead of going through your head. Had it done that, you would have been dead before you hit the ground. I've seen large caliber weapons deliver headshots, and I can assure you, it's fatal." He spoke with the authority of a man who knew exactly what he was talking about. "However, as I said, the bullet merely creased your scalp. There was a lot of bleeding, as is normal with scalp wounds. Too much bleeding, actually. If things hadn't turned out like they did, you would have bled to death where you fell. Which brings me back to how lucky you are. When we came in over the hospital, we saw you on the ground, and I had the men take you into the E.R. I was able to get enough plasma into you to stabilize you. There was some fear that you might start swelling under the skull, and to be honest, if you had, you probably would have died. I don't think that I would have been up to cutting your skull open in a hick E.R. Maybe, but I'm not sure. Thankfully, you didn't have too much swelling, so we'll never know, will we?"

A million questions bombarded Jeff at once. He tried again to think of what to say, but between the monstrous headache and the information overload this guy was laying on him, it was very difficult. Finally he managed to get out, "When you came in over the hospital? There *was* a helicopter?"

Hewes smiled and said, "Yup. We came over in a Blackhawk...excuse me *Sea*hawk...damn Navy... anyway, we came over in a bird, saw you on the ground, and put down on the hospital's landing pad."

"You said you had the men take me into the E.R.? Is the military still up and running? The government?"

Hewes grimaced. "In a fashion. When the Event occurred, anyone not shielded with lead or other radiation-retardant material was stuck blind. That included most of the military and most of the government. We've done over-flights of Washington and it's... well, let's just say that paying your taxes isn't going to be much of a concern for a while." He looked grim and paused for a moment, his eyes far away. He snapped back to the present and continued. "There were many places that were properly shielded from the Event. Nuclear subs, aircraft carriers like this one, although it was a stroke of luck that she was in port at Norfolk, because everyone that wasn't around the reactor and certain other areas was affected the same way as the rest of the world. Cheyenne Mountain came through just fine, and we've been getting our marching orders from there. A U.S. Senator from

Wisconsin was there when the Event occurred, and unless we can find anyone higher up the ladder than her, she is the President of the United States. First female President, yet *another* historic event. We've had isolated pockets of men coming in from all over, troops that made it through the Event and made contact through the military satellite channels. We go out after some, and others come in small convoys. At present, there are just about three thousand soldiers, sailors, airmen, and Marines here, or located nearby. We're in contact with about that many more, headed this way. We've been scouring the surrounding areas looking for those not affected by the Event for almost a week. In addition to the military personnel, there are about six hundred civilians housed either on board or at the base that we've set up on shore."

Jeff thought for a moment.

"You said you've been looking for people not affected by what you call the Event."

"That's correct."

"What about all the people that *were* affected?"

Hewes eyes grew dark. With a stony look, he said, "They are, I'm afraid, beyond our abilities to help at the present time." He saw Jeff start to protest and raised a hand to forestall him. "I did not say that I agree with that decision or that I enjoy it, but at the moment, we cannot deal with the problem."

Jeff snapped, "What the fuck do you mean, the *problem*? You mean the *problem* that there are millions of Americans dying right now while you comb through the debris to find the few that can still fucking *see*???"

Hewes' mouth drew in a tight line, but then with an effort, the man relaxed.

"You said it yourself, Mr. Della. The *millions* of Americans that are dying. Not to mention the *hundreds of millions* of Americans already dead. Americans like my wife, Mr. Della." The man took a steadying breath. "And beyond that, the *billions* of dead and dying all over the world. There are less than *four thousand* of us here. What would you have us do? We cannot possibly support them. As it is, we will be very fortunate if, by this time next year, there are a hundred thousand living, breathing Americans left. And as things stand right now, that number would be about a thousand times more than we could support. We have men clearing the town of Surry, Virginia of the dead. It isn't a huge town, but it's large enough to meet our needs for the immediate future. We have to deal with the bodies, Mr. Della, before we can continue. Disease doesn't care if you're blind or not."

Jeff looked away for a moment and then back at the man. He took a deep breath. "I'm sorry, Captain Hewes. I do understand what you're saying. I had started to realize the same thing myself, and I was just trying to take care of fifty people. And I'm very sorry about your wife, sir."

Hewes smiled sadly. "Thank you. I am sorry, too. About everyone's wife. Their mothers, fathers, brothers, sisters, grandparents, everyone. This is about the most hideous thing that has ever happened to mankind, and all we can do is try to survive it the best way we can. It's shit, to be honest. When I think of all those people out there…" he waved towards the port window, "I literally feel like I'm becoming paralyzed. Like I've abandoned everything I've ever stood for. I put on this uniform to protect my country, Mr. Della. How good a job am I doing, would you say?" His voice was brittle with ironic rage.

"You're doing all you can. Just like I was. I'm truly sorry if I offended you. I'm just sort of overwhelmed, I guess. Since you saved my life, I think I wouldn't mind if you called me Jeff, sir."

Hewes smiled. "Well, since you're a civilian, I think I wouldn't mind if you called me John."

Jeff stuck out his hand. "It nice to meet you, John. Thank you for not letting me bleed to death in a hick E.R."

Hewes laughed. He took Jeff's hand and shook it. "Think nothing of it. You're going to be fine, by the way. I'm personally going to see to it. We may not be able to do everything, but goddamn it, we're going to do *something*."

A thought suddenly occurred to Jeff. "You said you were only bringing in people who can see… what about the people I was with? Cynthia and Malcolm, Father Don, the kids from school, the people at the hospital…"

Again, Hewes held up a hand. "Chill, Jeff. I said we were combing the countryside for people that can see, yes, but I didn't say we were complete assholes, either. You had managed to keep almost a hundred people alive, all by yourself. We couldn't, in good conscience, let that sort of thing go unheeded. All your people are here, Jeff. The kids from the school, the survivors from the hospital, all of them. In fact, you gave us the idea that those that were born blind needed to be located just as much as those that were unaffected. They have a lifetime of knowledge to give to us about the condition. Schools and homes for the blind have been placed on our priority lists for reconnaissance. Because, who knows if the Event won't happen again? Then what? We need to be able to cope better than we did the first time. The truly blind, the *originally* blind, I guess you could say, can teach us a lot about how to cope."

"What the hell actually happened? I mean, you keep calling it 'The Event', but do we know what it actually was?"

The soldier shrugged. "They tell me that there are scientists from Cheyenne Mountain and some other government installations that were shielded that are working on that right now. Who knows? A solar flare was a hot bet for a while, but that didn't add up because it hit everywhere at the exact same time, as best we can tell. If it had been solar, then the folks on the other side of the planet wouldn't have been hit, no would they? At least, not like we were. No, whatever it was, it happened instantly, and it happened everywhere. They may never figure it out."

Jeff looked thoughtfully off into space. "Maybe it wasn't scientific. Maybe it was God."

Hewes shrugged again. "Maybe it was. I'm not a religious man, but I know that if I were God, I would be tired of dicking around with humanity. Hell, I would have been tired of it a long time ago." He spread his hands. "Again, we may never know."

Jeff smiled. "Well, my folks are here, I'm here, and I owe you a huge debt for that. If there's anything I can do, you just say the word."

Hewes gave him a pat on the shoulder. "From what I've been told, you deserve to be here, son. They told me about the Daniels individual. You were very brave to take him on like that. Most folks would have just turned their head and kept low. In addition to that, do you want to know something?"

Jeff nodded.

"As much as it pains me to say it, since we have begun doing over-flights and reconnaissance, Stone Grove, West Virginia is the *only* place where we found someone that had been unaffected taking care of those that were. Everywhere else, those that could still see were staying at home, taking care of their immediate families, just…keeping their heads down. Doesn't say much for the decency of humanity, does it?"

Jeff felt uncomfortable with the admiration in the man's eyes. He glanced away and said, "Well, I didn't have any living family, so it was different for me. If my family had been alive, I probably would have done the same thing as everyone else."

Hewes looked curious. "Do you really think so? I don't. I think you would have taken care of your own and then gone right on taking care of as many others as you could."

Jeff felt his face heat up. "I don't know. And like you said, we probably never will. I just had me and my dog to worry about at first... hey! What about my dog?"

Hewes laughed. "Waylon is the new official mascot of the U.S.S. Ronald Regan. He's currently in the mess hall, I believe, trying to score some grub."

Jeff grinned, relief painted on his face. "Yeah, that sounds like the furry bastard. When can I see him and my friends?"

"You can start having visitors today. You've got a few outside now, waiting to get in, as a matter of fact, so I'll get out of your hair and let you see them."

He started for the door, and then stopped. "By the way, how was it that you were unaffected? We *still* can't figure out why animals weren't affected, which lends more credence to the thought that this was an Act of God, but what were you doing during the Event?"

"I was cutting down a tree with Waylon in the woods behind my house", Jeff answered. He could see the confusion on Hewes' face and quickly related the story of the accident and his blindness, and the miraculous recovery from it.

By the time he was done, Hewes was shaking his head. "I said you were an extremely lucky man earlier. Now I am certain of that fact. Remind me never to play poker with you, all right, son?"

Jeff laughed as the man walked out of the room. The door hadn't fully closed when it came back open. Standing in the doorway with a Marine by her arm was Cynthia. Behind her, Jeff could see Father Don, Malcolm, and Jamie Cummings. They all had huge smiles on their faces. To the Marine helping Cynthia into the room, Jeff growled, "Hands off, Marine. That's my lady you're rubbing on." The Marine looked Cynthia up and down and gave Jeff an encouraging nod, followed by a lascivious wink. He grinned to show he was joking and headed back out of the room.

They all clustered around his bed, practically beaming at him.

"Well, howdy, folks. How's the grub here? It's bound to be better than Cynthia's cooking."

The others laughed, with the exception of Cynthia. She moved forward with a very determined look in her eye. Jeff was quick to caution, "Hey, remember I just got shot in the head, so if you're planning on beating on me, I'm gonna call that Marine back in here to…"

He didn't get to finish because she was kissing him. Very thoroughly kissing him. It hurt his head like hell, but there was zero chance of him asking her to stop.

Finally, they broke apart, both of them gasping for air. When he had caught his breath, Jeff reached down and took Cynthia's right hand. He slid the ring off of her finger. She looked confused until he took her left hand and slid the ring onto her ring finger, giving it a little twist at the end.

"There. Now, if you want to change it back, you go for it. But just so you know; even if you do, I'm just going to put it back where it belongs every time I catch you asleep."

Tears sprang to her gorgeous eyes. She looked down at him and again he was struck how much it seemed like she could actually see him. See him, or possibly see *into* him. "I love you, Cynthia Jordan."

She smiled through her tears. "I love you too, Jeff Della."

He grinned. "Good, that's settled. So, Father Don, do you do marriages if the contestants aren't Catholic, or do I need to convert or something?"

Cynthia grinned like a cat. "You sure do. After all, I'm Jewish."

"What?"

The sound of their laughter floated out into the hall. The Marine standing guard grinned. Laughter like that was rare, these days. It was nice to hear it again.

Epilogue

Jeff Della wished he had a cigarette. Which was odd, because he didn't smoke. He would also be asked to leave the room if he lit one up, and there weren't enough military men left on the planet to drag him from this room.

Holding Cynthia's sweating hands in his, he intoned "Breathe, baby, come on and breathe." If looks could kill, he would have dropped to the floor right there.

There was one final push, and the baby slid into the world. Jeff gave out a joyous laugh and kissed Cynthia all over her face. Cynthia took this in good grace and even gave him a few back. She turned her head toward the sound of her crying newborn. "What?" she asked, unable to express herself through her exhaustion.

The doctor (it wasn't Hewes, this one was an O.B./GYN that had been in an old hospital that still had a lead-clad room where the X-ray machine had been, ironically smoking a cigarette) lifted the baby and told the parents, "Congratulations, you've got a beautiful little girl." He placed the baby on Cynthia's chest, and she kissed the baby's head over and over. Jeff could do nothing but caress his daughter's back and look on in awe. After a few minutes, the nurses took the little girl from them and went through the process of weighing her, cleaning her up, and wrapping her in a warm blanket. The doctor checked the child out thoroughly, making sure that she was in perfect health.

There had been a great deal of to-do about the birth of this baby. She was the first child born in Surry since the Event. As far as anyone was able to tell, she was the first child born *anywhere* since the Event. There were several other expectant mothers, but Jeff and Cynthia Della had beaten them all to the punch.

The doctor put silver nitrate in the little girl's eyes and said, "Well, she's got eyes like her mother."

Cynthia drew in a trembling breath and let out a small sob. "Oh, I'm so *sorry*, Jeff."

Jeff shushed her with a kiss. "Be quiet. I don't care if she can see or not. She's perfect, just like her mother."

The doctor cleared his throat in embarrassment. "Uh, I hope you don't hit me, Mr. Della, but that's not what I meant. I'm sorry you both took it the wrong way."

Jeff turned to the doctor in confusion. "What?"

The doctor's face colored. "I meant that most of the time, babies all have the same colored eyes. They just look dark at first, and then you can tell the true color. With your little girl, she's got eyes the exact shade of green that your wife has."

Jeff was thrilled, but still confused. "I love my wife's eyes. But what did you mean about me taking it the wrong way? You aren't making a pass at her, are you?"

The doctor laughed. "No, sir, not at all. I just meant that her eyes are green. The baby isn't blind. She can seem to see just fine."

For a split second, Jeff almost *did* want to hit the dumbass, but then what the doctor had said filtered through and he grinned in delight. He turned back to Cynthia, her tears transformed from sadness to joy in an instant. He went back to kissing her until she laughed and told him to back off. "Shouldn't you go tell everybody that they are new aunts and uncles?"

He couldn't stop smiling. "Yes ma'am."

He kissed her one last time and went out of the delivery room and into the waiting room. The cluster of people there, both blind and not, looked towards him expectantly.

Father Don was the first to break the silence. "Well?"

Jeff said proudly, "Ladies and gentlemen, you are all the new aunts and uncles of Ms. Annie Renee Della, who is perfectly healthy in every way."

A roar of congratulations went up. All the kids from Second Sight were there, as was Malcolm, Father Don, and Captain John Hewes. To Jeff, Malcolm said, "Thank you. Annie… I'm so happy for you, man." Tears were running freely all around the room.

Jeff accepted hugs and kisses from everyone, even Waylon, who they had managed to sneak in past the nurse at the front desk, and then told them he needed to get back to his wife and daughter.

Jeff headed back into the delivery room, where his family now waited. As the door closed behind him and he started towards Cynthia and the baby, Annie's cry filtered out past the waiting room and into the night air beyond. It was the cry of a perfect child, born surrounded with love. The cry floated out into the night, where it was caught by the breeze and lifted away.

Even as the sound itself died, that breeze carried on, past the hospital through the city of Surry, and into the vast darkness that surrounded it. Like a tiny candle, Surry made a small beacon of light on an otherwise pitch-black continent. From Surry west, darkness ruled with an overpowering hand.

But so long as the candle burned in Surry, so burned hope. In time, that candle could be taken up and back across the darkened land. In time, the candle could be carried all the way from one sea to the other, lighting up the darkness as it went.

In time.

Ryan S. Pack was born and raised in Eastern Kentucky. He lives there still with his wife LuAnn and their four children. He was an Emergency Medical Technician for fifteen years before an injury ended that career. He has since spent his time in and out of college, where he remains one credit shy of a degree, and writing what he refers to as "My Ramblings". This is his second edition of Second Sight.

Ryan S. Pack

www.ingramcontent.com/pod-product-compliance
Lightning Source LLC
Chambersburg PA
CBHW071151250626
47159CB00001B/57